RACHEL VINCENT

SHADOW BOUND

RACHEL VINCENT

MIRA

Published in Great Britain 2012
MIRA Books, an imprint of Harlequin (UK) Limited,
Eton House, 18-24 Paradise Road,
Richmond, Surrey, TW9 1SR

© Rachel Vincent 2012

ISBN 978 1 848 45102 5

60-0612

MIRA's policy is to use papers that are natural, renewable and recyclable products and made from wood grown in sustainable forests. The logging and manufacturing processes conform to the legal environmental regulations of the country of origin.

Printed and bound by
CPI Group (UK) Ltd, Croydon, CR0 4YY

This one is dedicated to my editor, Mary-Theresa Hussey, who seems to see what I envision for a story even before I'm able to make that clear in the manuscript. This book was tough. *Shadow Bound* is the most difficult book I've ever written and there were days when living in Kori's head put me in a very scary place. My editor reminded me that shadows cannot exist without the sun. Kori needed balance. She needed Ian. And Mary-Theresa helped me find the man Ian needed to be, both for Kori and for their story.

I learned a lot with this book. Thank you.

One

Kori

If you live in the dark long enough, you start to forget what light looks like. What it feels like. You may remember it in an academic sense. Illumination. A possible source of heat. But after a while those abstract memories are all you have left, and they're worth less than the memory of water to a man dying of thirst.

I didn't know how long I'd been in the dark. Long enough for most of the pain to fade into dull aches, though the latest batch of bruises would still have been visible, if anything had been visible. Long enough that I couldn't remember what shade of gray the walls were. Long enough that when the light came on without warning, it blinded me, even through my closed eyelids.

I'd lost all sense of time. I didn't know when I'd last showered, or eaten, or needed the toilet in the corner of my cell. I didn't know when I'd last heard a human voice, but I remembered the last voice I'd heard, and I knew what the sudden light meant.

Light meant a visitor.

And visitors meant pain.

The door creaked open, and my pulse leaped painfully—fear like a bolt of lightning straight to my heart. I clung to that one erratic heartbeat, riding the flow of adrenaline because I hadn't felt anything but the ache of my own wounds in days.

If not for the pain, I couldn't have sworn I was still alive.

"Kori Daniels, rise and shine." Milligan was on duty, which meant it was daytime—outside, anyway. In the basement, it was always night. There were no exterior windows, and no light until someone flipped a switch.

The dark and I used to be friends. No, lovers. When I was alone, I walked around naked just to feel it on my skin, cool and calm, and more intimate than any hand that had ever touched me. The dark was alive, and it was seductive. We used to slide in and out of one another, the shadows and I, always touching, caressing. Sometimes I couldn't tell where the dark ended and I began, and at some point I'd decided that division didn't really exist. I was the dark, and the dark was me.

But the darkness in the basement was different. It was false. Broken. Weakened by infrared lights I couldn't see, but I could feel blazing down on me. Caging me. Draining me. The shadows were dead, and touching them was like touching the stiff limbs of a lover's corpse.

"Kori," Milligan said again, and I struggled to focus on him. On my own name.

The guard shift change had become the ticking of my mental clock—the only method I had of measuring time. But my clock skipped beats. Hell, sometimes it skipped entire days. If there was a pattern to the granting of meals, and showers, and company, I hadn't figured it out. They came when they came. But mostly, they didn't.

I didn't sit up when Milligan came in. I didn't even open my eyes, because I didn't have to. I hadn't sworn an oath to him, and I hadn't been ordered to obey him, so participation was at my discretion. And I wasn't feeling very discretionary.

I rolled onto my stomach on my mattress, eyes still squeezed shut, trying not to imagine how I must look after all this time. Skinny, bruised, tangled and dirty. Clad only in the same underwear I'd been wearing for days, at least, because humiliation was a large part of my sentence and I hadn't been granted the privilege of real clothing. My period hadn't come, which meant I wasn't imagining not being fed regularly, and water came rarely enough that I'd decided I wasn't being kept alive, so much as I was being slowly killed.

I'd been a bad, bad girl.

"Kori, did you hear me?" Milligan asked.

I'd had no problem with him on the outside. He'd respected me. At least, he'd respected the fact that the boss valued me. Milligan had never gotten grabby and he'd only leered when he thought I wasn't looking. That was practically chivalry, on the west side of the city.

Now, I hated him. Milligan hadn't put me in the basement, in that rotten fucking cell of a room. But he'd kept me there, and that was enough. If I got the chance—if I ever got out and regained my strength—I'd put a bullet in him. I'd have to, just to show Jake Tower that I was down, but not out. Beaten, but not broken.

Milligan would be expecting it, just like I would, in his position.

The door creaked open wider and I buried my face in

the crook of my arm, nose pressed into the dirty mattress, braced for whatever would come. Prepared to turn myself off and make the world go away. That was the only way to survive in the basement. Convince yourself that whatever they do to you doesn't matter. And really, it doesn't. How can it, if you can't stop it and no one else wants to? So I dug down deep, to a place where there was no pain and no thought. Not my happy place. Thinking of a happy place—*any* happy place—only reminded me that I wasn't really there. That I never would be again.

I went to my empty place.

"Tower's on his way," Milligan said. "I think you're getting out."

My heart leaped into my throat, but I didn't move. Surely I'd only heard what I wanted to hear. If I wasn't careful, I sometimes imagined things, and there's nothing more dangerous in the dark than unwarranted hope.

"Kori?" he said, and that time my eyes opened. "You're getting out today."

I sat up slowly, blinking furiously in the light, wincing over the residual pain from the gunshot wound in my shoulder. I'd heard him, but it took forever for the words to sink in, and even once they had, I didn't let myself believe it. It could be a trick. Jonah Tower—Jake's brother—had told me I was getting out before, but he only said it so he could watch me suffer when I realized it wasn't true.

"If you're lying, I'll fucking kill you," I croaked, my mouth and throat so dry my tongue felt like it had corners.

"I'm not—" Milligan glanced down a hallway I couldn't see as a set of firm, even footsteps echoed toward us. "Here he comes."

I swallowed a sob. I'd expected to die alone in this false dark. In these dead shadows.

Milligan stepped back, and Jake Tower replaced him in the doorway, a steel-spined symbol of power and authority in his white button-up shirt and suit jacket, sans tie. I hated myself for how relieved I was to see him, when he was the one who'd locked me up. I hated his clean clothes, and combed hair, and tanned skin. I hated the apple wood smoke clinging to his clothes from the grill, making my stomach rumble and cramp. I hated the slight flush in his cheeks that told me he'd had two glasses of red wine with his steak—never more, never less, because Tower was in control. Of everything. Always.

Jake Tower was the heart of the Tower syndicate. We—the initiates—were the lifeblood of the organization, but Tower was the pump that kept us flowing through the veins and arteries of this living machine. He pushed the buttons and pulled the strings, and we belonged to him, all of us, bound into service, sealed in flesh, by blood and by name. We lived and died according to his will. And we obeyed because obedience was a physical mandate. Even when our minds resisted, our bodies complied, helpless in the face of a direct order.

But I'd found a loophole. I'd disobeyed the spirit of an order, if not the order itself, and as punishment, Tower had thrown open the gates of hell and shoved me inside. He'd locked me up and given Jonah free rein, and for all I knew, Jake had forgotten I even existed until...

Until what?

Until he needed me. Why else would he be here? Why else had he let me live, if my current state could even be called living?

Rachel Vincent

Tower's nose wrinkled—I didn't smell good—then he closed the door at his back and sat on the edge of the bare foam mattress covering the raised concrete slab that was my bed. He grabbed my chin and tilted my face toward the light, studying me. I knew what he saw, though there was no mirror in my cell. Bruises. Dark circles and sharp cheek bones. Split lips. And the damage didn't end with my face. I looked like hell and I felt worse.

Tower looked…satisfied. "Does it hurt?"

"You fucking know it hurts." Everywhere. That was the whole point. With my existence reduced to fear, and pain, and dead shadows, surely I would never even consider another betrayal. "The lights?" I didn't want to ask, but I had to know. "Your idea?" Jonah wasn't smart enough to think of something like that.

Tower's lips curled up in a small smile, like he'd just remembered some distant childhood pleasure. "An irony I hope you fully appreciate. Absolute, inescapable darkness for the shadow-walker. Imprisoned by the source of your own abilities. How did that feel?"

I am a Traveler. A shadow-walker. I can step into a shadow in one room, then out of a shadow anywhere else I want to go, within my range. I can see better in the dark than most people. Sometimes I can look into one shadow and see through another one, somewhere else, like looking through a periscope, or one of those paper-towel-roll telescopes we used to play with as kids.

But the basement darkness was anemic, thanks to a grid of infrared lights, too high up for me to reach. So while my cell looked absolutely, claustrophobically dark to the naked eye, that darkness was too shallow for me to travel through. The shadows were dead. I was trapped in the element that had always been my ally. My escape.

How did that make me feel?

Like I'd been betrayed by my own body. Like I was lost to the rest of the world. Like I no longer existed at all, which would have been easy to believe, if not for the pain anchoring me to the reality of my own miserable existence. But I wasn't going to tell Tower that.

"It sucked, on ice. Happy?"

He said nothing. Whatever he wanted to tell me would come on his terms, and making me wait for it was just another way of making me suffer.

"Why?" I demanded, pissed off that my voice was as weak as the rest of me. "Why didn't you just kill me?" He'd killed others for far less than what I'd done.

"You needed to pay for your crimes, and others needed to know you were paying." He said it like he might explain that grass is green, as if it should have been obvious, and the emptiness in his voice was the scariest thing I'd ever heard.

"You told them?"

"You were an object lesson, Korinne. I showed them." He glanced at the slab of one-way glass in the top half of the interior wall, and my blood froze in my veins. I started to shake, and I couldn't stop.

"You let them watch?" He'd invited an audience to see me beaten, and broken, and humiliated, and… I closed my eyes against this new layer of humiliation.

"Only those who needed to see."

"Kenley?" No. *Please* no. I didn't want her touched by this. I didn't want her to know. If Tower was void of human emotion, Kenley was made of it, and she couldn't defend herself. That was my job.

Tower shook his head. "Your sister only knows that you're alive. She's anxious to see you."

I exhaled slowly and blinked back tears that would never fall, using them as fuel for the rage burning deep in my gut. Fury that would have no outlet for four more years. Anger that would fester and burn as I planned for the day when I'd be the one throwing punches and spilling blood. Jake Tower would *pay.* Jonah would pay. Milligan and the other guards would pay. Everyone who'd watched would fucking pay.

I would listen to them beg while they bled out on the floor.

But I'd have to survive to get revenge, and to survive, I'd have to play Jake's game. It was always his game, always his rules, and the only cards he dealt me were penitence and obedience. So I would play the shit out of penitence and obedience—anything to get out of the basement—and keep the cards I'd dealt myself up my sleeve. Until it was my turn to deal.

"I have an assignment for you, Korinne," Jake said. "A chance to redeem yourself."

I said nothing, because nothing was required, but my pulse raced so fast I had to lean against the wall to steady myself. Milligan was right. I was getting out of the basement.

"Ian Holt."

"Who?" I licked my lips, but my tongue was too dry to wet them, and now that I knew I was getting out, I found it hard to concentrate on the details, rather than the promise of regular meals, and showers, and relative freedom.

"He's a Blinder of extraordinary skill."

"You want him killed?" I'd never heard of him, which meant he wasn't ours. And if he could be used against us, he was a target.

"I want him whole. Preferably unharmed."

"Another acquisition?" In the weeks before I was locked up, I'd done quite a few of them, collecting whoever Tower wanted for his pet project.

"Only as a last resort. I want him on staff. Willingly." Because forced bindings were never as strong as those entered into freely. "Holt hasn't signed with anyone yet. In fact, he managed to stay completely off the radar until two days ago, when the JumboTron at an NHL hockey game caught him darkening the entire arena during a riot on the ice."

"How do you know it wasn't just a power outage?"

"Because he blinded the arena from the outside in, starting at the perimeter and moving toward the ice from all sides equally. The general public thinks he's just some idiot who saw the first lights go out before the camera did and pretended to be doing a magic trick. But I know what I saw, and I'm not the only one. Now that he's been exposed, everyone wants him. I've officially extended an invitation, and he's agreed to come to town as my guest and hear our pitch. You will be his liaison. You will show him the advantages of joining the Tower syndicate and make sure that he signs with us, or with no one."

"I'm not a fucking recruiter, Jake." I'd been part of Tower's personal security team. I'd killed for him. I'd kidnapped for him. I'd done other things I desperately wished I could forget, but recruiting was a specialized skill—one I didn't have. "I'm a soldier, and you need a salesman."

"You are whatever I say you are, and when Ian Holt gets here, you will be his recruiter. You will be his girlfriend, his best friend, his therapist, his mother, or his dog trainer, if need be. You will do whatever it takes to put a chain link on his arm." For emphasis, Tower glanced at the two black interlocking chain links tattooed on my own arm—the flesh-and-blood binding tying me to him until my term was up. "Whatever it takes, Korinne. Do you understand?"

I understood. "You want me to fuck him." And if I refused—if I refused *anything* Jake told me to do—resistance pain from violating my oath to him would shut my organs down one at a time until I died screaming.

"I want you to give him whatever he wants. And if he wants *you,* then yes, you will bed him, and you better be the best he's ever had, because if he refuses my mark, you will have to bring him in by force so I can drain him. And if that happens, I will kill you, and your sister will pay for your failure as you've paid for your latest mistake. She will serve out the years remaining on her contract in this room, under the same conditions."

My blood ran cold, and suddenly I couldn't breathe. "No one touches Kenley. You swore it when I signed on." My little sister would be untouchable, in exchange for my service.

"And *you* swore that you would guard my life and my interests with your own." Tower unbuttoned his shirt slowly, and I knew what he was going to do even before he pulled back the left half of the material to show me the fresh pink scar. "Your key card let the enemy into my house. Into my home, where my wife and children sleep. Your gun faltered where it should have fired, and I was shot in my own home, by my greatest enemy."

"I didn't mean—"

"You failed," Tower insisted. "You broke your word, and I have no reason to keep mine. If Ian Holt does not sign with me voluntarily by the end of his visit, I will have you executed, and your sister will pay the pound of flesh you still owe."

Nausea rolled over me, and if I'd had anything to vomit, it would have landed in his lap.

"You have two weeks to get back in shape and make yourself presentable. This is your last chance, Korinne. Save yourself. Protect your sister. Get me Ian Holt."

After Tower left, the lights stayed on, and I had several minutes to see the emaciated ruin my body had become. And to think. And to hate Jake Tower like I'd never hated anyone in my life. Then the door opened again, and my sister stepped into the room, a younger, softer reflection of the woman I'd been until Tower locked me up.

Kenley gasped. Her hand flew to her mouth, then she spoke from behind it. "What did you bastards do to her?"

Milligan stood behind her, staring at the floor. "I never touched her. I just work here."

"Where the hell are her clothes?"

Milligan shrugged. "This is how he sent her. You've got fifteen minutes to get her cleaned up." He backed out of the room and shut the door.

Kenley crossed the small space and set a canvas bag on the floor, then dropped onto her knees in front of me, brushing hair back from my forehead.

"How long?" I asked, staring at the mattress while she dug in her bag.

She pulled out a bottle of water and handed it to me. "Almost six weeks," she said, and I could hear the sob in her voice, though she tried to hold it back.

"I'm fine." I cracked the top on the bottle, scared by

how much effort that took, then unscrewed the lid. I'd gulped half of it before I remembered I should go slow.

"You're not fine. I thought you were dead. Jake kept saying you were alive, but he wouldn't let me see you. I was sure he was lying, just to keep me working." Tears formed in her eyes and when she blinked, they rolled down her cheeks.

"No. Don't cry, Kenni," I whispered, because they were listening. They were always listening, and they were probably watching through the one-way glass. I licked the moisture from my lips. "Don't ever let those steel-hearted sons of bitches see you cry. If they know you can be broken, they'll fuckin' break you just for sport."

Like they'd tried to break me.

She nodded, jaw clenched against sobs she was visibly choking back.

I opened my mouth to tell her it would be okay. I would *make* it okay. But then my stomach revolted, and I lurched for the toilet. I retched hard enough to wrench my injured shoulder, and the water came up. It was too much, too fast. I should have known better. I'd been sipping half handfuls of clean water from the back of the toilet tank since the bottles had stopped coming, but that was different from gulping half a bottle, ice-cold.

Kenley pulled my hair from my face and I sat up, wiping my mouth with the back of one bare arm. My stomach was still pitching, but there was nothing left to lose.

"No one knew where you were." She handed me the bottle again, and I rinsed my mouth, then spit into the toilet, thinking about how wrong she was. Some people knew where I was. Some of them had seen me, through the one-way glass. "Tower was shot, and you were shot, then he woke up and you disappeared. What happened, Kori? No one knows what really happened."

What happened? I'd been buried in the basement, at the mercy of the monsters. But that wasn't what she was asking.

"Liv said she needed my help, so I went. But it was a trap. They were waiting for me. They took my key and used it to break in." I was the breach in security that got one of our men killed, two more shot, and Tower's prize blood donor—my murdered friend Noelle's only daughter—taken. "Ruben Cavazos shot us both." I ran my fingers over the dirty bandage on my shoulder.

I should have run, regardless of the risk. I *would* have run, if not for Kenley. I couldn't leave her alone with Tower. Alone in the syndicate. My sister and I were a package deal, from start to finish.

"You're lucky he didn't have you killed," she said, but I shook my head.

"He can't. He still needs me." I had no clue why I had to be the one to recruit Ian Holt, but if Jake didn't need me, I would be dead.

"Let's get you cleaned up." She stood and headed for the canvas bag, but her shoulders were shaking and it took me a minute to realize why.

"Kenley, this isn't your fault." I used the edge of the toilet to push myself to my feet.

"Of course it's my fault." She dug in the bag and pulled out a bottle of shampoo, then crossed the room toward the narrow, curtainless shower stall in one corner. "I sealed the binding between you and Liv, so you have to do what she asks. Because of me."

Kenley was a Binder. A scary-good Binder. She was

so good Jake hid her from the world, to protect her and every contract she'd ever sealed for him. He kept her under twenty-four-hour guard, and he threatened me to control her, just like he threatened her to control me.

"It wasn't like that this time," I insisted, as she turned on the shower—it only worked when they wanted it to. "Liv didn't officially ask and I wasn't compelled. I went to help her on my own." Because it was the right thing to do. I was sure of that, even after everything that had come since.

"It's my fault you're here in the first place, Kori." Kenley aimed the shower spray at the opposite wall, then turned to look at me, arms crossed over her chest, and I sighed. I'd never been able to effectively argue with that one. But again, I had to try.

"I make my own decisions. We came into the syndicate together, and we'll leave together." Or not at all. "Four years," I whispered leaning with my forehead against her shoulder, while stray droplets of water sprayed us both. "We can do four more years, right?"

She nodded, but she looked far from sure. I'd been shot, starved, abused and locked in the dark for almost six weeks, but she was the one I worried about. Kenley was fragile, so I had to be strong enough for both of us. And Jake knew it. He knew what cards we held—what mattered to us—so he always won the game.

"Let me see your shoulder." Kenley blinked away more tears, and I leaned against the wall for balance while she peeled medical tape and gauze from my gunshot wound. I'd done my best to keep it clean, and I'd taken all the antibiotics Jonah had brought in the first couple of weeks, back when I was being fed and showered regularly, because *he* was the bulk of my punishment. But then Jake had figured out that his brother wasn't enough to break me, and that's when the darkness and isolation had dropped into place around me.

"It could be worse." Kenley wadded up the bandage and dropped it on the floor. "The stitches have dissolved and it's only a little red." Which kind of figured, because the rest of me was black and blue. "Get cleaned up. He's sending an escort for us in a few minutes," she said, while I stepped out of my underwear and dropped my grimy bra on the floor. Kenley kicked them into the opposite corner, then stuck one hand under the water and grimaced. "They could at least make it warm."

But they wouldn't. The basement cells weren't built for comfort. They were built for isolation and torture. They were built for hour after hour of darkness and silence, because when you can't see anything and you can't hear anything, you have no choice but to think about what you did, and how you would never, ever do it again.

But here's the thing. I would do it all over again, if I had the chance. I would take the gunshot wound, and the silence, and the darkness, and the worst Jonah could throw at me, if it meant sending Noelle's kid back home where she belonged.

I stepped into the shower and gasped as freezing water poured over my face and body. I let it soak my hair, then I opened my mouth and drank just a little, one hand propped on the tile wall for balance, because I hadn't eaten in days, and the room was starting to spin.

While I washed my hair slowly, shocked wide-awake by the cold water, my sister pounded on the one-way glass. "She's gonna need something clean to wear. Actual clothes, this time! And a towel!"

I lathered the cracked bar of soap while water and

shampoo suds ran down my body to swirl through the drain at my feet. It felt good to be clean on the outside, even if I might never be truly clean on the inside, ever again.

Five minutes later, clean and still damp, my hair dripping on clothes that weren't mine and didn't quite fit, I stepped out of the cell I'd spent almost six weeks in with one arm around my sister, as she half held me up. Milligan didn't look at me, and neither did either of the grunts Tower had sent to escort us to Kenley's apartment. But as the door swung shut behind me, literally closing on a chapter of my life I never wanted to reread, a man stepped out of the shadows in the hallway and crossed beefy arms over a barrel chest.

"Won't be the same around here without you, Kori," Jonah Tower said, cruel laughter echoing behind every syllable, and at the sound of his voice, my heart thumped painfully, pumping remembered pain and fear along with the blood in my veins. He stepped closer and whispered into my ear, too softly for Kenley to hear. "But I think you'll be back. And if you can't give Jake what he wants, I get to end you. Then the younger Miss Daniels and I are gonna get to know each other real well."

Kenley shied away from the hand he laid on her shoulder, and I stepped between them, close enough that I could smell the beer on his breath. "I'll be back all right, but you're not gonna see me coming. And if you've laid a finger on my sister, I'm going to tear them off one at a time and shove them down your throat until you choke on your own sins."

Two

Ian

"Have I told you you're an idiot?" Aaron asked, staring through the windshield at the tall iron gate and the even taller house behind it. If such a monstrosity could even be called a house. It was more like a modern fortress.

"About twenty times since my plane landed." I flipped down the driver's-side sunshade and checked my tie in the mirror.

"Has it sunk in yet?"

I glanced at him in the thick shadows of the car's interior, lit only by the green numbers scrolling across the radio's display in the dashboard. "Your puny verbal barbs are no match for my thick skull."

"You *do* have a freakishly thick skull," Aaron said, flipping through the stations on my rental car's radio. "But that won't stop a bullet. They may look civilized in tuxedos and sequins, but they're really monsters in men's clothing, every single one of them. They're going to eat you alive in there, Ian."

"Then may they choke on my corpse."

Aaron punched the button to turn off the radio, un-characteristically serious in concession to the job at hand. "Eight years since you left, and nothing's changed. You're still ready to charge in half-cocked and make the world bend to your will, consequences be damned."

"That's not true." The kid I'd been back then was idealistic but soft. Smart but naive. That kid had been burned by the real world—roasted alive—and I'd risen from his ashes, ready to breathe fire of my own. "Now I'm *fully* cocked, and well aware of the consequences. As are you."

He nodded at the somber reminder. "You sure you don't want me to go in with you? I could grab a monkey suit and be back in a second." Aaron was a Traveler, which meant he could step into the shadow of a tree outside my car and into his own bedroom in the space of a single breath, and be back just as fast. "You're gonna need someone you trust at your back."

Unfortunately for Aaron—or fortunately, depending on your perspective—traveling was one of the most common Skills in the world. Aaron's range was a little above average, but his accuracy was questionable at best, and unless his motivation was personal, no one would ever call him punctual. Which meant he had no value whatsoever to the Skilled syndicates.

That fact had kept him safe from their interest for years. So safe, in fact, I'd often wondered if he was faking his own incompetence for that very reason. He wouldn't be the first to try it. Hell, *I'd* tried it. But that wasn't why I couldn't use his help.

"Thanks, but no. If you show your face in Tower's house, within an hour they'll know you're an Independent."

They'd also know that Aaron was as good with a computer as he was bad with women, that he was late on the rent and quick with a punch line, and that he was addicted to those little melt-away mints people serve at weddings. His life was an open book, available to anyone who cared to read it. As were most people's lives. Which was why I was the only one who could do this job.

Because I had no life. No past. Officially, I didn't even exist, and if they ever figured that out, being seen with me could get Aaron killed.

"I need you to stay off their radar so you can be my emergency bailout, if this ends badly."

"Fair enough." Aaron sounded half relieved, half disappointed. He wanted to play badass assassin, but he didn't really want the risk that came with it. "Give me a call if you need a quick escape."

"I will," I said, as he pushed open the passenger-side door. But we both knew I wouldn't. There was nothing he could do to help me, if I couldn't get out of Tower's house on my own. The infrared lighting grid guaranteed that trespassers couldn't gain entrance through the shadows. His heavily guarded exits made sure no one got in the traditional way, either. Once inside, I would be on my own.

"If you survive this kamikaze mission, we should get dinner. And beer."

"Absolutely." But that was another lie. I had every intention of surviving, but wouldn't get the chance to hang out afterward, and I'd probably never be able to come back into the country at all, much less this particular city. If I accomplished what I'd set out to do, the price on my head would be high enough that preachers and Boy

Rachel Vincent

Scouts would fight one another for the chance to profit from my death.

"Good luck, man." Aaron stuck his hand out and I shook it, then he stepped out of my rental car and closed the door. I watched as he walked into the patch of woods at the side of the road. One step. Two. Three. Then he was gone, not just hidden by the shadows, but transported by them. Through them.

I took a deep breath and checked my tie in the mirror again—I hadn't worn a tux in years, and my distaste for formal wear had not faded. Then I shifted the car into Drive and pulled onto the street at the end of a procession of cars all headed the same place I was.

The queue of vehicles moved quickly, greased by proper planning and a well-trained workforce. When I rolled to a stop in front of the house, feet from the curved, formal steps, a man was waiting to take my keys while another spoke into his handheld radio, his steady but unobtrusive gaze taking in every detail of my clothes and bearing. They knew my face.

Before I'd even rounded the front of the car, a brunette in a long, formfitting peach-colored dress came down the steps toward me. She smiled like a pageant contestant and moved like a waitress, quick and eager to please.

"Mr. Holt." She threaded her arm through mine and guided me smoothly up the steps, without ever faltering in either smile or stride. "We would have sent a car for you," she said, leading me through a door held open by a man in service dress. She was smooth, and polished, and poised—an experienced people handler and a beautiful woman.

But she was *not* what I'd requested.

"Unnecessary. I wanted to see the city a bit on my

own." I stopped in the foyer, and she had no choice but to stop with me, because I still held her arm. "I'm sorry, I didn't catch your name."

"I'm Nina. Mr. Tower's personal assistant."

"And you're my escort for the evening?"

Her smile faltered a bit over my implication, and the dissatisfaction echoing intentionally within the question. But then she rallied from the insult and her smile beamed brighter than ever, if a little brittle now. "No, I'm afraid Mr. Tower has chosen someone else to keep you company during your stay. I'm just here to make the introductions this evening."

Nina led me through the wide foyer, generically ostentatious with its soaring ceiling and gold-veined marble tile. Even in his absence, Jake Tower exhibited his own affluence and power like a peacock displaying plumage. Wealth was evident in the expensive furnishings and decor, while his power was even more obvious in the stream of well-dressed guests, several of whom I recognized from political pieces on the nightly news.

At the base of each curved staircase, dressed in black and carrying handheld radios, stood a member of Tower's security team, monitoring the party in general and me in particular. I was unbound—I'd taken no oath of loyalty or service to Jake Tower—thus untrusted. They would watch me, prepared to intercept or incapacitate, until the day I bore Tower's chain link on my arm, marking me as his to command.

And that wasn't going to happen.

Once those milling in the entry had their chance to see me, Nina guided me into the main event. Into the snake pit, where every hiss would feel like praise and every bite

Rachel Vincent

like a deep, hot kiss. The venom would flow like honey, too thick to swallow, but too sweet to entirely resist.

I knew how extravagant and generous the syndicates could seem when they wanted something. I also knew it was all a lie. The party was an illusion, from every plunging neckline to each glass of chilled champagne. It was a show. A seduction. I was being courted by the Tower syndicate because I had something they wanted. And I would play along because *they* had something *I* wanted.

Heads turned to look when we entered the party. Hands shook mine and voices called out greetings, but the faces all blurred together. The names were a jumble of syllables I didn't bother to untangle. These weren't the important names. Not the important faces. Remembering would be a waste of effort.

So I smiled and nodded in the right places, agreeing when it was convenient, changing the subject when it wasn't. I sipped from the glass placed in my hand and ate the hors d'oeuvres Nina insisted I try. But I tasted nothing and hardly heard the words that came out of my own mouth. I was too busy scanning the crowd for the faces I'd studied. The names I'd memorized. The important ones, not necessarily in power circles, but vital to my purpose.

And finally, nearly half an hour after I arrived, a soft buzz spread through the crowd and I looked up to find Jake Tower coming down the main staircase with his wife on his arm and two black-clothed bodyguards at his back. The host had arrived, late enough to demonstrate that he lived life on his own schedule, but not so tardy as to be truly rude to his guests.

"Let me introduce you to Mr. Tower," Nina said,

taking my arm again. She led me through the crowd toward the stairs as Tower and his small entourage descended into our midst.

At the base of the stairs, a glass of champagne was pressed into Tower's hand, but he handed it to his wife before accepting another for himself. A heartbeat later, his gaze landed on Nina, then slid to me, and I swallowed a lump of eager rage before it could shine through my eyes and give me away. Tower wasn't my target, but that didn't mean I'd cry at his funeral. When the time came, I'd be raising my glass to whoever finally put the vicious, arrogant bastard in the ground, as would everyone else he'd ever tried to put his mark on.

"Mr. Holt, may I introduce Jake Tower and his lovely wife, Lynne. Mr. Tower, this is Ian Holt, your guest of honor."

Tower offered me his empty right hand and I shook it, making eye contact for the first time. Trying not to show that I knew more than I should.

I shouldn't know that Tower's first name was actually Jacob and one of his middle names was David. His wife was really Gwendolyn, and before she married, she'd been a Pierce, a great beauty by all accounts, but not burdened with enough brains or initiative to ever get in her husband's way.

"Mr. Holt, so glad you could join us. I hope you're enjoying yourself so far?" Tower's brows rose, and I nodded in reply.

"Of course. You have a lovely home, and an even lovelier wife." I took Lynne Tower's hand briefly, and she smiled, then silently sipped from her glass.

Over their shoulders, the bodyguards watched me, and their surnames filtered through my memory, triggered by faces matching the photographs and notes Aaron had fed me for days. The taller, darker man was Clifton, and the shorter, paler, broader one was Garrett. Their Skills, like their first names, were unknown, but based on their size alone, either could break a man in half.

The group around me shifted to accept a new couple into our power circle, and I realized with one glance at the newcomers that they weren't a couple at all.

"Mr. Holt, this is my brother, Jonah, and our sister, Julia."

"My pleasure," I said, shaking their hands in turn, and Julia's left eyebrow quirked over one deep brown eye, like something in my reply amused her.

Jonah only scowled. He was dressed like one of the guests, but even if I hadn't known from my research, I would have known from his bearing alone that Jonah would have been more comfortable wearing all black like the rest of Tower's muscle. He didn't like dressing up, and he didn't like playing nice. And he didn't like me—that much was obvious in his first glance my way.

Almost as obvious was the fact that his dislike of me would be very much mutual.

"Mr. Holt, if I may say so, that was quite an impressive show you put on at the arena a couple of months ago." Julia—Lia—raised her glass just a little, offering her own personal toast to my Skill.

"Oh, thank you, but it wasn't intended as a show at all." *Lie.* "I was just trying to help out where I could." That part was true, but intentionally misleading. I was trying to help myself into Tower's power circle.

"Still, you made quite an impression," Tower insisted. "Lynne and I were impressed, anyway."

"Unfortunately you weren't the only ones. The news

clip got quite a bit of airtime, and it's been viewed on the internet ad nauseam. If I'd known there were cameras aimed at me, I might have done things a little differently."

Another lie, and a big one that time. I knew there were cameras. The arena was chosen for that very reason. For my Skilled coming-out party. For the exposure that would bring me to Jake Tower's notice, during his favorite sport.

"And you're uncomfortable in the spotlight?" Julia asked.

"Or maybe scared of it?" Jonah added. "Darkness is more your thing, right?"

"I'm most comfortable in the absence of both light and attention, but scared of neither." I faked a nervous laugh. "However, I will admit to being unnerved a bit at first by interest from organizations like this one."

"You've had offers from other syndicates?" Tower's frown was small, but telling.

"Let's just say I'm keeping my options open for now. Though no one else has gone to quite this much trouble to impress me before." I gestured one-armed at the entire party.

"Obviously we don't stand around drinking and talking every day, but I thought a party would be the best way to introduce you to the syndicate as a whole."

"And what an introduction it is," I said, as one waiter took my empty glass while another replaced it.

"This is only the beginning." Julia smiled, dark straight hair framing a pretty face I couldn't quite read. "By the end of the week, you'll understand that no one else can offer you the benefits, security and career advancement potential that the Tower syndicate can."

"And here is the woman for the job." Tower smiled coolly at someone over my shoulder and I turned as he waved two more women into our widening circle. The first was a small, delicate-looking woman in light blue, her platinum curls tumbling over pale, bare shoulders. She was smaller and fairer than my personal tastes ran, but I'd requested an escort of her exact description, and when her brown-eyed gaze met mine, some small bit of tension inside me eased.

"Mr. Holt, this is Kenley Daniels."

I took her hand to shake it and couldn't help smiling in relief. There she was, my target, hand delivered to me by one of the most dangerous and powerful men in the country, though he had no idea that he'd played the very card I wanted most. All I needed now was to get her away from Tower and his security team, and...

"And this," he continued, before my hand had more than grazed Kenley's, "is her sister, Korinne. Kori will be keeping you company this week."

I blinked, confused, and glanced from Kenley Daniels to her sister, whose coloring matched Kenley's exactly—same platinum hair, pale skin, and deep brown eyes. Korinne was only an inch or so taller. She was a virtual match to the description I'd given Tower when he asked what I'd desire most in a liaison—the description of her sister.

"A pleasure," I said on autopilot, as I released Kenley's hand in favor of Kori's, still reeling from the bait-and-switch. Only it couldn't be a bait-and-switch, because Tower didn't know I'd had anyone specific in mind as my liaison.

And I hadn't known his mistake was possible, because *Kori Daniels* wasn't possible. She was dead. Every single one of Aaron's sources had said the same thing. She'd been a fixture at Tower's side for years—a strategically visible threat—then she'd disappeared several weeks ago. Gone, with no trace and no explanation.

In the syndicate, that can only mean one thing.

Yet there she stood, clearly alive and breathing, and waiting for me to shake the hand she held out. So I did.

She let go of my hand almost the instant we touched.

"Kori will be your tour guide," Tower continued. "She will also be your assistant, your chauffeur and your personal security while you are here. Anything you want, Kori will provide."

But Kori looked like she'd rather perform CPR on a leper than ever touch me again, even if only to hand me a cup of coffee.

My thoughts raced while I struggled to recover from surprise and frustration, without showing either. "You have security experience?" I said as if I didn't already know the answer, grasping at the only reasonable excuse I might have to reject her services. There had to be a reason she was no longer guarding the boss, and if he didn't trust her, why should I?

"Six years on my personal security detail," Tower said, and I was starting to wonder if my new liaison even had a tongue. "I assure you, Kori is everything you requested, and more."

Something silent and angry passed between Tower and the taller, older Daniels sister as her jaw clenched visibly and his gaze went hard. Kenley Daniels stared at her feet in the awkward silence, and Jonah Tower smirked when Kori flinched first, and looked away from her boss.

"Well, then, Mr. Holt, I believe we're scheduled to discuss business later, but tonight is for drinking, and dancing, and mingling. I have some other guests to greet, so I'm going to leave you in Korinne's capable hands for the moment. Please make yourself at home in my home."

With that, Tower guided his wife toward a couple I vaguely recognized from the cover of some financial magazine, and the rest of his entourage followed. Leaving me alone with Korinne Daniels, who held an untouched flute of champagne but showed no sign of sipping from it. Or of acknowledging my presence.

How could she be alive? Where the hell had she been for the past few weeks? I'd made sure that none of the other women photographed with Tower recently had pale blond hair, specifically to avoid this kind of mistake.

Weeks of research and study, down the drain.

"So…" I said, watching Kori watch the rest of the room, trying not to let frustration leak into my voice. "You're one of Tower's bodyguards?"

"Was," she said, and her posture tensed almost imperceptibly as she stared at something over my shoulder. I twisted to see Jonah Tower guiding her sister through the crowd with one hand at her lower back, and when I turned back to Kori, I found her eyes narrowed, one fist clenched at her side.

Were Jonah and Kenley involved? If so, Kori clearly didn't approve. Neither did I. Jonah Tower didn't like me, which could make it very hard for me to get close to Kenley if they were together. Unless her sister trusted me…

I studied Kori as she watched them wind their way through the crowd, trying to assess her more clearly now that I was over my initial surprise at being saddled with the wrong Daniels sister.

Korinne was slightly taller than her sister, but much thinner. Too thin, really. Her hip bones showed through the material of her dress and the points of her collarbone looked like they might pierce her skin at the slightest pressure. Her makeup was expertly applied, but couldn't quite cover the dark circles under her eyes or skin that looked sickly pale, in contrast to her sister's naturally fair complexion.

Still, she was pretty, in a hard-edged, angry kind of way.

Kori glanced up and caught me staring, and I held her gaze. "What do you do now?" I asked, trying to pick up the thread of a conversation that already seemed destined to unravel.

"Now I babysit you," she snapped, and I blinked in the face of such candor. Then almost laughed out loud. I'd expected Tower's people to be overaccommodating and ingratiatingly polite. Perhaps even sycophantic. Unvarnished honesty was a surprise.

"I meant, what do you do for Tower? What's your role in his organization?" When my question produced only a blank, half-puzzled look, like she wasn't sure she even knew the answer, I tried again from another angle. "Would it be impolite of me to ask about your Skill, considering you already know mine?"

"Hell yes." She flinched and rubbed her temple with one hand. Then she rolled her eyes at nothing. "I'm a Traveler."

A shadow-walker, just like Aaron.

"I assume you're good with a gun, since you used to be a bodyguard. Any other special skills?" But I could tell with one look at her closed-off expression that I'd picked the wrong approach.

Kori Daniels didn't want to talk about herself. She didn't want to talk to me. And she certainly didn't want to relax. She looked a little like she wanted to rip my head off and spit down my throat. "A *special skill?*"

I nodded, and too late I realized she'd found innuendo where I hadn't intended it.

I shook my head and tried to rephrase the question, but then she stepped closer, until she was in my personal space, not quite touching me, but so close air couldn't have flowed between us. She went up on her toes, like she might nibble on my ear, or share some dirty little secret. Then she whispered, so softly no one else could have heard.

"I do have a special skill," she murmured, her breath warm on my neck, her voice soft and low-pitched, with that hot, gravelly quality some women get when they're really turned on, and my pulse raced a little in spite of my very clear objective. "I'm pretty good with knives. I'm so good, in fact, that I could sever your testicles with one hand and slice open your throat with the other, and you'd go into shock so fast you'd die without ever knowing you'd spilled a fucking drop of blood."

Korinne settled back onto her heels and smiled up at me like she'd just promised to fulfill my dirtiest, most secret desire, and I felt the blood drain from my face.

This was *not* the woman I'd ordered.

Three

Kori

I sipped from my glass and enjoyed Holt's shocked expression so much that I'd taken two more sips before I remembered I hate champagne. And for the first time since I'd woken up in the basement eight weeks before, I felt a little better. A little more like myself. Until I saw Jake watching me from across the room, fury dancing in his eyes. He couldn't have heard me, but he could see that I'd scared his guest of honor—disturbed him, at the very least—and he was pissed. Jake tossed his head toward an alcove mostly hidden by the curve in the staircase, and I had no choice but to obey the silent summons.

"Be right back..." I mumbled to Holt, and cursed myself silently all the way across the room. I'd known better. I'd fucking *known* better, and I gave in to temptation anyway. I couldn't afford to scare off Holt or piss off Tower—Kenley couldn't afford my mistakes—yet I'd managed to do both after less than five minutes alone with the man whose Skill Tower valued more than he valued my life.

"What the hell did you just do?" Jake growled, hauling me into the alcove by one arm. I tripped over the stupid stilettos Kenley had insisted I wear and would have gone down on my face if Tower wasn't holding me up.

"He asked if I have any 'special skills.' He said it just like that." Like *special* meant depraved or perverted.

"Was I not clear before?" Jake's eyes flashed with anger. "I only pulled you out of the basement two weeks ago for this job. For *him*. I don't care what he says, or what he does, or what he wants," he growled into my ear, squeezing my arm hard enough to bruise, though I'd die before I complained. "You will answer him with a smile, and the answer is always yes. Do you understand?"

"Yes," I snapped, and it felt good to throw the word back in his face, even if it tasted bitter on my tongue.

He let go of my arm, but didn't back down. "I'm not going to bother listing all the things you are not allowed to say or do, because I recognize that while unsophisticated and often crass, your mannerisms have a certain crude charm, and for all I know, Holt might actually want to play 'tame the beast.' That's up to you to determine. But however this plays out, I swear on every beat of my wife's heart that if you don't have Ian Holt eating out of your hand in forty-eight hours, you will pay for it with your life. And your sister will pay for it with the balance of hers. Do you understand what I'm saying, Korinne?" he demanded, and I nodded, but that evidently wasn't enough, because he repeated the question.

"Yes. I fucking understand," I said through clenched teeth.

"Good." He stepped back and eyed me from head to toe without a hint of desire. Tower, for all his faults, worshipped his wife like she shit gold and bled wine, and I'd never once seen him even glance at another woman with any real interest. "You look like a lady for once. Now go pretend to be one," he said. "And try to remember that though a sledgehammer may be the most prominent weapon in your verbal arsenal, it is seldom the most appropriate."

"Jake, please," I whispered, swallowing the lump of bitter pride in my throat. "I'm not the best woman for this job. If you really want him, you need a recruiter." Someone who was used to wining, and dining, and kissing arrogant ass. Someone who was *good* at it. "Don't you think Monica would be better suited to this? Or Erica?"

Tower's gaze went hard, and I knew I'd overstepped. Again. "Without a doubt. But he doesn't *want* Monica or Erica. The only other person in my employ who fits Holt's description of his ideal physical type is your sister, and even if you were willing to let her wander all over town alone with a man she just met, I am not. I need her here, doing her job, where I know no one else can get to her."

I wanted to protect my sister from the realities of life in the syndicate. He wanted to protect a very valuable asset from being poached or exterminated. Still, in the end, our goals were the same, so I couldn't argue.

"Now take the man a fresh drink and apologize like you mean it. And do *not* give me a reason to have to repeat this conversation. That's an order." With that, Tower stepped out of the alcove and back into his party, smiling at acquaintances like he'd never had a sour thought in his life.

I started to make my way back to Holt so I could publicly choke on the crow Jake had shoved down my throat, but when I scanned the crowd, checking on Kenley out of habit, I found her with Jonah Tower, who smirked at me silently while he rubbed her bare back with one hand, until she shrugged out from under his touch.

And suddenly I wanted to vomit.

I backed into the alcove again and stayed there for another minute, fighting the flashes of memory that played behind my eyelids—a montage of pain and humiliation, overlaid with the terrifying certainty that if I failed, it would all happen again, this time to my little sister.

I swallowed compulsively to keep my dinner down, breathing deeply, like Kenley had showed me. So far, when the basement resurfaced in my head, the only thing able to beat it back when I couldn't take out my rage on the nearest boxing dummy was steady, measured breathing. Balancing each inhalation with an exhalation.

Kenley said I was imposing calm on everything else by instituting order in the most basic of involuntary functions. Or some shit like that.

I didn't care how it worked. All I cared about was that it *did* work. Usually.

When I opened my eyes again, the buzz of conversation and laughter roared back into focus and the looming darkness of the basement was gone, at least for the moment.

Remember who you were before, Kori. I had to remember and become her again, or I might die without the chance to claim vengeance or reclaim the woman I'd been.

I straightened my dress—stupid fucking sequins—and squared my shoulders, then took one more deep breath and stepped back into the fray.

That was the only way I could think of this night and hope to succeed. The party was a battle to be fought, not with bullets, but with pointless social gestures and small talk. I could do this. Every polite smile would find its mark. Every swallowed curse would block a blow. And every bitter concession made to polite society would bring me one step closer to the goal. To signing Ian Holt and protecting my sister.

If the party was a brawl, then Holt was my enemy, but he couldn't be beaten with fists or knives. He could only be lulled into submission—into lowering his guard—with subterfuge. With careful answers and gestures of compliance.

I could play that part. I'd *have* to play that part. Starting now.

I watched him as I closed in on my target, dodging hits from other combatants—Jake would call them guests—even as I armed myself with two fresh glasses of champagne from a tray carried by a passing waiter, an unwitting accomplice in my campaign.

Holt wasn't *bad*-looking. In fact, he was actually kind of hot, blessed with broad shoulders, a strong chin, and the smooth, dark complexion only mixed parentage could give. Or maybe that was the champagne talking. I could toss back vodka all day long, but I'd never been able to think clearly on anything fancy. Probably from lack of practice.

While I was still several feet away, two familiar silhouettes stepped between me and my goal. They were both brunette and curvy, and less than two years bound, yet eager to make names for themselves. They were also on Jake's shit list for refusing to believe after one crack at him that he could not be tempted to stray from his wife, even for a double dose of sin served hot and ready.

Within seconds of their arrival, Holt looked ready

to flee the premises. I exhaled slowly and donned my mental armor, then stepped back onto the front lines, right between the two brash sluts, who gaped at me like I'd just insulted their strappy footwear.

"You'll have to excuse us," I said, handing Holt one of the glasses so I could link my arm through his. I couldn't come up with a believable reason *why* they'd have to excuse us, so I didn't bother. I just steered him away from the wild hyena women and through the crowd, half enjoying the angry looks they shot my way.

A victory is a victory. The venue is irrelevant.

"Not that I don't appreciate the rescue," Holt said. "But I'm forced to ask, in the interest of self-preservation... exactly how well armed are you right now?"

I laughed, and it wasn't even forced. Probably because even with the smile hovering on the edge of his expression, his joke wasn't really a joke—he was actually asking.

"Guns leave unsightly bulges in an evening gown." Which I was only wearing under direct orders. "Tonight, what you see is what you get." Jake had made it clear that I had not yet earned back the privilege of carrying weapons in his territory, after letting him get shot. "But don't worry, there's enough security in here to rival the U.S. Mint. No one could possibly get an unauthorized gun through the door."

"I wasn't worried about getting shot," Holt said, as we wound our way through the crowd. "Perhaps ritualistically castrated and dismembered..."

"Okay, I'm sorry about the threat," I said, though that wasn't really true. "But they say you can't underestimate the value of a good first impression."

He stopped walking to frown at me. "Your idea of a

good first impression is to threaten a man's groin and his life in one breath?"

I shrugged. "Why? Would taking a breath in between improve the delivery?"

"I suppose not." He drained the last inch of champagne from his glass, then set it on an empty tray as a waiter passed. Then he turned back to me, his expression caught somewhere between confusion and amusement. "You're not what I expected from Jake Tower's envoy."

"What did you expect?" I was honestly curious.

"Someone like her." Holt nodded at something over my shoulder, and I turned to find Nina, Jake's personal assistant, schmoozing with the lieutenant governor, one hand on his arm, her gaze locked with his as she laughed at whatever asinine story he'd just told. I'd heard every story he had. They were all asinine.

I started to ask Holt if he'd rather have Nina show him around—surely Jake wouldn't make me play recruiter if the recruit didn't want me around after all—but he was already speaking again, this time watching a group clustered near the windows on the west wall. "Or someone like your sister."

I glanced at him in surprise, then followed his line of sight again to where Kenley stood against the wall, Jonah hovering near her like a kid eager to show off his prom date, and I realized Jake had probably told his brother to stick close to her, to remind me of what was at stake with this job.

Everything. That's what was at stake.

Kenley and our brother, Kris, were all I had left, and Kris had his hands full with our grandmother. Kenley was my responsibility, and I couldn't let her down. Even if that meant conning some clueless asshole into service at Tower's whims.

"Kenley would make a terrible tour guide," I said, more to myself than to him, still watching my sister play the wallflower. She wouldn't give Jonah any excuse to touch her. "She doesn't get out much."

"Out of what?" Holt asked, and I forced my mind back to the conversation at hand.

"Outside. Jake keeps her close at hand. Because of the nature of her work." And too late I realized how that probably sounded.

"Your sister lives here? In Tower's house? Do they…? Um…?"

I scowled. "No, my sister isn't screwing the boss." Nothing could be further from the truth. "She's his top Binder—the only one he really uses anymore—so he keeps her close to keep her safe. She has a small apartment near here." And she was always under guard.

"Oh." Holt looked relieved, and briefly I wondered why he cared who Jake was screwing. Was he a prude or a perv?

"I used to live here, though," I said, picking at the seams of his reaction. "In this house."

"You used to…?" He glanced from me to Jake and back, and I could practically see the gears turning behind his eyes as he tried to puzzle out a polite way to ask a crude question.

I rarely bother with polite. Makes things much simpler.

"Were you and he…?" Holt let the question trail off to its obvious conclusion.

"Do you ever finish a sentence?" I asked, and his cheeks darkened slightly as his brows rose in challenge.

"Do you ever think before you speak?"

I blinked, surprised. Jake said impulse control was my biggest character flaw. I'd always assumed he meant my tendency to hit first, then survey the situation as an afterthought, but Holt was clearly caught off guard by the verbal version of that.

"That's your problem." I backed slowly toward the foyer, leaving him to follow. "You think too much."

"I don't consider caution and forethought a problem."

"It takes you forever to order at a restaurant, doesn't it? And to pick out a tie?" I stepped closer and flicked his obnoxious little bow tie, then turned and stepped into the foyer, desperately hoping Kenley's stupid stilettos didn't seize that moment to betray me on the slick marble. Why do women insist on crippling themselves with footwear obviously designed by sadists?

Holt caught up with me, his mouth open to reply, but I spoke over him. "I tell you what. If you can dig up enough nerve to ask what you really want to know, I'll answer the question."

"Nerve isn't the issue." He stared straight into my eyes, practically daring me to argue. "What makes you think I care, one way or another?"

"The fact that you think too much. You overanalyze everything, like life's one big puzzle you can solve, if you can just find the pattern, and now you're thinking that neurotic tendency will help you figure out where you stand with one of the most powerful men in the country. You asked for a blonde liaison, and he gave you a blonde, so you're thinking—correctly—that that means he really wants you."

"You're on track so far," he admitted, amusement peeking around the edges of his skepticism.

"I know."

His eyes narrowed. "You're a Reader now?"

I almost laughed. "Hell no, I'm still just a Traveler." Readers, like Julia Tower, read the truth in a person's words. I read *people*. Their posture. Their expressions. The things their brains didn't even know their bodies were saying. That was the one quality I had that might actually come in handy for a recruiter.

Holt looked relieved, and I wasn't surprised. Readers make people nervous. Everyone lies, and no one wants to be called on it.

"So what else am I thinking?" he asked, and his grin said this had become a game.

I was not a fan of games, but when I played, I liked to win. So I swallowed my trepidation over the direction the discussion was headed and pressed forward, wearing my game face.

"You know Jake wants you. But now it's a little more complicated than that, right? If I'm Jake's sloppy seconds and you take a big bite, it's gonna look like you're satisfied with his leftovers. And that's going to lower your value. But on the other hand, he's given you what you asked for, and turning your nose up at a gift from Jake Tower could look like a massive insult. And you wanna play hard-to-get, not difficult-to-stomach, right?"

Holt's green eyes were huge. "And you think *I* over-analyze things?"

But I was right. I could see that much in the irritated way he crossed both arms over his chest, wrinkling his expensive jacket. He'd expected to study Jake, and his offer, and his people, but he hadn't expected a common escort to study him back. Much less be good at it.

I shrugged and smiled, then turned away from him

and started across the foyer, calling softly over one shoulder, "Fine. Then don't ask."

His shoes squeaked after me on the marble, and I knew I had him. "Okay, I give up," he called, grabbing my arm from behind. I froze at his touch and had to remind myself that it meant nothing. *I* was flirting with *him*—albeit under orders to seduce him on behalf of the entire syndicate—so I couldn't justify freaking out over evidence that I was getting the job done.

But neither could I stop myself from pulling my arm from his grip, though I tried to disguise the movement by ducking into an alcove, drawing us both out of view from most of the rest of the party. "I admit it," he said, stepping close enough that I wanted to back up, but there was nowhere left to go. "I want to know."

With the wall at my back and Holt blocking my path, I felt like the world was closing in on me. My pulse raced with encroaching panic. But I'd brought us here, out of sight, and I was still in control of this little word game.

"Then grow some balls and ask," I said, staring straight up into his eyes, silently daring him.

One eyebrow arched in response to my challenge. "Were you sleeping with your boss?"

I shook my head solemnly. "I have never once fallen asleep in Jake Tower's company." In fact, it was tempting to try to blink one eye at a time when he was around, so I could keep the other one on him at all times.

Holt rolled his eyes. "You know what I mean."

"I know what you *asked*." I couldn't tell if he was adorably old-fashioned, hopelessly shy, or simply reluctant to offend a syndicate representative with a question about a very powerful man's personal life. "If that's not what you wanted to hear, then say what you mean."

"You're bossy."

I laughed. "And you're nosy, so get it over with. No more euphemisms. Bite the bullet, or I'm gonna have to tell Jake you don't have the balls for this job." That was a total bluff, of course. Jake would like him better with neither a mouth, nor the balls to use it.

That time when Holt frowned, I couldn't tell if he was pissed off or intrigued. Until he stepped closer, leaving no room between us at all, and I realized he was a little of both. "Did you fuck your boss?" he demanded, his voice lower and grittier than it'd been a moment before.

"Hell no." I slid along the wall, sidestepping him, and my heart didn't slow to normal speed until I'd regained personal space, and both flight and fight seemed possible again. Just in case. "Jake doesn't screw around on his wife." He wouldn't, even if he weren't contractually prohibited from touching another woman. At least, that was the rumor. "And FYI, he'll have you shot for looking at her for more than a few seconds at a time, unless she's talking directly to you."

"That's crazy."

I shrugged. "That's love."

That hint of a grin was back. "Isn't that what I said?"

"Ah, a cynic." I sank onto a gold-padded bench against one wall of the foyer. "You may fit in here after all."

Holt sat next to me. "So, why did you live here, if you weren't...with him?"

And, the euphemisms were back. "Jake used to keep a small staff on hand at all times. But he moved everyone out a few weeks ago." The day after I'd accidentally punched a hole in his home defense system and gotten him shot. "Now it's just his family, the nanny, and whichever guards are currently on duty."

"Smart." Holt nodded thoughtfully. "And he really doesn't cheat on his wife? At all?"

"Nope. Not once, that I know of. Why?"

"I want to know who I'll be working for. If I sign on." He glanced to his right, toward the party still going on in the main part of the house. "A man like that, with plenty of money, in a position of extreme power over dozens of beautiful women..." He glanced at me, as if to say I was one of those beautiful women. Or maybe he was pointing out that I was powerless. "It has to be tempting to sample the goods. It'd be easy to get away with. In certain circles, it's practically expected, right?" he said, and I could only nod. "But Tower's loyal to his wife. That says something, doesn't it? Something about him, as a man?" Holt watched me closely, studying my reaction, and an uneasy feeling churned deep in my stomach.

Most syndicate employees didn't have the luxury of caring what kind of man Tower was, or what kind of business he did. They signed on because they were desperate for something they couldn't get for themselves. Usually money, protection or services only a syndicate could provide. Why else would you sign over even part of your free will to someone who doesn't give a damn whether you live or die, so long as you do both in service to the syndicate?

But Holt was different. He actually gave a damn. Which could make him very hard to recruit.

"Doesn't that also say something about the way Tower runs his organization?" He waited for my answer, staring into my eyes like he wanted to see past them and into my thoughts, and suddenly I recognized the ploy, and my teeth ground together.

Ian Holt wasn't naive enough to believe that a man

with Jake's power and breadth of influence had climbed to the top of the hill without stepping on a few heads. Or that fidelity to his wife translated into any kind of integrity in business. He knew what the Tower syndicate was like—at least, he *thought* he knew—and this was a test to see which I would choose: loyalty to my boss or honesty to the potential recruit.

Assuming I had any choice in the matter. And he had no way of knowing whether or not I did.

He'd see through a lie—he seemed to be expecting one anyway—but I couldn't exactly tell him the truth about Jake and the syndicate, even if he already knew most of it. Or even some of it. Which brought up an even bigger problem.

If Holt already knew what kind of man Tower was and what kind of business he ran, why did he accept Jake's invitation in the first place? I could only think of two possible reasons. First, Holt had no moral qualms about syndicate business or lifestyle. Or, second, he couldn't afford the luxury of indulging whatever moral qualms he did have. Which meant he was either corrupt or desperate.

But then a third, even worse possibility occurred to me and that uneasy feeling in my stomach swelled into a roiling discomfort. What if Holt was neither of those? What if he was just some curious, greedy asshole looking to get everything he could out of Jake before politely turning down our offer and walking away with his free will intact?

If that happened, I would have to harvest Holt's blood instead. And if I handed over nothing but blood from a venture this expensive, when what Tower really wanted was Holt's service, Jake would kill me. But first he'd give

Kenley to Jonah, down in the basement, so that the last thing I ever heard would be my sister screaming.

Bile rose in my throat, and I swallowed a sip of warm champagne to keep it down. And when I looked up, I realized that Holt was still waiting for my answer to a question I'd almost forgotten.

"Does Jake's fidelity to his wife say something about how he runs the organization?" I said, rephrasing the original question, and Holt nodded. "Yeah, I guess it does. There's nothing Jake wouldn't do for his wife, and even less he wouldn't do for the syndicate."

Including kill me and torture my sister.

The thought of damning someone else to the hell I was living in made me want to light my own hair on fire and take a bath in gasoline. But I would do it. I'd do whatever it took to make Holt sign.

I had no other choice.

Four

Ian

"Which is it you dislike, parties or champagne?" I asked, nodding pointedly at the virtually untouched flute in her right hand, as the party buzzed on without us.

Kori blinked, obviously struggling to refocus her attention, and twisted to face me on the ornate gold couch, both an expensive eyesore and an uncomfortable perch. "It's parties *with* champagne. And food served in bites too small to taste."

I laughed. "You'd rather drink from a trough and eat from a bucket?"

"I'd rather eat from a paper wrapper and drink from the fuckin' bottle."

"And your bottle of choice?" She had yet to say anything I'd expected to hear, and I couldn't help wondering what would come out of her mouth if we got a chance to talk about something more meaningful than appetizers.

"Vodka."

Any of the waiters could probably have gotten her whatever she wanted to drink, but I couldn't really talk to her surrounded by two hundred other partygoers, and if I couldn't talk to her, I couldn't make her trust me.

"And since you used to live here, you'd probably know where Tower might keep a bottle of vodka...?"

"I might."

"So maybe we could grab that and go for a walk on the grounds, free from the intrusion of pointless small talk as well as bite-size snacks."

Kori hesitated, and for a second, I was certain that she didn't want to be alone with me. Then she glanced at the guard stationed on either side of the front entrance. "They're never going to let you wander around the property without an escort from security."

"Aren't you an escort from security?"

She huffed, and I wondered what I was missing. "It's complicated. I protect you, but *they* protect Jake and his interests, which would not be served by giving an un-bound man free access to the grounds. We could sneak out, but the patrol would probably find us."

"Then it sounds to me like we have two options. We can ditch the party entirely and forage for a bottle of vodka elsewhere—"

"Jake would be pissed if we leave without telling him..." she said, and I nodded, not surprised.

"Or we could go upstairs, which—I'm willing to bet—isn't being patrolled."

She gave me a conspiratorial grin. "That's because no one's allowed upstairs. Jake's kids are asleep in the family wing, so there's a guard at the foot of both stair-cases." She glanced over her shoulder, and I followed her gaze to the closer of two mirror-image staircases, where a huge man dressed all in black stood directly in front of the bottom step, arms clasped at his back. He was obviously armed, and if his expression was any indication, he suffered from a severe lack of personality.

"But you used to be a guard, so you could take one of them, couldn't you?" I teased. "If I were to snatch a butter knife from the kitchen, you could bisect him from neck to groin in a single stroke, right?"

Her smile spread slowly, and her brown eyes practically sparkled. "Hell yeah. But Kenley will kill me if I get arterial spray on her dress." She slid one hand over her own hip to where the dress ended above her crossed knees, and my gaze traced the path, before I realized what I was doing.

Oh, *hell* no.

Don't believe a word they say. Don't let your guard down. And do not *make friends.*

I'd heard it over and over, from Aaron. Hell, I'd said it over and over to myself. I couldn't get personally involved. I couldn't afford to see any of them as real people. They were a means to an end. Tools for me to use, like a wrench, or a hammer. Kori Daniels was the hammer I'd have to swing to smash through Jake Tower's defenses and gain access to his prized possession, and you couldn't be attracted to a hammer. Right?

But she'd have to *think* I liked her, or she'd never trust me. And if she didn't trust me, she'd never let me near her sister. Kenley Daniels. The woman whose blood had the power to ruin lives—or end them.

"Okay, blood splatter is a problem," I admitted. "But you're a Traveler, right? So, you could just walk us both through a shadow down here and out of one up there, couldn't you?" I glanced at what I could see of the second floor for emphasis.

Kori shook her head. "Infrared grid. There isn't a true

shadow in this entire house, except for the darkroom. None deep enough for me to step through, anyway."

"What if there was?" I glanced around to make sure no one was listening, then I stood and started to tug her into the alcove she'd led me to minutes earlier. But she stiffened before I could touch her, and I realized I hadn't imagined her pulling away from me before. But I didn't understand it.

She was just a hammer to me, and I was just a job to her. An assignment. Korinne was the bait sent to reel me in, and for all I knew, she did this on a weekly basis. She flirted and cajoled, in a teasing, I-dare-you kind of way, clearly gauging my interest, and she probably knew far better than I did how to stay detached. How to attract without being attracted. How to engage without engaging your emotions, or even your desires.

So why the physical distance?

Was that part of Tower's pitch? Show me the menu, but don't let me order until I'd officially signed on? Or was Kori defining her own boundaries between work and play?

I was almost jealous of how well she played the game. And I was more determined than ever to keep in mind the fact that this *was* a game. A charade, of sorts. The woman, the party, the champagne and fancy clothes—they were nothing but a pretty mask covering an ugly beast that, behind its beguiling smile, waited to devour me.

"What if there was what?" she asked, standing without my help, and I had to drag my thoughts back on topic. Again.

"What if there was a true shadow upstairs? What if I could *make* a shadow? A real one? There's no way we could both get past the guard, but if you distract him, I could sneak up and make a shadow for you to walk through. Then you could find that bottle, and we could both forget about the crowd for an hour or so."

Because that part was real. She hated the party and the champagne, and the more comfortable—and less sober— I could make her, the better my chances of conning classified information from her. Like how well guarded her sister was at various times of the day. Or better yet, how to get into and out of Kenley's apartment in the middle of the night.

Her pale brows rose in surprise. "You can black out infrared light?"

I leaned closer and put one finger over my lips. "Shh. I'm pretty sure that's most of why Tower wants me. So yes, if you can get me upstairs, I can open a hole in the infrared grid, through which you could then join me."

"A cynic *and* a rule breaker. I like it." Her smile widened just a bit, and too late I realized I was returning it with one of my own. "And if we get caught?"

I shrugged. "I'll say I was giving you a demonstration of my Skill, for recruiting purposes." But she looked uncertain, so I tried again. "Tower told you to keep me happy, right?" No one had actually come out and said that, but it was no stretch of the imagination. Kori nodded, her smile fading fast. "So he can't get mad at you for doing your job, can he?"

She frowned, like she wanted to argue, but wouldn't. Or couldn't.

I arched one brow at her. "Never mind. If you're too scared…"

"Motherfucker…" she mumbled, rolling her eyes over my dare, and I couldn't resist another smile. "Fine. But it'll have to be the far staircase, and you'll have to be quick. And make sure no one else is watching."

"No problem."

"You ready?" she asked, and I could tell from the curve at the edge of her mouth that she was getting into the spirit of the adventure.

"Almost." I took the champagne flute from her hand and drained it with one gulp, then set it on the floor next to the wall. "What's your plan?" I asked, glancing at the guard on the far side of the foyer. "Flirt? Take him a drink?"

She shook her head. "He wouldn't buy either of those, coming from me. Don't worry about it. Just wait until he steps away from the stairs, then haul ass. And be quiet." Then she turned and headed across the foyer without so much as a glance back.

I tried not to watch her walk away, but failed miserably, and by the time I realized I was staring, she was in position. She walked right past the guard without a word, and I thought she'd changed her mind about the whole thing until he called out to her, though I couldn't make out more than her name, from across the large foyer.

I started across the floor, my hands in my pockets, prepared to claim I was looking for the restroom if I were accosted. The guard in front of the near staircase eyed me as I passed him, but when I didn't try to race up the stairs at his back, he turned to stare into the party again, obviously disappointed that his post wasn't closer to the action.

There was a broad expanse of floor between the two sets of stairs, and in the center of that, opposite the double front doors, was a smaller set of doors leading to a courtyard in the middle of the house. Several couples milled outside, sitting on benches, drinking and nibbling from plates of those hors d'oeuvres Kori hated. I stood near the door, blocked from sight by the curve of stairs, listening to her conversation with the second guard. Which turned out to be less conversation than argument.

"Look who's playin' dress up…" the guard said, but his tone was neither friendly nor flirty. "I've never seen you in a dress before." ·

"And you never will again, if I have any say."

"You don't, though, do you?" he said, and when she tried to keep walking, he grabbed her arm, hauling her close, his back to me and the staircase. And in that moment, I understood why she'd pulled away from me when I'd held her arm. "You don't have a say in anything anymore, do you?"

"Fuck off, David," Kori snapped, and I started to step in, thinking that her plan had gone awry. Then she jerked free from his grip and walked off. When he took several steps after her, I realized this was how she'd planned to distract him. Not by flirting, but by pissing him off. She'd known he'd follow. Maybe they had some kind of history. A grudge, or a former fling.

"I caught the show, you know," the guard said softly, like he didn't want anyone else to hear. Which meant he had no idea I was there.

I started to slip up the stairs, but then I noticed through the railing that Kori had gone still again, this time staring at the floor, fists clenched at her sides. "Shut up," she whispered.

The guard stepped closer, so close his chest almost touched her back, and I could see her tense when he leaned down to whisper into her ear, words so soft I had to strain to hear them. "All this time, turning your nose up at everyone who wanted a taste, busting balls and splitting skulls with impunity because Tower liked you. But look at you now. My, how the mighty have fallen…"

"I'm pretty sure that's a misquote," she mumbled, as he circled her slowly, and I ducked behind the staircase again, out of sight, unless the guard on the other side of the foyer turned to look.

"Fits, though, doesn't it. The taller the pedestal, the harder the bitch on it crashes to the ground. Do you want to know what we saw?"

"I want you to back the fuck off before I decide you'd look better with your nose on one side of your face."

"That was some messed up shit, Kori," he continued, like she hadn't even spoken. "I mean, I wanted to see you taken down a peg or two, but that was hard to watch, even for me. How you doin' in the aftermath? Need a shoulder to—"

The guard's voice ended with the *thunk* of flesh against flesh, and I came forward until I could see him through the railing, lying flat on the floor, bleeding from his nose. Kori stood over him, feet spread in those stupid stilettos, bloodied fist still clenched from the blow.

She thought I was already upstairs—I could tell by the look of pure rage on her face, something she wouldn't have intentionally shown a recruit. She didn't know what I'd seen or what I'd heard. Hell, *I* didn't know what I'd heard. But it made my stomach churn.

Aaron was right—they were monsters in human masks, and those masks were less convincing with every second I spent staring at them.

The guard coughed at Kori's feet and started to sit up, but she planted one pointy heel in his crotch to stop him. I glanced across the foyer at the other guard to make sure he wasn't watching, and when I saw that he was staring at the party still going strong in the main part of the house, out of sight from my current position, I jogged silently up the stairs—hunched over so she wouldn't see me—and into the first open, dark room I saw.

Faintly, from below, I heard Kori's heels click on marble, fading with each step as she headed for the front door.

For one long moment, I stood frozen, listening for anything that would indicate the west wing—the employee wing, where Kori'd once lived—was currently populated. But I heard nothing. So I pressed my back against the wall with the door still open to the hall and closed my eyes, slowly drawing darkness toward me from every shadowed corner and shaded nook in the room. I called to it, from every darkened crack beneath every door in thc hall. And thc shadows began to coalesce around my feet, curling around my shins, wisps of pure darkness rolling over me.

I lifted my hands, and the shadows rose with them, roiling around me, an inky oblivion, deeper and more satisfying than the shallow dark rendered useless by the infrared lighting grid I could feel overhead, blazing beyond the visible spectrum.

The darkness was cool and quiet. It was peace given form and function. I could feel it with every cell in my body, deep into the marrow of my bones. Into my soul. The darkness was mine to command.

Until half a minute later, when Kori Daniels stepped out of it and onto my right foot.

"Ow!" I laughed as the pointed toe of her dress shoe ground into my foot, and she stepped back immediately.

"Sorry!" she whispered, and I felt rather than saw

her trip over her own shoes in the absolute darkness. I reached out for her instinctively, but let go as soon as she'd regained balance. "You did this?" she whispered again, from inches away, and I realized that if I couldn't see her, she couldn't see me.

"Yeah."

"Holy shit, that's incredible," she breathed. Something moved between us, and it took me a moment to realize she was spreading her arms in the shadow I'd made, like a child in the rain. "It's like finding a watering hole in the desert. A shadow on the sun."

"Yeah, except I didn't find it. I made it." Couldn't hurt to remind her how valuable I was.

I began to let the darkness go, a little at a time, and slowly light filtered in again from the hallway, feeling much brighter than it should have, after the absolute darkness. "That was impressive," she said, when she could see well enough that her gaze met mine in the shadows. "No wonder Jake wants you."

"He's not the only one," I said, and her brows rose in interest as she stepped back and glanced around at the unoccupied bedroom.

"Oh? Who else is courting you, Mr. Holt?"

"Ruben Cavazos, most notably," I whispered, following her toward the door. "Along with a couple of the smaller syndicates on the West Coast."

"Cavazos." She practically spit his name, stepping out of the first of her shoes. "You don't want anything to do with him."

I laughed softly and tried not to notice the shape of her calves as she took off the second shoe. "I'd hardly expect you to endorse the competition."

Kori straightened, holding both shoes by the straps in one hand. "He fucking shot me."

"Cavazos shot you?" I could hear the surprise in my own voice.

Instead of answering, she pulled the left shoulder strap of her dress down to expose a puckered scar on her shoulder, still pink and fresh. "Two months ago."

"What happened?"

"Clash of the titans." Barefoot, she peeked into the hall, then gestured for me to follow her. "Everyone fights for one side or the other."

"Are we sneaking?" I whispered, nodding at her shoes, wondering if I should take my own off.

"Nah. There's no one in this wing. I just hate heels."

I followed her down the hall and around the corner to the right. Three doors later, she turned left into a room with a billiard table in the center of the floor and a full-size bar along one wall. "Close the door," she said over one shoulder as she dropped her shoes on the floor and headed for the bar.

I pushed the door closed softly, then crossed the room and took a seat on the center bar stool while she took up the position of bartender.

"What'll it be?" She leaned forward with her elbows on the polished dark wood surface of the bar.

"Scotch?"

Kori rolled her eyes. "Of *course* you drink Scotch."

"Are you calling me a stereotype?"

"Not yet, but if you don't pull some surprises out of your hat soon, I suspect that moment is coming." She dug beneath the bar and came up with a single short glass while I tried to decide how to respond to such a challenge. She wasn't ready for any of my real surprises, and she never would be. Which was why I couldn't get emotionally involved. Why I had to keep telling myself that she was just a hammer. A hammer with really nice legs, and eyes the color of good caramel, and...

Focus.

"Creating darkness wasn't enough of a surprise?"

She laughed. "It was a start. Ice?"

"Four cubes."

Kori scooped ice into the glass and set a half-full bottle of very expensive Scotch in front of me. I held it up, examining the label, reluctantly impressed with Tower's taste. "How much trouble will we be in if we get caught?"

"We're not going to get caught. If we hear footsteps, you make it dark, and I'll make us disappear." She produced a bottle of Grey Goose from beneath the counter, then circled the bar to sit on the stool next to mine. "There's snack mix if you want, but you're gonna have to serve yourself."

"What are you going to do?"

"This." She twisted the lid off the bottle and gulped from it once, twice, three times, without flinching.

"Rough night?" I asked, thinking about what I'd overheard.

"Any night that sees me in three-inch heels and sequins is a rough night." She set the bottle on the bar, the cork stopper still clasped in one hand. "But I've certainly seen worse."

I watched her, and after nearly a minute of staring off into space, she turned to face me. "What?"

"You drink like a man."

She shrugged and glanced at the bottle I had yet to pour from. "One of us should."

I wanted to ask, but at the same time, I didn't want to know. Whatever the guard—David—had seen done to her was none of my business, and it wasn't relevant to the job at hand. I already knew Tower was the scum of the earth, without having to hear the specifics.

And for no reason I could have explained, I didn't want her to know I'd heard.

"So, what do you think so far?" She tilted her bottle up again as I poured from mine, then she wiped her mouth with the back of one hand. "Seen anything yet worth signing over your soul for?"

"Is that what I'd be signing away? My soul?" I happened to agree, but I was surprised to hear it from her.

Kori blinked, like she'd just realized she'd said too much—that pesky honesty getting in the way again. But she recovered quickly. "Nah. Just five years of your life. The standard term of service for most syndicates."

"How close are you to the five-year mark?" I picked up my glass and sipped from it, savoring a liquor I could never personally afford, trying not to think about the fact that if I were alone with the other Daniels sister, this whole thing could be over in a matter of seconds. My objective hadn't changed, but the strategy certainly had. Use one sister to get to the other. And to do that, I'd have to pretend to be recruitable.

"Five years came and went nearly a year and a half ago." She twisted to show me her left arm, and the two interlocking chain links tattooed there. Marks of service. "One for each term."

I'd already seen them, of course, and I already knew what they meant. She was six and a half years into a ten-year commitment to serve Jake Tower and his syndicate. Her oath had been sealed with two linking tattoos, each containing a tiny bit of his blood—a flesh binding. Until the day her commitment expired and her tattoos faded into the dull gray of dead marks, she would be compelled to follow his orders, or she would die fighting the compulsion.

Syndicate service was a miserable way to live. And often a miserable way to die. Only three kinds of people joined voluntarily: the ignorant, the ambitious and the desperate.

Which category did Kori fit into? Which would be most believable for me?

"You must like it here, then, if you signed on for another term," I said, trying to embrace the part I had to play.

Kori blinked, then took another swig of vodka, straight. Then she shoved the corked lid back into the bottle and pushed the Goose away, like it might be to blame for whatever she was about to say. "This is my home."

I frowned. It felt like she was starting a new conversation, rather than continuing the one already in progress. "No, this is your job."

"You really don't understand, do you?" she asked, and I let my frown deepen, so she would explain what I already knew, and I would listen and respond, and ask all the right questions, and with every minute that passed she would trust me a little more, because she would know I was no threat. She had all the power, because she had all the knowledge.

And because she thought she could cut my balls off with one hand while slicing my throat open with the other.

Kori exhaled slowly, and a brief glimpse of guilt flickered across her face, like she was already regretting the pitch she was about to throw at me. That told me she was neither ambitious nor ignorant—at least, not after more than six years of service, which came as no surprise, after what I'd overheard on the stairs.

And that only left desperate.

"When you sign on with a syndicate—any syndicate, not just this one—you're not just taking a job, you're becoming part of a community. Like an extended family. You're getting job security, medical care, personal protection and virtually limitless resources. The syndicate isn't just employment—it's a way of life. A very stable, secure way of life."

"Sounds awesome." It also sounded like a very well-rehearsed speech. "What's the catch? Is it all the following orders? Because honestly, that's what I balk at." To say the very, very least.

"There's some of that, of course. But that's not really so different from any other job, is it?" she asked, and I couldn't help noting that now that I'd pointed out a flaw in the system, she was referring to it as a mere job again. "Any workplace is a hierarchy, right? There's a CEO, management, and the rest of the employees. Everyone has a boss, except whoever's at the top. That's how we operate, too."

"Yes, but in any other job, you can quit if you don't like the orders."

"That's not true." She smiled, like she'd caught me in a lie. "You can't just quit military service if you don't like the orders."

"So, would you say service to the Tower syndicate is more like military service than like a civilian job?"

She had to think about that for a minute. "Yeah, I

guess, only without the patriotism and gratitude from your fellow citizens. Large community. Great benefits. They even get chevrons for time in service." She twisted to show me her arm again, to emphasize the parallel.

But I knew what she wasn't saying—in the military, you can take the chevrons off at the end of the day, but the syndicate owns you for the life of the mark, twenty-four hours a day, seven days a week. You're never off the clock. And the word *no* has no meaning. I couldn't understand why anyone would ever sign on for that.

"Okay, obviously following orders is what's bothering you, and I can understand that. So why don't we just lay the truth out on the table?"

"The truth?" I watched her in interest. The truth was a rarity in life in general and even more so in the syndicate. Only the fearless and the foolish wielded it so boldly, and I already knew Kori Daniels was no fool.

"Blinders are rare, and you're the best I've ever seen. That makes you very valuable, and I'd bet my best knife that we're not the only ones who've made you an offer?" Her sentence ended on a question, and I could only nod. "Right now, everyone's playing nice and pulling out the best china because you're being recruited. But if that doesn't work, you'll be hunted. And eventually you *will* be caught, and when that happens, you'll be all out of choices. It's a winner-takes-all kind of game."

"I'm assuming there's a silver lining to this cloud of doom?" The cloud that had been hanging over me since I was twelve years old, when my mother explained how the rarity and power of my Skill would shape the rest of my life. As a kid, I'd thought she was being paranoid. As an adult, I'd learned better.

"The silver lining is that at this stage in the game, you

can still decide what mark you want to bear. Who you want to serve. Because you *will* wind up serving someone." Kori shrugged and glanced longingly at the corked bottle of vodka. "Hell, I'm not sure how you went unnoticed as long as you did."

Flying below the syndicates' radar hadn't been easy, and dipping beneath it again once this was over would no doubt be even harder.

"That's a rather ominous bit of truth," I said, committing to nothing.

Kori shrugged again. "It can't be changed, so you might as well understand your options."

"And those would be...?"

"The Tower syndicate, or some other, inferior organization."

Or...door number three, the option she either didn't know existed or didn't believe possible: hide.

"And the others are inferior because...?"

"Because we have the best of everything." She leaned closer, and I expected to smell vodka on her breath, but I couldn't, and suddenly I wanted to kiss her, to see if I could taste it. Or maybe just to taste her.

I blinked in surprise at the thought, but Kori didn't seem to notice. She was still talking.

"Jake wants you," she said, staring straight into my eyes. "I mean he *really* fucking wants you, which gives you more power going into negotiations than most people have. You could get just about whatever you want out of him."

Was it my imagination, or did she seem a little pleased at the idea of me taking Tower for all he was worth? More than pleased. She looked...excited. Her lips parted and her eyes shone with eagerness. She looked *fierce,* like the chain links on her arm could restrain her, but never truly tame her.

And as she watched me, probably waiting to see the gleam of greed that would tell her I was interested, I had a sudden, dangerous, treacherous thought. What would Tower give me, if I asked? Would he give me *her?*

I hated the thought as soon as I'd had it. People can't be given as gifts. They shouldn't be, anyway. Especially people like Kori Daniels, whose nature obviously couldn't be suppressed, even by direct orders. Giving her to someone else would be like caging a wild bird, only to see the bright, beautiful feathers you loved fall out and fade at the bottom of the cage.

But with that one lecherous thought, and the momentary failure of my own moral compass, I suddenly understood why someone might join a syndicate. Someone who wanted or needed something badly. Something he had no chance of getting on his own.

Everyone has a price. Tower's advantage in life was that he knew that and had no problem exploiting it.

"What is it you think I should ask for?" I turned my glass up and drank until the ice cubes bumped my lip, Scotch scorching its way down my throat, where I wished it could purge that lascivious thought from me. I couldn't afford to want the bait dangled in front of me. "What could I possibly ask for that would make it easier to take orders?"

"An extra chain link." She poured more Scotch into my glass, and I watched her light up with excitement over an idea I obviously didn't understand. She was beautiful in that moment. Intense, and dangerous.

"If I don't want the orders that come with signing on for five years, why the hell would I sign on for ten?"

"You wouldn't." Kori smiled and pushed the glass toward me. "You'd ask—no, you'd *demand* a second mark for free. A five-year commitment, with the seniority of a second-tier initiate. With two chain links, there are fewer people who can boss you around, thus fewer orders to follow."

"Why stop there? Why not ask for three or four links?"

Kori's expression darkened, and that spark in her eyes died. She leaned over the bar to grope for something and when she sat down again, she had a plastic jar of snack mix in one hand. "Seniority comes with responsibility. The more you ask him for, the more he'll want from you in return."

Things I wasn't going to want to do, obviously.

"Two is the perfect number." She unscrewed the lid on the snack mix and offered me the jar. "You have enough rank to avoid static from the bottom two rungs, but not enough seniority to obligate you to do…things above your pay grade."

I took a handful of pretzels and peanuts. "Things like what?"

Kori just scrounged up a small smile and shook her head. "Even if I knew what my superiors' duties were, I couldn't tell you. Some things—many things—you can't know until you bear his mark."

I wanted to pursue the issue. I wanted to ask her if Tower had ever given her an order she didn't want to follow. If he'd ever made her do something that made her skin crawl or rotted a bit of her soul. But picking at her emotional scabs—making her talk about things she obviously didn't want to remember—seemed cruel. *Too* cruel, considering what else I had to do. I hadn't come into Tower's territory to be recruited by Kori Daniels.

I'd come to kill her sister.

Five

Kori

I'd said too much. I could tell from the way he was sipping his second glass of Scotch, looking at me like I was some code he'd already started to crack. Like he could rearrange the words I'd spoken until they said what he needed to hear.

Holt knew what to ask. He knew what *not* to ask. I wasn't sure whether I was playing him or being played *by* him, and that scared the shit out of me. I had to regain the upper hand, or Kenley would pay for my failure.

"You done with that?" he asked, and I followed his focus to the bottle of Goose.

"Almost." I uncorked the bottle and took another swig, then pushed the cork back in.

"Well, you might as well take it with you," Jake said, and I turned so fast the room spun around me. He stood in the doorway, leaning against the frame like he'd been there all night. "No one else is going to want any, after your mouth's been on the bottle."

I wondered how much he'd seen. How much he'd heard. But I got nothing from his expression, as usual.

"The alcohol will kill any germs," I said, but I took the bottle with me when I stood. Never let it be said that I turned down good vodka. The shit under my bed at Kenley's would take paint off a car.

"Are you ready to rejoin the party?" Jake said, as Holt finished his drink, still seated, and evidently unhurried.

Holt set his glass down, the remaining ice cubes small enough to swallow now. "Actually I'm kind of tired from my flight. I think I'm going to call it a night."

Jake nodded. "Kori will drive you to your hotel. But I'm sure Nina and Julia would like to say goodbye before you go." He stepped out of the doorway to let Holt pass, and when I started to follow, Tower blocked the doorway with his arm. "Korinne will meet you at the front door."

Holt glanced at me, then nodded and headed down the hall.

Jake closed the door behind him, and my hand clenched around the neck of the bottle I still held. "Explain," he ordered.

"You said to do whatever it takes."

"And recruiting Holt required Scotch from my personal liquor cabinet, in the off-limits portion of my home?"

I shrugged. "He has good taste."

"Shall I assume the privacy helped you get to know each other?" he asked, and I nodded. "And does he like you?"

"I don't know."

"Does he want you?"

"I don't—" I started, and Jake frowned. "Yeah, I think he does." There'd been this look in his eyes a few minutes ago... "But it's not personal. Anyone will do. We could send one of the girls to the hotel with him—"

Jake shook his head. "He rented a seventy-five-thousand-dollar car and drank my fifty-year-old Scotch. He's either putting on airs or living beyond his means, but either way, he doesn't want a common whore, Korinne. He wants something worth more. Someone with a little class. So dig deep and scrounge some up."

I didn't give a damn about the insult. I'd been called much worse than classless. But Holt had already seen me barefoot, drinking straight from the bottle. If classy was what he wanted, I wouldn't be able to fool him. But I couldn't tell Jake that, because if he thought I was worthless, I was as good as dead.

"Drive him to his hotel and walk him up to his room. Eat a breath mint, say please and thank you, and don't trip over the damn heels," he said, running one finger over the toes of the shoes I still held in my left hand. "Act like you're worth something, and he might just believe it. And Korinne?"

"Yeah?" My cheeks were flaming now. I could feel it.

"If you ever come upstairs in this house again without my permission, I'll put you back in the basement and let the guards draw straws. David's eager to pay you back for the broken nose."

It took every ounce of willpower I had to keep my hands from shaking. To pretend nothing he said could scare me. Jake didn't buy it, but that didn't matter.

What matters is the face you show the world, not the quaking mess behind it.

Twenty minutes later, I pulled up to the entrance of the Westmark Hotel and shifted into Park. The valet was waiting when I stepped out and handed the key to him, and the doorman had Holt's luggage out of the trunk before I'd even rounded the car. He followed us inside with the bags while I led Holt to the elevator. I'd checked him in and picked up his key cards that afternoon.

Tower had reserved a three-room suite for him. It was nice enough to tell Holt he was valued, but not nice enough to inflate his ego. The suite said "we want you, but not as much as you think we want you." And that might have worked, if I hadn't already told him that he could pretty much get whatever he wanted in exchange for his signature—my little fuck-you to the puppet master pulling my own strings. Jake would get Holt in the end, but he would pay out the ass for him, if I had anything to say about it.

On the twenty-third floor, I tipped the bellhop, then closed the door behind him and made a mental note of all the rugs likely to trip me in Kenley's stilettos. Then I began the tour.

"This is Jake's favorite hotel," I said, pulling back the curtains to show off the view. "They have twenty-four-hour room service. If you want something that's not on the menu, just use Jake's name. They'll get you anything you want. And there's a Jammer on duty 'round the clock, so you can't be tracked while you're here."

"Wow." Holt stared out the window at the city, and even I had to admit the view was amazing. You could see the river from his room, and all the boats were lit up, like a string of white Christmas lights. And if you squinted just right, you could see where the river split, dividing the city into three parts: the east side, the west side and the south fork, like the bottom third of a peace sign. I rarely ventured out of the west side—Jake's territory—

because the chain links on my arm could easily get me killed east of the river, on Ruben Cavazos's side of town.

"There's no place like home, I know, but you'll only be roughin' it for a few nights," I said, turning away from the window to take in the leather couches, thick rugs and huge flat-screen television. "Think you can manage?"

Holt pulled the curtains closed. "Only if the chocolate on my pillow is Swiss and the bottled water was flown in from France."

"Hand-collected by crippled orphans from the fountain of youth itself," I said, and he laughed, while I headed for the bedroom. I pushed open the double doors and sucked in a deep, shaky breath at the sight of the bed against the middle of the far wall. "King-size bed with pillow-top mattress," I said, crossing the room with quick, efficient steps.

The bathroom was next and I breathed a little easier just being out of the bedroom—until I remembered that the giant whirlpool tub was built for two. As was the walk-in shower with dual showerheads. I stared, frozen, desperately trying to summon words that wouldn't come, until his footsteps echoed behind me.

"You okay?"

"Yeah." I turned to see Holt in the doorway, blocking my path whether he meant to or not. "This is the bathroom, obviously." I brushed past him before he could step back and headed straight for the front room, where the exit called to me with singular purpose. But I stopped at the cabinet beneath the television instead. "And the best part is the minibar, fully stocked with overpriced snacks and alcohol." I pulled open the door to show off the selection. "I recommend…well, all of it. Help yourself. Take everything you can carry, and call down for more if you get the munchies in the middle of the night. It's all on Jake."

I looked up from the minibar to find Holt watching me, his expression caught somewhere between amusement and confusion, which I wished I could clear up for him. But I couldn't. I headed for the door and had one hand on the knob before I spoke. "Is there anything else I can do for you?"

The words burned my tongue, and I wanted a drink to put out the flames. Something strong enough to make the next part easier. Bearable. Maybe.

"No, I think I'm good," he said, and I blinked, sure I'd heard wrong. He didn't want…?

But I wasn't going to question my good fortune.

"Okay, then, I'll see you in the morning for breakfast. Around nine? Or did you want to sleep in?"

"Nine's fine," Holt said, and I dropped the key to his rental car on the small table next to the door.

"Good night." I was in the hall before he could respond. The door closed on whatever he was saying, and I took off down the hall, only pausing long enough to step out of my shoes, half convinced that if I didn't run, he'd change his mind and call me back.

My heart racing, I jogged past the elevator and into the stairwell, hoping for a shadow deep enough to walk through, but the stairs were lit up like a fucking runway, and I couldn't reach any of the bulbs to bust them. So I jogged down the first flight, then stopped on the twenty-second floor to use the elevator—no way I was going to walk down twenty-one flights of stairs.

On the first floor, I crossed the lobby like my bare feet were on fire and only breathed easy when I stepped outside, into the night, and spotted the entrance to an alley at the corner of the building.

Unlit alleys are the downfall of many an airheaded horror-movie bimbo, but they were my escape. My own personal transportation system, with free, unlimited rides.

I dashed past the doormen and valet attendants, still holding my sister's shoes, and ran into the alley, already picturing my room in Kenley's apartment, kept dark for situations exactly like this. My bare feet pounded from the grass onto the broken pavement, and a rock bruised my foot on my second step. With the third step, my foot landed on carpet, and a step after that, I collided with my own bedroom wall, and the rebound knocked me on my ass.

Dazed, I dropped the shoes and leaned back against the foot of the bed. A second later, my bedroom door flew open and the overhead light flared to life. "What the hell was that?" Kenley demanded, one hand still clutching the doorknob.

"Sorry. I forgot how small this room is."

"No more running starts, Kori," she said, letting go of the door to cross her arms over her chest. "You're gonna break your nose on the wall."

I half hoped she was right. A broken nose would make me ugly. And if I was ugly, Jake might pull me off the Holt job in favor of a prettier face.

Of course, knowing my luck, he'd kill me as punishment for messing it all up, then carry out his threat against Kenley, even though I wasn't there to see her abused. It would be just like him to try to make my afterlife miserable, too.

"How'd it go?" Kenley gave me her hand, and I let her pull me up. "Did you have to sleep with him?"

"No." *Not yet, anyway.*

She turned me by my shoulders and unzipped my dress. Which was really her dress, loose on me now, where it would have been tight two months earlier. I let the material slide to the floor, and she picked it up when I stepped out of it. "Is it just me, or does he look familiar?" Kenley said.

"It's you, and half the planet. The whole world saw that news clip."

"I kind of feel sorry for him," Kenley said. "They'll all be after him now." They, being the rival syndicates, of course.

"Don't." I grabbed the T-shirt slung over the end of my bed. The one I'd slept in the night before. "Don't you dare feel sorry for him. He's the idiot who revealed his Skill on national television. He's gonna have to sign with someone. It may as well be Jake." Holt's imprisonment may as well keep me alive and keep Kenley out of the basement.

"What's he like?" she asked.

"He's fine. Normal. Kinda funny. He doesn't deserve this." What I was doing to him. What I *had* to do to him, to save myself and my sister.

"No one deserves this." Kenley laid the dress across the bed and pulled a hanger from the closet, then stood staring at it, like she'd forgotten what to do with it. "I'm so sorry, Kori," she said, and I could hear the unshed tears in her voice.

"No." I pulled the T-shirt over my head, then lifted her chin, making her look at me. "You have nothing to be sorry for, so don't start this again. Please."

Kenley burst into tears and I pulled her into a hug, holding her until the wrenching sobs fractured into smaller cries, then broke down into teary hiccups I could handle. "This is all my fault," she said, wiping her cheeks when I let her go. "I'm so sorry for getting you into this."

"You didn't know. You couldn't have."

Six years earlier, at twenty years old, Kenley had still been sheltered and naive, because we'd made her that way. Kris, Gran and I had tried to protect the baby of the family, and instead we'd turned her into a victim, ready-made for a world full of predators. I shouldn't have been surprised when one found her. And I couldn't let her serve her time alone. "Besides, I signed on voluntarily. I make my own damn choices."

"Not anymore," she insisted. "And that's my fault."

"It's not your fault. But I can't argue with you about this anymore." I let go of her, and exhaustion washed over me, pulling me toward sleep with a force I couldn't resist. "Not tonight, okay, Kenni?"

She nodded and picked the hanger back up. "I'm sorry. You're not well yet. Two weeks isn't enough time for anyone to recover from...whatever they did to you. You still look half-starved."

"Some women do this to themselves on purpose, you know. Others pay to get this look." I spread my arms, trying not to see how thin I still looked in the mirror.

"Those women are crazy."

"No argument from me." I pulled a pair of fuzzy socks from my top drawer and stuffed my feet into them, trying to make up for the abuse they'd endured most of the night.

Kenley slid the straps of her dress into the notches on

top of the hanger. "So, do you know what you're going to do? How you're going to snag him?"

I followed her with the stilettos when she carried the dress into her own bedroom. "I'm going to snare him with my demure manner and natural charm, of course."

Kenley laughed.

"I don't think Jake realizes how much he's bitten off with this one, and I've tried to tell him I'm not a recruiter, but he won't listen to reason."

"It could be worse, though, right?" She hooked the hanger over the top of her closet door and knelt to dig through the junk on the floor. "I mean, he could be making you throw yourself at someone hideous, like the Tracker Monica had to reel in last month. He's truly—" She flinched when she realized what she'd said. I'd been locked up last month. All month. And I had yet to meet whatever ogre Monica had recruited to replace Cameron Caballero, when Cavazos bought out his contract. "Well, trust me, he's hairier than a gorilla and he smells even worse. At least Holt's clean. And he's nice-looking, right?"

I dropped the shoes into the box she held open for me. "He must be, if *you* noticed."

Kenley flushed and slid the box onto a stack of others in one corner of her closet. "Like you didn't."

I shrugged. We'd never actually talked about her taste in men. Or lack thereof. But I didn't give a damn whether she slept with men or women, or both at once, so long as it was her choice. So long as she wasn't being used for anything except the bindings she'd been recruited to seal.

"What the fucking hell is this?" She slid one hand behind the dress still hanging on her closet door and pulled the material closer to her face.

"You sound like a kid playing dress up when you cuss. Give it up. You lack the skill."

Instead of answering, she held the dress out to me. "How did you manage to get blood on my dress at a formal party, Kori?"

"Shit. Sorry." I sank onto her bed and folded my legs beneath me. "I thought I avoided the spray."

"Whose?"

"David's," I said, and she waited, obviously expecting more of an explanation, so I rolled my eyes and sighed. "He started it."

"What'd he do?"

"Doesn't matter. The point is that if I let the bastard get away with something small now, he'll try something bigger next time."

Kenley hung the dress in her closet. "It was about the basement, wasn't it?" she said, and when I didn't answer, my sister sighed. "The blood's dry now, but there may be enough for a decent binding, if I dampen it. I could make him leave you alone."

"No." I shook my head. "I fight my own battles." As well as most of hers.

"What happened in the basement, Kori?" She spoke with her back to me, like she didn't want to see my face when I answered. Like she already knew I'd lie.

"Nothing." Some lies between sisters are okay. Some are forgivable. Some are unavoidable.

Mine was all three.

Kenley sighed, but she let it go. "Come on. I'll make you a sandwich."

"I'm not hungry."

"You're skinny. You need to eat."

"Yes, Gran." I rolled my eyes again, but followed her

into the kitchen and sat at the bar while she made two grilled-cheese-and-tomato sandwiches, both for me. My mouth was watering before she'd finished buttering the bread.

"How bad is this, Kori?" she asked, as she set the first one in front of me on a paper plate.

"Looks good from here." I picked up the sandwich and Kenley frowned at me—she knew damn well that I knew what she really meant.

"What's gonna happen if you can't sign him?" she asked, and I set the sandwich down, my appetite suddenly gone.

"That won't happen. I'll get him."

"But if you can't? If he's only here to eat, drink and be merry on Jake's dime? What's Jake going to do, Kori? Tell me the truth. You owe it to me."

She was right about that, but I couldn't give her all of it.

I exhaled slowly and met her gaze across the counter. "He'll kill me." Slowly. Jake wouldn't want me to die without having time to truly suffer first.

But I couldn't tell her the rest of it. I couldn't tell my sister what would happen to *her* if I failed.

Because I wasn't going to let that happen.

Six

Ian

After Kori left, I sat on one of the couches in the front room and stared at the door for a solid five minutes, trying to figure out what I'd said to send her fleeing into the night. I couldn't remember a woman ever running away from me before, and I certainly hadn't expected that from Tower's liaison.

Whatever I'd done, I couldn't afford to do it again. This was my only shot. Tower trusted me—as much as he ever trusted anyone who wasn't bound to him— because he'd approached me, rather than the other way around. If I got caught, he wouldn't fall for the same trick again. But it wasn't just *his* trust I needed.

I lay in bed half the night, trying to figure out how to get Kori to trust me enough to reintroduce me to her sister. Maybe even take me to Kenley's house, or leave me alone with her somewhere else. Anywhere else. Because the alternative was too horrible to contemplate.

I didn't want to kill Kori's sister in front of her, but I would, if I had to. I'd do it for my brother, and for everyone else who'd ever been bound against his or her will by Kenley Daniels.

Few could have done what Kori's sister had done to my brother—most Binders weren't strong enough to make a nonconsensual binding stick. But Kenley wasn't most Binders. She had an *extraordinary* amount of power, and as long as she wielded it like a weapon—or let someone else wield her power like a weapon—she was a threat to the general population. As was anyone pulling her strings.

Which was why Kenley Daniels had to die.

Bringing down Jake Tower was a bonus. It was also the carrot I'd dangled in front of Aaron, a die-hard Independent activist, to get him to help with the research and intel.

The plan had been simple, at least in theory. Kill the Binder, and those she'd bound would go free. By Aaron's estimate, in the six years Kenley Daniels had been working for Tower, she'd sealed bindings not only for most of the new recruits, but for most of the existing employees who'd reenlisted during that time period.

Jake Tower was the king of a castle built around a single, crucial cornerstone—Kenley Daniels. With her death, he would lose the majority of his workforce—the legion of indentured servants blood bound to follow his every order—and with them, his power and influence.

The whole recruitment ruse was intended to put her within my reach. She was supposed to be my liaison to the Tower syndicate; I'd described her in perfect detail.

Kori wasn't supposed to happen. She'd never even met my brother, and she hadn't bound anyone to Jake Tower, which made her useless to both me and Aaron. But she was all I had, so I'd have to make it work.

When she knocked on the door the next morning, I was as ready as I was going to get.

"Nice boots," I said as she stepped past me into the living area. "They should make it even easier to run away."

"Meaning?" But I could see the truth in the tense line of her shoulders. She knew exactly what I meant.

"You ran out of here last night like the hotel was on fire." I headed into the bedroom and her quick, angry footsteps followed me.

"I wasn't running, I was…drunk. Too much vodka. I didn't want to puke all over your hotel room."

I glanced at her from the closet doorway. She'd gulped from the bottle like a pro, without even flinching. Kori Daniels might have been a lot of things, but she was not a novice drinker. Yet there was something new and vulnerable in her expression—something fragile and caged—and that surprised me so much I decided not to push the issue.

I selected a tie and stood in front of the mirror to knot it, watching her reflection fidget while she watched mine. She was uncomfortable in silence, and her hands needed something to do.

Interesting.

"So, what do you want for breakfast?" she asked, when the silence became too much for her. "There's a restaurant in the hotel, or we could try—"

"I ordered room service," I said, giving the knot a final tug to tighten it. "Should be here in—" A knock came from the suite door. "Right about now."

She followed me to the living area and stood with her arms crossed over her chest while I signed for the food and the waiter laid it out on the table. "I thought we were going out for breakfast."

"We were. Now we're not." I handed the bill back to the waiter and he left, while she continued to scowl at me. "I ordered a little of everything. Take your pick." She opened her mouth to complain—I could see it on her face—but I spoke over her. "And don't tell me you're not hungry. I hate it when women starve themselves to achieve some stupid physical ideal that only looks natural on a twelve-year-old. Men don't want women who look like children. Not real men, anyway."

Her eyes narrowed and I could almost hear her teeth grind together. I crossed my arms over my chest and watched her, waiting to see her head explode. She opened her mouth to start what would surely have been an award-worthy string of expletives. But then she saw my face.

"You're baiting me," she accused, hands propped on her bony hips.

"Yes." I started uncovering plates, stacking the domed covers on the coffee table. "You are the most interesting thing Tower has shown me so far. But I do think you're too thin. Will you eat with me?" I sat at the table and pushed another chair out for her with my foot.

She stood for a moment, watching me. Considering. Then she glanced at the plates steaming on the hotel table. "Fine. But I call the waffles."

"I'll split them with you."

After another moment of consideration, she nodded.

We rearranged food on the plates, splitting the eggs and bacon as well, unwrapping silverware and passing salt, pepper and tiny bottles of syrup back and forth. When I was full and her plate was empty—Kori ate an entire Belgian waffle in under three minutes—I set my remaining food in front of her and leaned back in my chair, watching her from across the table. Studying her.

Reminding myself that she was a means to an end. A tool. Nothing more. No matter how fast my pulse rushed when she looked up, and I realized I'd never seen eyes with such depth, like everything she'd ever seen was still in there staring back at me, daring me to take a closer look.

One moment she looked vulnerable and bruised, and I wanted to bandage wounds I couldn't even see. Then a second later, that woman was gone, and in her place stood a fierce hellcat, angry at the world and spitting flames with every word, and I wanted to poke her just to see the sparks fly.

I couldn't figure her out. But the more time I spent with her, the worse I wanted to, and that was dangerous. *Kori* was dangerous. Tower knew what he was doing when he sent her. How could anyone spend more than five minutes with her and not be fascinated by her? Not want her?

Focus, Ian. Play to win.

"Okay, this is your moment." I crossed my arms over my chest and leaned back in my chair. "I am rested, fed and as receptive as I'm going to be. Tell me why I should join the Tower syndicate."

Kori hesitated with her fork halfway to her mouth, egg yolk dripping into a puddle of leftover syrup on her plate. "Right now? Just like that?"

I nodded. "Wow me."

She lowered her fork slowly and stared at me from across the table. I'd thrown her off balance, and I was a little relieved to realize that was even possible. "Well, obviously there's a steady paycheck. A nice one, considering the strength and rarity of your Skill."

I shrugged. "Every job pays. What will I get from the syndicate that I'm not already getting as a systems analyst?"

Kori laughed out loud, and I almost joined her. Then I remembered to pretend that it was perfectly plausible for me to sit behind a desk all day weighing the pros and cons of various software options for a billion-dollar company, when the truth was that I lived more than an hour from the nearest internet connection, connected to my family only by satellite phone.

Too bad that part of my cover story was set in stone.

"What's so funny?" I demanded, though I could easily have answered that question myself.

"Can I answer in the form of a list?" she asked, and I nodded, curious now. "The fact that you think you're getting *anything* out of being a systems analyst is hilarious. The fact that I don't even know what a systems analyst *does* is even funnier. Then there's the fact that you *are* a systems analyst. I knew that, but now that I've met you, I just…can't see it."

"People are rarely what they seem to be at first glance," I said, trying to pretend I didn't agree with everything on her list. "It's my job to analyze systems. It's your job to tell me why I'd like answering to Jake Tower more."

Her smile faded, and I wanted to take it all back. But I had a part to play.

"The apartment." She set the fork down and pushed her plate away. "I know you haven't seen it yet, but it's really—"

I shook my head. "Dig deeper. You're still throwing money at me, but this isn't about money."

Kori frowned, and her eyes narrowed like they did when she got irritated—a pattern I was already starting to recognize. "Of course it's about money. You wouldn't be here if you didn't need cash."

"Is that why you joined? For the money?"

Her frown slipped a little. "I don't give a shit about the money." But I'd already known that. She hated champagne and hors d'oeuvres. She preferred boots to stilettos. This was not a woman interested in wealth or social visibility. "I had my reasons."

I wanted to hear her reasons. Badly. But if she'd wanted me to know, she would have told me. "I have my reasons, too." And that may have been the truest thing I'd said to her so far.

"Does that mean you're going to join? Or have I fucked this up already?"

There it was again, that vulnerability. That depth in her eyes, and the way she held her breath waiting for my answer.

"That means I'm going to give you another shot. Tomorrow. Maybe by then you'll have figured out what carrot to dangle in front of me."

"This isn't a fucking game, Ian," she snapped, and I smiled. I couldn't help it.

"That's the first time you've said my first name. And of course this is a game. Right now, you're losing."

She stood, hands flat on the table, eyes flashing in anger. "You can put on a suit and sit in front of a keyboard every day for the rest of your life if you want, but that's not going to change who and what you are. You're a Blinder, and a risk-taker. A thrill-seeker."

I shook my head, ready to deny what I already recognized as truth—words from my own head, falling out of her mouth. But she cut me off before I could speak.

"I saw your face when you let the shadows fade around us last night, and I know that look. Darkness is in you, Ian. It's part of you. You're not going to feel whole until you're free to live in the shadows of your own creation, and that's not going to happen for you as a fucking systems analyst. But it can happen for you in syndicate service. And if you're going to join one, you might as well join the best."

"And do you really think the Tower syndicate is the best?"

Kori blinked, and I glimpsed something she was about to dance around, without actually denying—a trick syndicate employees learned quickly. "You will never find a better financial opportunity than what Jake is offering you. You'll never find a syndicate with better security or fringe benefits. But if you go into this thinking you can work Jake Tower with a smile and a joke, he will roast you alive, feast on your flesh, then pick his teeth with your fucking bones."

"That may be the most honest thing you've said yet." But I felt my smile slipping. "Colorful, too."

Kori sank into her chair again, and I watched her face as understanding bled into fear for a moment before her defenses slammed into place and left me staring at a carefully blank expression. But she couldn't undo what I'd seen. She'd shown me a glimpse of the gritty reality beneath the shining surface of Tower's empire, and that wasn't supposed to happen. At least, not until I had a chain link tattooed on my arm.

"So now what?" She gripped the arms of her chair like it was all that was holding her up.

"Now you take me out on the town. Show me the syndicate in its natural habitat."

"Why?" she demanded. "Is there anything I can show you that'll make a damn bit of difference?"

"Why else would I be here?"

Kori sat straighter, eyes flashing again, this time with new understanding. Possibility. "You need something from him." I could practically see the bulb flare to light over her head, and I wanted to smile. "I'm a bad recruiter. I'm a *suck-ass* recruiter, but you haven't even flinched over anything I've said or done, and that means you need something bad enough that you don't care what you'd have to sign to get it."

I arched one brow at her. "I do care what I'd have to sign over. But I also know that nothing in life is free."

She frowned, like that cliché meant more than it should have for her, and I wondered what she'd paid for whatever she got out of signing with Tower. "So tell me what you need, and I'll get it for you."

I shook my head slowly. "That's not how the game is played." Because if she knew that what I needed was her sister's corpse, she'd try to kill me where I sat. So why was I more disturbed by the thought of being hated by her than of being killed by her?

"Fuck the game. I don't wanna play."

"You don't have any choice," I said, and fury rolled over her in waves almost thick enough for me to taste.

"Don't *ever* say that to me," she growled, her hands clenched around the chair arms so tightly I was afraid she might break them off.

I exhaled slowly, backing carefully away from whatever psychological land mine I'd nearly stepped on. "That's not what I meant. You have to play the game because *I* have to play the game. I want something Tower won't want to give. Which puts me in a pretty difficult position."

Kori actually rolled her eyes. "I don't think you fully appreciate how badly Jake wants to secure your services. There isn't anything he wouldn't give you, if you ask nicely and do a little ass kissing. Money. Car. Apartment. Women. Hell, men, if that's what you like."

"I don't—" I started, but she spoke over me.

"Recreational chemicals..." Drugs, of course. "Fine art. Exotic pets. A surrogate mother for your unborn child. He'd give you nearly anything, short of his own wife and kids." She stopped abruptly, forehead furrowed with a sudden unpleasant thought. "Please tell me you don't want his wife. Asking for Lynne would get us both killed."

I scowled, repulsed by the thought. "No, I don't want his wife."

"What, then? Tell me, and I'll get it."

I arched both brows, trying to hide a grin. "You should be careful what you offer a man you just met. What if I asked you to kill someone for me?"

"You wouldn't." She leaned back in her chair, obviously comfortable with her assessment of me.

"You don't know me, or what I want, or what I'm capable of. But I'm telling you that what I need, Tower's not going to want to give me. So if you want to make your boss happy you may have to go around him to get it. Are you willing to do whatever that takes?"

Kori watched me, her expression carefully blank, her gaze steady and colder than I'd seen since the moment we met. "Maybe you belong here after all."

Seven

Kori

"It all begins with the grunts. The foot soldiers, with just one chain link," I said, when we were far enough from the doormen that they wouldn't overhear me explaining the inner workings of the Tower syndicate to a man without marks.

"The bottom layer of the pyramid?" Holt said as we crossed the covered hotel entrance and stepped onto the sidewalk, greeted by honking horns, the bite of exhaust, and what little breeze reached downtown from the river.

"Exactly." I wasn't sure how much he already knew, so I started from the beginning. "This is the rank I highly suggest you skip, and I don't think Jake will balk at that, if you ask nicely."

"What's he like?"

"Jake? He's disciplined. Patient." In the same way a cat is willing to wait as long as it takes for the best shot at its prey. "Jake likes order. Rules. Straight lines and neat little boxes. I couldn't walk a straight line even stone-cold sober and neat boxes tremble in my presence. Which is probably why I'm constantly in trouble."

"You? Trouble? I am shocked and appalled."

I glanced up to see Holt watching me with no hint of a smile. "You may be the most sarcastic man I've ever met."

"It's a gift." We stopped at the corner, but only had to wait a second for the light to change so we could cross the street. "So, what is a grunt's primary duty?" Ian asked as soon as we stepped onto the opposite curb.

"Depends on the color of the mark. Rust is the most common. A rust-colored mark means unSkilled muscle. They're sentries, on the lookout for anything that doesn't belong. And they're everywhere, whether you see them or not. They do much more than the police to keep crime rates down on this side of town."

Unauthorized crime, anyway. No one intervened when Tower ordered someone found, punished or killed. But that was one of the things we didn't talk about. One of many.

Ian glanced at the people all around us, carrying shopping bags, having breakfast at the outdoor tables spilling onto the sidewalk from various restaurants, or just rushing to and from wherever they had to be on a Saturday morning. "What's green?" He nodded toward a woman stepping out of a coffee shop with a cardboard container of steaming paper cups. The two chain links on her arm were the color of tarnished copper.

"Green is for unSkilled service. She's a secretary, or accountant, or something like that. She's not muscle, but she's not Skilled, either."

"And there are red marks, too, I assume?"

"Yeah. Red for the skin trade, same as for most other

syndicates, but they don't work on the street. Private appointments only. Their clientele is established and wealthy, and unlike Cavazos, Tower marks them on their arm, same as all the other initiates. He doesn't see the point of either degrading or hiding them by putting the marks on their thighs."

Holt's brows rose. "Prostitutes are people, too?"

"It's just another way to serve." I couldn't spit the lie out fast enough. "Of course, whatever you want would be on the house—at least until he marks you."

Ian scowled, and I wasn't surprised. Jake was right; Holt didn't want a whore.

"And your mark?" he asked, glancing at the half sleeve covering the top quarter of my left arm.

"Iron-colored links are for Skilled initiates, no matter what the position. I'm security, obviously, though no longer on Tower's personal guard."

"Why not? Did Tower get a splinter on your watch?"

Yeah. A big metal splinter to the chest. "Something like that."

"So, after you recruit me—*assuming* you recruit me—what will your job be?"

"I don't know." I would never work as Jake's guard again, nor would I be trusted to protect his wife or kids. "General security, maybe. Like the guards stationed everywhere at the party."

Ian grimaced. "That sounds boring as hell."

But I'd take boring over the basement any day.

"What would I be doing?" he asked, as we turned another corner.

"Whatever Jake needs done. Blinding the opposition. Punching holes in a defensive infrared grid, so his men can get in."

"But we're talking about crime, right? Criminal enterprise?"

I hesitated, trying to decide what he wanted to hear, and how best to merge that with the truth. "That sounds a little…"

"True?"

"Yeah." I frowned. "That sounds a little true. Also, insufficient. Not all of the syndicate's business is illegal. Some of it's just highly discouraged by legal, spiritual and political authorities."

"Semantics." He brushed off my reply with an ironic grin. "What are we talking about? What's his bread and butter?"

I hesitated, weighing my options.

"What's wrong?" Holt glanced at me as we stepped onto another crosswalk. The light changed before we were halfway across the street, but no one bothered walking faster.

"I'm not sure I'm allowed to answer the kind of questions you're asking now, but I'm supposed to do whatever it takes to keep you interested. Which means I'm walking the line between a couple of conflicting orders." And if I actually got caught between them, my body would tear itself apart trying to obey both at once.

"I'd never intentionally put you in that position," Ian said. "So if I ask something you can't answer, just tell me and I'll withdraw the question."

I frowned up at him, trying to decide whether or not he was serious. Nice guys didn't usually last long in syndicate life. Neither did nice girls, which was why I'd signed on to protect Kenley.

"Have you ever been bound?" I asked, and his sudden,

startled look darkened quickly into something I couldn't interpret.

"No. So, no, I've never felt resistance pain, if that's what you're getting at. Nor have I been caught between conflicting orders. Have you?" he asked, watching me carefully, and I nodded. "What's it like?"

"It's like dying, in slow motion. One piece of you at a time..." But my words faded into silence when a pair of unfamiliar eyes caught my gaze from several feet ahead on the sidewalk. I pretended not to notice, but it took real effort to keep tension from showing in my step. The stranger had glanced at me, but his gaze lingered on Ian, and his casual stance was as false as my grandmother's teeth.

The would-be poacher was young, which hopefully meant he was inexperienced, but I was unarmed, which automatically put me at a disadvantage.

I prattled on for several more steps without really listening to myself. Waiting. Hoping Holt wouldn't freak out when the shit hit the fan. You never can tell with civilians. And finally, as we stepped even with a narrow alley, a hand grabbed my right arm from behind and something sharp poked me to the left of my spine, through the thin cotton of my blouse.

"Scream, and I'll cut you," a young voice whispered into my ear, and I rolled my eyes as he pulled me into the alley. Ian didn't even get a chance to look surprised before a second man—this one bald—shoved him after us.

"You okay?" Ian asked me, his voice soft and taut with caution as he backed away from the bald man, who carried a knife no one on the street would be able to see. If anyone noticed us at all. With any luck, no one would.

"I'm good," I said, stepping carefully as I was tugged steadily backward. "They don't want me. You feel like being abducted today?"

"Wasn't on the agenda, no." Ian stopped with his back to the brick wall, halfway between the bald man and the one holding his knife at my back.

"Plans change," Baldy said. "Come with us quietly, or he'll gut your girlfriend."

I rolled my eyes again. This was a farce of an abduction at best. "First of all, I'm not his girlfriend. Second, it's kind of hard to gut someone from behind, dumb ass."

The hand around my arm tightened, and the first fiery threads of anger blazed up my spine. "Anyone ever tell you your mouth is going to get you in trouble one day?"

"Only hourly," I said, and Ian laughed without taking his attention from the bald man's knife.

"Last chance," Baldy said.

Ian glanced at me, brows raised in question. "What do you think?"

I shrugged, in spite of the knife at my back. "Well, they're not *total* morons. Knives instead of guns, so no one will hear gunshots. And they've got balls, coming after you in broad daylight. That one's a Traveler," I said, nodding at the bald man. "I'd bet my last drop of vodka on it."

Ian frowned. "How do you know?"

"Because the other one can't drag you through the shadows while he's threatening my life."

Baldy scowled, and I gloated silently.

"So should I go with them?" Ian asked, and I could hear the amusement in his voice. He was neither scared nor rattled, and I was pleasantly surprised.

"Nah." I twisted away from the knife at my back and

pulled the man holding my arm off balance. He stumbled, and I jerked my arm from his grip, then faced off against him with my feet spread for balance. "I'd hold out for a better offer."

Knife guy reached for me, and I kicked his kneecap from the side. He crashed to the concrete on one hip and swung his blade at my leg. I kicked the knife from his grip, then stomped on his hand, satisfied by the crunch of several bones, and even more satisfied by his howl of pain.

Something scuffed against concrete behind me, and I twisted to see Baldy lunge for Ian.

Shit! I started toward them, but stopped, surprised when Ian simply stepped out of his path, then slammed Baldy's wrist into the corner of the Dumpster. The knife clattered to the concrete at his feet, and Ian kicked it beneath the Dumpster. His motions were smooth and fast, and he hadn't come close to breaking a sweat.

The man on the ground in front of me pushed himself up with his good hand, and I squatted to snatch his lost knife. When he stood, I stepped up behind him and held his own blade at his throat. He stiffened, good leg holding most of his weight, arms out at his sides, and I almost laughed. "I take it back. You *are* a complete moron."

"Who *are* you?" he asked, in spite of the blade I held.

"Kori Daniels. Why? Were you expecting Little Miss Muffet?"

"Daniels? No shit? That's just my fuckin' luck," he said, and his voice shook, in spite of false bravado. "I bet two hundred dollars they'd find you facedown in the river."

I shook my head, though I'd had similar thoughts, myself. "So now you're stupid *and* poor."

The bald man grunted, and I looked up to see Ian's left fist crash into his face. Again. His head slammed into the brick wall—hard—and a cut appeared on his right cheek. Then his eyes closed and he slid down the wall to slump on the ground, unconscious.

Ian stepped out of reach in case the bald man woke up. A hint of a grin rode one corner of his mouth when he saw me gaping at him. "Why do you look so surprised?"

"Because I'm so surprised." Jake didn't know Ian could fight; if he had, he would have told me.

I considered that new information for a second, trying to decide how long I could get away with silence on the matter, while the man in front of me breathed shallowly in concession to the knife at his throat. "What's your name?"

"John Smith," he spat. And that was exactly the alias I'd expected—a generic fuck-you to the question no one with half a brain would ever voluntarily answer.

I slid the knife beneath the short left sleeve of John's shirt and he flinched when I split the material with one upward stroke. The cotton flaps parted to reveal a single iron-colored ring. No surprise there. "How much is Cavazos offering for Holt?"

"Hundred grand, unharmed. Seventy-five, if he's bruised or bleeding."

I glanced at Ian over John's shoulder, brows raised in appreciation. "Not bad. But he'll go higher." I stepped back from John and shoved him hard enough that he fell to his knees in front of me, facing Ian.

"What are you doing, Kori?" Ian said.

"Showing you what it feels like to suffer conflicting orders." I squatted and slid the knife across the concrete, and Ian caught it beneath the sole of his boot. "And

John's going to help." I circled John slowly, and he turned with me to keep me in sight. "To break an oath, you have to first be sealed into one. You give your word, and a Binder like Kenley seals it, with ink, blood or spoken promise. Or some combination of those. A verbal promise is the weakest. A blood binding is the strongest, whether sealed on paper, flesh or any other surface. John, here, has a blood binding sealed in his flesh by Ruben Cavazos." I glanced pointedly at his exposed biceps. "He's unSkilled muscle. And I mean unSkilled in every sense of the word," I said, backing out of reach when John lunged for me.

"Bitch!" he snapped, as I started circling him again, and I could see his bad leg shake.

"Kori, I know what a binding is," Ian said. "I grew up in the suburbs, not on Mars."

"But your understanding is theoretical, right? Like how I understand that the better part of valor is discretion, but I can't truly know what that feels like, since I've never tried it."

"You've never tried valor?" Ian's brows rose.

"No, discrction," I said, and he looked like he wanted to laugh. "My point is that you can't truly understand what you've never felt. But sometimes a good visual helps." That, and I really needed to hit something and I wasn't sure when I'd get another chance. "So watch closely."

I turned back to John, who still favored his right leg and was edging toward the Dumpster, probably in search of something to use as a weapon.

"When you break your word, you send your body into self-destruct mode. And when you're given conflicting orders, there's no way to obey them both, thus there's no way to avoid pain. First comes a real bitch of a headache."

I feinted to the right, then slammed a left hook into John's temple. He grunted and stumbled backward, and I followed while he was still off balance. "Next comes uncontrollable shaking and cramps. Then the loss of bowel and bladder control." I kicked John low in the gut for emphasis. He hunched over the pain in his stomach and I was already circling again before he stood.

"Then your body begins to shut itself down one organ at a time. Starting with the kidneys, and everything else housed in your gut." John lurched toward me, fists clenched, and I danced away from him on the balls of my feet. Before he could follow, I twisted into a midlevel kick, and my boot slammed into his right kidney.

John moaned, an inarticulate sound of pain, then fell to his knees.

"And in the case of conflicting orders, if one of them isn't withdrawn, the breakdown of your body continues until you die in a pool of your own evacuated fluids."

"Kori," Ian said, with a glance at the man curled up on the ground. "That's enough."

"Is it?" I grabbed a handful of John's hair and pulled his head back, one knee pressed into his spine. "What were you gonna do after you took me down?" I demanded. "How were you going to stop me from coming after you? Knife to the chest?"

John shook his head, and several of his hairs popped loose in my hand. "Across the throat," he gasped. "Then I was gonna throw your corpse facedown in the river and cash in on my bet."

Ian scowled, but didn't press his position.

I shoved John facedown on the concrete and put one

foot on the back of his neck. "Tell Cavazos I consider this a personal insult. If he doesn't make a serious effort next time, I'm shipping his men back in a series of small boxes."

Then I stomped on John's good hand, and his screams followed us as I knelt to pick up the knife I'd taken from them, then followed Ian onto the sidewalk.

The first of the resistance pain hit me as I folded the knife closed and slid it into my pocket—a flash of agony behind my eyes, accompanied by the glare of white light in the center of my field of vision. An instant migraine. And that was only the beginning.

"You okay?" Ian asked, when I staggered on the sidewalk, one hand pressed to my forehead, as if that could stop the pain.

"No." I stopped to lean against the wall of a dry cleaner's storefront and Ian stood in front of me, blocking me from view without being asked. If I hadn't been in so much pain, I would have questioned that kind of instinct, coming from a systems analyst.

I slid my hand back into my pocket and felt the smooth edges of the pocketknife, amazed by how calm the feel of the weapon made me, even as pain threatened to split my skull in two.

I'd been forbidden to arm myself, a fact I'd forgotten in the afterglow of the scuffle in the alley—even that little bit of expended energy had helped release some of my bottled-up rage. Carrying John's knife was an ongoing breach of the oath of obedience I'd sworn to Jake Tower, and I would hurt for the length of the breach— until I got rid of the knife, or my body shut itself down in protest.

Yet even knowing my life could end right there on

the street, my undignified death witnessed by an endless parade of strangers—not to mention Ian Holt—I didn't want to give up the knife. I'd won it in a fair fight. The knife was mine, and so were the skills needed to use it better than its original owner could ever have managed. Weapons were freedom. Power. Autonomy. And by denying me the right to arm myself, Jake had denied me all of those things, too. Intentionally.

I was still being punished.

While my head threatened to crack open like a pistachio seed, my hands began to tremble and my stomach started to cramp, and the pain was too severe to be hidden.

"Kori? What's wrong?" Ian's voice was tense with concern, and he glanced back and forth between me and the people passing us on the sidewalk, to see if anyone had noticed my weakened state. And that was all I could take, not physically, but logically.

Resistance pain weakened me and made me vulnerable, which made him vulnerable by extension. There were people—even my fellow syndicate members—who wouldn't hesitate to take advantage of that weakness, for any of a dozen reasons. And if I let Holt get hurt, Jake would kill me.

"Here. Take this." I pulled the knife from my pocket, my grip shaky, and Ian only hesitated for a moment before taking it from me. The instant the metal left my hand, the shaking stopped. The stomach cramps eased, and slowly, the pain in my head began to recede.

Ian glanced at the knife, then slid it into his own pocket. Then he met my gaze, silently demanding an explanation. When that produced no results, he tried again, verbally. "What's going on, Kori? Why can't you hold the knife?"

I exhaled slowly, not surprised that he recognized resistance pain for what it was. Then I braced myself for more. "I'm not allowed to carry a weapon. At the moment."

Another bolt of pain shot through my skull and into my brain—I wasn't allowed to tell him that, either.

I squeezed my eyes shut as my hands curled into fists at my sides, like I could actually fight the agony. But I couldn't. This pain was much stronger than the previous bout—literally blinding, for a moment—but shorter in duration, because telling Ian something I wasn't supposed to tell him was a terminal breach of my oath to Jake. Over and done with quickly, as opposed to an ongoing breach, like carrying a weapon would have been.

Ian's frown deepened. "Why not? What moment? *This* moment? Saturday morning specifically?"

"It's less a Saturday-morning thing than an until-further-notice thing." That one came with no additional pain—the breach was in the admission, not the details.

"How are you supposed to defend yourself?" he demanded, and I noticed that he didn't ask how I was supposed to defend him, which underlined for me the fact that he didn't need to be defended.

"Like I just did. I'm not untrained in unarmed combat, and I can use any weapons I gain. But I can't carry them once the fight's over."

Ian scowled like he had more questions, but he wasn't going to ask them, and I knew why. He didn't want to force me to answer any more forbidden questions. I could see it in his eyes. In the way he watched me in pity and concern, and I had the sudden, irrational urge to punch him, just so I wouldn't have to see either of them anymore.

I didn't need his pity or his concern, and I didn't want either. So I pushed off against the wall and started walking, and Ian fell into step behind me.

"Are you okay?" he asked.

"Fine," I snapped. "I'm not some delicate flower that's going to dry up and blow away at the first sign of pain."

"I never thought you were. In fact, you almost seem to be looking for a fight. Was all that really necessary, back in the alley?"

"That was a mercy," I insisted. "If I'd reported the incident, Jake would have told me to kill them both. But then there would have been no one to deliver my message."

"Your message daring Cavazos to bring his A game next time?"

"That's the one."

"And you really think throwing down the gauntlet was a smart move?"

I shrugged. "Couldn't let him think those clowns were a challenge. What is a gauntlet, anyway?"

"It's like a glove—" Ian shook his head, like he could jar loose all unnecessary thoughts. "That doesn't matter. My point is—"

"*My* point is that Cavazos will do anything to get you, and he won't be the only one. Why should we wear ourselves out swatting flies all day, so that we're too tired to fight when the eagle finally lands? With any luck, that message will piss Cavazos off enough that he'll skip the preliminaries and bring on the main event."

"Does that mean you're not going to report this to

Tower? Aren't you under some kind of contractual obligation to?"

"Nope. Jake's doesn't do much micromanaging
through direct orders. Sometimes that comes back to
bite him on the ass—those are my favorite times—but
usually that approach avoids much bigger messes."

"How's that?"

"Each command given is like a string that can't be
broken. Give too many to one person, and you're eventually just going to tie that person in knots, and when that
happens, nothing gets done. And sometimes people get
hurt." Not that Jake gave a damn about hurting people.
"Instead Jake saves direct orders for things he really,
truly means, and everything else is guided by a set of
standard expectations. For instance, I'm *expected* to
report any trouble we run into. But I'm not obligated to.
If I get caught, I'll be in trouble, but I won't suffer resistance pain from defying an expectation, whereas I would
from defying a direct order. And if I don't get caught..."
I shrugged. "No harm, no foul."

"And you're willing to take that risk?" Ian sounded
surprised, no doubt thinking of the resistance pain I'd
just suffered.

"What's life without risks?" But the truth was that defying Jake's expectations where and when I could was
the only way I had of striking back. Of showing him that
he might own my body, but he'd never own the rest of
me.

"Long," Ian said. "Life without risks is long. And
hopefully peaceful."

"And a long, peaceful life is what you're looking for,
Mr. Systems Analyst?"

"Who says I'm looking for anything? You people

called me, remember? You're the ones who're looking for something, and we both know that gives me the advantage."

"Yeah. That'd be believable if I didn't already know you need something from Jake, too. If he finds that out, you've lost your advantage, and you may as well drop your pants and bend over for him."

Ian flinched. "That's a rather indelicate metaphor." His frown deepened. "It *is* a metaphor, right?"

"Yeah. And it's only as 'indelicate' as the point it makes. If you don't thoroughly understand that Jake will fuck you over eventually, you need to turn around right now and start running."

Not that I could let him get very far. If he refused to sign, I'd have to take him in to be harvested.

Ian blinked, his green eyes narrowing. "You're right. You're a horrible recruiter. If I didn't know any better, I'd swear you were working for the competition...."

"I'm working for myself." And for Kenley. "Ultimately we're all working for ourselves, no matter who we're bound to."

"That sounds a little...mercenary."

I shook my head. "Simple self-preservation. No one's going to look out for you the way you look out for yourself. That's no different than in corporate America. Right?"

Ian blinked, like my question had caught him off guard. "I don't think that's a fair comparison. No one in corporate America has tried to kidnap me at knifepoint."

"And no one in the Tower syndicate has tried to bore you to death with spreadsheets and casual Fridays. What's your point?"

He laughed, and I was startled to realize I liked the

sound. A lot. I hadn't heard real laughter—the nervous kind didn't count—in a long time.

And he had a *really* nice smile…

No! Don't look at his smile, Kori! I couldn't afford to like Ian Holt, because then I'd feel guilty for damning him to a life of crime and violence, and once I let myself feel guilty for one horrible thing I'd been forced to do, all the others would crash down and bury me in regret for a lifetime of necessary evils. Unrelenting guilt was a crippling blow to any assassin, and one I had no plans to suffer.

Ian blinked, and his eyes narrowed. He was studying me again, and I had to squelch the urge to flinch away from his assessment. "You know, Tower might think he's scary, with his gun-toting guards and over-the-top security system, but I know the truth."

"And what's that?" *Why* did my voice sound so…frail?

"You're the most dangerous weapon he has, armed with nothing but the tongue in your mouth. And what a nice mouth it is."

Eight

Ian

"I…" Kori sputtered, blinking at me like the day was suddenly glaringly bright, leaving her exposed, and I realized that the only thing I enjoyed more than making her spew expletives was leaving her speechless. "What the hell does that mean?" she finally demanded, and I frowned. In my experience, most women love to hear how pretty they are and I'd never once pissed one off by saying so.

"It means exactly what I said. And by the way, the proper response to a compliment is 'thank you.'"

Her scowl was unrelenting. "You're not supposed to be complimenting me!"

"I'm not supposed to…?" My frown deepened, and my confusion only grew.

Kori squeezed her eyes shut and shook her head, but when she met my gaze again, she still looked mad, for no reason I could understand. "I mean…you don't have to do that. It's not necessary."

"Necessary for what?" I felt like we were suddenly speaking different languages, and hers was nonsense.

Kori glared at me through narrowed eyes. "This is all a game to you, isn't it?" she demanded, then rushed on before I could answer. "You better start taking this seriously, Ian, because Jake never loses and I don't like games."

"That's unfortunate, because you play them well." I snatched a handful of napkins from a pretzel vendor as we passed on the sidewalk and handed one to her, then wiped the bald man's blood from my hands. One of my knuckles had split open, but I couldn't have left enough of my blood behind to be of any use to someone else.

"I'm not playing," she snapped, swiping at the blood on her own fingers without ever slowing her step. "I'm telling you one fucking truth after another, most of which I'll probably get in serious trouble for, and you're treating me like some bimbo who can't see past her own reflection."

I stared at her, almost as fascinated as I was confused. "How the hell did you manage to twist my compliment into an insult? I think that qualifies as some kind of special skill."

"We obviously disagree on what qualifies as skill."

I stopped, and she went several more steps before turning to frown at me. "I don't understand you."

"You don't have to understand me."

"I do, though." I wanted to understand her worse than I'd ever wanted to understand anyone in my life, and I couldn't quite convince myself that my motivation was purely professional. Yes, the better I understood her, the easier it would be to use her to get to her sister. But the more time I spent with Kori, the harder it was to remember that she even *had* a sister, much less what I'd come into Tower's territory to do. "We're going to be spending a lot of time together over the next few days, and I'd like to know where the land mines are buried *before* I step on the next one."

"I think your best bet is steel-toed boots."

I laughed out loud at the thought of boots—any boots—protecting someone from a land mine. Even a metaphorical land mine. Then I wondered again why her landscape was so riddled with them. "Why are you telling me things that could get you in trouble?"

"Because they're…true." She shrugged, and her frown deepened as she searched for more of an answer.

"And you like the truth?" Interesting, for a syndicate employee.

"I'd call it more admiration than true enjoyment, but yeah." Kori frowned and dropped her used tissue in a trash can on the corner. "I guess you could say I like the truth."

"Why?" Every time I thought I was close to figuring her out, she said something that threw me for another loop, and though I'd given up trying to anticipate the dips and twists in the conversations, I couldn't help loving the ride.

"Why do I like the truth?" she asked, and I nodded. "I don't know. Because it's the truth. Why does anyone like anything? Why do you like coffee?" she demanded, when I glanced into a coffee shop while we waited for the crosswalk light to change.

"Because it wakes me up, it's warm in my hands and it tastes good. Your turn. Why do you like the truth?"

"I don't know how to answer that." And from the stubborn set of her jaw, I could see she didn't even want to try.

"Yes, you do. You're smarter than you think you are, Kori."

"How the hell would you know that?"

"Because I'm smarter than you think I am, too." I glanced at the crowd gathered around us, waiting for the light, then nodded toward the coffee shop and was relieved when she actually followed me to a rectangle of shade beneath its awning. "Why do you like the truth? Dig deeper."

She crossed her arms over her chest and thought about it, and for a moment, I was sure she would refuse to answer. But then she met my gaze with a shrug, understating how carefully she'd obviously considered the question. "Because it's right there for the taking. A lie, you have to think about, but the truth is… The truth is easy."

"No, it isn't. In my experience the truth is usually the hardest thing in the world to say. Or to hear." Or to see, lying on a bed, unmoving, staring at the ceiling with no sign of life.

Her mouth thinned into an angry line. "You don't want an answer, you want a fight. You're going to come up with an argument for anything I say, aren't you? Why does it even matter why I like the truth?"

"It doesn't matter to me," I said, my lie as steady as her anger. And I should have left it at that, but I couldn't help myself. Her steel spine and the occasional glimpse of vulnerability reminded me of Steven, and the bitter truth surged through me, scorching a trail through my veins. The memories. The loss. The rage still burning inside me.

Remembering should have made it easier for me to do what had to be done. But it didn't. Kori's mouth and her fiery grit—so different from Steven's quiet determination—made her real. They made it harder to picture myself destroying Kenley Daniels, if that meant destroying Kori in the process.

"Why you like the truth doesn't matter to me, but it should matter to you," I insisted, still trying to sort through it all in my head. "You can't recruit a man you don't know, and how are you supposed to get to know me in a matter of days when you don't even know yourself, after a lifetime in your own skin?"

"I know myself," she snapped. "And I'm starting to get a pretty damn clear picture of you, too."

"That first part, maybe." But she didn't know me. She couldn't. And if I was wrong about that, I was as good as dead. "So tell me why you like the truth. The real answer." I looked right into her eyes, practically daring her.

Kori glared at me, and I watched her, obviously pissing her off with nothing more than the fact that *I* wasn't pissed off. "The truth is real, even when nothing else is," she said at last, whispering so no one else would hear, dragging the words out like she didn't want to let them go. "It's steady. It doesn't change depending on the circumstances. It *never* changes. The truth will look the same in the dark as it does in broad daylight, and it quacks like the duck it is. That's a relief—knowing what you're getting. I like it."

I smiled. I couldn't help it. She was fascinating, and she obviously had no idea. Not that it mattered. I couldn't let myself want her, and I certainly couldn't *have* her; she'd want to kill me once I'd killed her sister. And even if by some miracle she could forgive that—though she wouldn't—she liked the truth, and my entire existence was one big lie. The reasons she had to hate me were too numerous to count and too huge to see around.

"Syndicate life must be hard for someone like you," I said, trying to drag my thoughts back on target, which proved almost as difficult as dragging my gaze away from her eyes. From her lips, half open, like she'd forgotten what she wanted to say. I wanted to taste her, right there on the sidewalk. Just once. Just for a second. And for one terrifying moment I was suddenly certain I wouldn't be able to concentrate on anything else until I'd done exactly that.

Then her frown grew skeptical, like she thought I was baiting her again. "*Life* is hard, period. Dying when there's another option is easy, even when it hurts, but that's the coward's way out. Sometimes it takes guts to live, and that's the fucking truth."

"So it is." I dropped my soiled napkin into the trash can a few feet away, and her brown-eyed gaze followed me. "Show me something true, Kori. Show me something real about the syndicate, even if it hurts to see."

Something horrible. I needed to see or hear something so terrible it would drive all other thought from my head and purge the sudden need tugging on my fingers like strings on a puppet. The need to touch her.

"You sure? I could show you lots of pretty lies," she offered, her voice delicate. Brittle. "You'd know they were lies, but they'd make you smile." I just watched her, denying myself what I had no right to want, and finally she nodded. "The awful truth it is. Let's go."

I followed her into the coffee shop without a word, and Kori pulled me into the ladies' restroom, then flipped the light switch by the door. Darkness descended and I exhaled slowly, enjoying the sudden calm it brought, like the start of an evening, after a glass of good wine. Everything seemed a little easier in the dark. Even with a strip of light shining from under the door and an emergency light flashing in the far corner.

Something touched my chest, and the breath I sucked in was loud in the silence. Her hand slid along my stomach, slowly, lightly, and I held my breath, wishing for more. I hated myself for that, but denying it would be pointless. I wanted greater pressure from her fingers. Longer contact.

I wanted to pull my shirt off so her hand would trail over my skin and I would know, just once, what her touch felt like.

Her hand kept moving until it reached my arm, then it trailed lower and her fingers intertwined with mine. Her skin was warm and dry, her fingers soft but strong. I wondered if the rest of her could possibly feel so smooth.

"When I squeeze your hand, take three steps forward, then stop. That part's important, unless you want to walk into a wall."

I nodded, then realized she couldn't hear my brain rattle. "Okay."

"Aren't you going to ask where we're going?"

"No. I trust you." I had no other choice, because I was helpless in that moment, in spite of years spent fighting, training for the inevitable. I was more vulnerable to her touch than I'd ever been to a gun, or a knife, or a fist.

"Don't," she whispered, and the words sounded like they hurt. "Don't trust anyone, Ian. Least of all, me."

Before I could respond, she squeezed my hand and tugged me forward, farther into the dark restroom. As my foot hit the ground on my third step, the air around us changed. It felt colder and dryer, and more sterile. And everything was dark. Truly dark. There were no shadows, because there was no light to cast them. There was no infrared grid, nor any glow from any kind of power indicator or exit sign. This was real darkness. My kind of dark.

"Darkroom?" I whispered, and the echo of my own voice told me the room was small, the walls not far beyond our shoulders, with us standing side by side.

"Yeah. Hang on, it's about to get bright." Her fingers left mine, and my hand felt cold and empty in her absence. Kori took a small step forward, then something clicked and light blazed to life all around us, violent and jarring, like we'd stepped into the middle of a roaring bonfire. There was no actual pain, but after such peaceful darkness, my eyes ached beneath the glare, and the sudden sense of exposure—of vulnerability—was more than enough to set me on edge.

Static hummed in front of me and I squinted into the light to make out a small monitor next to a door with no knob or handle. A moment later, the static on the monitor gave way to a man's face, scowling at us. "State your name and business," he ordered, eyes narrowed in irritation, as if he resented having actual work to do at work.

"It's me, Harkins. Open the door."

"Kori?" The man's eyes widened as he studied her face. "Tower said you wouldn't be making any more deliveries, so just turn off the light and slink back into the shadows before we both get in trouble."

"I'm not delivering. I'm tour guiding. This is Ian Holt." She stepped back so Harkins could get a better look at me, and I nodded in greeting. "Jake told me to show him around, so open the fuckin' door so I can do my job."

"Tower sent you? Then you won't mind if I verify that." He picked up a telephone receiver and held it in front of the camera.

Kori shrugged and crossed her arms over her chest. "He should be sitting down to lunch right about now, so you can probably catch him at the house. With his family."

Harkins scowled again and lowered the phone. "If there's trouble to be had from this, I'm aiming it all your way."

"What else is new?" she mumbled, as he made a show of pressing a button somewhere on the desk in front of him. The door to the darkroom popped open into the hall with the soft *whoosh* of a seal being broken.

"Stop by the front desk for visitor's tags," Harkins ordered, and then the screen went blank again.

"Was that an air lock?" I asked, as she stepped into the hall.

"Yup. So they can gas you without killing anybody else." She leaned back into the darkroom and pointed up, where two vents were nestled flush with the ceiling, side by side.

"You're serious?" I said, trying not to imagine why Tower might want to gas someone in his darkroom.

"Serious as gasping your last breath in a pool of your own vomit."

I frowned and followed her into the hall. "You know, you really have a way with words."

"I have a way with guns, too," she said, pushing the door closed behind us. "Let's hope I don't need one, because I am drastically under-armed today."

"Are you expecting another ambush in one of Tower's own buildings?"

She hesitated, then met my gaze briefly. "I don't have permission for us to be here, technically."

"Then why are we here?"

Another shrug as she led the way down the hall. "You wanted to see something true."

"Should I have specified that I want to survive seeing it?" She wasn't the only one drastically under-armed. For authenticity in the role of a systems analyst, I'd foregone even my bare essentials for the second day in a row.

Kori twisted to grin at me over her shoulder. "If you wanted boring, you picked the wrong tour guide."

"I didn't—" I stopped before I could admit I hadn't picked her. "I didn't say I wanted boring. Just nonlethal." For me, for her, and for whomever I'd have to kill to get my hands on a decent weapon if it came to that.

"Don't worry. You're too valuable to shoot." With that she headed down the long white hallway, and I had no choice but to follow, wondering what Tower was protecting with restricted-access darkrooms and gas vents.

We turned a corner to the left and Kori stopped at a rounded reception desk, where a woman with two green chain links on her exposed left arm handed us a sign-in sheet and slid two visitor's passes into plastic cases attached to lanyards.

UnSkilled service, I thought, staring at her arm.

Kori handed me a badge and I slid the lanyard over my head, then held the badge up so I could read it.

Heartland Pharmaceuticals

"You wanted to show me a pharmaceutical company?"

Her teasing smile lit a fire low in my gut, where it continued to smolder as long as her gaze held mine. "You got something against pharmaceuticals? You know, they may have a system you could analyze."

Before I could reply, she turned and crossed the lobby, then led me down another hallway and past several offices to a door with a keypad above the handle. "Wouldn't they have changed the code, if you're not supposed to be in here anymore?" I asked, as she started punching buttons.

"Why bother, when I wouldn't be able to get past the darkroom anyway?" She grinned and when a green light appeared on the keypad, she pressed on the lever and pushed the door open. We stepped into another hallway, identical to the first, as far as I could tell. More white doors with no windows. More featureless white tile floor. Security cameras on both ends, near the ceiling.

"Where are we?" I asked, as our footsteps echoed down the hall. I felt like I should whisper, but she hadn't, so it seemed stupid for me to.

"I thought you trusted me."

"I thought you said not to."

She stopped in front of the last door on the left and turned to look at me. "I don't know if I can actually get us in here. This one takes an employee-specific security code, and chances are good that they've stripped my clearance. Either way, I'm taking a big risk bringing you here."

"Why?" I said, more worried by what I saw in her eyes than by anything she'd told me so far. "Why would you break into a building you no longer have clearance for, just to show me something Tower obviously doesn't want me to see?"

Kori glanced at her feet for a second before meeting my gaze again, and again I was astounded by how much

I saw in her eyes, and how little of it I understood. "Because I can't truly balance the scales."

"I don't understand." I felt like a broken record, spouting that same sentence over and over again, but I couldn't help it. I'd never felt so unsure of anything as I felt when I was with Kori. I didn't understand her thought process and I couldn't interpret her body language, because it seemed to constantly broadcast contradictory signals. Her silence seemed louder than her voice, and even when she did speak, I felt like the parts she left out were more important than the things she actually said.

"Now that the syndicates all know about you, you're going to have to sign with someone, and it's my job to make sure that someone is Jake Tower. But no matter how badly he wants—or even needs—your services, he'll still have the upper hand in negotiations. He'll still have all the power."

"And you don't think that's fair?"

"I think it's unacceptable. But it's also inevitable. I can't give you even footing. The best I can do is arm you with information I haven't been explicitly forbidden to give you. That way, at least you'll know what you're up against. And what you're in for."

I studied her, trying to see what lay behind her eyes and hear what hid between her words. "You don't think I should sign with him, do you?"

She blinked, and her armor slid into place, as easy as if she'd just lifted an actual shield. "I think you have to," Kori said. "When there are no good choices, you pick—"

"The lesser of all evils?" I said, and she shook her head slowly.

"The evil willing to pay the most for you. You look that evil in the face, and you take it for all it's worth."

Was that what she'd done? Had she sacrificed liberty for the almighty dollar? Or was the money merely compensation for work she would have been forced to do, no matter who she signed with?

"But you shouldn't sign anything until you know exactly what you're signing on for," she said, before I could voice my questions. "Even if you can't change the terms."

"And what's behind this door will tell me that? What I'm signing on for?"

Another nod. "This is his most promising new business venture. Top secret. It's still on the ground floor, but Jake believes it has penthouse potential."

But she made the word *penthouse* sound more like a deep, dark dungeon, which made me both tense and incredibly curious. Intel wasn't my primary mission, but I had no objection to being handed information that could damage Jake Tower even beyond the blow I'd be delivering by killing Kenley Daniels.

"How bad will it be if we get caught?"

"For you? He'll make you sign a sealed oath swearing you haven't yet and never will reveal what you learned here."

"And if I don't want to sign an oath?"

Her brows rose. "You *will* want to, because the alternative won't be as simple or as pleasant."

I didn't bother asking what the alternative was. "What about you? What will happen to you?"

Kori's jaw tightened for just a moment. "Nothing. Because we're not going to get caught, unless you don't shut up so I can get us out of this hallway."

And there it was again—that fear I'd glimpsed earlier. It wasn't there when she talked about people dying in their own blood and vomit, or when she bluffed her way into a secure building, or when she took down armed men with her bare hands. I couldn't find any pattern to the things that Kori feared, and I was almost as worried by that as I was fascinated by it.

Kori started punching buttons on the number pad, but I only caught the first five of them. When she was done, the light flashed red. She groaned and let her forehead thump against the door. "Well, that was a lot of buildup for nothing, huh?" Her smile looked forced, but her relief—just a fleeting glimpse of it—was real. But before I could decide what to say, something clicked behind the locked door and it swung open.

A man in a white lab coat glanced at me, then his gaze found Kori and his eyes narrowed. "Korinne. Didn't they ban you from the building?" I glimpsed an ID badge hanging just below chest level, but his arms covered most of it when he crossed them, and I could only see his last name. Abbot.

Kori shook her head and clucked her tongue. "There you go thinkin' small again. I've been banned from *several* buildings. I'm a regular pariah."

"And who is your partner in exile?" Abbot asked, blocking the doorway with his own body.

"This is Ian Holt, the man whose ass you're going to be kissing in a few short days. Better practice your pucker." She shoved him into the room and stalked past him, and I followed when he stomped after her.

"Get out now, or I'll call security."

Kori shrugged, half sitting on a table covered in forms and file folders. "Call 'em. And while you're at it, tell them how you broke security protocol by answering the damn door. Anyone with the clearance to actually be in this room would have his or her own functioning code."

She picked up a clipboard and flipped through the pages clipped to it, too fast to have actually read anything. Then she looked up with her head cocked to one side. "You ever been on Jake's bad side, Abbot?"

"We all know *you* have." He snatched the clipboard from her and tossed it onto another table, then propped his hands on his hips beneath the lab coat, revealing brown slacks and a very poorly chosen button-down shirt. "You fell from grace, and I heard the landing was pretty damn rough. I wasn't on the guest list, but I heard that you—"

Kori swung before I even saw her pick up a weapon. She grunted with the effort and something I couldn't focus on slammed into the lab geek's head. He went down without a sound, out cold, a huge lump already forming on his left temple. "How rough was *your* landing...?" she mumbled, already squatting next to his still form. And only then did I realize what she'd swung. What had left its manufacturer's icon imprinted in the skin just below his hairline.

"An ink drum?" I wasn't sure whether to laugh or back away from her slowly.

"A *big* ink drum. If Abbot had upgraded his printer when Jake suggested it, he could have saved himself from a concussion."

"Or maybe a coma."

Her brows rose in interest. "A coma? You think?" She stopped digging through his pockets long enough to glance critically at his face. "Nice." Kori stood with a key card in hand. "Bastard deserves that and more."

"What did he mean?" I asked as she turned toward another door, and Kori went so still I wasn't sure she was even still breathing. "What did he hear? Why are you *persona non grata?*"

She clutched the key card like it might disappear if her grip loosened. But she didn't answer.

"Why do they hate you, Kori?"

"They don't hate me. Well, *some* of them hate me. The rest of them…" She turned slowly and looked up at me in shadows too shallow to be useful, thanks to yet another infrared grid. "You know how in school, there's always one kid who's just a little better than you at everything? His art gets hung in the hall. He gets to be the line leader, or the door holder, or, if it's high school, he gets to score the winning touchdown and fuck the cheerleader. You know that kid?"

"Yeah."

The frown lines across her forehead deepened. "You weren't that kid, were you? 'Cause that would kinda ruin my metaphor."

"No. I knew him, though." I wanted to touch her. I wanted to hold her, or squeeze her hand, but I understood that touching her would make talking harder for her. Might even make her words stop altogether.

"You know how you watch that kid, and you want to be him, but you also kind of want to see him knocked down a peg or two?"

"Yeah." Why did I have the urge to hold my breath, like that might somehow change the ending to a story we all knew?

"Did you see him fall on his face?" Her voice was harder than I'd ever heard it, and I nodded, feeling guiltier than I had since junior high. "When he fell, did you give him a hand up? Or did you kick him when he was down, to make yourself feel bigger? Or maybe you just watched someone else do that."

"I…"

"You don't have to say it, Ian. We're all grown-ups now. This isn't high school. But if it was, I'd be that kid, and he'd be the one kicking me." She glanced at the unconscious lab geek. Abbot. "They all would."

"And Tower?" I dreaded the answer, even though it wouldn't tell me anything. She'd painted a vivid picture without giving a single detail. "Who's he in this metaphor?

"He's the kid who pushed me down. Hard." She looked away again and stepped toward a window covered with dusty horizontal blinds ending an inch above the table she'd leaned against earlier.

I didn't want to ask. Knowing wouldn't change what I had to do. What I *would* do. But I wanted to know what had happened to her, and who had done it. I wanted to know if there was anyone I should kill with a little more than the necessary force and pain, when the time came.

"What does that mean, Kori? How hard did he push you?"

She turned slowly, still clutching the key card, and looked right up into my eyes, her pale hair the only spot of light in an otherwise dim room. "There are some questions it's not okay to ask. You just found one."

I held her gaze so she could see the truth in mine. "Fine. I can respect that." She didn't trust me, and why should she? "But you left out part of the story. In my school, that kid who tripped and fell? Or maybe got pushed? He got back up and fought until there wasn't another kid left standing, and he didn't do it out of courage or a need for retribution. He did it because that's who he was. He was a fighter, and fighters never back down."

"Fighters die young, Ian." She sounded older—she *looked* older—when she said it.

I nodded, watching her, my blood boiling in fury at whoever had hurt her, in spite of the fact that what I'd come prepared to do would hurt her even worse. "Yeah, sometimes," I agreed. "But they die fighting." Yet even as the words tumbled from my lips—words I'd been saying to myself for years—I remembered what she'd said earlier.

Sometimes dying is the coward's way out. Sometimes living takes guts.

She blinked, but her gaze never wavered. "What the hell are you doing here, Ian? You don't belong here."

I could see what it cost her to say that—another difficult truth that probably skirted the very edge of what she was allowed to reveal to a potential recruit. "Neither do you."

Kori frowned and turned away from me, reaching for the chord hanging down one side of the blinds. "This is what you'll be helping him do," she said, her voice hard again, as if she'd turned off whatever I'd seen in her. Like flipping a switch. As if it was that easy.

She pulled the chord and the blinds rose, clattering, to reveal a long observation window looking out over row after row of beds. Gurneys, really. Narrow, thinly padded carts on wheels, each of which held a single body. Or patient, as the hospital gowns seemed to suggest.

"What the hell is this?" Why were they all asleep? Or unconscious? The chills running up my back were so cold and ruthless my spine could have been carved from ice. "Who are they?"

They were alive. I could see the closest of them breathing, chests barely rising and falling. And they were all—every single one of them—attached to an IV bag hanging from a stand to the left of each cart.

"They're donors," Kori said, and I glanced at her to find her jaw clenched as she stared out at the sea of bodies. "And that's all I can tell you." There were dozens of them. Easily one hundred or more cots, and at the far end of the room was a single nurse in green scrubs, checking the IV bags one by one, stopping occasionally to lift an eyelid and check for…something.

"Can he see us?" I asked, staring at the nurse, who didn't seem to know he was being watched.

"Nope. One-way glass. He can't hear us, either, unless you push that button." She pointed to an electronic panel on the right side of the window. "So, don't push that button. This is an observation room. I can't get us in there." Kori nodded at the glass. "I never had that kind of clearance, and without Abbot's password, this is useless." She dropped the key card on the table.

"Donors…" I couldn't seem to make sense of what I was seeing. "What are they donating?"

"Look back there. The last two rows." She pointed, instead of vocalizing what she was obviously forbidden to say. And I looked.

"Carts." They were no higher than the beds themselves, but the one on the end of the second to last row was unobstructed, because the person on the bed next to him was too small to block the view. I didn't want to think about what that meant.

I squinted a little more and made out something on the cart. A bag of something dark, with something connecting it to the donor's right arm. A wire or a tube.

Yes, a tube.

"Blood," I said softly, horrified by the thought. "They're donating blood." Blood was dangerous. Blood was power. Putting any of your blood in someone else's hands was like turning over the key to your home and inviting the monsters in.

"Not just blood. What comes with blood sometimes?" Kori said, and I had to struggle through a fog of confusion and horror in order to look beyond her words to their meaning.

"They're donating Skills? How is that even possible? Why the hell would anyone ever donate Skilled blood?"

She lifted both brows in surprise. "I never said they were volunteers."

Words deserted me. The entire concept was unthinkable. "They're not… They didn't…?"

"Wake up one morning and decide to open a vein for Jake Tower? No. They were delivered here, for this specific purpose. After being identified and screened by a staff of specialists."

The implications were revolutionary and terrifying. The methodology was inhumane and unconscionable. The fact that she was showing me this at all…it made no sense. "Jake will kill you if he finds out you brought me here." She started to argue, but I spoke over her, whispering, as if the chances of us being overheard had suddenly increased, now that I better understood the stakes of the game. "Don't bother. I know you're risking your life by bringing me to see something that would send most recruits fleeing. What made you think I wouldn't have the same reaction?"

Kori shrugged. "The fact that you kept your cool in the alley, which tells me you're not easily rattled. The fact that you held your own in that fight, which tells me you don't run from trouble. And the fact that you need something from Jake, which tells me that you're here because you *want* to be here, not because he wanted you here. Don't get me wrong—he would have gotten you here anyway, but you didn't even make him work for it."

She crossed her arms over her chest again and silently challenged me to argue with her. "All of that together tells me that you may be a systems analyst, but you are *not* a corporate automaton with clean fingernails and an even cleaner conscience. This might shock and disgust you—and I'd be worried if it didn't—but it won't scare you away."

How the hell was I supposed to argue with that? Insist that I *was* easy to scare? This was why I'd wanted Kenley assigned as my tour guide. Ten minutes alone with her, and the whole thing would have been over. Without the psychoanalysis and flight-risk assessment from her sister. Not to mention the dangerous, top-secret information I was now burdened with.

"You shouldn't have brought me here," I insisted.

"I *had* to bring you here. You had to see what he can do, and that he can get to anyone. You had to understand."

And suddenly I did. I wasn't just looking at a collection of human vegetables being milked for the source of their Skills. I was looking at my own future. Kori was trying to tell me without actually telling me that Tower would get what he wanted from me, one way or another. I could serve him, or I could bleed for him.

She wasn't trying to scare me away. She was trying to scare me into signing, to avoid the alternative.

My head spun. My stomach pitched. But I stood

straight and swallowed everything I couldn't say. "I appreciate what you're trying to do, but at least three people have seen us, and if any one of them talks, we're both screwed."

Though I hadn't known about Tower's pet project when I started this mission, I was fully aware of the risk to my own life. Personal risk I could handle, but I didn't want her death on my conscience.

Hell, I didn't want her death at all.

"They're not going to talk," Kori insisted. "The receptionist and the security guard don't even know about this—Jake has half a dozen other projects going on in this one building. There are no cameras in here—" she glanced around the perimeter of the ceiling for emphasis "—because Jake won't risk the footage being seen by the wrong pair of eyes. Which is also why the staff for this project is smaller than you'd expect. And Abbot can't report us without getting into serious trouble himself. So as long as we're gone before his replacement comes on duty, we're all good. Unless..." Kori frowned and picked up the clipboard Abbot had dropped onto the table. She glanced at it for a second, then set it down again and crossed her arms over her chest. "Nope. No deliveries scheduled for today."

"Deliveries?" I'd seen a lot of sick stuff both stateside and overseas, but nothing compared to this. To people kept comatose and harvested for their blood. This made me sick. "Are these the deliveries you're no longer making?" I could hear the anger in my voice, and I could tell from the narrowing of her eyes that she heard it, too.

"I can't answer that," she said. "But I can say that I was removed from Jake's personal security squad about

half a dozen times to acquire a few of the more complicated things he required."

"Because you're a Traveler."

"And because I'm a petite woman, which makes me
slightly less threatening than your average hulking male
goon." I lifted one brow at her and she shrugged. "At first
glance."

"Why would you do this?" I demanded, my voice
lower and harder than I'd intended as I looked out at the
neat rows of cots and identically dressed donors. Everything was designed to strip them of identity. To dehu-
manize them, so the employees wouldn't be bothered by
that pesky sense of decency. Of human compassion.

"If you haven't figured that out for yourself by next
week, you can ask me again, and I'll answer."

But the answer was obvious. She'd had no choice.
And neither had any of the people she'd taken. Tower
had found a new way to rob people of their most basic
rights, and as important as my mission was to me, on a
personal level, I couldn't overlook what I was seeing. I
couldn't just walk away from all this when I'd done what
I'd come to do.

"Who are they?" I whispered, my voice an echo of the
horror roiling inside me.

"They're people," Kori said, staring through the glass.
"They're from all over the country. None from this city,
and few who would be missed by families or coworkers."

"Few? So some were missed?"

"That's inevitable. Some are presumed dead. Some
are missed as runaways."

"And you put them here." It wasn't a question. It was a
statement of fact I couldn't quite believe, and she couldn't
outright confirm.

"That's how this works, Ian. This is what's under all the fucking sequins and champagne. Stuff like this, and people like me and you, making it all happen."

Her voice was sharp, but her expression was empty, and I'd learned that when she looked like that—closed off and unavailable—she wasn't feeling nothing. She was feeling too much. She was blocking it all out. That was a survival skill, and her still-beating heart was proof that it worked.

"It's not your fault," I insisted. "You can't hold yourself responsible for something someone else made you do. Which would you blame, the gun that fires the bullet, or the finger that squeezes the trigger?"

For a moment, she was quiet, staring through the one-way glass. Then she exhaled softly. "Doesn't really matter who you blame, Ian. Either way, I'm his gun, and guns are only good for one thing."

But even after less than a day spent with her, I knew Kori Daniels was good for much more than what Tower was using her for, even if neither of them could see it.

Nine

Kori

"I need a drink. A strong one," Ian said. We'd left Jake's pet project behind two blocks ago, and he was still looking at me like he was disappointed in me. Like he'd started looking at me in the observation room, the moment he'd found out that I'd kidnapped for Jake. That I'd killed for him.

But that was stupid, because he didn't know me well enough to be disappointed in me.

"Never let it be said that I stood between a man and his liquor. If you want food, too, there's a decent Italian restaurant around the corner to your left."

He shook his head firmly. "I don't think I could keep it down, after what I just saw."

"Okay. My favorite dive bar is half a mile up the street. Or we could head back to your hotel." Personally I favored the bar, for the lack of beds and availability of liquor.

"What are the chances Cavazos would send men to ambush us in this bar of yours?"

"Slim to none, unless he wants them returned in pieces too small to identify. Dusty's will be crawling with locals at one on a Saturday, half of them bound to Jake."

"The bar it is."

Ten minutes later, I pulled open the door to Dusty's and descended two steps into familiar, comfortable shadows accompanied by the buzz of conversation, the clink of ice on glass, and the practiced cadence of sports announcers from several small, outdated televisions mounted in the corners of the main room. The floor was sticky, but the glasses were clean. This was one of my favorite places in the world.

"Who's Dusty?" Ian asked, following me to a booth along the back wall.

"No idea. The owner's a woman in her sixties named Patience." I slid into the booth, and before Ian could pick up the greasy, laminated snack menu, a waitress stopped beside our table, notepad in hand. "What can I get 'cha?" she asked, making a decent attempt to hide the gum in her mouth. She was new.

"Stoli and Coke. And bring me another one in fifteen minutes."

"And for you?"

Ian slid the single-page menu between the grimy, glass salt and pepper shakers. "Crown and Coke."

"Another in fifteen minutes?" she asked, with a grin that went unreturned.

"We'll take it play by play."

"Be right back." Then the waitress was gone, and I couldn't pretend not to see the way Ian was still looking at me.

"What's Tower doing with the blood?" he asked softly, when the silence between us became too much.

"I can't answer that, but you're welcome to draw your own conclusions. What's usually done with blood donations?" I said, leading him to deductions I couldn't confirm.

"Transfusions. Shit." His eyes closed, and he inhaled deeply before opening them again. "He's making transfusions of Skilled blood. Presumably for profit."

"A logical assumption," I said, and for once, that was truly all I had to add. When I'd last been allowed in the building, the project was only in its testing phase.

The waitress set our glasses down on white napkins, and Ian gulped half of his drink at once, then clenched his glass so hard his dark hands went pale at the joints. I understood his anger. The Skilled are generally uncomfortable even thinking about blood spilled in large quantities, and the personal security risk that represents. Thinking of it stolen and redistributed was enough to make me sick to my stomach, even though I'd had plenty of time to get used to the idea.

"Is it permanent?" he asked, when he finally lowered his glass. "Is Tower getting ready to arm the entire population with Skills?"

"I wouldn't worry about that," I said, already tired of dancing around things I couldn't say outright. "After any transfusion, it only takes a few hours for the new blood cells to be absorbed by the body."

The key to communicating points you aren't allowed to make is speaking in generalities and implications. I'd had six years to polish my skills.

"So, the transfused Skills are temporary," Ian said, but I couldn't confirm that, so I lifted my glass for the first sip, wishing for the days when one drink was enough to relax me. Mostly because those were the days before Jake, and the syndicate, and the loss of my free will, and the start of my body count.

"Does it work on those who already have Skills? Can he strengthen someone's existing ability, or give people multiple Skills?" His voice got deeper and more intense with each question, but his volume never rose.

"I honestly don't know. I've been out of the loop for a couple of months, but I haven't heard about anything like that." I drained half my glass, then caught the waitress's eye and held my drink up, wordlessly calling for another, several minutes early.

"So, what other criminal enterprises will I be aiding and abetting, once I've sold my soul?"

I swirled the ice in my cup, thinking about all the possible answers. Things that would paint an accurate picture for him, but wouldn't scare him or piss him off any worse than I probably already had with the whole black-market Skills operation.

"Well, there're the classics, of course. He does huge trade in black-market blood samples and names. That's where he got his start." And those were the common-knowledge kind of things I was legitimately allowed to talk to Ian about.

"Whose names and blood?"

"Everyone's. Anyone's. Politicians are big business. Right before a big vote, we typically get an influx of requests from various lobbyists."

Ian shook his head slowly and set his empty glass at the edge of the table. "I'd heard rumors... So they, what? Bind a congressman to vote a certain way?"

"Or to speak to certain key individuals whose opinions carry sway. Or to mention or avoid certain topics in interviews. Or whatever. There are about a million different ways to wag the dog."

He started to ask another question, then waited while the waitress set down our fresh drinks and took the empty glasses.

"And Tower just sells these names and blood samples to whoever wants them?" Ian looked horrified. Again.

"Of course not. You can't even get in to see him unless you have significant cash to flash, or some other resource he values. Usually important names and blood samples, or partial names and locations of potential new recruits."

Ian sipped from his fresh glass, and I could smell the whiskey from across the table. "Don't any of them notice that they're being…compelled to do things? Or not to do things?"

I shrugged, swirling the ice cubes in my glass. "Anyone who knows what a binding is would recognize the symptoms, but if you don't know who's bound you and the Binder was strong enough to seal a nonconsensual binding, there isn't much you can do to fight it, especially considering that resistance pain of just about any kind would keep you out of the big vote, or off the radio, or out of whatever spotlight you need to be in. So, worst-case scenario, whoever's being bound won't be able to push their own agenda, even if they manage to resist pushing yours." I shrugged and finished my second glass. "And, of course, all transactions are nonrefundable, so Jake's been paid either way. Win-win."

"Unless you're the one being bound."

"Well, yeah."

"And your sister's the one who seals these bindings?"

"Most of them. She's the best."

"The best Tower has?" Ian said, looking up from his glass to meet my gaze in the shadows.

"The best I've ever seen. The best Tower's seen, too. That's why he keeps her so close."

"So no one else can steal her?"

"Yeah." But it was more than that. The seals Kenley had put in place were *kept* in place by her blood and her will. If those stopped flowing—if and when she died— any binding she'd sealed would be broken. Most of Jake's indentured employees would go free. His deals with local politicians and businessmen would be void. His entire kingdom might very well collapse.

That's why he kept Kenley close, and under twenty-four-hour armed guard.

But I couldn't tell Ian that. I couldn't tell anyone that. Unfortunately those with the most potential to hurt my sister already knew exactly what she was worth.

I shrugged, then motioned for the waitress to bring me a fresh drink.

"Is drunk the goal for the afternoon?" Ian asked.

I glanced at him in surprise. "Is three drinks enough to get you drunk?"

His brows rose. "Lush," he accused.

"Lightweight," I returned, and his eyes narrowed.

"I'll have one more, as well," he said to the waitress, when she picked up my empty glass. Then he met my gaze again as she left. "Your sister's not his only Binder, though, is she? Surely he has a fail-safe. A redundancy, in case of system failure?"

I laughed. "Spoken like a systems analyst. And yeah, of course there's another one." But the truth was that Jake rarely used him. Barker was in his mid-sixties and already having health issues when Jake started the search for a new Binder seven years ago. In fact, Barker's failing health was *why* Jake had started looking. He needed a new Binder in place to start sealing all service oaths—both new enlistments and reenlistment—long before the aging Binder died, and his seals died with him. It hadn't taken Jake long to realize how powerful Kenley really was, and she quickly became the primary Binder. The single, fragile brick the entire structure rested on.

That was one of the few tactical errors I could point out in Jake's quest to own the whole city—he depended too much on my sister. He got away with that by signing me—someone who wanted Kenley safe even more than Jake did. I would do anything to protect my sister—unfortunately protecting her also meant protecting Jake's interests. Which he'd counted on.

"How long has Kenley been working as a Binder?"

"That's a complicated question. She's been getting paid—" and locked away from the world "—for six and a half years. But she's been binding since she was ten."

"Ten?" Ian's eyes widened and his mouth opened a little in surprise.

"Yup. In fact, I was part of the very first binding she sealed. It was an accident."

"She *accidently* bound you to something?"

"To three of my friends. We were just messing around, like girls do, promising to always be there for one another, and Kenley said we should write it down. Looking back, it seems obvious that she was feeling the first manifestation of her Skill, but at the time, we didn't know we came from Skilled blood. So we went along with her suggestion that we prick our thumbs and stamp them under this promise she'd scribbled on a scrap of paper, and that was that."

"Wow. How long did the binding last?" Ian asked, and my laughter that time sounded bitter and tasted even worse.

"It's still intact." Sixteen years ago, my little sister had bound me to my three best friends—Olivia, Annika and Noelle—and I'd been tied to them ever since. That oath was the reason I'd had no choice but to help Liv and Anne when they'd called. That oath was the reason I'd gotten shot, the reason Jake got shot and the reason I'd spent six weeks being tortured in his basement.

"How is that even possible?" Ian frowned, and there was something new behind his eyes. It looked like...fear. But surely that was just the dim lighting playing tricks. He wasn't scared of signing with Jake, so why on earth would he be scared of my little sister?

"I don't know. She hadn't had any training. My best guess is that the purity of her intent was off the charts. She *really* wanted us to be friends forever." Another shrug. "She thought of them as her friends, too."

"And did that work? Are you still close to the other three?" Ian looked fascinated, but I couldn't miss the tight line of his jaw and the way his hand still clutched his glass.

"The binding worked flawlessly. The intent failed miserably." And all of us had suffered from both.

"So you don't talk to them anymore?"

I shrugged. "Noelle's dead. Olivia and Anne...well, it's not safe for us to see each other," I said, and Ian frowned, like he wanted to argue. Like he might want to convince me that nothing was more important than our human connections—a concept my grandmother had drilled into me from the day my parents died. But I didn't need to hear that from him. "Bindings never favor those being bound, Ian. Ever. Even most married couples who are totally, sloppily in love when they say the words will one day resent the binding that ties them together."

His brows rose. "You don't believe in love?"

"Of course I believe in love," I admitted, and his eyes widened in surprise. "But I also believe that binding yourself to someone is the quickest, most efficient way to kill that love. Love should stand on its own feet, with no force or obligation."

"So, you'd never sign a sealed marriage contract?"

"Hell no. Binding yourself to someone else is like literally tying yourself to them. Eventually the ropes start chafing and you can't move without pain and the constant reminder that even if you wanted to leave, you couldn't. When love has to be defined by an inability to leave, it isn't really love. Real love is staying with someone because you want to be there, not because you have no other choice. Anything else is just lust, or obsession, or something less innocent."

The waitress set our third drinks on the table, and I asked for the check and two glasses of water. But Ian was still frowning, still thinking through my discourse on love. "Is Tower bound to his wife?"

"Not in the way that you're thinking." He wasn't obligated to stay with her, and the opposite was also true. "And she's not bound to the syndicate, either. She's his wife, not his employee."

"And you like that about him?"

"No." There was nothing I liked about Jake Tower, except the fact that he'd kept Kenley safe, even if he had his own reasons for doing that. "But I respect it."

Ian nodded faster, like he understood. "But you don't

respect his business—the political influence that is his bread and butter?"

"Names and blood are his bread and butter. Which sounds kind of disgusting, when you put it that way. But he doesn't limit himself to politics. He works with casting directors, record labels, and all kinds of the rich and soulless who'll do and pay anything to slant the odds in their favor. He also has a growing reputation with patent holders and inventors in the technical sector. You wouldn't believe how much money there is to be made in new tech. And how reluctant the designers are to give up their rights to their own inventions."

"Bastards. Where's their team spirit?" Ian's eyes sparkled in good humor for the first time since he'd seen Jake's pet project.

"Always thinking of themselves," I said, grasping at an opportunity to lighten the mood, because anything was better than the way he'd been looking at me earlier. "There's no *I* in intellectual property."

"So, where does Tower get these names and blood samples? I assume he doesn't just go jabbing strangers with needles."

"Don't assume anything." I drained the last of my drink and thanked the waitress when she set two glasses of water on the table. When she was gone, he watched me, waiting for me to continue. "Let's just say there's a nurse's uniform hanging in my closet, and it's not for Halloween."

"Stealth phlebotomy. Illegal, immoral and incredibly dangerous. But also devilishly clever. I'm impressed."

"Don't be. It wasn't my idea, and I'm not proud of it. There are a million other ways to do it, though. Shadow-walk into one of the older courthouses, where they still keep physical copies of birth and marriage certificates. Steal someone's wallet. Break into the bloodmobile while everyone's gone to lunch."

"And you don't feel guilty about that? About taking blood meant to save someone's life?"

I shrugged, hoping he couldn't read the thoughts behind my next words. "Guilt is one of those concepts that has no practical application." And the truth was that the blood I took did save someone's life. It kept Jake—not to mention my own body—from killing me for disobeying orders.

"So, what would I be doing, specifically. What did the last Blinder do?"

"Not as much as you'll be able to do, that's for sure."

"Because I'm stronger?" He looked vaguely uncomfortable as he spoke, like he wasn't used to honking his own horn.

"That and because you're…um…" I made a vague gesture at his face, reluctant both to admit the truth and to understand that reluctance.

"I'm…um…left-handed?" Ian grinned. "A democrat? A nonsmoker?"

I huffed in irritation. He was going to make me say it. "Because you don't smell like cheese, jiggle when you walk, or snort with every other breath because you refuse to get your sinuses flushed out. Also, you're not… horribly offensive to the eyes." I mumbled the last part, hoping he wouldn't hear, yet wouldn't ask me to repeat.

"Ms. Daniels, unless I've misinterpreted that colorful description of everything I'm not, it sounds like you just paid me a compliment."

"I'm pretty sure that's not what I did." In fact, I'd gone out of my way to make *sure* that's not what I was doing.

"Oh, I think it is. I think you just said that I'd be better at the job than Tower's last Blinder was because I'm not unattractive. First of all, thank you. Compliment accepted." He bowed his head slightly, like I'd just offered to crown him king of the universe. Then, in the next second, he pasted on a frown. "Second of all, I am offended on behalf of pretty people everywhere. I'm not just a chiseled jaw and eyes you could get lost in. I am worth more than the sum of my defined biceps, sculpted pecs and a six-pack you could scrub laundry on."

I nearly choked on an ice cube. "You have a six-pack?"

"Okay, maybe a four-pack. At *least* a carton of hard lemonade. But my point is that you have no right to judge my potential as a crime lord's lackey by my looks alone."

I nodded solemnly. "Don't hate you because you're beautiful. Got it."

His brows rose and I knew what was coming before he even opened his mouth. "You just called me beautiful."

"My point was that you'll be able to blend in when you need to and stand out when you need to, and Ray Bailey couldn't do either of those. You'll be able to flirt your way into secure spaces, then open the door for a Traveler to bring in the rest of the crew."

"You're saying that Tower will exploit me for my looks?" Holt asked, and at first I thought that was another joke. It seemed too obvious a statement to be serious.

"He'll exploit everything you are and everything you have. Your job description will read something like, 'whatever the hell Jake Tower wants from you.'"

Someone cleared her throat next to our table, and I looked up to see the waitress standing there with nothing in her hands. "Is there anything else I can get you two?" she asked, and I realized she was hinting at the check, which meant her shift was probably over.

"No, I think we're fine." I set my credit card on top of the bill—the syndicate would reimburse me after I filed the receipt—and she slid both into the pocket of her black apron. Then she picked up my empty short glass and when she turned to say something to Ian, the glass she held slammed into Ian's full glass of water. Which then slammed into mine. The water from both glasses poured over the edge of the table and onto my lap like a miniature waterfall. An *ice-cold* waterfall that splashed all the way up to my chin and soaked through my jeans so fast I may as well have been sitting on a glacier.

The waitress stared, frozen. And for a moment, I was too stunned to move.

Then that moment was over.

"Son of a motherfucking, ass-reaming, shit-eating, hell-dodging soulless bitch!" I stood too fast and my head swam, and the water poured down my pants to form freezing puddles in my boots.

Ian burst into laughter, the waitress burst into tears, and more profanity exploded from my mouth so fast I couldn't even tell what I was saying. But the whole damn bar heard it.

"I'm so sorry!" the waitress blubbered. "Here, let me help." She pulled off her grease-stained black apron and started wiping at my crotch until a growl rumbled up from somewhere deep inside me.

"Get. The fuck. Off me," I said, so soft I barely heard the words. She backed away, clutching her apron in one shaking fist.

"I'm so sorry. Let me take care of the bill." She set my credit card back on the table.

"It's coming out of your check," the bartender called from across the bar, and the waitress flinched.

"That's not necessary." Ian dropped a fifty and a twenty on the table, then grabbed my credit card and reached for my arm. But he stopped just short of touching me and held one hand out toward the back of the bar instead, gesturing for me to go first.

I stomped stiffly toward the bathroom, acutely aware that everyone was watching me. There was no sound, other than our footsteps. No silverware clanged. No ice cubes clinked. There was just me and my walk of shame.

In the back hall, Ian held the door to the tiny, one-person women's room for me, then followed me in and bolted the door while I cursed under my breath. "It's just a little water," he said, pulling handfuls of brown paper towels from the dispenser next to the sink.

"It's fucking Niagara Falls in my pants. With ice."

"There is a backlog of crude jokes in here just begging to be cracked," he said, tapping his own temple for emphasis. "But I want you to know that I'm holding them all back out of respect for your pain. I, too, have been the victim of an ice-water crotch deluge. There's no way to bear it gracefully."

"You're fucking right about that." And frankly, I was surprised to hear that he knew any crude jokes.

He chuckled again while I snatched the first handful of towels from him and started blotting my pants. "You can't help it, can you?"

"Can't help what?" I was cold. And wet. And starting to shiver, which pissed me off.

"Profanity flows through your veins like blood,

doesn't it? I bet you can't go a single day without bursting into a string of expletives foul enough to set a nun's habit on fire."

"The hell I can't," I mumbled, and he laughed again. "I said I could. I didn't say I *would*."

Ian stared down at me, green eyes practically shining with amusement, and my pulse spiked when I realized how small the bathroom was, and how close together we stood. "I dare you." The words were soft, his voice intense, like he was challenging more than just my proclivity for profanity.

I had to reach around him to drop the first handful of wet paper towels into the trash, and for one dizzying second, the full length of his body was pressed against mine, because there was nowhere else to go. "What are we, twelve?" I asked, desperately hoping he didn't notice the tremor in my voice.

"No self-respecting twelve-year-old would balk over a simple dare."

"I'm not balking," I insisted, suddenly short of breath now that the shocking cold of spilled water had given way to the body heat building between us in the small space. "This is not what I look like when I balk."

"You're right." He tilted his head, pretending to study me from another angle. "This is definitely the face of cowardice. It's a subtle difference."

"Smart-ass." I took the next handful of tissues as he offered them. "Fine. But for the record, this is a stupid fucking dare. What are the terms?"

"It's a bet, not a contract negotiation." He shrugged. "Don't cuss. If you do, you lose."

I frowned up at him, trying not to see the flecks of brown in his green eyes, almost mesmerizing from such a close vantage point. "You're a piss-poor negotiator. Do yourself a favor. Take a lawyer with you when you meet with Jake."

"I kind of feel like I need one now."

"You and me both. State your terms." Was the air-conditioning even on? How could I be so warm now, when I was freezing a minute earlier?

"Twenty-four hours. No cussing. No exceptions."

"What about life-and-death situations? No one could keep from cussing with a knife in her back or a bullet lodged in her chest," I said, plucking at the wet material clinging to my legs—until my hand brushed his thigh, and I froze, half embarrassed, half…intrigued.

"Are you planning to be shot or stabbed in the next twenty-four hours?" he asked, like he hadn't even noticed, and I wasn't sure whether to be relieved by that or insulted.

"Were you *there* in the alley? If I get hurt, it'll be in the line of duty, keeping your ass from getting poached."

"No exceptions," Ian insisted. "But if that's too much for you…?"

I frowned up at him. "You are such a child. Fine. No cussing for twenty-four hours. Starting now." I pulled my phone from my pocket to glance at the time. "Two thirty-four p.m. What do I get when I win?"

He smiled and spread both arms, and for a moment, I thought he was offering himself as the prize, and I flushed at the thought. For just a second. "My undying respect."

I didn't even bother to hide my disappointment. "You'll have to do better than that."

His left eyebrow rose. "My respect has no value to you?"

"That's not what I…" In fact, for no reason I could explain, considering that we'd just met, I *did* want his respect. But I also wanted free will, a billion dollars and a bathtub full of Häagen-Dazs, and I wasn't going to get any of those, either. "How 'bout we assume the fair market value of your undying respect is…a bottle of Grey Goose. The big one. Because your respect means that much to me."

He laughed. "Oddly, I'm flattered."

"But are you ready to put your money where your mouth is? I dare you to go the rest of your visit without slacks."

His mouth actually dropped open a little in surprise. "You want me to take off my pants?" he said, and when I realized what my dare had sounded like, I could feel my cheeks flame. But I couldn't make my tongue work right.

"That's not what I… I mean, I dare you to wear jeans for the rest of your visit, instead of slacks. And no tie. I bet you can't go the next four and a half days without your stuffy, corporate zombie clothes."

His grin seemed to warm his face, like he might still be thinking about that first misinterpretation of my dare. "Why four and a half days? You're only on the hook for twenty-four hours."

"To make up for the difference in the degree of difficulty. Unless you don't think you can do it."

"You're on. And if I win?"

"What do you want?" I asked, and regretted the words as soon as they were out of my mouth.

Ian stared down at me again from inches away, so close I could feel the heat from his skin through both layers of clothes. I could see what he wanted—some hint of it, anyway—in his eyes. And again, my breath deserted me.

"A compliment."

"What?" His answer was so unexpected I couldn't even make sense of it.

"If I win, you have to tell me what you like best about me. With a straight face."

"That's it?" Was his ego that malnourished?

"That's it." His smile was a quiet challenge, and I couldn't help wondering if this was some kind of trick.

"Fine. Let's get out of here." I unbolted the door and turned off the light, and his hand slid into mine like he'd been planning that since the moment he'd closed the door behind us. I stepped forward—there was only room for a single step—and he walked with me. A second later, we were in the bathroom of his hotel room, left dark on purpose that morning.

He let go of my hand and pulled the door open, and light poured in from the bedroom, but I stayed put when he stepped into it. "I have to go change, and I need to report to Jake after that. Will you be okay for a couple of hours?"

"I've been staying home by myself since I was nine, Kori."

"So you've got it down by now, right? I'll see you back here at four."

Ian nodded and started to close the door, then stopped and looked at me, and there was something in his expression I couldn't quite identify. "Will we be working together?" he asked. "If I sign with Tower?"

"Maybe." I shrugged. "Probably. But you never can

tell with Jake. Why? Is that a deal-breaker?" I was joking. At least, I was trying to. But he didn't laugh.

"Quite the opposite. I think that may be the only thing that would make wearing his chain links bearable."

Ten

Ian

I don't know why I asked her that. It wasn't fair. And it didn't matter, because I wasn't going to sign with Tower. Kori and I would never work together.

The damn dare was a mistake, too. If she won, I'd have to present her with a bottle of vodka, right around the time I killed her sister, like some kind of morbid condolence for the crime I'd committed. I'd be lucky if she didn't beat me to death with it.

What the hell are you doing, Ian?

When Kori was gone, I glanced at my watch, then picked up my cell phone. Aaron answered on the second ring. "Hello?" he croaked into the phone, and springs creaked as he rolled over in bed.

"Get up. I need a lift."

"Night shift, man. I gotta get more sleep."

"This is the only chance I'm going to have, and I have to be back in two hours. Get dressed."

More springs creaked, and Aaron groaned. "Where are you?"

I gave him the hotel's address and the room number, then hung up. Five minutes later, the bathroom door creaked open and Aaron padded into the living room of my hotel suite in huge, dog-shaped slippers and a pair of navy boxer briefs.

"Where the hell are your pants?"

Aaron shrugged. "You said you were in a hurry, so I rushed right over."

"Did anyone see you?"

Aaron scowled on his way to the minibar. "Do I look like an idiot?" When I only glanced at his slippers, he rolled his eyes. "Do I *normally* look like an idiot?" Before I could answer, he knelt in front of the minibar and opened the fridge. "I need a drink."

I slammed the fridge closed. "You can make coffee when we get there. There's a robe hanging on the back of the bathroom door."

Aaron put the robe on, then stepped into the bathroom while I pulled my phone from my pocket and autodialed Meghan's number. "Ian? Why isn't it done?" she said into my ear, after only a ring and a half.

My eyes closed. *Of course* she knew it wasn't over. She'd be able to feel it when the binding was broken. "Turn off the light. We're coming over."

Meghan hung up without a reply, and Aaron turned the bathroom light off as I pushed the door closed. He took my arm, bared by the sleeve I'd rolled up, and a second later we stepped into another bathroom thirty miles away, in the suburbs.

This bathroom felt familiar, even with the lights off. It smelled like fruit-scented shampoo, bleach and the slightly scorched scent of every scrap of blood-soaked material that had ever been burned in the old-fashioned iron tub. When I stepped forward and reached for the light switch, my foot landed on ceramic tile, not as old as the tub, but older than I was, by several years. The tile was yellow, like the wallpaper exposed when I flipped the switch and let the light in.

The floors in the rest of the house were real wood, scarred from use and warped in places from the spills and drips of three generations. Aaron and Meghan had grown up here, as had their mother. This house was as safe a rendezvous point as any other, and a good deal safer than Aaron's apartment in the city.

Meghan stepped out of a bedroom and into the hall, pulling the door closed behind her. She waved us into the living room without a word, and she didn't even seem to notice that her brother wasn't wearing pants.

We followed her down the hall, through the living room, and into the small eat-in kitchen, where Meghan sank into a chair at the table and scrubbed her face with both hands. Long brown hair tumbled over her shoulders, and Aaron paused to set one hand on her head—a wordless, comforting gesture—on his way to the coffeepot.

"How is he?" I asked, and I regretted being the one to break the silence before the words had even fallen from my tongue.

"No better. A little worse, maybe," Meghan said, and for the first time in more than two weeks, the exhaustion in her voice outweighed the accusation. She couldn't do this for much longer. Not on her own. But it would be over soon, one way or another. If I couldn't kill Kenley Daniels and break the binding, he wouldn't last much longer anyway.

But no one wanted things to end like that, least of all me.

"Can I see him?"

"I don't want to wake him up. He doesn't sleep much anymore." Meghan sighed, and the weight of the world slipped a little on her shoulders. "What happened?" she said, as Aaron filled the pot and poured water into the reservoir. And the accusation that was absent from her voice found its way to her eyes, where it simmered quietly, waiting for the moment to flare into true flames and roast me alive.

I sank onto the chair opposite her and rubbed one hand over my head, trying to decide where to start. A minute later, the scent of coffee drew my thoughts into some semblance of focus. "Remember my brilliant plan to get Kenley Daniels assigned as my tour guide-slash-recruiter for the duration of my visit?"

"I take it that plan's proven less than brilliant in hindsight?" Aaron took a mug down from the cabinet and leaned against the countertop as the machine spit the first drops of coffee into the carafe.

"I stand by the simple brilliance of the plan. The flaw is in the execution. Kenley has an older sister who fits the same general physical description." Though the more I got to know Kori, the less she looked like her sister, at least to me.

Aaron turned with the pot in hand. "Korinne Daniels is Kenley's sister?"

"Who's Korinne Daniels?" Meghan said, glancing from her brother to me, then back.

"Tower's guard dog bitch. But she's dead." Aaron glanced at me with both brows raised. "Didn't we already determine that? Every source we spoke to said the same thing."

I shrugged. "She's a little less dead than the rumors indicated."

"You got the *wrong sister?*" Meghan demanded, and I nodded.

"The same thing happened to Jacob in the Old Testament," Aaron said. "He worked seven years to earn Rachel's hand in marriage and got her sister Leah instead. That poor fool then worked *another* seven years just to earn Rachel as his second wife. If you think about it like that, you got a bargain."

"This isn't the Old Testament, Aaron," Meghan snapped.

Aaron poked the pause button on the coffeepot and filled his mug without turning. "All that means is that Ian's not gonna get to bed both sisters."

Her fist clenched around the edge of the table. "This isn't funny!"

"Maybe not 'ha, ha' funny, but we're in some pretty deep shit here, sis, and if we lose our sense of humor, what do we have left?" Aaron said as he poured dried creamer into his cup.

"Nothing." Meghan folded her hands on the tabletop, but she couldn't keep them from twisting, as if her fingers were trying to tear each other apart. "I'll have nothing left, without Steven."

Aaron frowned over the implication that he meant nothing to his sister, but we both knew that wasn't what she'd intended. She was too tired to think clearly.

A moan echoed from behind the bedroom door Meghan had closed, and I stood, but her hand landed on my arm. Her fingers were cold, her skin was pale, and her eyes were damp, but she never hesitated. "Let me."

I started to argue, but Aaron shook his head at me

over her shoulder, and I sank back into my chair as she crossed the living room toward the hall again. "She needs to do this," he whispered, once his sister was out of sight.

"If Steven wakes up to find her dead of exhaustion, he'll kill us both," I said, and Aaron gave a bitter laugh, no doubt picturing Steven just as I was. Healthy, happy, in good humor, and willing to slay any dragon for Meghan.

"It's your job to make sure that doesn't happen," Aaron said, sinking into his sister's chair with one dog-slippered foot crossed over the opposite knee, the hotel robe gaping over his thin chest. "So what's this Leah like? Is she going to be a problem?"

"Her name is Kori. She's smart, but she doesn't know it. She's funny, but I don't think she knows that, either." I shrugged, trying not to see her in my mind, a little frightened to realize I could picture her with almost perfect recall, down to the freckle on her left cheek, about an inch in front of her ear. "She's a little thin, but she makes one hell of a temptation. Which is exactly what Tower's paying her to be." The carrot dangled in front of the ass, guiding him toward the farmer ready to put him to work.

Naturally I was the ass.

"Well, that's more than I asked for." Aaron's brows rose, like he'd heard more than what I'd actually said. "Can you use her?"

"Do I have any other choice? I'm almost twenty hours into this mission and the only time I've even been in the same room with the target is when I shook her hand at that damned party, in front of two hundred other people."

Aaron shrugged and sipped from his cup, then swore beneath his breath when he burned his mouth. "That's an easy fix. Just tell Leah—"

"It's Kori," I corrected again, leaning back in my chair.

"Fine. Tell *Kori* that you want to meet some of your future associates. Have her get a group together. If she's any kind of sister at all, she'll invite Kenley, and you can get her alone and put a bullet in her head. Problem solved." He leaned back in the chair, cradling his coffee and looking quite satisfied with himself.

An unexpected flash of anger licked the base of my spine. He wouldn't be so indifferent if we were discussing shooting *his* sister.

"Yeah, that might work," I snapped. "If not for the fact that Kenley is under twenty-four-hour guard, to prevent exactly the kind of idiotic plan you just rattled off. I might be able to put a bullet in her, but not without taking a few myself."

Dying for the cause was the worst-case scenario, and things hadn't gotten quite that bad yet.

"Oh, right. You wanted to survive." Aaron shrugged and blew over the top of his mug. "So what are you going to do?"

"The fastest, easiest solution I've come up with is to get Kori to bring her sister along on a tour of Jake's side of town. Surely Tower will let her come without her usual bodyguard, since Kori has security experience and more motivation than anyone to make sure Kenley is safe."

But when I thought about that for too long, I started feeling nauseated. This wasn't some armed, hostile insurgent or terrorist. We were talking about killing someone's little sister.

Kori's little sister.

That part shouldn't have bothered me any more than the rest, but it did. In fact, the more time I spent with her, the more the whole thing bothered me. But if I didn't kill Kenley, Steven would die, and if she refused to give up on him, Meghan would die with him.

"Wouldn't it be easier to shoot her in her sleep?"

"Yeah. If I knew where she slept. But that's the bit of classified information Kori is least likely to give up."

"Maybe so, but she's not going to let you near her sister—even in broad daylight—until she trusts you completely. Can you make that happen?"

"I think we're almost there." I glanced at my hands, suddenly wishing I'd poured some coffee, too, so I'd have something to do with them.

Aaron set his mug down and cleared his throat to catch my attention. When I glanced at him, he frowned, studying me. "No, Ian," he said, finally.

"No, what?"

"You know what. I know that look."

"What look?"

"That look that says you've found a wounded puppy and you want to nurse it back to health. And keep it, like that dog that got hit in front of your house when we were kids."

"That wasn't me, that was Steven."

"Bullshit. It was you," Aaron insisted, and I didn't bother arguing. "Korinne Daniels is no wounded puppy, Ian. She's a fucking Doberman, and she'll rip your throat out if she finds out what you're really doing here."

I forced a laugh. "I was in the marines, and you don't think I can take a one-hundred-pound woman in a fight?"

"I think you won't fight her, because you want to *keep* her, but she is not a fucking puppy, Ian. You can't have her, you can't keep her, and you sure as hell can't let her get in the way of what you're doing here."

"I know." But I also knew that Kori didn't deserve what was coming. Neither of them did. I scrubbed both hands over my face, yet couldn't scrub away the guilt.

Aaron set his coffee on the table. "Don't lose sight of the goal here, Ian."

"You don't think I should feel bad about shooting her little sister?"

Aaron eyed me sternly. "Don't do this to yourself. Don't overthink it, and do *not* get emotionally involved. You're here to save your brother's life, and keep my sister from killing herself by trying to save him. I'm as sorry as I can be for your girlfriend's impending loss—it's the same loss you and I are both facing right now—but let's not forget that this whole thing is Kenley Daniels's fault in the first place."

"I know."

"And it's not like Korinne is a Girl Scout, either. She's got blood on her hands."

"So do I."

Aaron growled in frustration. "You killed men with guns, to keep them from killing anyone else. She killed people who got into Tower's way. There's a big fucking difference, Ian."

Maybe.

Kori and I had fought in different wars, but I wasn't naive enough to believe that her life in the syndicate was any less a battle than what I'd seen overseas.

"Look, we can argue about this all day if you want, but that's not going to change the facts. Kenley Daniels has to die to keep your brother and my sister alive. Where does your loyalty lie, Ian? With your own flesh and blood, and friends you've known your whole life? Or with a woman you met yesterday?"

"Here. My loyalty is here. Why else would I be here?" Steven and I had had our problems over the years, but I couldn't let him die, and that would have been true even if it wasn't my use of his name that had gotten him into this mess in the first place. He was my brother.

Blood mattered.

"Good. It better stay that way, too," Aaron said. "I am *not* going to tell my sister that her fiancé's liberator fell not to a bullet, but to one of cupid's fucking arrows." When he caught me staring at his coffee, he stood and pulled another mug from the cabinet. "Please tell me you know you're being played."

"I know I'm being played." But so was she.

"You're being played like a fucking *harmonica,* Ian." Aaron dumped sugar into the mug and followed it with creamer he didn't bother to stir. "She's getting paid to do what you want done, show you what you want to see and say what you want to hear, but she'd kill you in a heartbeat if Tower told her to. Do whatever you need to do. Fuck her, kill her, stuff her into a crate bound for China, for all I care. Just don't let her get in the way of the mission."

Meghan cleared her throat from the doorway, and Aaron's mouth snapped shut. He set my mug in front of her when she sank into an empty chair at the table.

"Any change?" I asked, eyeing the circles beneath her eyes. Had they grown darker since she left the kitchen?

"His kidneys," she said, her voice a weak whisper. "He's better for the moment. Sleeping again."

Aaron's hand shot across the table so fast I barely saw him move. He grabbed his sister's left wrist, and she tried to pull away from him, but obviously lacked the strength. Aaron pushed her sleeve back, and we both groaned at the sight of her arm.

Her skin was pale, nearly translucent, and every vein and artery below her bunched sleeve showed through. But they weren't blue. They were black. Every single one of them, like they ran with tar, rather than blood.

"You're killing yourself," Aaron said through clenched teeth.

Meghan shook her head and pulled her sleeve back into place when he let her go. "I'm saving him." But she couldn't hold out much longer, which was exactly what Aaron's accusatory glare at me said.

He stood and started pulling food from the refrigerator. "You need to call Dad, Meghan. If you don't, I will."

"I'll never forgive you," she whispered, and he flinched as he piled meat onto a slice of bread. It was the same argument they'd been having for two weeks. Their father was a Healer, too, and he could help her save Steven. He could share the burden. But she wouldn't call him because of what he'd say, and what he'd do.

Meghan's father would tell her she was championing a lost cause—no Healer can save someone from death by broken binding, because as soon as she repaired one organ, another began to shut down.

And he would take her away, by force if he had to, to keep her from dying alongside her doomed love. My doomed brother.

"Eat." Aaron set the sandwich in front of her, then pulled a carton of milk from the fridge. "This is crazy, Meg."

She ignored him and turned to me as she lifted the

sandwich. "What about the binding? Have you at least figured out what that bitch bound him to?"

"I haven't had a chance to talk to Kenley alone," I said. "She's definitely strong enough to do it." I'd never heard of a Binder using her skill at ten years old, and Kori's story had scared the shit out of me. "But are you sure she's the one? I've never seen her before, and she didn't seem to recognize me or my name."

"It's her," Meghan insisted. "That Tracker cost nearly every dime we had saved up, and he swears it was Kenley Daniels. He's come across her work a lot, with people running from the syndicate. Her blood sealed the binding, and it's strong. But he can't tell what kind of binding it is."

In a way, that was the worst part. Steven was mostly conscious, but usually incoherent from the pain, and even during his rare lucid periods, he hadn't been able to tell us what binding he'd accepted, and from whom. And there were too many questions the Tracker couldn't answer.

All we really knew was that it was a name binding, and that meant that whatever had happened was my fault. Steven and I had switched names years ago—when we were still kids—to give ourselves an extra layer of protection. If anyone tried to track my name, they'd find Steven and assume they'd made a mistake.

But the plan we'd concocted in childhood had backfired on us as adults.

At some point—we had no idea when—Kenley Daniels had bound Steven to something using her blood and his real name. But I'd been answering to Steven's name since we were eighteen years old, which meant she'd actually meant to bind *me*.

Steven was inches from death's doorstep, and it was all my fault.

Mine, and Kenley Daniels's.

Eleven

Kori

That time when I shadow-walked into my bedroom, I stopped a foot short of smashing my nose on the wall. Two weeks, and I was finally getting the hang of the tight space, which Kenley had used as an office before I'd moved in. Well, before Tower's men had moved my stuff in, while I was still in the basement. Eventually I'd get my own place. Once I was sure I was going to live long enough to need one.

I felt my way along the wall to the light switch and flipped it up, then peeled my wet pants off, cursing in my head. I wasn't sure whether profanity in the privacy of my own room—away from Ian's ears—would violate the terms of our bet or not, but you can't police someone's thoughts. That was one of many, many truths I'd learned working for Jake—the only one that brought me any comfort.

Clad in fresh, dry clothes, I crossed the tiny hall—really just a square of floor with four rooms opening into it—and pushed open the bathroom door, where I blinked in surprise and nearly jumped out of my own skin.

A young woman—not my sister—stood in my bathroom, staring at herself in the mirror over the pedestal sink. Her first name was Vanessa, if memory served, but I didn't know her last name. I only knew she was one of Jake's unSkilled computer geeks, and that Cam Caballero had been forced to recruit her for Tower after he killed the Binder who'd sealed her in service to Ruben Cavazos a couple of years earlier.

"Hey." Van turned to smile at me. "I'm done, if you need in here."

"Why are you in there in the first place?" I demanded. Then I noticed that she was wearing Kenley's robe. And nothing else, if the lack of clothing lines beneath satin meant anything.

Kenley's bedroom door opened behind me, and I turned to find my little sister staring at me, legs bare beneath one of the long T-shirts she usually slept in. "I thought you'd be out all day," she said by way of explanation, and for a moment, neither of them moved. Obviously waiting for my reaction.

"So did I." I squeezed past Vanessa to get into the bathroom. "And I would have been if some clumsy—" I stopped just in time and turned to Kenley with a frown. "Hey, if I accepted a dare to stop cussing for the next twenty-four hours, does that mean I can't cuss at all, or just when I'm with the person who dared me?"

Kenley grinned for several seconds when she realized I wasn't going to make a big deal about catching her in postcoital glow with her new friend. Then what I'd said sank in. "You agreed to stop cursing?" Suddenly she looked concerned. "What were the terms?"

"No terms. It's not a contract…it's just a stupid dare." I ran water into the bathroom cup, then drained it in several gulps.

"Who dared you?" Van asked as they both followed me into the living room.

"It was Holt, wasn't it?" Kenley said on her way into the kitchen as I pulled open the front closet and squatted in search of a dry pair of boots. "Why would you take that dare? How many times do I have to tell you that 'Na na na boo-boo' is not proper motivation for engaging in self-destructive behavior?"

"Where was that voice of reason half an hour ago?" I turned with my second-favorite pair of boots in hand to find Van and Kenley both blushing furiously, which explained exactly where they'd been half an hour ago. "I withdraw the question."

"We were gonna make waffles. You want some?" Van asked, pulling a box of Bisquick from the cabinet over the toaster. And that's when I realized this wasn't her first visit. *I* didn't even know where we kept the Bisquick.

"Waffles at two in the afternoon?"

Van shrugged. "It's Saturday," she said, like that should be explanation enough.

"Thanks, but I have to go meet Jake."

"That should make this whole 'no cussing' thing interesting," Kenley said, pulling a carton of eggs from the fridge. "At least it's just a dare, and not a sealed oath."

I stepped into my first boot. "What, you don't think I can do it?"

My sister looked up at me from across the counter. "I think profanity is your native language. That makes it a hard habit to break."

I thought about that as I brushed my hair and teeth. And I decided she was right.

I started to tell Kenley and Van that I was leaving, but sudden suspicious silence from the kitchen made my pulse spike in warning and drew me forward before I remembered that I was unarmed. But instead of an intruder, I found only my sister and her girlfriend, leaning against the counter in front of the steaming, hissing waffle iron, holding hands and just staring at each other.

It was so sweet I couldn't stand to watch. So I backed up without drawing their attention and closed myself into my room again with the light off. A second later, I stepped into Jake's darkroom. I hadn't been there in two months, but I'd been hundreds of times in the past six years, and it still felt exactly the same. A little bigger than most of the darkrooms at his various other facilities, and a little colder. And as dark as a void, like space with no stars.

I started forward, my hand outstretched, and three steps later, my fingertips bumped the switch on the wall, next to the door. Light flared to life overhead and I squinted while my eyes adjusted. Then I pressed a button on the small full-color display set flush with the wall next to the door. Static appeared on the screen, and a moment later a familiar face replaced it.

"Kori?" Danny Larimore stared out at me from the screen. "What the hell are you doing? There's a big red sign next to the monitor in here that says your darkroom privileges have been revoked. It's laminated and everything."

Which was why I didn't have the key card that would have gotten me access to the rest of the house without having to deal with someone in the security room. "I know, but I have to talk to Jake. Buzz him if you need to. Tell him it's about Ian Holt. He'll tell you to let me in."

"If this backfires and he decides to shoot the messenger, I'm comin' in there to kick your ass."

"Whatever." I could take Larimore even unarmed. "Just buzz him."

The screen lapsed into static again, and I filled the silence by running through the list of reasons I wouldn't recruit Ian, if I had any choice. Then I started on the number of ways I could kill Jake Tower—if that wouldn't be the worst strategic mistake in history.

I was up to boiling him alive in the blood of his own murder victims when Larimore appeared on-screen again. "He's sending someone to escort you to his office."

"I know the way."

"And he knows *you*. Sit tight." Then the screen went blank again, and again I was alone with my thoughts— a situation I found increasingly less comfortable with every occurrence.

A couple of minutes later, the door swung open into the hall, and David scowled at me, a strip of medical tape over his broken nose, dark bruises circling both eyes.

Great.

I stepped into the hall and the door swung closed behind me. David crossed both thick arms over his chest. "Make one suspicious movement, and I have permission to drop you where you stand."

"I think we both know how well that worked out last time." I turned to the right and headed for the staircase. "How pissed was Jake about you lying down on the job?"

David growled, and when I reached the top step, his

footsteps stopped behind me. "You know, I could just kick you down the stairs and say you fell."

I shrugged and turned to face him, careful not to grip the railing, which would make me look scared. "You could. And even if I don't manage to take you down with me, I'd be dead at worst, hurt and pissed at the least. Either way, that leaves you to explain to Jake that with me out of the picture, he's lost all the headway I've made recruiting Ian Holt. And you know how Jake deals with bad news."

With that, I made myself walk down the stairs, trying not to look like I was worried about being shoved with every step. Because I knew from experience that logic doesn't always trump anger and humiliation, and I'd fed David heaping helpings of both.

In the foyer, he grabbed my arm and pulled me close. "You look like you might be about to run off," he said, and I realized this was a power play. He wanted to be seen hauling me through the house like he'd caught me making trouble. I wanted to laugh. His little show wouldn't make the damage to his face look any better.

Jake's office was just off the foyer, and when we got there, before David could knock on the double glass doors, I spun and pulled my arm from his grasp, then punched him in the nose. Again.

David howled, and blood poured from his face. Again. While a couple of housekeepers came running with disposable towels and bleach, I knocked on the door and waited for a response. When Jake called for me to come in, I pulled open both doors and stepped inside, while behind me, two women in simple black uniforms tried to staunch the flow of blood from David's nose.

"What happened to your escort?" Jake asked as I pushed the door closed behind me.

"Ran into something." I dropped into one of the chairs in front of his desk. "I bet he'd be a real hazard on white carpet."

"Would your fist happen to be what he ran into?"

"Could be." I pretended to examine the blood on my hand. "My knuckles are suddenly sore."

Jake chuckled, and I exhaled silently in relief. "I always could count on you to test the weak points in my security." He handed me a wet wipe from the carton on his desk and I scrubbed the blood from my knuckles, then tossed the tissue into the gas fireplace, where he incinerated it with one press of a remote control button.

There would be no consequence for busting David's nose. No consequence for me, anyway, because Jake was in a good mood. Or because he was already pissed at David. Or maybe because his horoscope said he'd find humor in unexpected places today.

As for David… He'd been taken down two days in a row by an unarmed women five inches shorter and eighty pounds lighter. That meant he wasn't pulling his weight. I wouldn't be surprised if he found himself on much lighter duty in the very near future.

Jake leaned back in his chair and crossed his arms over his chest. "I assume you're here to report that Holt is eating out of your hands?"

I shrugged. "Well, he hasn't bitten off my fingers yet, so it's looking pretty good."

"Does he like you?"

"Yeah, I think he does. But I'm actually here to report something else. Cavazos made a play for him this morning. Two low-level musclemen in broad daylight. It was insulting."

Jake frowned. "On the west side?"

I nodded. "Less than half a mile from the hotel."

"Casualties?"

"None. Like I said, they were in over their heads. It looks like they found out where he was staying and waited for him to show up on the street. They may even be recon guys who just saw an opportunity and grabbed it. Cavazos will try again, though, and the next team will be more competent. I need a weapon, Jake."

"No, you don't. Cavazos won't send anyone he can't afford to lose past the river, so just stay out of the east side." Jake's brows rose in challenge. "Or should I assign David to protect you?"

"I don't know, he's kind of delicate," I said. "I'd hate for him to get hurt again."

Jake chuckled, but his eyes weren't laughing. "So you can handle this on your own, then?" he said, and that question only had one acceptable answer.

"Of course."

Sure, I could walk all over downtown in possession of the second most valuable piece of human commodity in the city, armed with nothing but quick fists and a sharp tongue. No problem.

Jake watched me, and I was careful not to fidget or to look away, or to give him any nonverbal hint that I was less than sure of myself. Appearing confident is half the battle with Jake.

The other half is being willing to grab the man next to you and use him as a human shield.

"Good," he said at last. "Where did you take him today?"

"He wanted to see the city, so we walked around downtown and I explained the basics of syndicate structure."

"What's his disposition toward signing?"

I shrugged, and the leather upholstery creaked beneath me. "Understandably hesitant, but interested."

"Have you come across anything we can use to make him less hesitant?"

"Not yet." That was mostly true, because I didn't yet know what Ian wanted from Jake. And since Julia wasn't there to read the tiny kernel of a lie buried deep in that larger truth, I would get away with it.

"So you walked, talked and dined all day long, and you didn't come up with anything useful?"

"Um... He's left-handed, a democrat and a non-smoker," I said. Jake was not amused. "In my own defense, liquor was the main course at lunch, so it's not like we lingered over conversation and coffee."

"What about his things? What name is on his license? What numbers are in his phone? Are there pictures in his wallet? Credit cards?"

"I didn't realize I was supposed to be spying on him."

"You're supposed to be convincing him to join the syndicate. Whatever that takes. Too many credit cards could mean he has heavy debt. Pictures of kids in his wallet could mean he has someone we can threaten."

"But you already ran a credit check, and a background check, and every other kind of check there is." I'd seen the results. Ian's parents and only brother were dead, and he had no other close living family members. He lived alone, and well within his means. He had $17,000 in savings and no stock portfolio. He owned his car outright—a two-year-old midlevel sedan—and rented a two-bedroom house. He was an ordinary man with a good sense of humor and an extraordinary Skill.

"That won't tell me what bastards he fathered on the sly, or what debt he's racked up under someone else's name."

"He's not a thief, Jake." Or a deadbeat dad. He just wasn't.

Jake rolled his chair backward and pulled open a mini-fridge built into the credenza behind him. "You're a lot of things, Kori. A steady hand, a good shot, a beautiful face, a foul mouth, an abrasive bitch and, recently, a very big pain in my ass. But one thing you've never been is naive." He pulled a bottle of water from the fridge and pushed the door shut, then rolled his chair back to his desk and scowled at me over it, bottle in hand. "You don't know what he is, and the minute you start thinking you do is the minute you've failed this assignment. You only know what he lets you see, and the reverse damn well better be true."

I nodded—you can never go wrong with a noncommittal answer.

"Only two kinds of people join the syndicate. Those who have something to hide and those who have nothing to lose. It's your job to figure out which one of those descriptions fits Ian Holt."

"What if neither of them fits? He hasn't said he'll sign yet," I said, and immediately regretted reminding him of what I hadn't yet accomplished.

"He's here for a reason, Korinne. Find out what that is." Jake cracked open his water bottle and took a long drink, but his gaze never left me, disapproving stare intact. "Where are you taking him for dinner?"

I shrugged and, too late, I realized he probably wasn't going to like my answer. "I thought I'd let him choose."

Leather creaked as Jake sat straighter in his chair. He leaned forward, arms crossed over his desk blotter. "So, he ordered his own breakfast, you neglected to feed him lunch, and you've made no dinner reservations? The plan is to weaken him with hunger? Starve him until he signs?"

Making concrete plans for dinner honestly hadn't occurred to me. I never ate anywhere that required reservations unless I was with Jake—he took two bodyguards everywhere he went—and even then, his assistant always did the reserving.

"I can make some calls," I mumbled, digging my phone from my pocket.

"What, the fry cook at Denny's owes you a favor?"

I had no good response to his piercing sarcasm, so I bit my tongue. Until it bled.

"I'll make dinner arrangements. You go fetch my guest. I'm ready to discuss business." He reached for his desk phone and waved one hand at me in dismissal.

"Can I get a key card?" I said, standing.

Jake looked up at me, anger flashing in his eyes. "When and if I want you to have unlimited access to my home, I'll give you a key card. But don't expect that to happen anytime soon."

I nodded curtly, pretending that didn't sting. I didn't want it to. I didn't want to give a damn that he still didn't trust me, because I'd never trusted him a day in my life. But it did sting, and beyond that, it was a hell of an inconvenience, not being allowed into the syndicate's headquarters without being personally cleared by security every time I traveled into the darkroom.

I excused myself and made my way back upstairs alone and was not surprised to see that Jake had sent another guard to make sure I went no farther than the darkroom. This one didn't grab my arm. He didn't even speak to me.

He must have liked his face the way it was.

Twelve

Ian

I didn't know Kori was there until she stepped out of the bathroom without warning, and I nearly jumped out of my own skin. I'd met shadows that made more noise. "You know, you should give a guy some warning. What if I'd been naked?"

She shrugged and followed me into the living room. "I could use a good laugh."

"Ha ha." But unless I was mistaken, she didn't look horrified by the possibility.

"Your presence has been requested at syndicate headquarters," Kori said, perched on the arm of the nearest couch.

"Now?" I asked, and she nodded. "And headquarters would be where?"

"Jake's house. But don't let that lull you into a misplaced sense of comfort."

"Wouldn't dream of it." I opened the minifridge and pulled out two sodas, then tossed one to her. "What does he want?"

"To talk business. And probably to apologize for your mistreatment at my hands."

My brows rose in surprise and I spread my arms to take in the elegant suite around us. "If this is mistreatment, you can abuse me any day, Ms. Daniels."

She laughed, and I watched her. Making her smile felt like a victory.

"So, what if I don't want to report to Tower? What if I'd rather sit here and finish this soda with you?"

Her smile died a slow death. "Then I'd have to assume that you're not seriously considering our offer. And I'd be obligated to relay that to Jake."

"Obligated?" I said, and she shrugged.

"I can't lie to him."

I twisted the top from the plastic bottle and the soda inside fizzed briefly. "I take it he doesn't bear bad news gracefully?"

Kori blinked and seemed to consider the question. "Honestly, he doesn't get much bad news. Messengers tend to go out of their way to make sure they only bring him good news. Many a decision has been changed at the last minute by a messenger with a will to survive."

I watched her, waiting for a smile, or a laugh, or even one sharply arched brow to tell me she was joking.

She *had* to be joking. Right?

I wasn't going to take the chance, either way. I couldn't afford to piss off either Kori or Tower until I had a clear shot at Kenley Daniels.

Standing, I screwed the lid back on my bottle and set it on the coffee table. "So, anything I should know about this meeting?"

Kori shrugged and sipped from her own bottle. "Don't

promise him anything. Ask for more than you expect to get, so he can talk you down a little and save face."

"But I haven't agreed to sign yet."

"Exactly. This is his chance to try to buy you. Later, when you *do* agree to sign, the first draft of your contract will reflect whatever the two of you hash out in his office today. Nothing's official until the ink has dried, but you want a good starting place. You *need* a good starting place."

Except that I didn't want to start anything with Jake Tower and his organization. I'd come here to finish things.

An hour and a half later, after endless rounds of verbal posturing, thin pretense and precisely worded defensive blocks from us both, Tower leaned back, hands resting on the padded arms of his desk chair, evidently satisfied.

I'd been very careful to ask for more than he'd give the typical recruit, to show that I knew my own value, but I only pushed the issue on a couple of points, mostly because I had no real intention of signing and I didn't want to waste any more time making demands I would never see met.

In the end, Tower was satisfied that he was getting the better end of the deal, but not suspicious that his victory had come too easy. And by the time he pressed a button and asked his sister to bring in a round of drinks— signaling the end of our "business talk"—I was mentally exhausted. I'd had very little experience with negotiation, and overthinking everything I planned to say before I could say it had given me one hell of a headache.

When Julia Tower arrived with a tray of drinks, Kori

opened the door for her, then followed her in from the foyer, and I felt myself relax a little at the sight of her.

Then I realized that was *not* the reaction I should have to the woman who was trying to get me to sign over my free will. Tower wanted me to be comfortable with her. He wanted me to trust her. He wanted me to be blinded with need every time I glanced into those big brown eyes, so I wouldn't have the clarity and focus to understand what I'd be signing away when he put that pen in my hand.

But it wouldn't work.

Sure, I wanted her. But if I let my guard down even for a second in this den of lions, one of them would bite my head off.

Tower frowned up at Kori from his desk chair. "How much of the business side of things have you shown Mr. Holt?"

She froze, and I remembered what she'd said about being unable to lie to him. Fortunately there was nothing stopping *me* from lying to Tower. "Not much," I said. "Today I wanted to see downtown and get a feel for the syndicate's structure. Kori was kind enough to oblige me."

It wouldn't occur to me until later that night to wonder why I'd lied for her without a second thought.

Tower glanced at his sister, then his gaze slid to me, and I felt the weight of it. This was different from how he'd looked at me at the party. This look was skepticism and surprise, and for a moment, I thought he'd call me on my lie. But then he only turned back to Kori and nodded, and Kori turned toward the door. We'd obviously been dismissed.

"Mr. Holt," Julia Tower called, and Kori's hand froze on the doorknob. "How are you enjoying your stay?"

"Very well, thank you," I said, and Kori turned to face her slowly, dread written in every line on her face.

"I assume Korinne is treating you well?"

"Of course. She's gone to great lengths to accommodate my curiosity."

"Good." Tower stood and rounded his desk toward the door, brushing Kori aside as he gestured for me to walk with him. "I've made reservations for you both in my name at Philemon's. Best filet in the city."

"Thank you, but that really wasn't necessary," I said, and Tower frowned.

"I'm afraid it was. I'm confident that Kori is an excellent tour guide, and she has certain other gifts to share, I'm sure, but her perspective on the syndicate may be a bit…narrow." He stopped in the middle of the foyer and turned to look right into my eyes, ignoring Kori and his own sister like they weren't even there.

"Your Skill is formidable and your strength is very rare. That makes you much more valuable than any common Traveler, if I may be blunt, and the trajectory we foresee for your future soars far higher than hers, which, frankly, has already declined from its peak. So go out tonight and eat and avail yourself of any other amenities we have to offer. But please keep in mind that while Korinne is at your disposal, we have many other, more sophisticated treats for you to sample, should your appetite change."

He glanced at her on the last word, and Kori's fists clenched at her sides, but she stared at the floor.

Tower pulled her aside then, while his sister tried to distract me with pointless small talk, and I could barely hear the single sentence he growled at her, his hand tight around her arm, though he flinched as if his grip hurt him, as well. "No. More. Bars."

Minutes later, after another trip through Tower's darkroom, we stepped into my hotel suite and Kori sank onto one of the couches, her expression carefully blank. She just sat there, staring at her hands, perpetuating the longest silence I'd endured since meeting her.

"He's full of shit, you know," I said when I couldn't stand to see her like that anymore. Kori was like a bonfire, blazing with bright light and sometimes harsh heat, and Tower had just kicked dirt all over her, smothering the flames. I didn't like seeing her light put out. In fact, sitting there watching her, I realized I hated it. "Ninety-five percent of sophistication is pretense. The other five percent is good wine, and I prefer the latter without the former."

"What does that even mean?" she asked, without looking up.

"It means that I don't want to trade you in for a more sophisticated model. I like the sharp edges and surprises."

I told myself it was okay to say that. To admit a truth of my own, after all the truths she'd already shown me. I even tried to convince myself that telling her was part of my job. I needed her to like and trust me. But I'd obviously managed to say the wrong thing.

"Yeah. You like sharp edges," she spat. "That's why you wanted me to stop cussing, right?"

Damn.

"That was just a game, Kori. A stupid game to push your buttons. To see how you'd react, because…" I took a deep breath and leaned forward, hoping to catch her gaze. "Because you never do what I expect. But you're right. It was a stupid game. Forget about it. The bet is off."

"Oh, no, the bet's still on," she snapped, and a flare of anger finally burned through the shield of ambivalence she'd erected. "I'm not going to break my word. But for the record—" She stopped suddenly and looked away, hands clenched around the edge of the cushion she sat on.

"What? For the record, what?" I could practically taste the gritty honesty of whatever she'd been about to say, and I wanted to hear it, because whatever it was, it came from her soul. It was a truth about her.

"Nothing."

"No, that was something. I want to hear it."

Her eyes flashed in anger again. "You can stop pretending we're on an even playing field, Mr. Holt," she snapped again, and I flinched over her cold, formal use of my surname. "Until your signature is dry on Jake's contract, you hold all the power here and I can't afford to say anything that will make you mad."

I blinked, surprised. "Why? You think I'm going to go tattle to Tower if you hurt my feelings? Is that really what you think of me, even after I lied about what you showed me today?" I demanded, and her anger faltered, just for a moment. "Tell me what you were going to say, Kori."

Let me in. Just a little.

"Fine." She sat back, arms crossed over her chest in a pose that was probably supposed to look unaffected, but really looked defensive. "For the record, I don't *care* whether you like sharp edges or sophistication. I don't care what you like in a woman, and I don't care what

Jake thinks about my social status. If you want to trade me in for a different 'model,' go ahead. You won't be hurting my feelings."

I shook my head slowly. "That's not it," I said, trying not to look disappointed. "That's not what you were going to say. I can see it in your face." I *would* be hurting her feelings if I traded her in. Which seemed to imply that she did, in fact, *have* feelings.

And finally she nodded. "This job—recruiting you—is my chance to get back into favor with Jake. I'm not cut out to be a recruiter, Ian. But I have to recruit you to get my life back."

That felt closer to the truth, but there was still something she didn't trust me enough to show me. But pushing would only drive her further away.

"Fine, then let the recruiting continue," I said. "I believe we have reservations tonight, on Tower's dime? Some fancy restaurant?"

"Philemon's. They *do* have really good lobster." And we'd missed lunch, as my growling stomach was quick to point out.

"Then we'll both get one. Maybe two. Let's go recruit me in style," I said, and finally she smiled, a glimpse of a rainbow after the storm. "What's the dress code at this fancy restaurant?"

Kori frowned. "You're gonna need a suit. And they'll probably make me wear a dress."

"I thought you hated dresses."

"I do."

"And I have a bet to win. So we'll both wear jeans?"

Her smile grew just a little. "Mr. Holt, I think we may make a rebel of you yet."

After a quick trip back to her sister's apartment, Kori

stepped out of my bathroom in a low-cut, drapey black silk blouse that bared a two-inch strip of skin down the center of her torso, all the way to the bottom of her sternum. I wasn't sure how the damn thing even stayed on, and I caught myself holding my breath when she turned, watching for accidental gaps in the material.

"Wow, you look beautiful," I whispered when she stepped into the light, trying not to stare. I hadn't meant to say it. The words fell from my mouth before I could call them back.

"Does this cover all my rough edges?" She held her arms out hesitantly, like she wasn't sure she wanted to be inspected. "'Cause I feel like it doesn't cover much of anything."

"Your rough edges are thoroughly hidden. But it's good to know they're still under there," I said, my voice deeper than I'd intended it to be, my gaze glued to hers. My stomach twisted with nerves like I hadn't felt since junior high. I clasped my hands at my back because that was the only way I could control them. I wanted to reach for Kori.

I was dying to touch her.

"I feel kinda stupid in the blouse," she admitted, plucking nervously at the material. "But Kenley insisted this would keep me from getting tossed out of the restaurant."

"Your sister has wonderful taste." I crossed my arms over a pressed button-up shirt, tucked into my spare pair of jeans. Then I made myself think about Steven and Meghan—the mental reminder I needed in order to focus on the job at hand, rather than the woman in front of me. "Do you think she'd like to join us? Your sister?" Kori frowned, and I slid my hands into my pockets. "I'm interested in her role in the syndicate. I haven't met many Binders."

"She's...with someone tonight."

I shrugged. "So ask her to bring him. I'd love to get multiple perspectives on life in the Tower syndicate."

Kori's frown deepened. "I don't think they're ready to be seen out together. In public. Yet." She reached for the bathroom doorknob. "Are you ready?"

"Yeah." I buried my frustration, along with a sizable amount of guilt over the fact that I was about to dine in a five-star restaurant, while my brother lay dying, hidden away in his girlfriend's childhood bedroom. "Let's go."

Kori took us through my darkened bathroom once again, this time into an alley behind the restaurant, deep with shadows in the setting sun. "Not the most glamorous way to travel, I know," she admitted, as we stepped out onto the sidewalk. "But it's definitely the fastest."

Inside, the hostess wore an ankle-length black dress and a too-tight bun, and looked down her nose at our jeans. "We have a reservation for two," Kori said.

"For what time?" She didn't even look at the reservation list, as if she'd already decided we were lying.

"Actually I'm not sure. I didn't make it," Kori said, and the hostess's gaze hardened even more.

"Mr. Holt? Ms. Daniels?" A man in an expensive suit plucked the list from the podium, brushing the hostess aside without even a glance. We both nodded, and the manager—who else could he be?—smiled like he was made of sunshine. "Mr. Tower reserved your table for the entire evening, so please take your time and enjoy your meal. Erin, if you don't mind?" he said, gesturing for the hostess to show us to our table.

She took us to a quiet corner of the restaurant, where

I somehow felt both sheltered and exposed, and before I could even glance at the menu, a waiter appeared to pour two glasses of red wine, explaining that Mr. Tower had selected it himself.

"Did he order our food, too?" Kori mumbled, and the waiter chuckled.

"No, but he did offer suggestions."

We ordered several courses, and while we waited for the first of them, I sipped from my glass, watching her. "Tell me something about yourself. Something I don't already know. Something about your family."

"Aren't we supposed to be talking about the syndicate?" she said, staring into her wine skeptically.

"Okay, then, tell me something about your family *and* the syndicate. Is this the family business, or is it just you and Kenley? Are your parents bound? Any other siblings?" I knew I was pushing my luck, but I had to find some way of bringing her sister back into the picture before too much time spent with Kori made me forget my purpose, or hell, even my own name. She was Calypso, and I was starting to worry that she'd caught me. And the scariest part was that in spite of the guilt, and the lies, and the ugly truth of my mission, I wasn't sure I wanted to be released.

Kori hesitated for one long moment, like she was trying to decide whether or not she could trust me. Then, finally, she spoke. "Kenley and I have an older brother, but he's not syndicate, thank goodness. He's his own brand of trouble, even without criminal ties."

I didn't ask her brother's name, and she didn't offer it. Either would have been a big faux pas among the Skilled, who know that names, like blood, carry power.

"What about your parents? Are they bound to Tower?"

"No, they died when I was a kid," she said, and I blinked in surprise.

"Mine died a few years ago," I said softly, and I recognized the echo of old pain in her eyes. "Who raised you?"

"My grandmother, and no, she's not syndicate, either. In fact…" Kori exhaled, like she couldn't believe what she was about to say. "In fact, she doesn't even know Kenley and I are bound. If my parents knew, they'd probably come back from the dead just to yell at us."

"So, how did you wind up bound to Tower?"

"I…um…" She stared at the stark-white tablecloth. "That's kind of a personal story, and it's not entirely mine to tell."

Not entirely hers? My curiosity doubled. "So just tell me your part," I said. "You have my word it will go no further. If that means anything."

I desperately wanted my word to mean something to her, but at the same time, I was fully aware that it shouldn't. I had been lying to her all along, and the lies would have to continue, but this part was true. I wouldn't betray this trust.

"I signed on to be with Kenley," she said after a moment of thinking it over. "I couldn't leave her here alone. She's not like me. She doesn't have any hard edges or any self-protective instinct. She's sweet. And nice. She would have been eaten alive."

But that didn't make any sense. The only thing I knew about Kenley Daniels—other than what I'd learned from Kori—was that she'd sealed my brother into a nonconsensual binding strong enough to kill him. And she must have done it by accident, because my brother didn't use his own name. She *had* to be aiming for me.

How could someone with enough power to seal the wrong person into a binding he hadn't consented to possibly be the sweet, innocent sister Kori had sold herself to Jake Tower to protect?

"You okay?" Kori asked, but I barely heard her, and I only distantly noticed the tray of one-bite salmon and rice appetizers the waiter set in the center of the table.

"You joined to protect your sister?"

She nodded. "I joined to try. But there's only so much I can do."

"What makes you think she needs protection?"

Kori frowned, like she may have heard me wrong. "The fact that she's here. Kenley got into some trouble when she was in college, and one of Jake's scouts swooped in promising to clean up her mess, in exchange for her services. She was terrified, and naive, and very young. She thought she had no other way out, so she signed up. Two days later, she showed up at my brother's New Year's Eve party in tears, begging for my help. But there was nothing I could do. She's a piss-poor negotiator and her binding had already been sealed. All I could do was negotiate protection for her in exchange for my own services."

"What kind of protection?"

Kori exhaled heavily and fiddled with the knife next to her plate. "I'm not allowed to discuss the specifics of my contract with Tower. But life in the syndicate can be really hard for a pretty twenty-year-old woman with only one chain link on her arm. Especially one who doesn't know how to shoot or fight. So I negotiated for a position with enough power to protect her. Then I defended that position by taking down everyone who got in my face, to make sure they all knew what would happen if they messed with either of us."

She shrugged to punctuate what felt like a confession, and I could only stare at her, trying in vain to reconcile the beautiful, almost dainty-looking woman with the warrior I—and the entire west half of the city—knew her to be.

Kori picked up one of four silver spoons on the platter and sniffed at the single bite it held, then set the spoon down again and made a face. "I think the salmon is underdone."

She was obviously trying to change the subject, and I decided not to push the issue. I didn't know what to do with what she'd already told me, and I wasn't sure how much more I could take with her sitting across from me, barely-but-elegantly draped in thin black silk.

There was nothing under that blouse. There couldn't be. Nothing but her.

"It's smoked," I said, picking up one of the spoons, just so I'd have something else to look at. And something to occupy my hands and my mouth, which seemed to be forming an alternate plan of their own, involving thin ribbons of black silk, bare skin and any room with a decent lock on the door.

"So it's raw?" Kori looked horrified. "People actually pay someone to not-cook their food? Even cavemen had fire."

I laughed. "Try it. You might like it." I ate one of the bite-size appetizers in demonstration, but she only frowned. "Am I going to have to dare you?"

"Low blow," she mumbled, choosing one of the three remaining spoons. "If I get sick from raw fish, I'm blaming you."

"If you get sick from a thirty-five-dollar smoked salmon appetizer at one of the best restaurants in the city, I'll nurse you back to health myself."

That time she smiled. And ate a spoonful of smoked salmon. But she obviously had to force herself to swallow.

"Not for you?" I asked, laughing at the face she made. In answer, she pushed the platter toward me and took a drink of wine, but that only twisted her expression into a stronger display of dislike.

"I'm two minutes away from ordering a burger and a beer," she threatened, pushing the wineglass away, too. "How can you drink this sh— Uh, this stuff?"

"It's an acquired taste," I said, lifting my own glass. "Much like the syndicate, I suppose."

"I guess." Kori shrugged and watched me from across the table. "The big difference between Jake and uncooked salmon is that eating what he serves *will* eventually kill you."

Thirteen

Kori

After the waiter came to refill his glass—mine was still full—Ian excused himself to go to the bathroom. I watched him make his way across the restaurant, pointedly ignoring my wine, wondering for the millionth time in the last twenty-four hours what Ian was looking for from Jake. And how I would be able to live with myself once he was bound, knowing I was the one who'd led the sheep to slaughter.

Halfway to the bathroom, Ian turned to speak to someone, and my heart nearly stopped when I saw Julia Tower stand from the table where she and Jonah had just been served their own appetizer. No doubt Jake had sent them to make sure I was getting the job done. Treating Ian right.

She and Ian spoke, and she laughed at whatever he'd said, and suddenly I desperately wished I could read lips. She would hear the truth—or lack of—in whatever he said. As a Reader, Julia was her brother's best and most trusted source of inside information. And one of my least favorite people in the world.

After another minute, she let him escape to the restroom, and if he'd come to hate her half as much as I had, the urinals in the men's room must have been a much more welcome sight than her face.

When he disappeared around the corner, she looked right at me, then started across the restaurant in my direction.

Fuck!

"I have to say, you've impressed me with this one," Julia said, sinking into Ian's empty chair uninvited.

"Because I'm still alive?"

"Because he actually likes you. And he thinks you like him." She picked up my wineglass and sipped from it, then held it as she crossed her legs and leaned closer, like she'd let me in on a secret. "I must admit, you're playing this one very smart. Jake will be pleased."

"Um...thanks?"

I never knew what to say to Julia, because I was never quite sure what she was talking about, but if I lied, she'd know it. So I usually treated her like I'd treat any snake in red satin—I avoided her like the plague. And when avoidance wasn't possible, I tried my best to dodge both fangs and venom.

She twisted the glass, swirling the red wine, and I found myself watching the way light shone through it. Anything to avoid eye contact with her. But I couldn't stop her from watching me.

"Uh-oh." She set the glass down and lifted my chin with one finger. I slapped her hand away, but it was too late. She'd already seen...something. Or maybe she'd pretended to see something. I never could tell with Julia. Her silence was as toxic as her words. "He's right, isn't he? You actually like him."

I didn't answer, because the answer didn't matter. If I told the truth, she'd know. If I lied, she'd know. Silence was my only defense.

"Don't do this to yourself, Kori," she whispered while my blood rushed fast enough to make me dizzy. "You know this isn't real. The reality is that he's champagne, and you're malt liquor." She spat the last phrase like it actually tasted bad, and my fingers twitched in my lap, itching to curl into fists. But if I punched her, that punch would be the last I ever threw. "His career path will take him soaring, and yours has already landed you in the basement."

"Shut up," I growled, itching to call her all the names running through my head.

"I'm trying to help you, Kori. I'm trying to keep you from hurting yourself."

That was a lie. It had to be. She would never help me, unless helping me somehow benefited her. But what could she possible gain from this?

"Just let him play his game. Let him fantasize until he's satisfied, then he'll sign with Jake and you'll be off the hook. There's no reason for you to get hurt by this."

I shouldn't have asked. I *knew* better than to ask. Just because she could read the truth didn't mean she would speak it. But after everything I'd already shown Ian—everything I'd told him—if I'd given him that much power over me and he was playing some kind of game, I was screwed.

"What game?" I hated myself for asking. For giving her that opening. But I had to know.

Her eyes widened and her jaw dropped open in a

staged display of surprise. She didn't even try to make it believable. "Seduction, Kori. The game of seduction." Fake surprise melted from her expression to expose her natural look. Malice. The snake was about to strike. "Don't tell me you haven't noticed."

I rolled my eyes. "He is *not* trying to seduce me."

"I think this has gone beyond 'trying.'"

"You are so full of...crap."

She lifted one brow over my uncharacteristically tame language. "So, he hasn't told you you're beautiful? He doesn't try to make you smile? He doesn't look right into your eyes when he talks to you, so you feel important?"

"That doesn't mean anything, except that he's a nice guy." Too nice for the syndicate. Too nice for me.

Julia leaned closer, looking deep into my eyes in search of what every predator wants: fear. "Then why did he lie about what you showed him this afternoon?"

Of *course* she knew he'd lied. She'd probably smelled his intent before he even opened his mouth.

"Why do you think Jake let him get away with that?" Julia demanded, her voice hard now, a little too angry to be truly taunting. "Why do you think he let Holt cover for you?"

"Because he didn't know?"

Julia's frown deepened, and I realized she hadn't wanted Ian to get away with his lie. She'd wanted Jake to punish me. "Jake knows everything. I make sure of that. He let Holt lie for you because that's part of the game. Holt was playing the hero, protecting the damsel to win her over, and you fell for it."

"You're lying." But I couldn't even make myself believe that.

"Think about it, Kori." She leaned back in her chair,

arms crossed confidently over her chest. "Why would a man like Ian tolerate a woman like you? Why would he put up with brash and impulsive when he could have friendly and willing from any girl in Jake's stable?"

I couldn't answer. I *had* no answer.

"He's kept you around for the same reason a lion would rather kill its own dinner than eat from a dish. He wants the hunt. He wants to play the game. Even if the game is rigged." She shrugged, and her eyes flashed with cruelty. "After all, he *will* win. He gets to pretend to win you over with no chance of failure, because in the end, you're a sure thing. Right? The key is to never let him feel like he's hunting caged prey. The harder you feign disinterest, the more he will want you." Julia leaned even closer, staring into my eyes, enjoying whatever she saw there. "You can do that, right? You can make him feel like this is real? Like he's really working toward a prize?"

I couldn't speak. I couldn't think past the horrible ache in my chest. I didn't want to know what that pain meant, or how it could possibly hurt worse than what I'd lived through in the basement.

"I'm sorry, Kori," she said, her words sweet, her tone vicious. "I guess Jake just doesn't understand how badly a girl can be hurt by a game, if she doesn't know she's playing." Julia drained the wine from my glass, then set it down. "Or maybe he doesn't care." She smiled sweetly, then, and made her way back to her own table, where Jonah sat watching us both.

I sat at the table alone when she left, silently cursing Ian for accepting Jake's invitation, Jake for forcing me into this assignment and Jake's mother for giving birth to any of her three hell-spawn children in the first place. But by the time Ian got back to the table, just as the waiter brought out two bowls of soup, I'd moved on to cursing myself for ever believing a word any of them said. I could blame Jake, Julia and Ian until the day the sun devoured the entire planet, but that would never erase the fact that I'd broken my own number-one rule.

Trust no one.

Me, Kenley and Kris. It had been the three of us against the world since the day our parents died, leaving us with a grandmother who hadn't wanted kids of her own, much less grandchildren. They were the only ones I could trust. The only people I could lean on. Except that Kris was an hour away, and now Kenley had Vanessa. I was alone in a mess of my own making. And I had no idea how to get out of it.

"You okay?" Ian asked, lifting a spoonful of soup to his mouth.

"I saw you with Julia Tower," I said, stirring my own soup with my spoon. "What did she want?"

"She was asking about you," he said, and I watched him carefully, wishing for the first time in my life that I was a Reader rather than a Traveler. Shadow-walking had always made me feel safe and kind of stealthy, because I could get out of almost any situation armed with nothing more than a decent shadow. But whether or not Julia had been lying, she'd showed me one thing for sure—I could shadow-walk away from danger, but I couldn't walk away from the truth. Hell, lately I couldn't even identify it.

What if I'd been wrong about Ian from the start? What if it *was* all a game and everything I thought I knew about him was a lie? What else could I have been wrong about?

"What did you tell her?" I asked, when he studied my face, frowning.

"I told her you've been the consummate hostess. That you're beyond reproach, and that her brother couldn't have chosen anyone better to show off his empire and its many, varied offerings."

But Jake hadn't chosen me. He'd just given Ian what he asked for.

"So, you're enjoying yourself?" I heard the hollow note in my voice, but I couldn't fix it. I didn't know how to act like I was having fun when Julia had just pulled the rug out from under my feet and stuck around to watch me stumble off balance. I was angry, and confused, and more scared than I would ever admit, and it took every ounce of self-control I had to keep from spewing profanity into the heavens.

Unfortunately self-restraint was a poor substitute for gratitude and a love-struck gaze, or whatever Ian expected to see, if Julia was telling the truth. And suddenly I realized she'd known that. Had she set me up to fail, by telling me about Ian's game, knowing I couldn't play along if I knew I was playing at all?

Or was the whole thing a lie intended to make me paranoid and even more shrewish than usual?

"Well, this isn't exactly a vacation," Ian said, answering a question I'd forgotten I asked. "Why? What's wrong, Kori?"

"Is there something you want from me that you haven't gotten?" I demanded softly, holding his gaze. Silently daring him to tell me the truth, if there was anything to be told.

"Well, yes." He frowned. "Last I heard, you were still trying to figure that part out."

Right. Whatever it was that would make him sign. "And what you need from Jake, it's not some kind of game, is it? You're not just playing a game here?"

Ian pushed his soup bowl toward the middle of the table and leaned closer, his gaze holding mine captive. "No, Kori. I know I joke a lot, and the truth is that I like to see you smile. You don't do enough of that. But I'm not playing games with your boss. I came here with very serious intent. I swear on my own free will."

And that I believed. But whether he'd meant to or not, he'd misunderstood what game I was talking about.

"What brought this up?" he asked, handing his half-empty bowl to the waiter who already held mine. I hadn't taken a single bite. "Did Julia say something to you?"

"We don't get along," I admitted. "Which sucks, because Jake listens to her."

"Well, I gave her nothing negative to report, so try to forget about her." He smiled at something over my shoulder. "Your lobster is here."

I made it through the rest of the meal without losing either my mind or my temper, mostly because the food—the parts I recognized, anyway—was amazing and when I got back from my own restroom break, Ian had ordered something with vodka in it to replace the second glass of wine I'd turned down.

I tried to tell myself that he was being nice, not manipulative, but that was hard to believe because in my world the reverse was almost always true. Even a second drink and a huge slice of the most delicious chocolate cake I'd ever tasted weren't enough to completely settle my nerves. Julia's interference led me to look for hidden meaning in everything Ian said. She made me overanalyze every smile, every second of eye contact. And she wasn't finished.

After dinner, I ducked into the restroom one more time, and when I came out of the stall, she was standing at the row of sinks, watching me in the mirror. "It'll be tonight," she said, her mouth hardly moving as she dabbed gloss onto her lower lip. "He sounds like he's ready to move in for the kill. So to speak."

I squirted citrus-scented sanitizer on my hands. "What, you're psychic now, too?"

"You don't have to be psychic to see what's obvious. When you drop him off, he'll ask you to stay for drinks. Then he'll just ask you to stay…"

She turned to leave, then twisted to glance at me in the mirror one last time, her palm flat on the door. "Don't make it too easy for him, okay? Even a caged rabbit struggles a little before it's caught." Then she pushed the door open and left me staring at my own reflection, breathing too fast, my blood pumping fear and anger through my veins.

I tried to breathe, like Kenley had shown me. In and out, exhaling all the hate and pain. But this time it didn't work. This time memories weren't the problem, so burying them couldn't help. If Julia was telling the truth, I was trapped as thoroughly now by my own bindings as I'd ever been by the basement walls. And knowing what was coming didn't make it any easier to deal with.

You can do this. You have *to do this.*

I sucked in one last deep breath, then turned for the door, determined to cling to dignity until the last possible moment. But then the rage inside me crested and a wordless shout of fury erupted from my mouth. I whirled toward the sink and my fist slammed into the glass above it. The mirror shattered and slices of it fell everywhere, breaking into smaller shards in the sink basins and on the floor at my feet. And for about three seconds, I felt better.

Then I realized I'd just spilled my blood in a public restroom and had no good way to clean it up.

I snatched a cloth from the stack on the counter and tied it around my cut hand, then picked up the bottle of hand sanitizer and read the contents. Alcohol. I exhaled in relief, then upended the bottle and squirted a glob onto every single drop of blood I could find. I was still on my knees in the mess when the door opened behind me and the hostess came in.

She gaped at the destruction around me, her mouth open wide enough to catch a whole swarm of flies.

"The mirror fell right off the wall. Could have killed me," I said, dropping the nearly empty bottle of sanitizer in the nearest sink. "I might sue." Then I marched past her and out the front door to the sidewalk, where Ian was waiting for me.

He took one look at the cloth around my hand and lifted one brow. "Do I even want to know?"

"Probably not." I lead the way into the alley again without offering further explanation.

"Do you find trouble everywhere you go?"

"Sometimes it finds me."

I took him back to the hotel and he called downstairs for a first-aid kit, then refused help on my behalf from the man who brought it up. I cleaned and bandaged my cuts in the bathroom, then I stoppered the sink and dumped the bleach from Ian's travel kit—no Skilled person travels without bleach-solution in a spray bottle, even if it has to go in the checked luggage—over the cloth stained with my blood. Bleach would destroy the blood enough to keep it from being used against me.

"You want to tell me what happened?" Ian asked, glancing at my bandaged hand from the doorway.

"No." I didn't want to tell him anything until I knew whether or not Julia was lying.

"Kori, I can see that something's wrong."

"I'm fine." And maybe if I said it enough, we'd both eventually believe me.

In the front room, I glanced around at the view, and the couches, and the huge television, and the bottle of champagne sitting in a bucket of ice on a tall table against one wall—it had obviously been sent up moments before we'd arrived. This hotel suite probably cost more than I made in a month.

No one had ever wanted me as badly as Jake wanted Ian. But I knew better than anyone that the more Jake gave, the more he'd expect in return.

Angry, I marched across the room and plucked the small, embossed envelope from the tray the champagne sat on, trying to guess whether it had been sent by Jake or by Julia. But before I could take the card from the envelope, Ian gently pulled it from my hand. I looked up at him and immediately wished I hadn't. There was something there. Something in his eyes when he looked at me. Something important, but I didn't know how to interpret it. I'd lost all perspective.

Julia had *stolen* my perspective.

Ian looked worried—nervous—but I couldn't tell if that was because he genuinely cared that something was bothering me, or because his game wasn't working out the way he'd planned.

He stared into my eyes, and my palms started to

sweat. My head felt like it was floating above my body, not truly attached. I couldn't make sense of what I was feeling. Everything was all tangled up in a knot so complicated I couldn't follow the threads. And I had no hope of untangling them.

He wanted me. I could see that in his eyes. In the way he stood close, but not quite touching me. In the way he kept glancing at my lips, like he wanted to kiss me.

Some part of me wanted to kiss him, and that scared me so badly I couldn't breathe. I needed to back away. To put some space between us. But that same part of me remembered what things were like before the basement. Before every touch bruised and every mouth bit.

Ian didn't look angry. He didn't look nasty or cruel. He wasn't stalking or skulking. He just looked…interested.

If we'd met somewhere else.

If my life and Kenley's well-being weren't in Ian's hands.

If I were someone else, and *he* were someone else.

If the moment hadn't been manufactured by Jake Tower.

If any one of those things had been true, I might have wanted more than a kiss from Ian. I might have wanted to be with him. For a night. For a week. Maybe for more.

But this was… I couldn't do it. Not like this. Not when I had no choice. I couldn't breathe past the bitter lump in my throat or make my head stop spinning. I couldn't mute the voice in my head—*my* voice—shouting for me to run. Fight. Leave, before he said something neither of us could go back from.

"So, you all set?" I asked, and even to my own ears, my voice sounded brittle, like it might break any moment. Like I might break with it.

"Stay and have a drink with me." Ian waved one hand at a minibar. "No champagne, I swear."

I opened my mouth to say no thanks, and that's when the rest of me discovered what my brain had already known, at least in theory. I couldn't say no. Even *trying* to say it sent pain shooting through my temple, half blinding me. My hands started to shake. Jake had told me to do whatever Ian wanted me to do, and Ian wanted me to stay for a drink.

Just like Julia had said he would.

Ian was playing a game—*I* was his game. And I was going to lose.

With that realization, I knew what I had to do.

Turn it off. Turn everything off. Whatever happens, happens. But I didn't have to feel it. I didn't have to truly be there. No matter what Jake made me do or say, he couldn't shove his greedy fingers into my head. He couldn't control my mind, or where I sent it.

No one could.

"Fine. Just one," I said finally, and my hands stopped shaking. My voice felt empty, like the prerecorded message on my voice mail.

Ian pulled the bottle of champagne from the bucket and scooped ice out with a plastic cup. I flinched when the cubes clinked into two glasses. I sat on the edge of the leather couch with my hands clasped in my lap while he pulled tiny bottles from the minibar. A minute later, he turned around with two drinks and gave me one as he sank onto the couch next to me. "What should we toast to?" he asked, holding his glass up between us.

"Whatever you want." That was the game, right? The winner gets whatever he wants?

My glass smelled like vodka, a clean scent. Astringent. If I drank enough of it, could it make me clean on the inside? Could it wash the blood from my hands? Bleach the stains from my soul? If I started drinking right that moment and didn't stop until it was over, maybe I wouldn't remember anything in the morning. And if I didn't remember what had happened, I could tell myself nothing had happened.

A lie is always easier to believe if there's no evidence against it.

"Oh, come on. There must be something you want to toast. Dinner on someone else's dime? Low heels?" Ian glanced at my sandals. "Borrowed blouses?" He touched the short, flared sleeve of Kenley's shirt, and my hand clenched around the glass. He wasn't going to let me check out. Ian wanted to hear the wind-up doll speak.

"To free will," I said finally, looking right into his eyes.

He laughed, like I'd made a joke, and chills broke out on both my arms. "To free will," he repeated. "That most fabled of civil rights. May we all one day truly understand what we've lost." He bumped his glass against mine with a *clink,* and my stomach clenched around my lobster dinner.

"You don't know what real loss is," I said through clenched teeth, refusing to drink. He couldn't possibly.

Ian's smile died and he lowered his glass, frowning at me over it. "What the hell does that mean?"

"It means exactly what I said. You don't know a thing about loss. If you did, you wouldn't be sitting here in a suite paid for by a man who's just waiting to teach you what that word really means."

His gaze hardened and he set his drink on the coffee

table. "You're not the only one who's ever lost someone, you know."

"This isn't about dead parents," I snapped.

"Then what is it about? What did I say wrong this time?"

"Nothing. I wish you *would* say it. I wish you'd quit with the drinks, and the chitchat, and the deep eye contact. This doesn't have to be so much work. I'm a sure thing, Ian. No seduction required. Didn't you get the memo?" I turned my drink up and drained it in several long gulps, and when I finally set the glass down, he was frowning at me, his expression stuck somewhere between confusion and exasperation.

"What the hell are you talking about?"

I needed another drink. If he was playing the game Julia said he was playing, I'd just ruined the illusion of the hunt. And possibly tied a noose around my own neck.

"Nothing. I just… I'm sorry." I stood and headed for the minibar. "I just can't pretend anymore. Playing your game is one thing, but pretending it isn't a game is too much."

"What game, Kori?" The couch creaked at my back as he stood, but there were no footsteps.

"You. Me. Recruitment. Fringe benefits." I plucked another tiny bottle from the minibar and cracked the lid without even glancing at the label. Then I turned and met his gaze from across the room. "I'm what you asked for. I can't say no. So I wish you'd quit trying to make this feel like something it isn't and just tell me what you want me to do, so I can get it over with."

His eyes widened. Then his dark eyebrows sank low over green eyes and his hands curled into fists at his sides. I knew that look. Hell, I'd perfected that look. He was going to hit something.

Me? Was he going to hit me, because I'd ruined whatever fantasy he was playing out in his head? And if so, how many punches could I throw before the resistance pain kicked in again? Would this be like it was with Jonah, brutal and violent? Or would this be a civilized conquest, grown-ups playing pretend, polite until the last stroke?

In the basement, I'd been trapped by dead shadows and crippled by direct orders. Mentally fighting hands and teeth I couldn't see, crushed by weight I couldn't bear, pinned, humiliated, hurt. Wishing for death, but too scared to reach for it.

Would I have the guts to end it this time? To fight back until I couldn't move, drawing death closer with every punch I threw, in spite of the pain...

"Kori, what are you saying? Whatever I tell you to do, you have to do?"

I rolled my eyes and drained half the tiny bottle, wincing at the burn. "You knew that. You've known it all along."

"No, I... I hadn't thought about it like that. I hadn't realized..." He closed his eyes and sank onto the couch, his head in both hands. Then his hands fell away and his head snapped up. His gaze met mine and held it. And I realized I believed him.

Ian truly hadn't known. There was no game, except the one Julia was playing.

His forehead wrinkled, and each breath he released sounded angry. "Tower told you to...?"

My stomach tried to revolt, and I held down my dinner with nothing but willpower. If he hadn't known what I'd been ordered to do, then he hadn't thought of me as a whore. Until now.

"He told me to do whatever you want. He said if I wasn't the best you've ever had…" But I couldn't finish that sentence. I couldn't admit the consequences to him. Not with him looking at me like that. Not with disgust dripping from his words, revulsion written in every line on his face.

It was obvious what he thought of me now. I may as well have a red chain link tattooed on my arm.

"That soulless son of a bitch." He stared at the floor, fists opening and closing. Then he looked up at me with something new shining through the surface of his obvious anger. Was that…disappointment?

And suddenly I understood that I wasn't the only one hurt by this. If Ian's jokes, and obvious desire, and genuine conversation weren't part of some game he was playing, then…he'd meant them. He'd meant it all. And somehow that realization cut even deeper than the latest knife Jake had shoved into my back.

"So, this isn't real?" Ian demanded, anger edging out whatever pain I'd glimpsed from him. "Dinner? Telling me about your family? Was any of that true? Did any of that mean anything to you?"

I inhaled deeply. Slowly. I could admit that in spite of my orders and my own common sense, everything I'd said and done with him was real. That I liked him, and that's why I'd tried to paint an accurate picture of life in the syndicate, even as I roped him tighter with Jake's noose. But that wouldn't be fair to either of us. We couldn't be together, ever, even if Jake hadn't ruined anything we could have had by ordering me to sleep with Ian. Julia had been right about that much. Once Ian officially joined the syndicate, he would quickly outrank me. And even if my lower standing didn't put him off, association with me would do him no favors.

So I put on my work face. My stone-cold-bitch face. Because he was hurting just like I was hurting, and this time, the truth would only make that worse.

"This is a job. You are a job. Nothing more." It was the most difficult lie I'd ever had to tell. And it wasn't over. "After you, there will be another job. I don't know what that job will be, since I'm clearly the world's worst recruiter. But whatever that next job is, I'll do it. Just like I'm doing this one. So..." I swallowed and met his gaze, refusing to let mine falter. I could do this. I had no choice. "So just tell me what you want me to do—what it'll take to get you to sign with Jake—and I'll do it."

"I don't believe you." He said it softly, but his words were drenched in anger. I closed my eyes, desperately wishing I'd heard him wrong. Wishing I hadn't seen the pain in his eyes. The denial. "I don't believe you, Kori. The reason you're a horrible recruiter is that you're bad at selling something you don't believe in, and you don't believe in what you're saying right now."

"Yes, I do." I turned and reached for the tiny bottle again, but he was there in an instant, pulling it out of my grip.

"No, you don't. I can tell when you're lying, and you're doing it now."

"Don't pretend you know me," I snapped, reaching for the bottle, but he tucked it behind his back. "We just met. You don't know anything about me."

"The hell I don't. I know you love your sister more than you love yourself. I know you hate Jake Tower, even if you can't ever say that out loud. I know that you cuss

like a fish swims, but you haven't spoken a single profanity in the last seven hours, and as near as I can tell,
the only thing stopping you is the fact that you gave your
word. I know that he makes you do things that rot your
soul, and that you do them because you have to, but that
you'll never really forgive yourself."

I stared at him, stunned, knowing I should argue.
Knowing that for both of our sakes, I should have the
courage to lie and tell him he was wrong. That he didn't
know me and he never would. But words had deserted
me, for maybe the second time in my entire life.

"And I know they did horrible things to you. Things
you never talk about. I know they tried to break you,
but they failed, and that's why Jake talks about you like
you're trash, when we all three know that's not true. I
think he hates you because even though he tried his best,
he couldn't break you. Which means he won't ever really
own you, no matter what he tattoos on your arm or anywhere else."

His face blurred right in front of me, and it took me
several seconds to realize why. To realize there were
tears standing in my eyes and that I couldn't get rid of
them without letting them fall.

"You don't know what you're talking about. He does
own me." And he would, as long as he owned Kenley.

"No one owns you, Kori. People like you can't be
owned. Putting chain links on your arm is like putting a
lion in a cage. He may be locked up, but he'll always be
wild, and he'll eat his handler the first chance he gets.
You're that lion, Kori, and I see you watching. Waiting
for your moment. And it will come."

"No, it won't, because it's not just me in that cage, Ian.
Kenley's there with me, and she can't bite."

He blinked, and something passed over his expression too fast for me to understand. Something complicated and...conflicted. Then he shook that thought off, whatever it was, and captured my gaze again. "So you bite for her, too. You fight for the people you love, no matter what."

I shook my head, and to my horror, those tears fell. "I can't." I hadn't cried in the basement. I'd screamed. I'd even begged. But I'd never cried. Yet here I was in no danger whatsoever, and I couldn't stop the burning in my eyes, the hot trails down my cheeks. "I can't."

"So you're just going to give up? You're just going to do whatever he tells you to do? Let him pass you around to all his friends like a lit joint, until you're all used up and worthless?"

A sharp bolt of anger shot through me and I swiped tears from my face with both hands. "That's not... This is the first time. It's not a regular thing."

"And you really believe it won't be?"

I didn't have an answer for that. I hadn't thought beyond getting through this one job, because there was a significant chance that wouldn't actually happen, and if I was dead, I wouldn't have to worry about the next assignment.

Ian studied my face, looking for something, and when he didn't find it, he set the small bottle on top of the minibar. "So, if I'd asked you to stay the night, you would have done it? Not because you wanted to, but because he told you to?"

I sucked in a breath so deep my chest ached. "I wouldn't have had any choice."

"And last night, after the party? After knowing me

less than eight hours? Would you have slept with me then?"

I could only nod miserably.

"And if I was a real asshole who hurt you and called you names? Would you be allowed to stop me?"

"Stop it. You already know the answer."

"Yeah, I know it. I'm waiting for you to hear yourself say something awful enough to make you want to fight back."

"I do want to fight!" I shouted, fury buzzing beneath my skin like an army of wasps. "But it doesn't matter. That's the real problem here, Ian. After everything I've shown you and everything you've figured out on your own, you still think fighting back is an option. You still think that if I close my eyes and wish hard enough, I'll suddenly be able to break an oath sealed by one of the strongest—quite possibly *the* strongest—Binder in the world. But if there was a way out of this, you can bet your fancy rental car that I'd have found it myself. But there isn't. Kenley and I are stuck exactly where we are, doing exactly what we're doing, for the next four years."

Assuming I lived that long.

I exhaled and met his gaze again, digging deep for the anger that fueled my heart like gasoline in an engine, because I'd rather be mad than wallow in the pain my next words would bring. "Now unless you're actually planning to make me do what Jake told me to do, I'd like to leave. But as much as I hate to say it, I can't go without your permission."

He watched me, and emotions flickered over his face too fast for me to identify. But in the end, there was anger. Raw, pure anger of the highest quality. Rage. Ian wasn't just angry, he was enraged.

I knew exactly how that felt.

"Go home, Kori," he said through clenched teeth. "I think you should go home. Now."

I nodded in acknowledgment, because I couldn't bring myself to thank him for doing the only decent thing. Then I stepped into the hall and pulled the door shut behind me, and too late I realized I should have gone through the shadows in his bathroom. But I wasn't going back into that hotel room. I couldn't. Not after that.

For several seconds, I couldn't move. I could only lean against the wall outside his suite, sucking air in through my throat over and over, only to lose it an instant later. He hated me. Worse, he pitied me. I'd seen it in his eyes. He was disgusted by what Jake had turned me into, and even more disgusted that I'd let it happen.

And the worst part was that I couldn't argue with a damn thing he'd said. And if he told anyone—if Jake found out what I'd told him—Ian's recruitment would be reassigned and I would wind up in the basement again.

I couldn't survive it again. I *couldn't*.

You should have just let it happen. I should have just kept my mouth shut and stayed the night, and he'd never have known I was under orders. So what if he thought it meant more than it ever could? So what if letting Jake dictate what I did with my body made me sick to my stomach? So what if just thinking about that brought memories of the basement roaring to the front of my mind, so vivid and horrifying I could smell the sweat and taste my own blood?

I raced for the elevator, but my stomach lurched after less than a minute of staring at my own reflection in its mirrored wall, so I punched buttons until the elevator stopped, then ran down the last four flights of stairs. I burst into the alley behind the building, but I couldn't make it to the Dumpster. My dinner came back up in the middle of the alley, all over Kenley's sandals. I vomited until there was nothing left, trying to purge the memories along with the food, but they wouldn't go. I felt every blow. Relived every humiliation. I saw Jake closing the door on that very first night, leaving me alone with his brother, half-naked and still oozing blood from a gunshot wound.

When the retching finally stopped, I sank onto the concrete with my knees pressed against my chest, curled around the ache deep inside me. But finally I could breathe again. Finally the pain was gone, and in its place was a blessed numbness.

My stomach was as empty as the rest of me. That was the only way I knew how to be.

I closed my eyes and I heard Jake's words again, echoing from my memory. He'd pronounced my sentence in three words with one hand on the doorknob, a cruel smile on his face.

"Don't fight back."

That's how my hell had begun. And it had yet to end.

Fourteen

Ian

For almost a minute after she left, I stared at the door, willing her to come back, though I had no idea what I'd say if she actually did. How could she let him use her like that? How could she let him just *give* her to a man she barely knew? What fucking century were we living in?

And the worst part was that she'd thought I'd known. She'd thought I was party to forced prostitution and rape. That I was playing some kind of sadistic game with her, just waiting for the perfect moment to—

I couldn't think the words, but I couldn't purge them from my mind, either. I was caught between thinking it and not thinking it, an endless cycle of self-torture that built inside me until rage finally burst out of me like shrapnel from an explosion.

My hand closed around something I didn't even see and I hurled it without looking. Ceramic crashed into the door and rained shards of broken table lamp on the floor. The crystal shade shattered, reflecting tiny rainbows all over the room, but the cheerful colors only further infuriated me. So I stomped the shards into the floor until I couldn't see a single color.

Then I sank onto the couch with my head in my hands, trying to draw the chaos in my head into some semblance of order.

The mission was screwed. *Steven* was screwed. Kori would never trust me enough now to let me anywhere near her sister, and the more I learned about her and her reasons for serving Tower in the first place, the less likely it seemed that she ever would have anyway.

And just as suddenly as that thought occurred to me, I realized I didn't care. I couldn't let my brother die, but I couldn't hurt Kori to save him. She'd been through enough, and even if the grief from losing Kenley didn't destroy her, being left to bear the brunt of Tower's rage certainly would.

With sudden insight, I understood what I should have known all along. If I killed Tower's Binder and toppled his empire, he'd kill Kori for letting it happen. And I wasn't naive enough to think her death would be either quick or painless.

I dug my phone from my pocket and my fingers pressed buttons automatically. Aaron worked the night shift, but he answered on the third ring. "Is it done?"

"I can't do it, Aaron." I let my head fall against the back of the couch, one hand over my eyes to cut the glare from the light overhead. "I can't kill her."

"Fuck." For a moment, there was only silence, except for the distant sound of heavy machinery running in the background. Then Aaron groaned. "I'm coming over."

Several seconds later he walked out of the darkened bathroom in stained jeans and a T-shirt stamped with his company logo. He took a glance around, then headed straight for the open minibar, where Kori's half-empty bottle still sat. "So what's with all the drama?" He sniffed her minibottle, then drained it. "Go ahead and air your girly feelings so I can laugh at them, then kick your ass back into the game."

"This isn't a game. I can't do it."

"Which part?" He grabbed another tiny bottle, then dropped into an armchair and stared at me over the coffee table. "The part where you get wined and dined and put up in a fancy hotel room while Steven and Meghan are slowly dying in a great deal of pain? Or the part where you get to spend all week with a beautiful woman at your beck and call, while I work my ass off in a factory to keep all three of us fed and clothed while they can't work? Because in case you can't tell from the ripe scent of man-sweat I'm rubbing into your chair, in the real world, this doesn't qualify as a hardship." He spread both arms to indicate the luxury Tower had thrown at me.

"Tower is psychotic. He's fucked her up beyond what I can explain, and I can't kill her sister after everything she's already been through."

"So we're talking about the sister, not the target?" he said, and I nodded. "What's she been through?"

"She won't tell me. But it's bad. They talk about her like she's a piece of trash he just hasn't gotten around to throwing out yet. And he's using her like human currency."

"Meaning...?"

"He told her to sleep with me."

Aaron shrugged and cracked open the minibottle. "I'm still waiting for the psychotic part."

"Aaron, he fucking gave her to me, like she's some

thing he can use however he wants. Like she's part of the signing bonus. How would you like to see your sister treated like that?"

Aaron leaned forward in his chair and tossed the bottle cap onto the coffee table, where it slid across the surface and clattered to the floor. "*My sister* is in no danger of being treated like a slave or a whore because she wasn't stupid enough to sign away her free will in exchange for paycheck and a tattoo."

"Kori only joined to protect her sister, and she signed on as security. She never agreed to be used like this."

Aaron drained his minibottle and stretched to set it on the end table. "She had to know it was a possibility, and *you* knew what this would be like. You know he has whores as well as assassins and you know damn well that one's just as dangerous as the other. But you *swore* to my sister that you would save them both. Now you're backing out because you're too sensitive to call a whore a whore?"

"She's not a whore." Frustrated, I scrubbed my face with both hands, wishing I had something to shoot, or hit, or stab, so I could pretend I was killing Jake Tower with all the enthusiasm that task deserved. "You should have seen her. She couldn't even leave without my permission, and I think telling me that actually made her sick."

"Did you fuck her?"

"Hell no! I didn't touch her."

"Then you'll come out smelling like roses. You're the honorable man who didn't take the bait. So pull up your big-boy pants and apologize for the misunderstanding. Explain that you didn't realize this was supposed to be a full-service tour and you would never have made her do anything she didn't want to do. The facts will back you up on that, since you didn't touch her." Aaron shrugged. "*Voilà*. You're right back on schedule."

"On schedule to kill her sister."

"Well…yeah. That *is* what you came here to do."

"When exactly did you forget that Kori's a victim in this?" I demanded.

He rolled his eyes. "Around the time I started asking questions about her." Aaron sighed and stared at his hands for a moment, then made eye contact. "After I dropped you off this afternoon, I called a few of my local contacts and asked them what they knew about Korinne Daniels, other than the fact that she's evidently back from the dead."

"And…?" I said, certain I already knew at least part of what he had to say.

"The word from a couple of former syndicate members—guys willing to talk so long as their names never come up—is that she impressed Tower from the start. Not his most powerful Traveler, but she's a hell of a fighter and she's got nerves of steel. Word has it she disabled half of his household security team in a matter of minutes, just to get Tower's attention. That got her assigned to his personal security detail pretty quickly. One of the guys says he took a special interest in her. Nothing dirty, from what I can tell—"

"He doesn't screw around on his wife," I supplied.

Aaron nodded. "But he got a kick out of seeing her take down men twice her size. He treated her like a niece, and while she was in good standing, her sister was untouchable—a personal favor from Tower."

"Meaning?"

"Meaning hands-off. Completely. No one hit her, no

one screwed her. No one so much as breathed too close to Kenley Daniels, like she was made of glass. It was like that for years. But then something went wrong."

"She fell," I whispered, hearing Kori say the words in my head. Aaron frowned at me in question, but I just waved him on. "What happened?"

"None of my sources were still active in the syndicate recently enough to tell me that, so I had to go digging on the other side of the river." Aaron grinned. "You're welcome."

"Thanks. Now spill."

"I found a loose tongue—one of Cavazos's men—who claimed that a couple of months ago, Ruben Cavazos led a small team right into the heart of Tower's territory. They broke into his fucking house, in the middle of the night. I haven't been able to verify that with any secondary source—makes sense that Tower would have covered up an embarrassment that big—but the timing lines up."

"You think Kori had something to do with the break-in?"

Aaron shrugged. "She was still working security at the time, and within days of when Cavazos's man says this happened, she disappeared. I mean, gone. No one saw her. No one heard from her. I got ahold of her sister's cell record—I'd tell you how, but then I'd have to kill you—and it looks like she was panicking. She called their brother several times a week, and she also called this chick who works for Cavazos, of all people. So I looked her up. Turns out this other chick—Olivia Warren—went to high school with your girl Kori."

Olivia... Could this be the Olivia that Kenley bound Kori to when they were kids?

"Which gives Kori a connection to Tower's biggest enemy," I said, thinking aloud.

"Right. So what I'm thinking is that—intentional or not—Kori had something to do with Cavazos and his team getting into Tower's house. And if I'm right about that, it's a miracle she's still alive."

But I could still see her face when I closed my eyes. "I don't think she's feeling very miraculous."

Aaron shrugged. "Well, I'm sure she'd feel better if she was free from Tower. And she will be, if you do what you came here to do." Because killing Kenley would break Kori's binding to Tower. "We'll call that the bright side."

"You're an asshole."

"Yeah, but I'm also a fucking genius with a Wi-Fi connection and a keyboard."

I stood, pacing to burn off angry energy. "She's messed up. I mean, she's *really* messed up, and I think the only reason she's still alive is because her sister needs her. If I kill Kenley, what does Kori have to live for?" I stopped pacing to look at him. "I can't do that to her."

"So you're just going to let Steven and Meghan die?" he demanded. But I could see what he wasn't saying— that he couldn't let that happen. If I didn't kill Kenley, he would try. Which would get him killed. Then I'd have all three of their deaths on my head.

"Hell no, I'm not going to let them die. But there has to be another way."

"A way other than killing Kenley?" Aaron frowned. "If she's half as powerful as word on the street says she is, there's no other way, short of getting her to break her own bindings."

"Can she do that?" I frowned at him. Why hadn't anyone mentioned that possibility before?

"Is she physically capable?" Aaron shrugged, looking up at me from his chair. "In theory, yes. Is she allowed?" He shook his head firmly. "No way in hell. The first thing Tower would have prohibited her from doing is breaking her own bindings. That clause may only include the bindings she sealed for him specifically, but that depends on whether or not she insisted on tightening the language from the broad, basic phrasing." Which, according to Kori, she had not.

"Okay, so she's probably not allowed. What if she tried anyway? People breach sealed contracts all the time, right?"

"Yeah. There'd be resistance pain, but how strong that is depends on how strong the seal on her contract is, and whether or not she swore on her life not to breach it. If she just swore and signed, she'll be in pain—probably a lot of pain—but it'll eventually end. But if she swore on her life, then breaches the contract, she'll die."

Great. That was no better than shooting her myself.

"But, Ian, the consequences aren't the problem here. The real hurdle is convincing her to break her own seal. Seals are held intact by will of the Binder. You can't just hold a gun to her head and tell her to withdraw her will from the binding. She has to *want* to break the seal. And if you can't get within shooting distance of her, what makes you think you can get close enough to explain what you want and convince her to want it, too? Steven doesn't have forever, you know. Meghan can't hold out much longer."

I exhaled slowly, my brain racing. This should have been a no-brainer. My brother and his girlfriend—my

best friend's sister, whom I'd known her whole life—
or a woman I'd known less than thirty-two hours. I
couldn't let Steven die, but every time I thought about
killing to protect him, I saw Kori in my head. Pale hair,
petite build and pixieish features alternately reflecting fierce determination and haunted pain. I wanted to
touch her. I wanted to make her smile. I wanted to protect her.

I wanted her not to die a prolonged, agonized death,
screaming my name in fury, hating me until her last
breath.

I sank onto the couch again and met his gaze over the
coffee table. "One more day," I said. "Can Meghan hold
on for one more day?"

Aaron looked at me like I'd lost my mind. "What is it
about this girl? You've only known her for a day."

"You'd understand if you met her. She needs my help."

He leaned back in his chair, shaking his head slowly.
"She doesn't need you. She doesn't even *want* you—you
said that yourself. And even if she did, she's not worth
it. She's a killer!"

"If she's killed, Tower made her do it."

His frown deepened. "And you think being bound to
follow orders absolves her of any guilt?"

I exhaled slowly, trying to swallow a sudden surge of
guilt and anger when what I really wanted to do was un-
leash it on him. "*I've* killed under orders, Aaron."

"You were a soldier."

"That doesn't make it right. I'm no more innocent
than she is, so if you think hating Kori will make it
easier for you to kill her sister to save yours, you may
as well hate me, too. She had nothing to do with what

happened to Steven." But we both knew I had, even if inadvertently.

"You've lost perspective," Aaron said, and he sounded sad.

He was right. Being near Kori was like standing on an iron plate holding a compass. I couldn't tell which way was north. I couldn't tell what was right. I only knew that I couldn't kill her sister, and just knowing one plan was impossible made the other look more doable. "One more day, Aaron."

He frowned. "Ian, I'm not going to let my sister die."

"I know. Just ask her for one more day."

Aaron hesitated. He stared at me. And finally he sighed. "I'll ask her. But if you haven't broken the binding by this time tomorrow, I'll do it myself."

"It won't come to that," I insisted. But I couldn't tell if he believed me.

Hell, I couldn't tell if I believed myself.

Fifteen

Kori

I shadow-walked into my bedroom and didn't even have to stretch to reach the light switch, possibly the only advantage to living in very cramped quarters. I had Kenley's ruined sandals off before I even reached the door and I pulled her blouse over my head as I left the room.

The bathroom was two steps to the right of my room, but the door was closed and a line of light glowed beneath it, so I tossed the shirt through my sister's open bedroom doorway and ducked into my room for a T-shirt, then stomped through the living room as I pulled it over my head. In the kitchen, I opened the cabinet over the microwave and stared at a half-empty bottle of cheap vodka.

Another drink wouldn't fix anything. But it couldn't hurt, either, and I'd thrown up everything I drank at Ian's.

I was trying to decide whether to bother with a glass or gulp straight from the bottle when the bathroom door creaked open and Vanessa stepped into the living room, wearing her own robe this time.

She'd brought a robe.

"It's getting crowded around here." I set the bottle down and reached for a clean glass from the dish drainer.

"Sorry." Vanessa shrugged and sat on the arm of the couch. "I didn't think one extra toothbrush would make that much difference."

I pulled an ice tray from the freezer and dropped it on the counter to break up the cubes. Kenley always over-filled it, so they never came out easily. "I don't know if you've heard," I said, dropping the first cube into my glass, "but Kenley is off-limits. Untouchable." At least until Tower decided whether or not to kill me.

"I did hear that." She crossed the room and sank onto a bar stool across the counter from me, as if I didn't scare her. But that couldn't be right.

"Being a girl doesn't exempt you from that." I dropped in another cube, then poured an inch of vodka into the glass. Then I poured another inch.

"No, it doesn't. What exempts me is the fact that she wants me here."

I stared into Van's eyes, trying to see the truth, to believe that what I wanted for my sister was even possible in the syndicate. Trying to believe in human connection that wasn't based on a lie or born in pain. Could a new relationship possibly take root in Jake's world without being choked by the bitter weeds he'd planted?

What if Vanessa was one of those weeds? I knew nothing about her, and Kenley couldn't know much more. What if he'd sent her to get close to Kenley and earn her trust—maybe even her affection—so that after he'd killed me, he'd still have someone to threaten in order to control her.

"What are your intentions with my sister?" I said, twisting my glass on the counter when I couldn't read anything definite in her eyes. I thought she'd laugh. I wouldn't have taken that question seriously in her position. But her eye contact remained steady and she answered without so much as a smile.

"I intend to love her for as long as she'll let me. Then a little longer than that."

I blinked. Then I frowned. "You love her? You don't even know her."

"Love is supposed to *last* forever, Kori. Not take forever. But if it makes you feel any better, Kenley and I had been together almost a month before Jake locked you up."

I pushed aside the dark flash of memory her reminder dredged up—it hadn't been far from the surface anyway—and focused on the middle part of her statement. Three months. They'd been together for three months, and I hadn't known?

"Why didn't she tell me?"

Vanessa shrugged. "You'll have to ask her that. But here's why *I* didn't tell anyone. You know how when you're a kid and you get a shiny new toy, you don't want to share it for a while? You just want to keep it to yourself? It's like that."

I frowned. "Are you calling my sister your toy?"

"I'm calling our relationship shiny and new. And I'd really appreciate it if you could resist the urge to smudge it up for a while."

"Why would I smudge up your shiny new relationship with my sister?"

"Because you're worried about her. Or jealous. Or maybe both."

I wanted to tell Van she was full of shit, but that didn't feel true. I *was* worried about Kenley. Constantly. And as much as I loved her and as willing as I was to do anything to protect her, I'd never been more jealous of anyone in my life.

I hated myself for even thinking that, but it was true. I was jealous of the cocoon I'd wrapped around Kenley. Jealous of the decisions she'd never had to make. I was jealous of the fact that she could be with whomever she wanted, without wondering whether what she felt was real or was manufactured by a powerful man pushing her around a life-size chessboard like a pawn to be sacrificed at will.

I was jealous of how well Kenley slept at night, free from nightmares about a darkness she couldn't master and a sentence she couldn't escape.

Desperate to reclaim the numbness, I picked up my glass.

"That won't help," Vanessa said, before I could take the first sip. "In fact, drinking can make the flashbacks harder to fight. Anything that impairs your concentration will."

"You don't know what you're talking about," I snapped, then drained the glass, leaving only ice to clink in the bottom.

"Yes, I do." She exhaled slowly. "You're not the only one, Kori."

"Get out." I couldn't talk about it. I couldn't even think about it without feeling sick and wanting to break something. Some*one*. It was easier to drink until I didn't have to think about anything.

Vanessa didn't get out. She didn't even get off the bar stool. "You need to talk to someone, and you obviously don't want to talk to your sister."

"How do you know that?"

"Because you haven't told her." Van ducked to catch my gaze. "But that doesn't mean she doesn't know."

"Go away, Vanessa. This isn't social hour and I don't need your fu—" I'm not sure why I swallowed the word. I didn't give a damn about that stupid bet, and I'd consider us all lucky if Ian hadn't already called Jake and told him what I'd said. What I'd done. "I don't want to play group therapy."

"I understand. Just let me say one more thing, and I'll let it go."

"If you say it wasn't my fault, I'm going to punch you in the face." And I meant it. I wasn't in denial and I had no patience for stupid therapeutic clichés. Or for therapy at all, for that matter.

"That's true, but it's not what I was going to say." She leaned on the counter with both elbows and looked right into my eyes. "I was going to say that it will get better. Eventually, there will be days when you won't think about it. Days you won't see his face when you close your eyes."

"I don't see his face when I close my eyes," I insisted, pouring another inch of vodka over the melting ice cubes. My flashbacks were all pain and the stench of his sweat. His breath. The fact that I hadn't been able to see well enough to focus on his face was the only mercy. "But I do see him when they're open. I see him every day, and every day I want to kill him. And one day I will."

"Do you think that will fix it?" Van asked, and it took

me a second to realize she was honestly curious. "Will killing him make you feel better?"

"I don't know. And I doubt it matters. If I get the chance to kill him, it'll be the last thing I ever do." Because Jake would have me killed for killing his brother. "But at least he'll get to hell before I do."

After Vanessa went back to bed—Kenley slept through our entire conversation—I lay awake in my room, trying to assess the damage I'd done to both my life and my sister's. Based on the fact that no one had burst into the apartment to haul us out, I had to assume that Ian hadn't reported the night's events yet. But there was no guarantee that he wouldn't, and I had to be prepared for that very real possibility.

I needed a plan. Even worse than that, I needed a way out, if not for me, at least for Kenley.

The next morning, after a scant four hours of sleep, I waited until I heard Kenley get in the shower—I could tell it was her by the off-key singing—then I hurried into the kitchen, where Vanessa was starting a pot of coffee.

"How much do you love my sister?" I asked, sliding onto a bar stool in front of her.

She eyed me from across the counter. "As tempted as I am to demonstrate how incredibly none-of-your-business that is..." She set the bag of coffee grounds between us and met my gaze head-on. "I love her enough to be terrified that her feelings aren't as strong."

"And what if that's true? Do you love her enough to protect her even if she doesn't love you as much as you love her? Do you love her enough to fight for her?"

Vanessa tied her robe at her waist and planted both hands flat on the counter between us. "Kori, my dad sold me into the skin trade as a teenager," she said, and for a second, I couldn't think beyond the horror that thought brought with it. "Your sister is one of only two good things to happen to me since I was fifteen. The other was Cam Caballero. I lost my best friend when he left, and Kenley is the only thing I have left. I would do anything for her."

I smiled in relief. "That's exactly what I wanted to hear."

"Should I be worried?" she asked, pouring grounds into the filter.

"Terrified. We all should be." I took a deep breath, then launched into a quick summary of the trouble my sister and I were in. "If I can't get Ian Holt to sign with Jake in the next couple of days, I'm under orders to… make sure he can't sign with anyone else. And if that happens, Jake will have me executed." Though I doubt I'd be lucky enough to score a simple bullet to the brain. "But not before he puts Kenley in the basement. He's going to make her pay for my failure."

Vanessa dropped the bag and coffee grounds spilled out onto the counter. "I assume you have a plan?"

"Not much of one. I need you to stay with her today and text me if there's so much as a knock on the door. Text me if you guys go anywhere and let me know who he sends as security." Because Kenley wasn't allowed out alone. "And if her guard gets a text or phone call, let me know."

"Why?" Vanessa scooped most of the spilled grounds into her cupped palm, then dropped them into the trash. "Why today?"

"Because last night I messed up, and if Holt tells anyone, we're all screwed."

"Okay, so why don't we just run? Or hide, if we're not allowed to run," she said, and I had to remind myself that Vanessa was unSkilled, and even though she worked for and was bound to Jake, she wasn't as familiar with my world as she should have been. As she'd need to be, to help protect Kenley.

"Because if Jake tries to get in touch with Kenley and can't find her, he'll know something's wrong and he'll send them after us. Why set off an alarm when we may not have to? Holt obviously hasn't told anyone yet."

"Do you think he will?"

"I don't know. And it may be worse if he doesn't." After what I'd told him, I couldn't imagine Ian being willing to sign with Jake, no matter what he hoped to gain in the negotiations. And him refusing to sign would be much worse than just tattling on me. "But either way, if someone comes for Kenley, I need you to take her and run. Don't look back and don't stop for anything. Don't use public transportation or credit cards. And destroy your phones. Steal whatever you need, and get out of town, then call me from a pay phone. If I don't answer, call my brother. Kenley knows his number."

"What if he doesn't answer?"

If Kris didn't answer, that would mean Jake had already gotten to him, too. He wasn't syndicate, so he'd be harder for Jake to find than I would be, but Jake *would* find him, and he'd use Kris to get to Kenley.

He'd use anything and anyone to get to Kenley.

"If Kris doesn't answer, keep running and don't look back."

Vanessa nodded solemnly. She looked scared but determined, and I felt a little better knowing that I'd made the right call in enlisting her help. Other than me and Kris, no one would work harder to protect Kenley.

The shower stopped running in the bathroom, and I leaned closer to Van over the counter. "Don't tell her about this unless you have to run," I whispered. "She'll put herself in Jake's path if she thinks it'll help me."

Vanessa nodded again, and this time she wasn't just watching me, she was studying me. "I never had a sister..." she said, and I wondered how her life would have been different if she'd had someone to look out for growing up. Or someone to look out for her.

The bathroom door opened and Van blinked, then slid the filter into place above the coffeepot.

"Hey," Kenley said, and I turned to find my sister standing in the doorway wrapped in a towel, her hair dripping on the floor. "You staying for breakfast? I'm thinking omelets."

"Can't. I gotta grab a shower, then head out." I brushed past her into the hall, then stopped and tugged her into my tiny bedroom with me. "Why didn't you tell me about Vanessa?"

Kenley frowned. "That I'm gay, or that she's my girl-friend?"

"That you've been together for three months. How could you get so serious with someone without even telling your sister you're dating?"

"We're not really dating, exactly." She flushed and glanced at the ground, where her toes had curled into the carpet, a nervous habit she'd had since she was a kid. "And I didn't know if it would go anywhere at first. Then you disappeared, and I *couldn't* tell you."

"I've been out for two weeks, and you never mentioned it."

"Yeah, I don't have an excuse for that part." Kenley shrugged, holding her towel closed at the seam. "And I really don't know how serious this is. It still feels new."

I exhaled slowly, trying to decide how much I had a right to tell her. "She really likes you, Kenni," I finally said. "And she hasn't had it easy, so don't hurt her. If you're not serious, you owe it to her to tell her."

My sister eyed me skeptically. "This coming from a woman who loses interest in a fling before the sweat's even dry."

"We're not talking about me, we're talking about you," I said, but she wasn't listening. She was too busy trying to catch a glimpse of Vanessa around my door frame.

"Did she say that? She said she likes me?"

"Just trust me. And trust her, if something goes wrong."

"What does that mean?" Kenley frowned up at me.

"Nothing. I gotta get going." I stepped around her and into the bathroom before she could argue. Twenty minutes later, clean and dressed, I stepped through the shadows in my room and into the darkness in Ian's bathroom, my hair still damp from the shower.

Heart pounding, I stood there for nearly a minute, listening for voices, or snoring, or footsteps. Anything to tell me where Ian was and whether or not he was alone. But I heard nothing.

My pulse roaring in my ears, I pushed the door open and stepped into the suite. The bedroom and living room were empty. Had he left? Just completely bailed on Jake's offer? If so, I was dead.

I wiped my suddenly sweaty palms on my jeans, then walked silently down the hall and back into to the bedroom, intending to see if the sheets were still warm, and on the way, I glanced into the bathroom. I'd left the door open and the room was still empty, but his toothbrush lay on the counter.

When I got to the bed, I threw back the comforter—and nearly shrieked in surprise.

Ian was there, sound asleep, so motionless he could have been comatose. If not for the soft rise and fall of his chest, I might have thought he was dead.

Ian groaned and reached down for the covers in his sleep, and I backed silently away from the bed. When he couldn't find the covers, his eyes opened and he sat up slowly, one hand rubbing his forehead. He winced, then his eyes opened. He blinked. Then he turned and looked right at me.

I froze, but he managed a smile. "Hey," he said and flinched, like speaking hurt. Which made sense, considering the half-empty full-size bottle of whiskey on the nightstand. "You'll have to give me a minute here. Gravity's a real bitch this morning."

Sixteen

Ian

"You're hungover," Kori said, but there was no accusation in her voice. She sounded...relieved.

"Little bit, yeah." I ran one hand over my hair, then scrubbed my face, trying to wake up.

"We have to talk." She sank into a chair in the corner and sat with her hands in her lap, alternately staring at the floor and at me.

"I don't think I can manage more than single syllable words without some coffee. And maybe a shower." And definitely a toothbrush.

"I'll make coffee." She stood and looked at the open bathroom door, then headed for the hall.

The shower felt good—dual massage heads—but I did not. I hadn't been that drunk or that hungover in a long time.

Soaked, dizzy and nauseated, I stepped out of the shower and grabbed a towel, and only then realized that my suitcase and all my clothes were in the living room.

With Kori. Fortunately there was a fresh white terry-cloth robe hanging from the back of the bathroom door.

Wrapped in the robe, I followed the scent of coffee into the living room to find Kori leaning against the counter over the minibar. I reached for the suitcase against one wall. "Just let me get—"

"Did you tell him?" she interrupted, setting an empty coffee mug on the counter.

"Did I tell who what?"

"Jake. Did you tell him about last night? About what I told you?"

I set the suitcase down, resisting the urge to close my eyes and slide down the wall to sit on the floor. "Think about how hungover I am now and how drunk I must have been last night and see if you can follow that thread of logic to its natural conclusion."

Kori rolled her eyes, and just watching that made me dizzy. "Quit talking like an asshole and just tell me. Please. Did you report me to Jake?"

I crossed the room slowly, drawn as much by the thread of fear in her voice as by the promise of caffeine. "No. I haven't spoken to anyone in the syndicate since we left the restaurant last night." And frankly, I was a little insulted that she thought I would tattle on her, even though logically, I knew she had no reason to trust me.

Kori took a deep breath, then met my gaze. "What will it take to keep you from reporting me?"

I frowned and gripped the back of the couch for balance. "Are you trying to bribe me?"

"I'm negotiating." She opened the cabinet next to the minibar and pulled out a sugar dish full of packets of artificial sweetener. "And it'd be a lot easier if you'd give me a starting point."

"Why?" I sank into an armchair across from her, acutely aware that I was nude beneath the robe, and tried to catch her gaze again. "Why are you negotiating? Why do you live life like you're constantly volleying for position or looking for an advantage? Life isn't a contract to be negotiated, Kori."

"Mine is, and you're only making that harder."

"Okay, if you don't mind, I'm going to offer an amateur diagnosis." I'd come into the room for underwear and wound up playing shrink instead. "But please keep in mind that I'm extremely hungover at the moment. Either the room is spinning around me, or I'm actually tilting in this chair."

"You're tilting." Kori tore open a sugar packet and a million tiny crystals spilled onto the counter. "What is it you think you're diagnosing?"

"Your life. Your problems. Because frankly, I think those are one and the same."

"Well, you got that much right." She poured coffee into a second mug and dumped a packet of powdered creamer into it. "What's your diagnosis?"

I took a deep breath and closed my eyes until the room stopped spinning. Then I met her gaze. "I think the reason you value the truth so highly, even when it hurts, is that you don't experience much of it. Syndicate life seems to be lie after lie, strung together with cruel manipulation and brutal compulsion. So let me be completely honest with you for a moment." Well, as honest as I could be without getting us both killed. "I like you. I like you a lot."

Her eyes widened, and I couldn't tell if she was surprised by what I was saying, or by the fact that I was saying it at all.

She started to reply, but I cut her off. I wasn't done. "Yes, I wanted you to stay for a while last night, but not because I was playing some kind of sadistic game. I wanted you to stay because I like your company."

Kori stuck a stirrer in her coffee. "Now I *know* you're lying." But her grip on the mug was tense, like she didn't want to believe her own words.

"Why? Why is it so hard for you to believe that some-one could want to be with you with no ulterior motive?"

"Because it's never happened." She set the full pot on the coffee table in front of me, along with an empty mug. "Everyone wants something. Even my sister needs me for protection."

"Okay, but I bet she'd do as much for you as you've done for her, if she had the chance. Every now and then, someone may just want to be near you, Kori. Or do you honestly think Kenley would kick you out if you were no use to her?"

"No. But she's my sister. You're…"

"A job. I know." And even hearing it from my own mouth stung a little. "But even if that's all you see in me, that's not all I see in you. I have no intention of report-ing what happened last night to Tower. Nor will I report anything that happens today. I won't tell him anything you don't want me to. I swear on my life."

"You're serious?" She frowned, but I knew her skepti-cism ran much deeper than a cynical expression. "Why?"

"Because believe it or not, I'm not trying to hurt you, and I don't want someone else assigned as my recruiter. So nothing that was said here will leave this room." Except what I'd already told Aaron. "Think of this suite as our own personal Las Vegas. What happens here…"

"Stays here," she finished, and I nodded. Kori sank

onto the couch across from me and glanced at the coffee-pot. "I'm not going to serve you. Unless that'll get you to sign on. Or have I already ruined any chance of that?" She said it casually, but her eyes didn't match her tone. My answer mattered. A lot.

I picked up the coffeepot and filled my mug, glad my stomach was finally starting to settle. "What will happen if I don't?" I asked, but she only stared into her coffee. "The truth, Kori. You owe me that."

And finally she looked up, anger flashing in her bold, aggressive gaze, like she was daring me to disagree with something she hadn't even said yet. "If I can't get you to sign, he'll hurt Kenley to punish me. Then he'll execute me."

A bolt of anger burned through the center of my chest, and my jaw clenched. "Execute?"

She lifted her mug with shaking hands, and I felt like I was burning alive, consumed by my own rage. "Death by conflicting orders."

"That's sick. That's not death, it's torture."

"It's both. It's also an object lesson. Public executions tend to keep the masses in linc."

I wanted to beat Jake Tower into the ground until the earth accepted him back.

"I'll sign," I said. My words were a lie, but my intent was true. I would do whatever it took to protect her from him, but that wouldn't involve signing with Jake Tower. I wanted to free her from him, not enslave myself along-side her.

"Are you sure?" She looked so suddenly hopeful, yet so skeptical. So...guilty. Because she thought she was condemning me to a life like her own.

"Yes," I said, and her obvious relief was like a ray

of sunshine parting dark clouds. "But not today. I want today off. My last day as a free man. And I want you to spend it with me. If you want to." I had to know that she wasn't just following orders.

"Now more than ever. But don't read too much into that." She was actually grinning. "It's a nice suite."

There was something in her eyes when she said it. Something I liked. I wanted to know what scared her and what made her smile. I wanted to know what she'd wanted out of life before she'd joined the syndicate, and if that was what she still wanted.

"Was any of it true, Kori? About your parents, and your grandmother? Or was that just part of the role he made you play?"

"I can't tell you everything," she said, meeting my gaze. "But nothing I said was a lie." She took another sip from her coffee, and the stiffness in her shoulders eased. She looked almost relaxed, and I realized she'd been tense since the moment I'd met her, and probably for years before that.

My lie had set her at ease and given her a borrowed sense of security. But I wanted her to have those both permanently. I wanted her to have a real life, free from compulsion, humiliation and pain. And I only knew of one way to make that happen.

I needed to talk to her sister alone—a chance to convince her to do the right thing, not just for Steven, but for Kori, too. Kenley Daniels was the source of so much trouble, but she might also be the solution.

But Kori couldn't know what we were planning, because she'd have to report me to Tower.

"So, what do you want to do today?" Kori asked, and I struggled to wipe my thoughts from my expression.

She couldn't know what I was thinking about until it was done.

"I don't know," I said, stirring my coffee. "How would you spend your last day as a free woman? What should I absolutely see before I sign?"

"The fork in the river," Kori said without hesitation. "My favorite place in the city. There's a park on the south side, right where the river splits, and you can see all three districts from there. And there's this vendor in the park that serves the best hot dogs in the city. The secret is the potato bread buns."

"Hot dogs?" I laughed.

Kori shrugged. "Jake said no more bars. He didn't say anything about hot dogs in the park."

"Do they have sauerkraut?"

"Of course."

"I'm in. Let me get dressed."

I threw on some clothes, and then Kori and I took a cab to the fork in the river, because she couldn't shadow-walk into a park in broad daylight. I don't know what I was expecting to see, but the carousel surprised me.

"My parents took us here once when I was a kid," she explained, leading me along the waist-high wrought-iron fence containing a crowd of children waiting their turn for a ride. "I was about five, so Kenley would have been three, and Kris was probably almost seven. I rode that black one, with the gold reins."

"Of course you did." The carousel horse she'd pointed out was one of only three not painted in some pastel shade with a white mane. Her horse was more dignified, and probably a little creepy from a child's perspective, its lips pulled back from its teeth like it was in midwhinny.

"I fell off and busted my knee on one of the bolts on

the floor," she said, watching the carousel turn. "My mom swooped in to pick me up while my dad sprayed all the blood with bleach solution." She stopped walking and crossed her arms over her chest. "I wonder if any of it's still there, in the cracks."

"If so, there's no way it's viable," I said, but I'd misunderstood her intent. She wasn't worried. She looked… interested.

"Isn't it weird, how we leave little bits of ourselves everywhere we go? Like, there's part of me in that carousel, and part of it in me. I still have the scar on my knee." She frowned then, and looked away from the carousel. "There's a part of Jake in me, too." She rubbed her left arm, where the tattooed chain links would be beneath her sleeve. "They're sealed with his blood. Not enough to use against him, unfortunately. Just enough to make it feel like you don't belong to yourself anymore."

And that was true. That was the whole problem.

"So, where are those hot dogs?" I asked, eager to change the subject. Smart-ass Kori was fun, and even angry Kori was usually entertaining. Scared Kori made me want to fight. To find a way to accomplish the impossible. But I didn't know what to do with melancholy Kori. She seemed directionless. Lost. Not like Kori at all.

"It's a little bit of a walk, but it's worth it," she said, altering our course toward a winding sidewalk.

"Does Kenley like these dogs, too?" I asked as we walked. "Think she'd like to join us for lunch?" Admittedly, my approach was less than subtle, but I was running out of time and options.

"Kenley's a vegetarian. Which is why I eat out so often."

"Oh. Well, maybe—" I started, but Kori grabbed my

arm and pulled us both to a stop, suspicion thick in the arch of her brows.

"What's with your interest in my sister? She's not into you, and Jake would never…"

"No, it's nothing like that," I insisted, but she didn't look like she believed me. So I told another lie, and I wasn't sure whether I should feel guilty or grateful that I'd had enough practice to carry it off. "I've never been bound to anything, and I feel like I'm diving right into the deep end with this. I just…I want to get to know the person who's going to be sealing the binding. I want to know I can trust her."

"You can't," Kori said, and I frowned. "You can't trust any of us," she continued, and that didn't make me feel any better. "Soon, you won't be able to trust yourself."

"That's comforting."

"Don't get me wrong. You'll like Kenley. Everyone does. But she has to do whatever Jake tells her to, just like the rest of us."

"What was she like before the syndicate?" I asked. If I couldn't talk to her directly, maybe I could at least get a feel for her personality in preparation.

"She was sweet, but gullible. Powerful, but naive."

"You said she got into some trouble?"

"Yeah. Kenley had trouble making friends as a kid, and that got worse in college, until her roommate found out about her Skill. Poor Kenni thought this little bi— um, this little monster was really her friend, so she gave her a little bit of her blood. The roommate said she needed it to get an aggressive ex out of her life. Kenley didn't realize she was being used until this Tracker tracked her down through one of the bindings and scared the shit out of her. Turns out the roommate had been using Kenni's blood for everything from revenge on a volleyball team rival to making sure her boyfriend stayed faithful."

"The boyfriend she was trying to get rid of?"

"That was a lie—she was actually trying to keep him. And he wasn't technically her boyfriend. But she used Kenni's blood to tie him into a particularly nasty Love Knot." A binding preventing him from committing to anyone else.

"Damn. So, how did Tower get involved?"

"The Tracker was working for Jake, looking for a new Binder. He hit the jackpot with Kenley."

I wasn't seeing the park anymore, in spite of the children racing past every now and then on their way from the playground to the riverbank. I could only see half-formed connections—threads that didn't quite meet.

Kenley had bound Steven to something unknown, at some time in the past, but he didn't recognize her name or her picture. But Kenley wasn't the only one who'd used her blood to seal a binding. Was it possible...?

"Wait, how would that even work? It's a Binder's will that actually seals a binding, right? If Kenley didn't know what her blood was being used for, how could her will be there?"

Kori shrugged. "Evidently by giving her roomie permission to use the blood, she was contributing her will to whatever the roommate decided to use it for."

"That's scary as hell," I said, and my voice sounded hollow.

"No sh—" Kori cleared her throat and started over, but I was too distracted to find humor in her near miss. "No kidding. Which is why she's not allowed to hand her blood out anymore."

We walked half a mile or so as we talked, following the sidewalk around the playground, a set of basketball courts and large patches of grass beneath sprawling trees. All around us, kids played and joggers jogged, enjoying their weekend in one of few green patches within the city limits. But I hardly noticed any of it. I was thinking about my brother and his girlfriend, and the invisible ties connecting them to Kori's sister, and me to her by extension. How long had those connections been there? How had Steven only breached this mysterious binding two weeks ago, if it had been in place for the past six years, if my hunch was right.

At the dock, a line had formed as people waited their turn for boat rides, and just past that, Kori led me to a quaint walking bridge spanning one branch of the river. My footsteps echoing on wood was what finally brought me out of my own head.

"Is this still the west side?" I asked as we reached the apex and she stopped to lean over the rail, staring out at the river flowing beneath us.

"Technically, this is nowhere. This is the space above the river, and no one owns the river."

"Like standing with one foot on either side of a state border?" I asked as she leaned so far over I was afraid she'd fall in.

"More like standing on neither side. I like it here. There's no ground beneath us, so it feels like this place doesn't really exist. And if it doesn't exist, then I don't exist when I'm here. And if I don't exist, no one can make me do...anything."

"Do you come here a lot?" I asked when she showed no sign of wanting to move on.

"No. If I did, it wouldn't be special." And she needed

this place to be special—this place, where she didn't exist—and I felt privileged to not-exist there with her.

"So, if that's the west side..." I said, pointing back the way we'd come. "Then that must be the east side. Is the hot dog stand on the east side? Are we allowed to go there?"

"Yes, because that's the south side. Neutral territory. The east side is over *there*." She pointed over the bridge and I saw the actual fork in the river, beyond where we stood, and the east side, on the opposite side of the thicker part of the river, before it branched.

Kori finally turned away from the water and we crossed the rest of the bridge slowly, side by side. "Neutral territory, huh? So it's safe for everyone?"

"No one is safe. No place is safe. The south fork is only neutral because no one's been able to take total control of it yet. Cavazos has a regular presence here, as does Jake. If either of them backed down, the other would claim the fork and have a larger territory. So really, it's land in flux. The heart of the struggle. Not coincidentally, the south fork has the highest crime rates of any area of the city."

"And the best hot dogs?"

She laughed. "And the best hot dogs. The stand is just over there." She pointed, and I followed her gesture to find a wheeled vendor's cart with a faded, striped awning and a line of customers stretching out beyond it.

We were almost to the cart when Kori stopped in the middle of the sidewalk. Her shoulders tensed and her fingers curled and uncurled at her sides. I started to ask what was wrong but before I could speak, a woman said her name.

"Hey, Kori."

I looked up to find a man and a woman on the sidewalk in front of us, carefully spaced to block our path. We could have gone around them, of course, but their positions were more statement than true barrier. A command to stop. As was their identical stance, feet spread wide, as if they were expecting a fight. Jackets unbuttoned, for easy access to whatever weapons they were carrying.

The woman was unfamiliar, but I knew the man from Aaron's research on the Tower syndicate. Cameron Caballero. The only man alive known to have gotten out of his contract with Tower before the term was up. Now he worked for Cavazos—a lateral move at best.

"Olivia," Kori said. "I wondered when you'd show up."

Seventeen

Kori

"I assume you know why we're here," Olivia said.

Cam flexed his fingers at his sides, like he wanted to be holding his gun, and I knew the only thing keeping his hands empty was his respect for me and the six years we'd both spent chained to Tower. Though we'd rarely actually worked together, Cam was the closest thing I'd had to a friend in the syndicate.

Until he'd left.

"You're here because Cavazos's first attempt was laughable." And because I'd dared him to send someone more worthy, hoping he'd choose at least half of the pair now facing us. This was my only opportunity to talk to them without disobeying a direct order from Jake, and I *needed* to talk to them. I needed to understand why Liv had used me and Cam had abandoned me.

Yes, they'd been under orders, but so had I, yet I'd done everything I could to help them. And I'd paid for that in the basement.

"Olivia Warren?" Ian asked, and I actually looked

away from the double threat of my former friends to glance at him in surprise. If Olivia and Cam hadn't also been caught off guard, my mistake might have cost me my life.

Jake would kill me if I lost Ian.

Liv frowned. "How did you...?"

"Your reputation precedes you," Ian said, and I did a quick mental inventory of every conversation we'd had since meeting at the party not quite forty hours earlier. I hadn't told him Olivia's last name. Names are power, and I wouldn't have given him that much power over a friend. Even a friend who'd ambushed me, tied me up, stolen my key, and ruined both my career and my life. "I'm guessing this isn't a friendly visit," Ian said, and Cam actually chuckled over the understatement.

"This is business. But we're free afterward if you want to get a drink."

"I'm sorry, Kori," Liv said. "This isn't how we want it."

"Any chance you could just claim you never found us?" Ian asked. "As a favor to an old friend?" He glanced at me for emphasis.

"That's not how it works." Olivia sighed, a sound heavy with reluctance, and directed her next words to Ian. "Ruben Cavazos extended an invitation, and it went unanswered. Come with us now and meet with him voluntarily. Pretty please."

"And if I decline?"

"If you decline, there will be weapons and threats. Inevitably Kori will say something she doesn't really mean and Cam will get his feelings hurt, and I don't think anyone wants that kind of drama in a public park."

"Is she serious?" Ian asked, and I nodded.

"Is she armed?"

I nodded again, my own fingers itching from lack of a weapon. "Gun on her right hip, blade on her right ankle. Unless something's changed in the last two months."

"A lot has changed," Olivia said. "But not that." She pulled her jacket back to reveal a pistol in a holster on her hip, then raised one brow at me in challenge. "As long as we're playing nice, what's your count? Three blades and a nine mil?"

"We're unarmed," I admitted, because she'd figure it out soon anyway, and Olivia laughed out loud.

"She means it," Cam said, studying my eyes, and I realized he knew me better than Olivia did. I'd gone to school with Liv, but I'd truly grown up in Tower's service, with Cam. "Jake won't use her as security anymore, after what happened."

"No thanks to you," I snapped, my temper wound so tight I was afraid that if I inhaled too deeply, something would pop, and I'd just explode. "I have yet to earn back the right to bear arms." No matter what the second amendment said. But I could use whatever I took from them until this little conflict was over.

"Sorry, Kori." Olivia pulled her gun, aiming at the grass between us, but I held my ground and directed my reply to Ian, who looked just as calm now as he had in the alley the day before.

"She's not going to shoot you, and she can't shoot me," I said softly, glad none of the other park-goers were close enough to see Liv's weapon. But if things escalated, we were in for some very public trouble.

"Because of the childhood binding?" Ian asked, and Olivia glanced at me in surprise.

"Have you been telling stories, Kori?"

"Only the ones that are true." My next words were for Ian, though I couldn't take my attention off Liv's gun. "She can't intentionally hurt me, and if I ask for her help, she has to give it. Which, I'm willing to bet, would put her smack in the middle of two conflicting compulsions. Right, Liv?"

Olivia's eyes narrowed, but both her gun and her voice held steady. "That sword cuts both ways, Kori. Don't make me ask you for help taking Holt to Cavazos," she said, and I groaned, mentally.

"I don't think it'll come to that," Cam said, pulling his own gun smoothly.

"You're not going to shoot me," I insisted, desperately hoping I was right.

Olivia shrugged. "He shot *me*."

"He was under orders."

Cam took aim at my leg. "That hasn't changed. Holt comes with us, or I shoot you. Don't make me shoot you, Kori." He didn't want to spill my blood in a public park—more blood than I could possibly clean up—but he would.

"You owe me. Both of you." I could hear the fury in my voice, and saying that was like popping the top on a shaken can of soda—the rest just came shooting out. "You used me. You got me shot, then you left me there to—" I bit my sentence off before the words could fall out into the daylight and leave me exposed by the truth. "You defected, without a word. Kenley heard it from one of the da—" Another pause, while I rerouted my sentence and I barely noticed Cam's surprise over the aborted expletive. "From one of Jake's secretaries."

I studied him, trying to understand what had happened two months earlier, and latent anger at Cam crashed over me with the weight of every wrong I'd suffered in the basement. Alone. Because when he'd switched sides, he'd left me to bear the brunt of Tower's fury.

Ian glanced from face to face, trying to make sense of a discussion he couldn't possibly understand. "What am I missing?" he said finally, but no one answered.

"I had no choice," Cam insisted, and I could read the guilt on his face. But I couldn't see any regret. "Cavazos was going to let Olivia die unless I signed, and I didn't have a chance to tell you. But I tracked you every day, to make sure you were alive."

"He put me in the basement." I shrugged and spoke through clenched jaws. "Obviously death is a mercy I haven't yet earned."

Cam looked like I'd just punched him. "I'm so sorry, Kor," he said. "Tracking you was the best I could do."

"Well, now you have a chance to make it up to me. Leave. Just tell Cavazos Ian is using a fake name and you couldn't track us."

"His name's real and Ruben already knows we found you." Liv's gaze shifted to Ian. "Ruben knows everything he needs to know about you, which means you're either stupid or naive for sticking with Tower when there's a better offer on the table." Liv frowned and her gaze slipped to me before centering on Ian again. "Or maybe it's not Tower you're sticking with…"

I ignored her inference and focused on the implied threat. "Whatever Cavazos knows, Jake knows, too," I insisted. "And Ian's made up his mind."

"Really? Is that what he told Meghan Hollister?"

Ian froze at my side, and I glanced at him quickly before turning my attention back to Olivia's words and

Cam's gun, trying to pretend I hadn't seen Holt's reaction. "Who's Meghan Hollister?"

When Ian didn't answer—I couldn't even tell if he was still breathing—Olivia took over once again.

"Meghan is Ian's girlfriend. They've been together for twelve years."

I tried not to react, not to let my disappointment and anger show through on my face. Ian groaned, but I could practically feel his posture relax, his arm brushing mine. He seemed relieved. What had he thought she'd say?

"That's not true," he said to me, without taking his gaze off the threat. "She's got her wires crossed. Meghan is my brother's girlfriend."

"Bullshit." Cam bit the last syllable off, leaving a sharp edge to the word. "Your brother died seven years ago. KIA overseas. What kind of a gutless loser pawns off his lies on a dead serviceman?" Cam demanded, and Ian's entire bearing changed, though he didn't move a muscle. He was just suddenly taut. Furious. Wound so tight the slightest vibration might set him off.

"They don't know what they're talking about," Ian said through clenched teeth. "I swear on my own name. Just please believe me, Kori. Trust me."

I didn't know what to believe. I didn't know who to trust. Nothing had made any sense since I got out of the basement.

Cam laughed, and again the sound was bitter. "Shows how well he knows you, huh?" Then he turned back to Ian. "Kori doesn't trust anyone. She just doesn't have it in her."

"I don't anymore," I spat. "The last person I trusted was you," I said, and Cam flinched.

"I'm sorry, Kori," Olivia said.

But I couldn't concentrate on yet another worthless apology, because I was busy trying to figure out something else. "Why are you still with Cavazos, anyway?" I asked Olivia, stalling for time to come up with a new plan, since the "you owe me" attempt had gone south. "I thought your mark died."

"It did." Olivia scowled. "Then this big dumb ass signed on for a fifteen-year term to pay for my medical care."

Cam transferred his gun to his left hand, which wasn't a handicap for him, unfortunately, and lifted his left sleeve. Above the three chain links that had connected him to Tower—now the pale gray of dead marks—were three freshly inked black rings, one and a half of which were already dead and gray, like the chain links beneath them.

"She died, Kori," Cam said. "I killed her, under orders from Tower, and Cavazos had doctors on hand, just standing there with a crash cart. He wouldn't let them touch her until I signed."

"So why are the marks half-dead?"

Olivia twisted to show her own bare arm, where there were two more rings, one half-dead. "Ruben said I could let Cam serve his fifteen years alone, or I could take half of it. Seven and a half years each, served together. A ring and a half for each of us."

"Liv..." I moaned, my anger at Cam momentarily swallowed by my ache for her. "You were free."

"And I will be again. But for now, Ruben's still calling the shots, and if Holt doesn't come with us peacefully, Cam has to put a bullet in your leg."

Cam strengthened his aim with a double-handed grip, and Ian exhaled.

"Fine, I'll go." He held his hands, palms out in the universal posture of surrender. "Just leave her alone."

"Ian…" I said, but he ignored me and stepped slowly toward Cam and Olivia. "Ian, stop." I reached for him, but he stepped around my arm.

"Can we at least keep this civil?" he asked when Cam pulled a plastic cinch lock from his pocket. "Most hosts don't tie up their guests."

Cam didn't even consider it. "Sorry, man. Turn around." He handed the strip of plastic to Olivia, who holstered her gun to accept it.

The moment her gun disappeared beneath her jacket, Ian leaned to the left and kicked her square in the chest. She flew backward, and I lost an instant to surprise, then I lurched into motion.

Cam aimed at me, but Ian stepped between us, and wouldn't move when I tried to shove him out of the way. "He can't shoot me, which means he can't shoot you *through* me," he insisted, and I'll admit it—I was impressed. He was both smart and evidently fearless. No matter what Jake paid for him, he'd be getting a bargain.

Olivia tried to get up, but I planted one foot on her chest, then squatted and snatched her nine millimeter from its holster while Ian danced the combat waltz with Cam, trying to stay between me and his gun. Then I stood and backed away from Olivia to aim at Cam.

My possession of a gun evened the odds. Their unwillingness to shoot Ian tipped the scales in our favor. Barely.

"How about we call it a draw, and retreat to neutral corners?" Ian suggested as we backed slowly away from them, while Olivia stood, fuming. "That way, everyone lives to die another day."

"Sorry, can't do it," Cam said.

"I *will* shoot you," I warned him, aiming at his thigh for emphasis.

Cam's aim rose. "Likewise."

"Okay, there has to be a way around this," Ian said, backing slowly, carefully toward a gathering of trees that would block us from the hot dog stand. No one had noticed us yet, but that wouldn't last. "You don't want to shoot each other."

Cam barked a bitter laugh and raised one brow at me. "Does he believe in Santa, too?"

"Kori, *please,*" Olivia said, and I could hear the stress in her voice. She loved us both and we were going to kill each other, if something didn't change soon. We had no choice.

"Don't say it, Liv," I warned when I realized just how bad this was about to get. If she asked me for help, I'd have to respond in kind, and the conflicting compulsions and resulting pain would complicate things beyond recovery.

"Okay, let's take this over there, out of sight of the general public." Ian tossed his head toward the small grove of trees.

Cam glanced at Olivia without altering his aim, then he nodded. "Run, and I'll shoot her." He was talking to Ian, but still aiming at me.

"No one's running." I backed slowly toward the trees with Ian, and Cam and Olivia followed. As we walked, I talked, my brain racing, desperate for a way out. "What are your orders, exactly? Maybe there's a loophole. A way we can all walk away from this."

"There is—so long as at least three of us are walking east," Cam insisted. "That's the only way we're all going to live through this."

Eighteen

Ian

Some measure of tension inside me eased as my left foot settled into the first patch of shaded grass, where I'd been subtly leading us since that first step off the sidewalk. I could feel the shadow against my skin, cool, like the first foot dipped into a swimming pool. Another step and I could feel it in my bones. Shadows always called to me, but that call was never stronger than when I actually needed the dark.

Unfortunately, the mottled shade cast by the trees was shallow and sparse. But it would have to be enough.

"Okay, then, why don't we all go?" I said, stepping farther into the shade with Kori at my side, still aiming her appropriated gun at Cam's leg. "We'll go see Cavazos together and discuss this like civilized adults. No weapons. No restraints."

"No," Kori said, and I bit my tongue to keep from groaning. I wasn't actually going to *go* with them. I was just trying to back us into deeper shadows to make for an easier escape. Then I realized I could let her argumentative tendencies serve as a distraction from what I was doing.

"Why not?" I glanced at her, careful not to let effort show on my face as I pulled the shadows toward us, letting them gather at our feet. If anyone had been looking at the ground, they would have seen the shade actually roll across the earth toward us from its natural placement, leaving spots of light where none should have fallen through tree branches and leaves.

But they didn't notice. They were watching and listening to Kori because she was armed with a weapon they could actually see.

"If you put one foot on Cavazos's property, you won't step back out unless you bear his mark," Kori said. "And I sure as hell can't take you there myself. Jake would kill me."

But it was her first statement that echoed in my head, momentarily distracting me from the stealthy gathering of shadows. "Cavazos would kill me if I don't sign?" I glanced at Cam and Olivia, trying to glean the truth from their reactions. But they didn't bother lying.

"Without even blinking," Olivia said. "He can't let you sign with someone else."

Cam nodded. "And Tower will do the same."

I glanced at Kori for confirmation, but she wouldn't look at me. Which had to mean that he was right.

I'd known Tower would go to any length to sign me—hell, Kori had warned me from the beginning that if I couldn't be recruited, I'd be hunted—and deep down, I'd probably known all along what would happen if the prey couldn't be caged. But I hadn't given serious thought to preserving my own life, because I was busy trying to save Steven's. And because I'd planned to disappear once I'd done that anyway.

But this revelation presented a new problem. If Tower would kill me to keep anyone else from signing me, he'd do the same to Steven, who would resume using my name once I'd disappeared.

And I wasn't going to disappear without Kori. I would not leave her alone in the syndicate. Not like Cam did.

"Isn't that a little extreme?" I said, faking ignorance to distract from the shadows I was gathering faster now.

Cam's aim never wavered, though his arms had to be getting tired. "It's common sense."

Olivia elaborated. "Mr. Holt, the strength of your Skill is unheard of, and it may never be matched. I don't know how you escaped notice as long as you did, but the display you made of yourself at that hockey game was idiotic, at best. The whole world knows what you can do now, and that's not ever going to go away."

"What does that mean?" The shadows were as thick as I could make them, but I let them simmer at our ankles for another minute, fascinated to hear Olivia saying the same things my mother had warned me and Steven about from the time we were old enough to listen.

"That means that even if you sign with Tower tomorrow, you're not going to be able to just walk away at the end of your commitment," Olivia continued. "He'll use everyone you love—hell, everyone you even *know*—to manipulate or just plain force you to stay. If you don't believe me, ask Kori why her sister's still with Tower."

But I didn't need to. As long as Kenley still had a brother, grandmother, or anyone else she cared about, Tower would have a way to control her.

"It'd be the same with Cavazos," Kori said as I pulled

the building shadows up to our shins. I couldn't go much farther than that without them being noticed. "That's how he got the two of you."

Olivia nodded. "And neither of us are anywhere near as powerful as you are," she added, looking straight at me. "You're going to wind up serving someone. Your only real choice is who that will be."

"Maybe," I said, and the shadows built higher, churning faster as my pulse began to race. I wrapped one arm around Kori's waist, sliding my hand beneath her shirt to make necessary skin contact without compromising her aim. "But last I checked, that was still my choice. Give my best to Cavazos." Then I pulled the shadows up around us like a cocoon, as fast as I could. Faster than I'd ever done it before.

"Hey!" Olivia shouted, as we disappeared behind the shield of darkness I'd built in broad daylight. But there was no gunfire. Cam couldn't risk hitting me.

Kori laughed out loud, a giddy release of tension and a celebration of the darkness that was a part of both of us. Then she tugged me forward. A single step later, everything changed.

We were inside—I could tell from the silence, and the absent scents of grass and trees. Those were replaced almost instantly with other familiar scents.

Dust. Wood. Wine.

I let the darkness around us melt into the ambient shadows, revealing a dimly lit wine cellar. A *huge* wine cellar. This wasn't someone's private collection. This was the real thing.

"Where are we?" I said, and I only realized my hand was still on her stomach when she turned to scold me with one finger pressed against her lips.

"Shh."

I let her go reluctantly, missing her warmth the minute it was gone. "I take it we're not supposed to be here?" I whispered.

"Not without an appointment and a traditional front-door entry. This is a local winery—the closest place I could think of that would be dark during the day. They have a vineyard outside the city, but this was closer and safer to travel into, since I've actually been here with Jake several times. They make his favorite wine."

"Wow." I pulled a bottle from the nearest rack and glanced at the label. I'd never heard of the brand, but that wasn't surprising, since it was local. "Are they any good?"

Kori shrugged. "You're asking the wrong person."

"You just haven't found your favorite yet. Or you're drinking it at the wrong temperature. Either of which can be remedied." I slid the pinot noir back into its slot and went in search of a good starter wine.

"Hold it down," she repeated, following me through the cellar, which was obviously used as more than storage. When I turned the corner around the next floor-to-ceiling rack, I found tables and chairs set up for a wine tasting, though nothing was set out at the moment.

"Can you point me to the whites? Maybe a pinot grigio…" I mumbled, rounding the nearest table toward another set of racks on the other side.

"No, I can't." Kori grabbed my arm with the hand not still gripping Olivia's gun. "Ian, we have to go. I have to tell Jake that Cavazos tried again."

I stopped and met her gaze, unable to quell the nerves churning in my stomach. "Are you under specific orders to report the very event that only *almost* took place? No one was hurt. No guns were fired. There was no public spectacle."

She thought about that for the moment and finally slid the safety switch into place on Olivia's nine millimeter and handed it to me—she couldn't carry it now that the fight was over. "I guess not. But if he finds out from someone else—"

I tucked the gun into my waistband for lack of a holster. "If he finds out, I'll take the blame. I'll tell him I wanted to explore his favorite winery." If we reported a second poaching attempt, Tower might assign extra security, which would render my plan completely useless. And that was the best-case scenario. "If we go make your report now, what are the chances that he'll ask me to sign on the spot?"

Kori shrugged. "Pretty good. But what does that matter, if you're going to sign anyway?" Which I'd told her I'd do. The lies were getting complicated.

"That would be robbing me of my last day of freedom, and I really want this last day, Kori. If I'm going to be stuck either bound to or running from the syndicate for the rest of my life, I'm damn sure going to have one last day of freedom. If you'd known what was coming before you signed, wouldn't you have wanted the same thing?"

"I still want that," she said, and the truth of the statement echoed in her words. And suddenly I had to know.

"Was Olivia right? If I refuse to sign, will Tower kill me?" I could hardly see her eyes in the dim light, but I saw enough to know there was something she hadn't wanted to say in front of Olivia and Cam.

"Yes. And if you were a normal potential recruit, he'd probably put a bullet in your brain. But because you're special and everyone wants you, if I can't recruit you I'm under orders to take you to Heartland Pharmaceuticals."

"You'd turn me into a vegetable?" The choice wasn't hers. I knew that. But it still hurt to hear her talk about my death.

"Not me. Jake. And no, not a vegetable. The whole world knows about you, Ian, and half the city knows Jake's trying to recruit you. If you disappear, people will try to track you, and if you're alive—even as a vegetable—they'll find you. If I can't recruit you, Jake won't be able to use you as a blood cow. So he'll have you completely drained."

Nineteen

Kori

Ian's eyes widened, but he looked more hurt than surprised. He'd known, at least on some level, that there were only two ways out of the mess we were both in: service or death.

And with the latest betrayal to slide off my tongue, most of my secrets were out. "I'm sorry. I should have told you that this morning, but then you said you'd sign, so I didn't see any reason to threaten you with death and the posthumous sale of your blood."

"You'd really do it? You'd turn me over to be drained just because Tower told you to?" The disappointment and betrayal in his gaze stung like little else I'd ever felt.

"I—" The answer was there, ready to go. It didn't require thought. So little did, with Jake pulling my strings. But the words wouldn't come out, and the new thoughts blocking them made me close my mouth. Then my eyes.

What good would it do to turn him over to Jake? Both Kenley and I were screwed anyway, if things went that far south.

"I honestly don't know," I said at last. "Physically, I'd have no choice. Resisting the compulsion would kill me unless Jake rescinded the order. And he won't. But if I turn you over to him, he'll kill me anyway, for failing to recruit you. So…"

And suddenly it all looked so clear.

"No, I wouldn't." Because I was going to die either way, and at least this way, I'd go out without having first killed an innocent man. Ever. And that might just be the only point of honor for me to look back on if my life really flashed before my eyes in those last few seconds.

I'd killed for Jake, of course. I'd had no choice. But he had never—up till now—ordered me to kill someone who wasn't at least as guilty as I was.

Ian's gaze never left mine. He was watching me think, and I wondered if he could read any of those thoughts on my face.

"You know none of that matters, though, right?" I said. "If I don't hand you over to Jake, someone else will."

"None of it matters, because I'm going to sign," he said, and again I wished for just a second that I was a Reader. He looked like he meant it, but he also looked like there was something he wasn't saying.

I thought about demanding the whole truth, right there on the spot, but then, in an unprecedented display of common sense, I held my tongue. Some secrets are kept for a reason and spilling them prematurely can mean spilling blood, as well. His silence was meant to protect someone. Probably himself, but maybe me. So I decided to wait.

Then I hoped I'd made the right decision.

"We should take Tower a bottle," Ian said when he

finally looked away, and some small bit of the tension inside me eased. "What does he like?"

"I don't know. Something dark red."

"You've eaten with him, right? What does he order most often?"

I'd spent years shadowing Jake. Protecting him. I'd seen him order dinner a thousand times.

He liked a thick cut of tenderloin, still cool in the middle. His baked potato came with salt and butter only, his mashed with a hint of garlic. And to drink, he ordered...

"Cabernet Sauvignon. Sometimes Bordeaux."

"Okay." Ian nodded. "Bordeaux is a blend, and I'm not familiar with this label, so the Cab may be a better bet." He started pulling bottles from the racks, reading the labels then sliding them back into place, working his way down one aisle and into the next until finally he read a label and smiled. "This should work." He held the bottle up for me to see, but other than the familiar icon on the label, I had no idea what I was looking at. "And maybe one for us..." He handed me the wine, then turned back to the rack.

I studied the bottle I held, surprised by how thick the glass was, especially at the bottom, where there was a pronounced dip in the base—a mountain of glass rising into the dark liquid. In the movies, I'd seen people whack bad guys with beer bottles, but holding my very first bottle of wine, I was convinced that it would make a much more effective weapon. Assuming I could compensate for the greater weight. Maybe an empty bottle...

I swung experimentally, and in one smooth motion, faster than I would have thought possible, Ian's hand shot out and the bottle *thunked* into his palm in the middle of my swing. "That is *not* a weapon."

"Everything's a weapon, if you know how to use it."

His brows rose. "You're holding a two-hundred-dollar bottle of wine, and all you want to do with it is bash someone's head in? I think that statement clearly illustrates the source of your problems. Everything doesn't have to be a fight, Kori."

"And *that* statement clearly illustrates the source of *your* problems." I enjoyed throwing his own words back at him. "You're chin-deep in the fight, and you don't even know it."

"I know it," he insisted, and suddenly that seemed possible. The rare somber look in his eyes hinted at some dark depth I hadn't truly seen yet. "My point is that some weapons are more suited to a delicate touch than to blunt-force trauma."

"I'm a blunt-force trauma kind of girl, in case you haven't noticed."

"I have. And so has Tower. Part of your problem is that he knows what to expect from you. So let's give him something new." Ian held the bottle up, like he was modeling it for a commercial. "Think of Jake Tower as the fly, and this bottle as the honey."

"Ooh, are we going to poison the honey?"

His brows rose higher. "No."

"Then how is it a weapon?"

"It's a distraction meant to outshine any report of trouble in the park. More a shield than a sword."

"Just as well." I sighed. "Killing Jake isn't an option." And it never would be. In fact, I dreaded the day of his death almost as much as I dreaded every breath he took.

When Jake died, something worse would rise from his ashes to claim his kingdom.

Ian was watching me again, like maybe he'd heard more than I'd actually said. Then he handed me the bottle with a warning frown and turned back to the racks.

"Why do you know so much about wine?" I asked as he read label after label.

"My father was an enthusiast. He tried to make his own several times when I was a kid, but by the time I was old enough to share his passion, he'd admitted defeat and committed to enjoying the fruits of someone else's labor."

"Oh. My dad drank tequila. The kind with the worm in the bottle." In fact, that was my clearest memory of him. "Your dad teach you about fighting, too?" I asked, and Ian chuckled.

"My dad was a pacifist. He marched in antiwar rallies before I was born."

"And your brother was a soldier? I bet Thanksgiving was interesting at your house."

"Yeah." Ian glanced at me, then pulled another bottle from the rack. "Where'd you learn to fight?" he asked, and I got the impression he was trying to change the subject.

"My grandmother said I needed a healthy way to burn energy and express my natural aggression, so she enrolled me in my brother's martial arts class when I was ten. I loved it."

"I'd say it loved you, too," he said, and before I could reply, something creaked from the other side of the cellar—a door swinging open—and light flooded the entire room. I froze, my heart racing. Footsteps clomped down a set of stairs I couldn't see from our position, and my hand clenched around the neck of the bottle, now slick with nervous sweat.

I backed toward the end of the aisle, my boots silent on the floor, and Ian followed, both of us peering through the open racks at what we could see of the rest of the cellar. High stools around high tables. The dark wood bar that had been lined in wineglasses and manned by two servers at every event I'd accompanied Jake on. And the open space in the middle of a cellar full of racks, where guests would mingle, and gossip, and examine the collection surrounding them.

Jake's wine-tasting parties were interminably dull, and I'd sometimes wished someone would try to kill him, just to bring a little excitement into the most boring room I'd ever stood in.

Now I had excitement, and I wanted nothing more than the dark, quiet cellar back.

"As you can see, there's plenty of room for the event, and we can set up more tables," a man said, and I recognized the slightly nasal voice of John Yard, the winery's events coordinator.

"How are you fixed for lighting?" Another man asked as their steps echoed closer. "This is nice for ambience, but my wife will fuss if the light isn't sufficient for people to admire her shoes."

"That's not a problem."

A switch flipped somewhere and another set of lights came on. I flinched, though the cellar was still much dimmer than the park in broad daylight. This was starting to feel too familiar. An underground room. No windows. Someone standing between me and the exit. Darkness that should have been a comfort to me, made terrifying by the light source caging me.

There were huge differences between Jake's prison cell and the wine cellar. But knowing that didn't stop my pulse from racing or my next breaths from sliding in and out of my mouth too fast to satisfy my need for air. Logic couldn't stop my feet from carrying me backward across the concrete, as quietly as I could move, my heart pounding, until my back hit something warm and solid, and I gasped.

A hand closed over my mouth before I could scream and another took the bottle of wine from me before I could drop it.

I clawed at the fingers over my lips and stomped on the foot between my own, and Ian sucked in a breath, so close his chin stubble caught in my hair. "Kori, relax," he whispered, so soft I understood more than heard the words. "Don't move, or they'll see us."

When I nodded, he let go of my mouth and stepped back to give me space, still holding the bottle he'd taken, and I concentrated on breathing slowly. Counting the breaths. This wasn't Jake's basement. Ian wasn't Jonah. I wasn't being punished.

But we both would be, if we got caught. Stealing a bottle of Jake's favorite wine as a gift to him was one thing, but getting caught looting his favorite winery was something else entirely.

I stood as still as I could, waiting for Ian to pull darkness around us again, so I could walk us out of trouble. The cellar was much darker than the park had been, so it shouldn't have been any problem. But no shadows gathered at our feet, cooling me from the toes up. No darkness built. And the voices only came closer.

I turned to glance at Ian and found him much closer than I'd expected. He was trapped between me and the wall, obviously trying to give me as much space as possible. I opened my mouth, but he pressed one finger against his own lips, still holding the bottle in his other hand.

I rolled my eyes and stepped closer until I was pressed against him, going up on my toes to whisper in his ear, acutely aware of how solid his chest felt against mine. "Make it dark, and I'll get us out of here."

"Can't," he whispered in return, so softly that it took me a minute to figure out what he'd said. Then he pointed at something behind me and I turned to find my cell phone lying on the floor across the main aisle from where we stood. It must have fallen out of my pocket, and thanks to the rubberized case, neither of us had heard it land.

We couldn't leave without it. I wasn't allowed to keep syndicate names or numbers programmed into my phone, but I hadn't cleared the call list since last night, and it would only take a cursory glance through the contents to figure out who the phone belonged to, and only a phone call after that to link my name with Jake's.

He was going to kill me.

My pulse raced again, so fast the room started to go dark around me, though the lights hadn't faded. John Yard and his customer came closer, still discussing whatever event they were planning, and I could see them now, through the single floor-to-ceiling rack of wine separating me and Ian from the main open area. Which meant they could see us, too, if they glanced our way. Or if any movement from us drew their attention.

"Shh..." Ian whispered into my ear, and I inhaled slowly, then exhaled slower still. His free hand slid down my right arm and I stiffened and would have pulled away if I weren't afraid to move. But then his hand brushed my palm and his fingers twined around mine, and I clung to his hand, not out of fear, but out of relief. I wasn't alone. I may have been feet from getting caught and minutes from facing Jake's wrath, but for the first time in years, I wasn't alone in either predicament.

Ian wouldn't let me take all the blame or bear the brunt of the punishment, even if Jake and I both tried to give it to me. He wouldn't desert me like Cam had. He'd said he'd sign—he'd promised to commit the next five years of his life to a monster—to keep Jake from killing me.

Ian wouldn't leave me.

I let myself lean against his chest, my heart pounding in some intoxicating combination of fear and indefinable need, and his hand tightened around mine. And for a minute, I couldn't breathe.

I'd never done this. I'd never felt anything as intimate as the feel of his hand in mine. His breath against my ear. His chest warm against my back.

I'd had sex. I'd even had sex multiple times with the same man, and until that moment, I would have considered that intimacy—the fact that I could tolerate one man enough to sleep with him more than once. But I was wrong. With Ian pressed against me, his heart beating in sync with my own, I understood that no connection I'd ever made had been more than physical gratification. Mutual back-scratching. I'd never *lingered* with anyone else. Never touched just to touch. Just to feel.

I'd never truly experienced or been experienced by anyone.

When Yard took his customer into another section of the cellar without noticing my cell phone, I breathed a little easier. They were still close enough that we could hear their voices, but far enough away that they wouldn't notice our movement if we were quiet. So I turned and looked up at Ian in the shadows, and his dark-eyed gaze searched mine. Waiting. Silently asking a question words couldn't have clarified.

I let go of his hand, and he looked disappointed—until I laid it on his chest. His breathing deepened, and his heart raced. I could feel it through his shirt. I slid my hand up slowly, over his sternum, then his collarbone. My fingers rounded the curve of his neck, scratchy with stubble, and I pulled his head down as I went up on my toes. Then I kissed him.

Twenty

Ian

Kori kissed me. I'd half expected her to rip my arm off for touching her hand, but instead she kissed me, and every bit of spark in her—every blaze of temper and passion she smothered just to survive in her world—it all burned bright in that kiss. She'd found an outlet for everything she felt but couldn't show, and I took it all. I swallowed her pain and her anger. I devoured her isolation and frustration. And I reveled in the hunger she was showing me, and in my own need, awakened by hers.

When she finally dropped onto her heels again, her hand trailing down my neck and lingering on my chest, I couldn't look away. I couldn't see anything but Kori, and the confusion and desire warring in her eyes. Flickering across her expression, one side of her face shadowed, the other illuminated by light shining through the racks from the lit section of the cellar.

Then the men's voices grew louder, accompanying their footsteps toward the cellar entrance. They'd have to pass by us again to get there, and if they got a sudden craving for an eight-year-old Cabernet—or even just glanced to their left—we were screwed.

Kori's breathing grew shallow and quick. She turned toward the sound of their steps and her gaze flitted back and forth as she tried to spot them through the racks all around us. I knew what she was thinking. What were the chances that they'd miss us twice? How could they not spot her phone?

I pulled her close, careful not to grab her arm and trigger automatic resistance, and with her pressed against my chest, her cheek on my shoulder, I wrapped the shadows around us. Not true darkness—an anomaly like that would be noticed in a semilit room—but just a thickening of the existing shadows, decreasing the chances that a casual glance our way would reveal us.

We both wore dark clothes, which blended easily into the shadows, leaving her face and hair the only pale spots in my darkness. So as the voices came closer, the footsteps echoing from mere feet away now, I wrapped my arms around her and turned us both carefully, putting my body—my own dark head and clothing—between her and the rest of the cellar.

She tensed, but didn't object, and I knew she wasn't used to being sheltered. Kori was the type to throw herself in front of a bullet to protect someone else, but I wanted her to know it didn't always have to be like that. That she didn't have to fight the world alone. That I wanted to fight with her. If she would let me.

The host and his customer passed our aisle, and I turned my head to watch their progress across the open area. And as I rotated us again, I couldn't resist touching her hair, where it trailed down her back. It was so impossibly soft, as if her hard edges couldn't quite tame that one feature, or disguise its beauty with function.

When the lights went out and the cellar door finally closed, we both exhaled in relief. But I held her a second longer, with no good excuse. And when I let her go, she stayed pressed against me for one more second, and my heart beat harder. I wanted to freeze that moment in time and live there for eternity. Alone in the dark with Kori. No immediate threats. No fear strong enough to push her away from me. No lies standing between us.

However, like all good things, that moment expired and real life descended again, bringing with it bitter obligations we couldn't ignore. But things were different now. Real life had been changed forever by that moment, at least for me, because Kori had let me in. She'd trusted me, and I didn't have to be told how rarely anyone saw past her shields to the woman beneath.

But with her trust came an obligation to prove myself worthy. If I let her down—if I betrayed her trust just once—I would lose her forever.

When I couldn't figure out how best to acknowledge what had passed between us without scaring her off, she finally gave me a tiny smile, then brushed past me to grab her phone from across the aisle. "You know, it's a minor miracle that we're not being drawn and quartered by Jake at this very moment," she whispered, shoving her phone into her pocket.

"That's a rather antiquated form of punishment," I said, handing her the bottle I'd picked out for Tower. "Please tell me you don't mean it literally."

"I've never actually seen anyone ripped limb from limb, no, but Jake's certainly pulled people apart figuratively, and that's bad enough."

"No argument from me…" I pulled another bottle of Cabernet from the rack to my right, then headed deeper into the cellar in search of something lighter and fruitier.

"Ian, we're not shopping, we're escaping. Let's go."

"One minute…"

"Thirty seconds," she conceded, following me past the blushes and into the whites. "Then I'm leaving you here." But she wouldn't, and we both knew it.

I pulled a bottle of pinot grigio from the nearest rack, crossing my fingers, since I was unfamiliar with the label, then I let her pull me into the shadows. A moment later, we emerged in the unlit bathroom of the hotel suite.

Kori followed me into the living room, where I set all three bottles on the occasional table against one wall. "I believe you still owe me lunch," I said, pulling open the minifridge. At which point I realized I was too hungry for snack food. "But I'm guessing going back to the park would be a bad idea."

"I think leaving the west side at all would be bad, with Cam and Liv after you. But if your stomach's set on nitrates, there's a decent street vendor a couple of blocks over."

"Or, we could order in." I held up the room service menu. "There's a vegetarian section, if you think your sister might like to join us."

Kori frowned. "Okay, I get that you want to get to know the person who's about to bind you to Jake Tower. But if I invite Kenley over, her bodyguard of the day will come, too, and I really don't want to spend the next hour with someone who'll report everything we do or say directly to Jake."

"Okay. No problem. What do you want from room service?"

"A burger. A big one."

Kori ducked into the bathroom and I placed an order, then texted Aaron for an update on Steven and Meghan. I'd just hit Send when I heard the bathroom door open, and when the message went through, I deleted it from my phone, just in case. I wanted to tell Kori the truth. I *would* tell her. But I couldn't, while the chain links on her arm were still live marks. And to fix that, I needed to talk to Kenley. Alone.

When Kori walked into the living room, she wasn't looking at me. She was looking at her phone. Staring at it. "What's wrong?" I asked.

Instead of answering, she dropped onto the couch across from me and handed me her phone.

On the screen was a picture of a framed photograph on an end table. It was a photograph of Meghan. And me.

"Okay, that's not what it looks like," I said, but she waved off my explanation.

"Don't bother. You don't owe me an explanation, and you never swore not to lie. But now I need the truth."

"About Meghan?"

She shook her head and gestured back and forth between us. "About this. About us. I'm not a Reader—though Jake does have Readers. I can't tell you who they are, so just…don't lie to him—but I know you were telling the truth last night. You didn't know I was under orders to do whatever you want. But today, you've been lying."

"It's not what you think," I insisted, setting her phone on the coffee table.

"Look, I don't care who you were screwing before two days ago. I don't care how long the two of you have been together, or how cute and sweet she looks, or what kind of jam she spreads on your fucking toast before she sends you off to analyze systems every morning," Kori said, and I had to glance at my watch to verify that it had indeed been more than twenty-four hours since she'd agreed not to cuss for a day. "What I want to know is whether or not what happened in the wine cellar means anything to you. If not, fine. No hard feelings." But now *she* was lying. I could see it in the line of her brow and hear it in the tone of her voice. "But if that meant something...I need to know."

"Yes, it meant something," I said, and she studied my expression so intently I felt exposed, like she was seeing more than I meant to be saying. "It meant a lot. And that's not me." I pointed to the image on her phone, and Kori rolled her eyes. "Seriously. That's my brother." I took a deep breath, then let it out slowly, preparing to say the part we never voluntarily told strangers. "My twin."

"You had a twin?" she asked, and I nodded, but I couldn't tell whether or not she believed me. "Seriously? Because now you sound like the subject of a made-for-television movie."

"I can't help what it sounds like. Twins are actually a pretty common natural phenomenon."

Kori laughed. "No wonder your ego's the size of Texas. You think you're a born phenomenon." She glanced at the picture again. "Identical?"

"Fraternal. But we always looked a lot alike."

"Okay..." She wanted to believe me. I could see it. "But your brother's been dead almost seven years, and Liv says this picture was taken an hour ago."

"Olivia sent you that?" It was from Meghan's apartment. It had to be. Thank goodness she and Steven were staying at her parents' house.

Kori nodded. "That, and an offer from Cavazos. He'll 'make every reasonable effort' to buy my contract from Jake if I take you to him."

For a second, I couldn't breathe. "Is that what you want?"

"Hell no. I'm not leaving Kenley. And Jake wouldn't sell my contract anyway—not if I take you across the river. Cavazos is getting desperate." She picked her phone up again and stared at the picture. Then she looked up at me, and this time she was studying me for a different reason. "He looks just like you. Like you look *now*. But this has to be at least seven years old. Right?"

I shrugged. "I've aged well," I said, and when she smiled, I exhaled in relief. "Kori, the wine cellar meant a lot to me. I understand if you don't believe me, but…I wish you could. I want more of you."

She stiffened, and I wanted to take the words back.

"I didn't mean that as any kind of order. I'm not asking for anything," I said. "But I am offering…whatever you want."

"Ian, I don't know where this is going." She looked like there was more she wanted to say, and there was definitely more I wanted to hear. "I don't know if it *can* go anywhere. So if that's really you in the picture, you should just—"

"That's not me. And this can go wherever you want it to go. Your marks won't always stand between us." I let her think that was because I'd soon have a mark of my own, but I'd never been more determined to find a way to rid her of hers, and her next words only underlined that fact.

"No matter what happens, Jake will be in the way," she said. "That's how he likes it—his hand in every pie, so that even couples who've been together for years know that's only because he lets them stay together."

Chills were building at the base of my spine, spreading icy fingers out from there. "How the hell does he justify dictating the terms of his employees' private lives?"

Kori shrugged. "Why would he bother justifying it?" she said, and my chills became a river of ice flowing up my back and down my legs. "If a match doesn't benefit him in some way, he'll dissolve it."

"If you want to be with me—even on a trial basis— I'm not going to let Jake Tower stand in the way of that." Since I was painting fantasies with a palette of lies, I might as well paint something nice for her. For us. "That'll be the first contractual demand I make—Tower and his people have to keep their fingers out of my personal life."

Kori met my gaze, her eyes swimming in guilt. "I never wanted this assignment. Not even for a single second. But I've never wanted it less than I do right now. I don't want to be the thing that ties you to Jake. I don't want to be the reason you sign away your free will. And I *really* don't want to be the person who makes you look like the sun just set and it'll never rise again."

My chest ached. "This isn't your fault, Kori." But I couldn't truly absolve her of her guilt without admitting my own, and I couldn't do that while she was still bound to Tower. "Besides, the dark is my natural habitat, remember? Who cares if the sun never rises again? We'll thrive in the dark together."

"No one thrives in the syndicate. No one worth knowing, anyway." Her eyes flashed with anger, and my pulse raced in response. I wanted to touch her. I wanted to kiss her again, and find out if anger made her as passionate as fear did. I wanted to snatch her away from the world and keep her for myself, so no one could ever put out the fire she breathed with every thought that sparked in her brain and every word that left her mouth. "He'll change you. He'll make you do things. Hurt people."

And finally I understood. "You're not responsible for what Tower makes you do. *He* is."

"You don't know—"

"Yes, I do," I insisted softly, wishing the coffee table wasn't between us. "I know he's used you as a weapon, but even when you're the gun, he's still the one pulling the trigger. The blood is on his hands."

"I've done horrible things, Ian. You may have heard, but you don't really know. You can't really understand. And I can't forget." Her voice cracked, but no tears came, and again I was floored by how incredibly strong she was. How determined to hold everything together, when her world was clearly falling apart beneath her feet.

I loved that she was so strong. But I hated that she had to be.

"What if we left?" I said. "What if we just go get Kenley and you take us as far as you can go? And farther still, from there? We could do it." I'd lived off the grid for the past seven years. "I could keep us safe."

She shook her head slowly, and that blaze of anger in her eyes evened into wistful frustration. "Even if defaulting on our contracts wouldn't kill me and Kenley—and it would—he'd find us. He knows our real names. Part of them, anyway. And if he couldn't find us, he'd go after my brother. My grandmother. Kenley's girlfriend."

My brow rose a little at that unexpected bit of information, but she was still talking, constructing verbal obstacles to every exit strategy I could possibly have come up with.

"Whoever you have, Jake'll find them, too. And they don't have to be bound to him to suffer at his hands. Or his surrogate hands."

I thought about Steven, and Meghan, and Aaron. I thought about everyone I wouldn't want to see hurt, any more than they already had been. But above all of them—above everyone I'd ever shared a cup of coffee or a kind word with—it all came down to one thing.

"You," I whispered, staring down at her. I hadn't realized how empty my life was, so far from everyone I'd ever loved—until I met her. "I care about you, Kori."

She blinked up at me, her eyes sad, and more scared than I'd ever seen them. "Then that's how he'll get you."

Twenty-One

Kori

Ian was up to something. I could tell from the way he kept glancing at me out of the corner of his eye as he stacked dirty plates beneath a silver room service tray cover.

"Don't tell me," I said from the couch. I was trying desperately to hang on to the rare, vague sense of contentment I got from watching him clean up, like we were some normal couple staying in a hotel on vacation. Like our lives weren't both at serious risk. But that look in his eyes was making me nervous.

"Don't tell you what?"

"Whatever you're planning. If you tell me, I'll have to tell Jake. So don't tell me. And stop plotting."

"Even if I'm plotting to whisk you away to some isolated homestead in the middle of the Australian outback, where we can forever live in peace and privacy, far from the meddling hands of both egomaniacal mob bosses and the IRS?"

He said it like it might actually be possible.

"*Especially* if that's the plan."

Ian rounded the couch toward me. I should have backed away, but I couldn't do it. I let him sit and wrap his arms around me and I cursed myself silently when my hands slid over his stomach and around his back, feeling hard planes and solid ridges. I couldn't help that, either. I wanted to touch him. I wanted to be touched by him.

And that thought terrified me.

He kissed me, and I kissed him back, and for that minute, with his arms around me, the taste of him on my lips, I forgot all the reasons this was a very bad idea.

I forgot that I was dooming him to serve a human monster. I forgot that my life and my sister's well-being depended on his compliance. I forgot about everything except how good he felt, and how much I liked the version of myself I saw reflected in his eyes.

Then he pulled away with a satisfied moan, his eyes still closed, and reality came crashing down around me again, the pain sharper, the aching hopelessness deeper than ever after the brief distraction.

"You know we can't do this," I whispered, clutching his shirt in both fists, my forehead resting on his collarbone. I wanted to hold him, but I needed to push him away, because the longer this went on, the harder it would be for both of us, when Jake ripped him from my grasp.

Jake might actually agree not to mess with Ian's personal life, but he could still do whatever he wanted with me. How would Ian react if Jake sent me to recruit someone else, under the same circumstances? Jake would do that—and worse—just to prove he could. To punish me. And maybe to punish Ian for trying to protect me.

"We can't do what?" Ian's hands slid up my back, touch demanding nothing. Offering everything. I'd never met anyone like him. I could step back, and he would give me space, but he'd still be there, ready to accept more whenever I was ready to give it.

"This. We can't do this. It won't last. It can't."

"I don't like how easily you toss that word around." He frowned, his green-eyed gaze narrowed on me. "Why is everything 'can't' with you?"

"I speak from experience."

"Not this time, you don't. If this had ever happened before, it couldn't be happening now. That's what they mean by 'once in a lifetime.'"

"I don't know what you're talking about." But that was only half-true. I might not have followed whatever convoluted logic his words mapped out, but I knew what he meant. I could feel it, too.

"I'm talking about you. Us. You can't possibly know how this is going to end, because this doesn't fit into the boxes you shove all your other issues into. This is bigger than that. This is bigger than you, and bigger than me, and it's sure as hell bigger than Jake Tower." He ducked, drawing my gaze back up with his, and the look in his eyes was so intense my pulse started *whooshing* in my ears almost loud enough to drown out his words. "Kori, I—"

"Don't." I stood and backed across the room in mounting panic, trying to hold myself together by pushing everything else out. "Don't tell me how you feel, and whatever you do, don't tell Jake. But don't lie about it, either, because he has Readers, and he'll know the moment you tell an outright lie. And he'll know you're hiding something even if you only *think* about lying. It's a trap. The whole thing is one great big trap and we're flies flapping our wings, trying to pull free from the sticky paper. But the harder we flap, the tighter we're caught."

Ian frowned and came closer, but I backed away again. "You're starting to sound paranoid, Kori."

"I *am* paranoid." The bitter laughter that bubbled up my throat actually burned. "But that doesn't mean he isn't out to get me."

"Okay, calm down."

I shook my head and backed around the glass coffee table, but he followed me slowly. Persistently. "You don't understand. You don't know what happened. I can't come back from what I did, and even if I could, I don't think I want to."

"I know what happened." Ian reached for me, but I backed away again. I couldn't help it. I wanted to let him hold me, and that's how I knew I should keep distance between us instead.

Wanting things is dangerous—it gives people power over you.

Wanting things you can't have is even worse.

But giving in to desire just because you want something is weakness. Inexcusable weakness of character and will. I didn't get many opportunities to exercise my own will, and I wasn't going to let any of it slip between my fingers just because his arms felt strong. Just because it felt good to let someone else stand guard for once. I wasn't that weak.

I couldn't be.

"How do you know?" I didn't want to believe him. If he knew what I'd done, he might also know how I'd paid for my crimes. And I desperately didn't want him to know that.

"People talk and I listen even when they're not talking to me."

That was the truth, and part of me was glad he respected me enough to give it to me without the sugarcoating. But the rest of me... The rest of me was...

I don't know what I was.

Something crawled beneath my skin, fighting to get out, and I wanted to scratch, but that would bring no relief. My throat ached from holding back words I couldn't say. My eyes burned from holding back tears I couldn't let fall. And in my head, one word played over and over, and I couldn't make it stop.

Nonononono...

"Kori..."

"No! Stay there." I backed toward the short hall, instinctively pulled toward the dark bedroom. Toward escape.

"Okay. I'll stay here." Ian stopped in the middle of the living room, reaching for me with his palms out. Unarmed. Unsure. "But you stay, too. Don't go, Kori. Please."

"I got him shot." The room blurred beneath my tears. "I was supposed to protect him with my own life, and I let Jake get shot instead. His kids could have been killed. He hates me now, and even though I'm out of the basement, I'm still being punished, and that's never going to stop. I'm poison, Ian." I looked right into his eyes, trying to make him understand how serious my predicament really was, because the words alone weren't enough. I wasn't overreacting. I wasn't unreasonably paranoid. My fear was justified, for us both. "I'm the most dangerous thing that could ever have happened to you."

"No. It wasn't your fault."

"Doesn't matter." I shook my head, and I couldn't stop. I couldn't make my hands stop shaking, and my breaths were coming too fast again. "If you try to stay with me after you sign, you'll piss him off, and you'll go down with me."

"You're not going down, and neither am I. No one can hold a grudge forever, and you were one of his favorites, right?" Ian asked, and I nodded, trying to see whatever possibility he was seeing for my future. I needed that light at the end of the tunnel. "When you bring me into the fold, all will be forgiven, and you'll get your place back. You'll get your job back. It'll be just like it was before."

I couldn't tell whether he meant that or was just trying to calm me down. I could feel panic building beneath me, a spiral of dread and alarm waiting for me to take that final step over the edge. And once I lost control, I wasn't sure I could ever regain it.

But that didn't really matter. None of it mattered anymore, because of the truth I hadn't been able to voice before. The truth I shouldn't have voiced, even then.

"I don't want it back, Ian. I *hate* him, and I'm scared that if he gives me my job back, the next time I have a chance to protect him, I just…won't. I'll just let the bullet fly right past me, or I'll pull him through the shadows a second too slow."

Pain exploded in my head, in reaction to thoughts I had no contractual right to speak, but I kept going because the pain in my head could never hurt worse than my memories. Than the gnawing deep in my gut as the nightmares and flashbacks ate at me slowly, devouring the me I'd been to make way for this new me—a whimpering coward I didn't want to face in the mirror.

"It'll hurt, but it's a terminal breach, so if I can ride out the initial pain, I'll survive, and that's too much temptation for me to resist. I want to kill him, but I can't. Letting him die is the best I can do."

"So let him die." Ian reached for me again, and again I backed away, and the walls of the narrow hallway closed in on me.

"I can't." I shook my head, trying to clear it. Trying to slow my breaths like Kenley had shown me. "I mean I *can,* but if Jake dies, everything'll be worse. So much worse. There are clauses in place. If he dies, every contract and piece of property not already in his wife's name automatically transfers to his heir, and we'll be so much worse off then."

"Who's the heir?" Ian asked, and I almost missed the note of quiet danger his voice held. He'd stopped advancing, so I'd stopped retreating, but I couldn't let him come any closer. This wasn't the kind of problem a little cuddling and some vodka could fix. "Do you know who it is?"

"I know, but I can't tell you. No one can. We're all sworn to silence."

"So, killing Jake Tower wouldn't free you?"

I shook my head slowly, watching him through narrowed eyes. I could see what he was thinking. Hell, he'd practically said it. "That wouldn't free me or anyone else. You can't kill Jake. And I can't let him die. And we can never, ever have this conversation again."

Ian

Kori sat in the hallway for almost an hour, one bare foot stretched into the unlit bedroom, like just the touch of darkness soothed her.

I wanted to touch her—to hold her—so badly my arms ached from emptiness. But I was afraid to get any closer for fear that she'd bolt into the bedroom and out of the shadows before I could even call her name.

I didn't know how to fix what was wrong with her, and it killed me to see her sitting in the corner—both literally and figuratively—when an hour before, she'd been ready to spit nails at anyone who crossed her path. I didn't know what had triggered this meltdown, and at first I thought it was me. I thought kissing her—or maybe touching her—had triggered some memory she couldn't conquer. And maybe that was part of it.

But when I replayed everything she'd said, I realized there was more than that. She wasn't afraid of me. She was afraid *for* me. Afraid that being with her would put me in danger. And because that wasn't a logical fear, she couldn't be reasoned out of it. So I didn't even try. Instead, I sat at the other end of the short hall, leaning with my back against the wall, my legs stretched out in front of me. And I talked to her.

"There are things I wish I could tell you," I said, and she glanced up, a cautious arch of curiosity in her eyebrows.

"There are things I wish I could hear. But it's probably better if we don't even start down that road."

I nodded reluctantly, and for several more minutes, we sat in silence. Then I tried again. "Do you remember much about your parents?" I didn't think she'd answer, so when she started to speak, it took every bit of self-control I possessed to keep from cheering over my minor success.

"Mostly my mom. My dad was gone a lot."

"Was your mom a Traveler like you?"

She exhaled in a small huff, like there was some humor in my question. "She was a Traveler, but not like me. She only walked the shadows in emergencies, and I only know that because my grandmother told me. My parents were totally paranoid about exposing us as Skilled. I didn't even know I could travel until after they died. One day I got in trouble for using the ground beef my grandmother thawed out for dinner as viscera for my brother's army men when I blew them up."

"You blew them up?" I wasn't sure whether to laugh or cringe.

Kori shrugged. "With Black Cats. They're more noise than anything, and Kris didn't care. My grandmother was pissed, though. She grounded me, and I stomped into my room, thinking about how I'd rather be with my mom and dad, and the next thing I knew, I was in the cemetery, three feet from their graves. Twelve miles from home."

"Wow."

"Yeah. But the real bitch was that I didn't know how I'd gotten there, so I didn't know how to get back. And that was way before I had a cell phone. I had to walk a mile and a half to a pay phone and call my grandmother collect. I thought she'd be pissed, but she looked kind of relieved. I guess because she didn't have to keep the secret anymore. And maybe because I didn't get my dad's Skill instead."

"What was his Skill?"

"He was a Silencer. I think she was afraid I'd suck all the sound out of a room when I got mad and nothing pissed my grandmother off worse than not being heard."

I laughed, and she relaxed a little more.

"What about your parents?" Kori asked. Then she frowned and seemed to reconsider. "Not their Skills.

Don't tell me anything Jake could use. Just…what were they like?"

I closed my eyes and leaned my head against the wall, remembering. "They were good parents. More in love with me and my brother than with each other, but they held it together. My dad died when I was in college, and my mom followed him five years ago."

"I'm sorry." Kori pulled her foot out of the bedroom and folded it beneath her, and I took that as a good sign. Like she was literally stepping out of the darkness. To be with me.

"I want to tell you something," I said, trying to hold her gaze in the shadows. Kori had trusted me with everything she had, and I owed her something in return. Something real and personal. Something that meant as much to me as the things she'd told me about herself.

"Maybe you shouldn't."

"You're probably right. But I'm going to say it anyway, and it would mean a lot to me if you'd listen."

"Okay." She turned to face me, giving me her full attention, though she still sat inches from the bedroom and the dark escape it represented.

"My brother's still alive."

"Steven?" Kori whispered, and I frowned. Then I realized his first and last names were public record, and of *course* Tower had done his research. "But he was killed in action. I saw the obituary. There was a funeral."

"It was a memorial," I said, trying not to outright lie to her, even as I let her believe her own misassumptions. Because this one truth was all I could give her at the moment, and I shouldn't even have done that. "Because there was no body. Because he didn't really die."

"He faked his death?" she said, and I was grateful that

she didn't really expect an answer to that. "Why would he do that?"

"To avoid this," I said, spreading my arms to indicate not the suite around us, but interest from the organization that had paid for it. "We knew from the time our Skills manifested that they'd attract the wrong kind of attention from the wrong kind of people. Our mom was paranoid, but she was right about that."

"So he thought it'd be easier to fake his own death than to avoid notice from the syndicates?"

I scooted closer, praying she wouldn't back away from me. "Faking death *was* to avoid notice from the syndicates."

"So, that picture of him with Meghan? That's not really seven years old?"

"Probably not," I admitted, and it felt good to voice even that little bit of truth.

"What's his skill?"

"I can't tell you that. I shouldn't have even told you he's alive—that wasn't really mine to tell—but you've told me so much…"

"You don't owe me anything, Ian. And I won't tell Jake about your brother. Even if he asks." I started to object, but she spoke over me. "If he wants me to suffer, I'll suffer. The question I refuse to answer is irrelevant."

I stared at her, awed by her strength and determination. She'd done time in a hell I could only imagine, and come out intact. "I feel sorry for all the people who will die without ever meeting you, Kori. But the selfish part of me is happy, because I don't even want to share you with the people you already know. Most of them don't deserve you."

Tears shone in her eyes, and my heart cracked within

my chest. "You okay?" I asked, aching to move close enough to touch her. "I didn't mean to make it worse."

"You didn't. I just... I need you to understand that whatever this is between us, it can't last once you're bound. I think we need to keep that in mind." The words came out slowly, like she wanted to pull them back in before they'd even fallen.

"Why can't it last?" I scooted closer across the floor, and she didn't back up. "Jake can't take this away, Kori," I said, scooting another foot closer to her, wishing I could explain that I wasn't going to be bound to Tower, and soon neither would she. He would have no power over us.

"He'll try. He'll renege on the apartment, and the car, and he'll take back any privileges he offers, unless you get them down in writing. I wouldn't blame you for bailing."

"I don't care about any of that. And I'm not bailing."

"He'll throw women at you. Beautiful women. Women who wear nice dresses, and drink champagne, and don't cuss."

"I don't want those women. I want you."

Kori shook her head slowly. "You don't even know me."

"I know enough to know I want to know more. I know I want to *kill* everyone who had anything to do with whatever happened in that fucking basement."

She sucked in a deep breath, and the next few came quicker, like she couldn't get enough air. "I don't need a knight, Ian. I can fight for myself."

I nodded. "And everyone else around you. I know. That doesn't mean I don't want to help."

Kori glanced at the floor and spoke while she picked

at the hem of her jeans. "I don't…I don't know how to do this. I've never really done the relationship thing, unless you count a few three- or four-night-stands."

"The only thing you learn from any relationship is how to be in that specific relationship. So even if you'd been married a dozen times, this would still be new. It's new for me, too. It's supposed to be."

She looked up then and met my gaze. "I'm kind of a wreck right now, and I can't promise that'll get any better."

"We're all messed up, Kori. We all have secrets. We all have problems. Part of the process is figuring those things out. One at a time."

"What if I scare you off?"

I scooted closer, and we were only two feet apart now. "You couldn't possibly. I know what I want." I leaned forward and hooked one hand behind each of her calves, where her legs were bent at the knee. When she didn't object, I pulled her closer, until our knees were touching. "I want you. I want *only* you. I want *all* of you. But I'll take whatever you're ready to give."

Twenty-Two

Kori

Ian kissed me, and I kissed him back. I couldn't get enough of him and how good he felt. How eager, but safe.

Kissing was fine. Kissing was *good*. There was no kissing in the basement, and kissing Ian made me feel like I was fifteen all over again, and just discovering the art. Innocence and adventure. Power, because he wanted to kiss me, but I could pull away and he'd *still* want me, but he'd let me go.

Kissing Ian was like starting all over. Clean slate. No memories. No past. Just…us.

When I finally pulled back, desperate for both air and perspective, I couldn't hold back a groan. "You're playing dirty," I moaned, letting my forehead fall against his shoulder.

He laughed, his face pressed into my neck, and his words seemed to melt right into my skin. "Not yet. But I'm open to that."

"I mean you and your words. You always know exactly what to say." That he wanted me. That he'd take what I was willing to give. "Does that silver tongue work on most women?"

Ian leaned back so I could see his eyes. Or maybe so he could see mine. "I'm not feeding you lines, Kori. If I were I'd have told you how hot you are and how badly I want you. Both of which are true. But neither of which are how I want to start this."

This.

This is a mistake. Alarm bells were going off in my head. I knew better than this. This was going to get us both hurt, and not just emotionally. But for the first time in my life, the risk felt worth it.

"So, how *do* you want to start this?" I couldn't believe the words, even as they came from my own mouth.

"I want you, and not as a signing bonus. I want to *be* with you. I want to fall asleep touching you, and I want to see you first thing in the morning. I want you to answer the phone and smile when you hear my voice. I want to be the only one you ever look at like you're looking at me now. That's what I want. What do *you* want?"

"I want...I want to try it. No promises and no hard feelings if either of us changes our mind," I said, and though he nodded immediately, I couldn't help wondering if he would have agreed to anything right then, just to make me happy.

Then I realized it didn't matter. If he was that determined to make me happy, who was I to complain?

I kissed him again. Then I kissed him some more. And somehow, we made it from the floor to the leather couch, where he let my hands explore hard planes of muscle through the soft cotton of his shirt. My mouth trailed over the rough stubble on his chin and down his neck.

Ian groaned, and his hand glided over my hip. He felt so good. Sooo good. But then his fingers slid beneath the hem of my top, and—

"Wait…" I sat up, pushing him away, and after less than a second, the confusion in his eyes gave way to caution and understanding too raw for me to look at. I didn't want his sympathy. I didn't need to be coddled like a baby or seduced like a virgin.

I needed…time. Just a little more time.

"I'm hungry. Let's get some food."

"You okay? Is this too much?" That look—pity—lingered on the edge of his understanding smile, and I couldn't stand it.

"Don't look at me like that," I snapped, and I could hear the anger in my voice, but I couldn't control it. "I'm not fucking broken. I'm just hungry."

But that was a lie. I *was* broken, and there was no bandage in the world big enough to fix me.

"I'm sorry. I was just trying not to—"

"It's fine," I said, purging the anger from my voice with a staggering effort. "I really am hungry. I was going to take you to this awesome steak house in the south fork, but after what happened in the park this morning, we probably shouldn't leave the west side. There's a place a couple of miles away that's not too bad…?"

"Let's bring the food back. I don't feel like sharing you with a restaurant full of people."

I called in our order and gave the restaurant Jake's credit card number, and since our food wouldn't be ready for twenty minutes, we decided to walk. It was a beautiful night, cool for early summer, and the cloud cover had lifted, so if we'd been anywhere but the middle of the city, we could have seen the stars. Not that I knew what any of them were. But suddenly I missed the suburban sky view I'd grown up with, because as I walked next to Ian on the sidewalk, I realized I hated the city.

But that wasn't quite right. It wasn't the city itself I hated. It was how much of Jake Tower I found represented on the west side, everywhere I looked. His sentries stood on most corners of the main drag. He owned several apartment buildings and businesses. And everywhere I turned I found another arm bared to show tattooed chain links.

They all knew me, even the ones I couldn't have named for my life, because for years, I'd been at Jake's side, responsible for his safety and elevated by the job. And they all knew those days were over.

I could feel them staring. A few looked sympathetic—no one wanted to be on Jake's shit list—and that was almost worse than those who gloated, pleased by my fall.

Ian could tell I was tense, and he tried to distract me with small talk, but I couldn't relax, and being with him made that even harder. I wanted to touch him, but I was hyperaware that anything we were seen doing would be reported to Jake, who would either understand that we'd excised him from our relationship—which would piss him off—or misinterpret the reports as me seducing Ian on his behalf. Which would piss *me* off.

Finally the restaurant appeared in front of us. Inside, we had to wait for several minutes before the hostess handed me a receipt to sign, then exchanged it for a thick paper bag with twisted twine handles and an embossed logo. I resisted the urge to stick my head inside the bag and inhale the scent of beef grilled with onions.

Ian looked like he wanted to do the same thing.

Outside again, we headed for the alley behind the restaurant, intending to return to the apartment through the shadows so the food wouldn't get cold. But the minute I stepped into the alley I knew something was wrong.

I stopped, one hand clenching the bag handle, the other groping at my waist for a gun I wasn't yet allowed to carry. I reached for Ian's arm to warn him silently, but before I could, someone grabbed me from behind and hauled me away from him, nearly jerking me off my feet.

I grunted in surprise, and Ian spun toward us, but before he could reach for me, someone stepped between us, gun—plus silencer—pointed at the ground, but ready to take aim at either of us in an instant.

Cam.

I dropped the food bag and started to twist away from the hands holding me, but before I could, my right arm was released and something cold and sharp was pressed against my throat, just beneath my jaw.

Shit. Another alley and another knife fight. A blade at my throat could spill my blood and sever my vocal cords in one stroke—a silent death, in the middle of my own territory.

"Mr. Holt, no one needs to get hurt here, and if you come with us now, no one will," Cam said. "But you should know that if you refuse, my associate has instructions to kill Kori in an effort to motivate you. Should you *still* refuse, we have instructions to kill you, as well." Because like Jake, Ruben Cavazos didn't want someone as powerful as Ian working for his enemy. "I'm sorry, Kori," Cam said, and I could hear the strain in his voice.

I shrugged his apology off. He was the foot soldier, not

the commander, and I could certainly sympathize. And it's not like I'd never been threatened with death before.

"Liv...?" I called softly, moving my throat as little as possible, because of the blade pressed against it.

"Ruben rarely makes the same mistake twice. Unless it's a mistake he enjoys," said a female voice with a familiar Hispanic accent. Anger flared inside me when Michaela Cavazos stepped out of the shadows next to a large Dumpster, and I understood how they'd gotten into the west side without being spotted. Cam had tracked us, probably waiting for us to leave the hotel, and Meika was a Traveler. She was also Ruben Cavazos's wife.

Fuck. Without Olivia, who was obligated to help if I asked her to, we were screwed.

"I didn't know Ruben ever let you off your leash," I snapped, but Michaela only shrugged.

"It's a very long leash."

"Your husband still fucking every bitch with a gap between her thighs?"

Another shrug, like she didn't care, but I could see the truth in her eyes. In the perpetually angry line of her jaw. "He sets them up, I knock them down," she said, and my temper burned hotter. She wasn't kidding.

I owed Michaela Cavazos a knife to the gut, and the one currently pressed into my throat would do the job nicely.

"Holt?" Every muscle in Cam's body was tense and ready for action.

"I'm not leaving her," Ian said, looking straight at me, his hands open at his sides, his stance steady and confident.

Cam glanced at me in surprise, then back to Ian, and comprehension surfaced on his features, obvious even in the near darkness. "I understand," Cam said. "But if you don't go with Michaela right now, Stan will kill Kori, and I couldn't stop him even if I were allowed to. Please go. I can't do anything for Kori anymore, but you can."

My mind raced, looking for a way out. If I could get the knife away from my throat, I could take Stan—I was sure of that without even having seen him. I could take down most guys twice my size in a fair fight.

"If I leave her here, Tower will kill her," Ian said, and I flinched. That wasn't something I'd planned to broadcast.

Cam glanced at me again, brows raised in question, and I could only nod carefully to confirm the fact.

Michaela whistled, and what little light made it into the alley glinted off the knife she spun over and over on her open palm. "Sounds like you signed on with the wrong side."

"There is no right side," I said, and I'd never believed that more.

"What's it going to be, Holt?" Cam asked, and at my back, Silent Stan's grip on my arm tightened, his knife shaking almost imperceptibly at my neck. He was nervous. Or maybe eager.

"There's no good choice here," Ian said, and Cam nodded in acknowledgment. There was nothing he could do about that. "If I go with you, Tower will kill Kori. If I opt to stay here, you'll try to kill us both."

"*Try* isn't in my vocabulary," Michaela said, and Ian's brows rose.

"I suspect there are a great many words missing from your vocabulary," he said, and she bristled. "But my point is that in the absence of a good choice, a bold one will often suffice."

Meika scowled. "What the hell does that mean?"

Ian drew a gun from his waistband and aimed over my shoulder before I'd even realized he'd moved. Before Cam could even lift his own weapon. Ian fired, and the flash from his gun blinded me as gunfire echoed through the alley. I didn't have time to be scared or surprised, which was good, because if I'd realized what was coming, I'd have ducked, and that would have pulled Silent Stan out of Ian's aim.

The bullet *thunked* into flesh inches from my head, and for a moment, the knife pressed harder into my skin. Then Stan's hand fell from my arm and his blade slid lightly across my neck in a downward arc.

I shoved the knife away, but not before it sliced a long, shallow cut from the left corner of my jaw almost to the center of my throat. I hissed at the sudden pain, then cursed over my own spilled blood—the biggest security risk possible.

Turning, I glanced at the still form on the ground behind me, then another gun flashed in the dark, and I heard the muted *thunk* of a silencer as Cam returned fire. But Ian was already moving. Cam's bullet slammed into the brick wall just behind him. Ian fired again, and Cam shouted in pain. His gun clattered to the concrete and he slapped his left hand over his right arm.

"Leave, before they come for you," Ian said, both his gun and his gaze trained steadily on Cam, and I could already hear footsteps pounding our way from across the street.

I gaped at him, one hand pressed to the sticky, bloody wound on my neck. Ian was fast. And he was *good*.

Systems analyst, my ass. Ian Holt had serious training.

"I can't go back without you," Cam said, and movement on my right drew my attention to where Michaela stood with her back to the Dumpster, feet spread for balance, a knife in each hand, ready to be thrown.

Ian shrugged at Cam. "Stay and let Tower's men kill you. I don't give a damn." He turned to me then, his free hand open and waiting for mine though his aim at Cam never wavered. "Kori?"

I took one step toward him, then froze when gravel crunched behind me. I spun, one hand still pressed to my wound, and kicked the knife from Michaela's left hand as she lunged for me. She swiped at me with her other hand and I kicked her in the chest, afraid that any use of my hands would splatter my blood all over the alley.

Michaela stumbled back and I kicked again. Her knife arced toward my leg. The blade hit my boot and snagged in the leather, but didn't break through. I kicked one more time, and her knife clattered to the ground, then slid beneath the Dumpster. She howled in pain and clutched her arm, and as the first onlooker appeared in the mouth of the alley, I wasted one precious moment hoping her arm was broken. A lot.

"Stay back!" Ian shouted, waving his gun at the crowd starting to gather. Several ducked out of sight again, speaking into phones, but no one came closer. Not even Tower's men, and surely there were at least a couple already reporting the incident.

"Michaela, take Cam and get out of here!" I whispered, as anger at him battled with my sympathy for the position he was in.

"I'm bleeding," he protested as she tried to pull him into the darkest patch of night, on the other side of the Dumpster.

"Give me your bleach, and I'll clean it up," I said,

holding my free hand out as Ian retrained his gun on Cam. He wasn't taking any chances. And I couldn't afford to use my own pocket-size bleach solution on Cam's blood. But neither would I leave a viable sample of it in the alley to be used against him.

Cam hesitated, glancing from me, to Meika, to Ian, then back at me. Then he dug in his pocket with his good hand and tossed me a small clear plastic bottle, just like the one I carried at all times. Because you never know when you're going to be attacked in a dark alley by a psychotic bitch and a former friend and coworker.

"Thanks," he said, then he and Michaela stepped into the darkness and disappeared.

"Got a light?" I said to Ian as soon as they were gone. Then I realized I couldn't open Cam's bottle—not to mention my own—without the use of both hands.

"No." Ian flicked the safety switch on the gun and shoved it back into his waistband, then glanced at the mouth of the alley, where the crowd was reforming. "Anyone got a flashlight?"

After a moment of hesitant silence, three people produced key chain penlights and a fourth pulled a sizable LED flashlight from the pocket of his cargo pants. With their help—I recognized chain links on the arms of two of the men—we scanned the alley quickly but thoroughly for blood and poured bleach everywhere we spotted it.

Only once we'd destroyed both mine and Cam's blood did I realize that Ian was bleeding, too. Cam's bullet had grazed his upper arm before slamming into the concrete wall and his sleeve was dark and wet. None had dripped beyond the cloth, that I could tell, but that couldn't last forever.

"Let's go," I whispered, even as my phone began to

buzz in my pocket. I thanked the flashlight volunteers, then pulled Ian into the darkness with my good arm. A moment later, we stepped into his hotel bathroom, and I flipped on the light to see him holding the paper bag from the restaurant. Somehow, in spite of killing one man, shooting another, and being shot himself, he'd managed to salvage our dinner.

I laughed out loud. I couldn't help it.

"What?" Ian shrugged and set the bag on the marble bathroom counter. "You said you were hungry."

"Wow. What would you do if I said I was angry?"

"I would make fire rain from the heavens to smite your enemies with the flames of our shared rage."

My eyebrows arched halfway up my forehead. "That sounds like poetry and feels like war. I like it."

"I thought you might."

"You don't see that very often in the city. There isn't enough smiting with flames."

"No, but there's more than enough blood." He held up his arm, which was still dripping blood down his sleeve, and one glance in the mirror showed me what I'd already felt—that my neck and shirt were soaked in my own blood. "I'll call down for another first-aid kit," he said.

"I'm going to run home and clean up, but I'll be back as soon as I can, okay?" I said, and he nodded from the hall, already heading for the room phone.

I turned the bathroom light off, then stepped through the shadows and into my own room.

"Kenley!" I shouted, before I even had the light on, and she called back from the living room.

"In here."

"I need some help." I pulled my shirt off on the way to the bathroom and dropped it into the tub, then grabbed a clean rag from the rack over the toilet and pressed it to my neck.

Kenley stepped into the hall and her eyes widened with one look at the rag and the blood staining both my chest and my bra. "What the hell happened?" She took the rag from me and gasped at the sight of my wound.

"Looks worse than it feels."

"Good, because it looks like someone tried to slice your head off."

"Pretty much. And I think Jake's already heard about it," I said when my phone buzzed in my pocket again. A headache had already started—resistance pain from not answering his call immediately.

"Want me to talk to him?" She pushed me toward the toilet, where I closed the lid and sat while she dug beneath the sink for first-aid supplies.

"No, just patch me up and I'll call him myself." I didn't want her to have anything to do with Ian. Jake didn't need any more of an excuse to hold her responsible for my failures.

Kenley poured peroxide onto another clean rag, then pressed it against my neck. I hissed at the sharp sting, but I let her hold the rag in place while I reached back to unhook my bra then tossed it into the tub with my shirt.

Then I took the rag from her and returned Jake's call while my sister dumped bleach into the tub to destroy my blood.

"What the hell happened?" Jake barked into my ear, in lieu of a greeting.

"Cavazos moved on Holt," I said. "Ambush in the alley behind Sutherland's. One dead, two wounded, on their side." No need to mention that Cam was one of them… "We had to leave the body because we're both bleeding, but two of your men were there."

"They're already on it," Jake said, and some small measure of tension eased inside me. Even on the west side, where Jake's authority was almost absolute, gunfire could bring the police. "Witnesses say Holt fired two shots."

"Yeah. I'm unarmed, remember? Perhaps you'd care to revisit that issue now?"

"I'll take it under consideration. If Holt fired two shots and hit two people, that means he didn't miss."

"Yup." That's as much as I was willing to commit to.

"Any thoughts on why a pencil pusher from the suburbs knows how to shoot?" His voice was steady, and the silence that followed it was expectant. He knew something. Or he knew I knew something.

I closed my eyes and took a quick, quiet breath. "He's a man of many talents?"

"Obviously." But that wasn't the end of the issue. It couldn't be. "Where'd he get the gun, Korinne?"

I closed my eyes, bracing for what would follow. "I took it off Olivia Warren in the park this morning."

Silence.

Dangerous, tense silence, during which my stomach tried to devour the rest of me whole.

"What park?"

"The south side of Durham Park, at the fork in the river."

More silence, and I could almost picture Jake sitting behind his desk with his eyes closed, controlling his temper on the outside while it raged unchecked just beneath the surface.

"How badly was Holt hurt?"

I shrugged, though he couldn't see me. "He wasn't, this morning. From tonight, just a graze. He's fine. I am, too," I added, though he hadn't asked.

"I have a body to get rid of and witnesses to deal with. Get Holt patched up, get yourself patched up, and consider yourselves grounded for the night. Neither of you are to leave his suite before the sun rises. And I want you in my office alone at eight in the morning, or you'll be back in the basement five minutes after that."

Fuck!

"And, Kori, if I have to come looking for you, there won't be enough of you left to bury."

Shitshitshit! I hung up my phone and immediately set a timer for seven-thirty the next morning, because I knew from experience that Jake would be setting his for seven fifty-nine, and I couldn't afford to be late.

"Go on." Kenley took the bloody rag and handed me a thick gauze bandage to replace it. She looked sick, and I wondered how much of that she'd heard. "I'll take care of this." She dropped the rag into the tub with everything else I'd bled on and lit a match, then dropped it onto the pile. Flames flared behind me as I hurried into my room.

Holding the gauze in place with one hand, I plucked a hand wipe from a package on my dresser and carefully wiped all the blood from my neck and chest, then dropped the used wipe in the trash. The blood on it wouldn't be viable, thanks to the sanitizer. Then I left the gauze in place—it was stuck with drying blood anyway—while I put on a fresh bra and carefully shrugged into a clean shirt.

"Here. Wear this." Kenley stepped into my room with a gauzy blue scarf. She taped the bandage to my skin, then arranged the scarf around my neck to mostly cover it. Tower would still notice, and Ian knew what had happened, but with any luck, no one else would notice anything wrong.

"Thanks." I hardly recognized my own reflection with the scarf on. I looked like Kenley, only skinnier. "Where's Van?"

Kenley flushed. "She doesn't live here, you know."

But suddenly I kind of wished she did. I didn't want to leave my sister alone when Jake was pissed at me.

"Call her. See if she'll come hang out with you."

The blood drained from her face with one glance at mine, and she nodded without question. If I sounded worried, she knew she should be, too, and she rarely wasted time arguing. For which I was grateful.

"I have to stay with Ian, then report to Jake in the morning. But I'll check back in afterward, just in case."

"Okay. Be careful, Kori."

I hugged her, then she flipped the light switch for me and I tried to step back into Ian's apartment, only to find the opening blocked by blazing light in the visible spectrum, which could only mean one thing. He was in the bathroom.

Frustrated but not really surprised, I closed my eyes and reached out mentally until I found a patch of darkness in his suite big enough to step into. I walked forward and a moment later I slammed right into the inside of the closet door.

I opened the door and stepped into the bedroom, and was greeted with the sound of water running in the bathroom. "Hello?" I called, but there was no answer. "I had to come into the closet since you're—"

Half-naked and dripping wet...

Ian stood in bathroom doorway, hair dripping, wearing nothing but a towel he was just then tying loosely at his waist. His chest and stomach were bare, dark and defined against the thick white cotton, and beaded with clean water.

Carton of hard lemonade, my ass. That was a full-on six-pack.

I couldn't stop staring. He was beautiful.

Twenty-Three

Ian

I stepped out of the shower, still tucking the towel in at my waist, and looked up to find Kori standing in the bedroom in fresh clothes, a blue silk scarf only half hiding the bandage on her neck. Her conflicted gaze met mine, then traveled lower, and I let her look.

She took a few hesitant steps forward and her hand twitched, like she wanted to touch me, but also wanted to run from me. But she kept coming, slowly, and I stood still, afraid to spook her, because she kind of looked like a deer caught in oncoming headlights. Like she was mesmerized for the moment, but any small distraction could send her fleeing into the night.

"We're grounded," she said, her voice a whisper.

"Like a broken airplane?"

She shook her head. "Like a naughty child."

"What does that mean?" I asked when she stopped on the threshold, one hand clutching the bathroom door frame, like her grip was the only thing keeping her from fleeing. Or maybe from coming in.

"He knows about the park, and he knows about the alley," she said, still standing in the doorway, and I wondered if she was stuck there. Not in, but not out. Hovering in that liminal moment between realizing there's a choice to be made and actually making it. "So we're supposed to stay here all night."

I fought the urge to pull her closer. "Tower's punishment for not telling him about the park is to lock us up here together? All night? I'm not sure he understands how punishment is supposed to work."

"It's not punishment. It's a safety precaution."

Right. Normally I'd feel the need to remind Tower that I don't take orders from him yet. But I wasn't going to object to a night spent with Kori, even if we did nothing but play cards and watch TV all night long.

"How bad is it?" I asked, eyeing the scarf around her neck.

She shrugged. "It's just one night." Then I reached for the scarf, and she understood. "Oh, the cut. It's fine. It's hardly bleeding anymore." My fingers brushed the silk, feeling the rough texture of the bandage beneath. Then I pulled her hand away gently and tugged on the scarf. The filmy material fell through my fingers, and she sucked in a breath, like I was removing something more intimately located than the scarf around her neck. Her gaze locked with mine as I tucked her hair behind her shoulders and unwound the last layer of scarf.

The silk slipped over her arm as I pulled the material loose and let it fall to the floor between us. Her hands found my chest, but there was no clear intent in her eyes. She didn't have a goal, and for once she wasn't overthinking things. She was just…touching.

I closed my eyes as her hands skimmed my bare,

damp skin, skittering over my ribs toward my stomach. Her touch was light, just enough contact to make me desperate for more, and I wanted to lean into her. Offer her more. But she had to set the pace. That was the only way this would work.

Her fingers traced the edge of my towel, playing over the skin south of my navel, and my next breath was shaky. My fingers twitched at my sides, itching to touch her. To explore her like she was exploring me. It took every bit of willpower I had to let my hands hang empty, giving her free rein.

She bit one side of her bottom lip, and I wanted to taste it. Her hands shook at the tuck in my towel, and I wanted to steady them. Her gaze held mine, and I saw fear in her eyes, but I wasn't sure if she was more scared of giving in to the need gripping us both or resisting it. When she did neither, I grinned, my brows arched in challenge.

That did it.

Kori leaned into me, her hands on my sides for balance, and I didn't realize what she had in mind until she licked a drop of water from the left side of my chest. I groaned, and my hands clenched around air, aching to grip her hips instead.

She bent for another taste, and this time she moved from drop to drop, her tongue leaving a hot trail across my skin, higher and higher, weaving back and forth until finally she licked a drop beaded on my right nipple, and that was all I could take. I reached for her waist and pulled her closer.

Kori looked up at me and her hands stilled. Her mouth opened and I leaned in to kiss her, my heart beating so hard I could almost hear it. Then my phone buzzed from

the counter and she jumped, startled by the sudden interruption.

Kori glanced at the screen. And froze.

I followed her gaze to see a text from Meghan.

Can't do this anymore, Ian. Tell her whatever it
takes to get the job done. I'm counting on you.

I reached for the phone, but it was too late. She'd already seen the message. "What job?"

"It's not—"

"*What job,* Ian?" She shoved me away, and I stumbled
backward, toward the mirror.

"Kori…" I said, but she was already backing away
from me. She spun sharply in the bedroom, bypassing
the dark closet in her haste and anger. I caught up with
her halfway through the living room, and in my desperation to keep her from leaving, I forgot.

"Kori, *wait!*" I grabbed her arm, and she turned on
me, already swinging. Her fist slammed into my jaw and
my head rocked back sharply, pain spreading across my
face.

"Damn it!" I dropped her arm to rub my chin, and
when I reached for her again, she smacked my hand away
and spun into a wide, high kick. Her boot slammed into
my chest, and I stumbled backward, and had to grab the
back of a chair to keep from falling.

"Don't fucking touch me, you lying, traitorous son of
a bitch," she spat, and by the time I'd regained my balance, she was nearly to the front door.

I jogged to catch up with her, one hand clutching the
towel at my hips, and I slid in front of the door just as she
reached for the lever. "Wait. Please." I held both hands

up, palms out, careful not to make my request sound like an order. "I won't touch you. Just please hear me out. It's not what you think."

"Fuck off." She backed up two steps, and rubbed her forehead so hard it looked like she was actually trying to shove her fingers through her skull. "Jake's going to kill me. You're some kind of a spy, or a…a *mercenary*."

"No. Kori, let me explain…"

"The fighting. The shooting. I *knew* you couldn't be a fucking systems analyst. You never had any *intention* of signing, did you? You don't give a shit about me or my sister." Then her eyes widened. "*Kenley*. Fuck!" She dropped into a squat, clutching the back of the couch with one hand and her stomach with the other, like all the pain from my betrayal had settled there, and my own chest tightened in response. "You're here for Kenley. You're a fucking poacher, aren't you? The whole thing was a setup, to get you through Jake's defenses."

"No! Well, yes." I exhaled slowly, trying to figure out how much of the truth I could tell her without spilling the beans she'd then have to feed to Jake Tower.

"The hockey game. I should have known. You're too smart to accidentally reveal yourself like that." She stood, angry tears building in her eyes. "You've fucking *screwed* us both!"

"No, Kori, I'm not going to let him hurt you or Kenley."

"Who do you work for?" she demanded.

"No one. I'm not a poacher. That's not what this is about, I swear on my life." I stepped closer, aching to hold her but she backed away. Her eyes lost focus. She wasn't hearing me. She wasn't even really seeing me.

She was seeing the consequences to come in what little future she thought she had left.

"I don't want to do it," she mumbled. "I don't want to let him drain you, but you *lied,* and I'm as good as dead, and the only chance Kenley and I have now is if I hand you over and beg for mercy in exchange for turning in a mole."

"Kori, please."

She woke up then, and focused on me with startling clarity. Resolve surfaced behind her eyes, hardening her gaze like a shield slipping into place between us, and my heart hurt like someone was squeezing it, milking the life from me drop by drop.

"Get the hell out of my way, or I will break your jaw," she growled through clenched teeth.

I crossed both arms over my bare chest and stood firm in front of the door. "Fine. Do it. I won't hit you back. I don't want to hurt you, Kori. I just want to explain." She came at me, fists clenched and ready, and I rushed ahead, words spilling from my mouth like blood from a gaping wound, and I wanted to take them back as soon as I heard them because they were true, but they weren't *the truth.* They were facts out of context, wielded like sword and shield. I said them to protect her, but I hated myself for it. For the foundation of lies supporting the most fragile and precious relationship I'd ever tried to build.

"The hockey game was a setup, yes, but I'm not here to poach your sister. I just needed to get Tower's attention. Quickly. I need something from him." Technically that was true. I needed his Binder. But I wasn't going to poach her for someone else.

"So you're not a systems analyst?" Her fists were still

clenched, but they hung at her sides now. Her eyes were still narrowed in suspicion, but she was listening.

"No. I only type thirty words a minute and can barely work a cell phone."

"But your name's real. What kind of spy uses a fake backstory, but his real name?"

I shrugged. "What kind of recruiter shows her recruit the dark side of the syndicate, instead of the advantages?"

"I'm not really a recruiter," she said.

"And I'm not a spy. Tower would have known inside a minute if I gave him a fake name."

"So what are you doing here? What do you need from Jake?"

I exhaled slowly, working up to the last part—the truest of these truths out of context. "Tower has the resources I need to break the seal on a binding."

Kori frowned. "Can't be done. The best you can do is destroy the binding itself. Burn the paper it was sealed on it. Assuming it was sealed on paper?"

"It's a name binding, so it probably was," I said. "But we have no idea where that paper is. If it even exists." For all I knew, Steven's binding could have been sealed in graffiti on some wall a thousand miles away. The binding itself was a dead end. We had no choice but to break the seal.

"And 'we' includes Meghan? Who is she, really?" Her gaze held mine, demanding truth while trying to hide how much my answer actually meant to her.

"She's really my brother's girlfriend. Well, technically his fiancée, now. He proposed a couple of weeks ago."

Kori frowned as the implications sank in. "Oh, shit, your brother's the one who's bound."

"Yeah."

"What's he bound to?"

"I don't know. He doesn't know, either. It's bizarre, and scary, and infuriating. I *have* to get him out of it. That's why I'm here."

"So, you need to break the seal on a binding you can't locate or identify..." she said, thinking out loud, and I nodded. "What makes you think Jake can help?"

"You said he did it for Kenley, when she got into trouble in college."

"*That's* why you keep asking about Kenley..." Kori looked so relieved I didn't have the heart to correct her. Not that I could have anyway. Not while she was still bound to Tower.

"Do you know how he did it?" I asked, but she only shook her head.

"She never told me and I never asked. A lot of things go unsaid around here."

"So, can I talk to her?" I was pushing my luck, and I knew it. But Steven didn't have much time left, and I couldn't tell Kori anything else until her binding was broken.

"We can't leave here tonight, and she can't come over without Jake's permission and an escort. And I doubt he'll let her, considering how much trouble I'm in right now. But I guess I can call her..."

I swallowed a moan. This wasn't a phone-call kind of conversation, and it certainly wasn't anything I could say in front of Kori, while Tower's marks were still live on her arm. "It can wait until tomorrow," I said at last, desperately hoping that was true. I was less than a day from losing both my brother and his fiancée, and I'd be lucky if my recruitment ruse with Jake Tower lasted that long.

The clock was ticking.

The noose was tightening.

And Kori was looking at me like I held her life in my hands. Because I did.

"You're still going to sign, right?" she said, and there was a thread of steel beneath the fragile surface of her voice. "Or was that part of the act, to get you in the door? Because you know that whatever Jake did for Kenley, he won't do that for your brother unless you sign."

"I know." But I had no intention of letting Tower anywhere near my brother. Or anywhere near Kori, if I had my way.

I took her right fist and uncurled her fingers until her hand lay flat in mine, and I placed my other hand over hers. "There are things I haven't told you. Things I *can't* tell you while your marks stand between us. But soon none of that will matter. What matters is that I am *not* going to leave you and your sister here. I would swear to that right now, if there was a Binder here. I'll do whatever it takes to be with you. To stay with you. If you want me." I stared into her eyes, trying to see past the anger she wore like a mask to cover fear and vulnerability. I tried to see past all of that, to the part she never showed anyone else.

"Do you want me, Kori?"

Kori

I couldn't make sense of the tangle of emotions balled up inside me. I was frustrated, and scared, and angry, and somewhere in there, I felt a tiny kernel of hope, struggling to survive in such harsh conditions. But every last thread in the jumble of conflicting emotions led back to Ian, through one twisted route or another.

He was hiding something, yes. He'd practically admitted that. But he'd shielded me in the wine cellar and refused to leave me in the alley. He'd talked me down from panic and he'd said I was a lion that could not be tamed. He knew what I'd had to do for Jake, and what Jake had done to me in return. And he wanted me anyway.

And I wanted him like I'd never wanted anything else in my life. So I pulled him down with one hand and kissed him.

Ian groaned against my lips. He tugged me closer, then his mouth opened beneath mine, pulling me in. My hands wandered on their own, slowly exploring the hard planes of his back until I realized his towel was loosening, and my fingers were damp with water from his shower, and we were pressed so tightly together I could hardly breathe. But his hands hadn't moved. One cradled my jaw, trailing beneath my ear. The other sat at my waist. Above my clothes. There, but demanding nothing.

Did that mean he didn't want to touch me?

No. I could feel how badly he wanted to touch me. But he had patience. Self-control. It almost felt like... manners.

"You okay?" he asked, when I pulled away and looked up at him.

In answer to a question I never wanted to hear again, I tugged him through the living room, hall and into the bedroom, where I let go and started to unbutton my shirt.

Ian's brows rose, but his gaze never left mine. "Are you sure?"

I nodded and pushed another button through its hole.

He watched me for another second, then he was there again, kissing me, and my hands fell away from my shirt so his could take over.

My pulse rushed too fast and the room spun, a blur of dark wood and rich fabrics, shadowed on the edges by the fear I pushed aside with every breath I took. I threw myself into that kiss, letting the taste and the feel of him chase everything else away.

When the buttons were undone, his hands slid beneath the cotton and gently pushed the material down my arms. He kissed my shoulder and unhooked my bra, and I let it slide to the floor. Then I reached for the towel at his hips and pulled it loose.

His towel fell off and he moaned, his lips pressed to the unbroken side of my neck. His arms slid around me, guiding me as he walked us backward, and I felt the mattress against the backs of my thighs.

I sat, then lay back, and for a moment, I couldn't breathe. Darkness closed in on the edges of my vision, and with it came flashes of memory I couldn't push back. Dead shadows trapping me. A weight on my chest. A cruel hand twisting, and pinching, and bruising, and invading.

Ian lay beside me, naked, reaching for me, and my throat tried to close.

"I can't," I whispered, and his hands fell away. I pulled the rumpled blanket over me, confused, and humiliated, and drowning in frustration. Pissed off by my own fear.

He propped himself up on one elbow and I made myself look at him. "It's okay. There's no rush," he said, brushing hair from my cheek.

But it wasn't. It wasn't fucking okay, and it never would be until I could push past the fear and anger devouring me from the inside out. Until I could touch and be touched and just live in the moment, without reliving other hands. Without feeling like the world was spiraling in on me, constricting around me, compressing me until I couldn't move. Couldn't fight. Couldn't breathe.

Why now? Why did I have to meet him *now,* when I couldn't tell from one minute to the next whether I wanted to touch or hit, kiss or bite?

This wasn't okay. And it wasn't *going* to be okay until I could do whatever the fuck I wanted with whoever the hell I wanted. Until I could take control back, not just of my body, but of my mind. If I gave up now—if I let fear chase me from what I wanted—the next time would only be harder.

Ian stroked my hair, spreading it over the rumpled comforter. Touching me without touching me. And suddenly I wanted to cry. He was so patient.

I looked up at him, and he was still watching me. Not smiling. Just watching.

"Make it dark," I whispered, and he frowned for a second. Then he sat up and reached for the bedside lamp.

"No." I laid one hand on his arm, and he turned back to me. "Make it dark. True dark." The kind I knew. The kind I loved. The kind I could escape into whenever I needed to.

The kind Ian carried in his soul and could gather at will.

He smiled, and the darkness rose around us, faster than ever before. Cool and calm. Quiet. Soothing. Like it had been there all along. Waiting.

I couldn't see a thing, but I'd never been more sure of where I was.

I reached for him and my hand found his stomach. I

trailed my fingers up the hard lines of his chest and over his collarbone, then around to the back of his neck. I pulled him down, and his mouth found mine. He couldn't see me, but he could feel me, and that was more than enough.

I kissed him. I couldn't taste enough of him. His hand found my side and threatened to linger there in chaste caution until I arched into his touch, and his fingers wandered up slowly. Gingerly.

The dark settled around me, touching me everywhere he didn't, and I reached for him, pulling him closer. His hand found my breast, his fingers brushing my nipple, and when I moaned into his mouth, his hand tightened, bolder now. I arched into him, fumbling with the button on my jeans, and his hand trailed down to brush mine aside. A second later, the button was free, my zipper down.

Ian sat up on his knees and his hands slid down from my waist, slipping beneath the material at my sides, sliding it over my hips so slowly I squirmed in anticipation, my eyes closed. He followed the material all the way to my feet, leaving a trail of kisses down my left leg. Then he kissed his way up the other leg, his hands blazing the same trail in advance.

When I couldn't wait anymore, I pulled him up, opening for him, reaching for another kiss. He settled between my thighs, and I could feel him, hot and hard, and ready.

"Are you sure?" he asked again, whispering in my ear this time. "I need to know that you want this."

I blinked in the dark, and hot tears trailed silently down both sides of my face. "Yes. I want you, Ian."

He exhaled, and I felt the tension in him ease. He slid one hand over my hip and down to my knee, then lifted my leg, guiding my ankle around his waist. My heart thumped almost painfully as I tucked my other leg behind him and pulled him down for another kiss.

He entered me slowly, and I gasped, sucking air from his mouth. Rising to meet him. When he was all the way in, he stayed for a moment, and I sucked his lip into my mouth, holding my breath. Reluctant to move.

Then he withdrew and slid inside me again, and we found our rhythm.

I clung to him, arching with him, holding him close. He buried his face in my hair, holding me with one arm, supporting his weight with the other. And everything else faded away, swallowed by the darkness he wrapped around us.

I remembered nothing but Ian. I felt nothing but him. I wanted nothing but him. And I never wanted that moment to end.

Then the rhythm changed, and I rode the waves, coasting toward an edge I could feel building, tighter and tighter. He moved inside me and I rose to meet him over and over, faster and faster, and the fire burning between us consumed all conscious thought for one precious moment. Then that fire crested to spill over the rest of me in a hot, desperate wave of pleasure and I clung to him again, riding it out to the finish.

Ian collapsed on the bed next to me and I rolled over to face him, unable to quell the languid smile I could feel forming. He leaned forward to kiss me, then I rolled onto my back again and put one hand on his chest, because I wasn't done touching him. I never wanted to be done.

Slowly he let the darkness fade, and as the light rose to replace it, I found him watching me. And for the first time in months, maybe even in years, I felt safe.

Twenty-Four

Ian

I couldn't stop watching her during dinner, after we'd heated up the meal that had almost gotten us killed. I loved the way she cut her steak into bites, then ate them two at a time and refused any sauce. The way she picked every single tiny sliver of carrot from her salad, then offered to trade them for my cucumber. I loved the way she laughed when I dribbled wine from the lip of the bottle because I was too busy watching her to pour with anything resembling competence.

She made a face over the red wine, but she liked the white enough to have a second glass after dinner. She was different now. More comfortable. More confident. Still brash, but less angry. She was funny and quick-witted, and on the rare occasions that night when her smile slipped, I suffered a renewed, intensified hatred for everyone who'd ever so much as bruised her, body or soul.

After dinner, I asked her if she wanted to stay the night—Tower's order wasn't good enough for me—

careful to phrase my question so that she had an out, just in case.

She stayed, and we made love again, and afterward, with her head on my shoulder, my dark hand splayed against her pale stomach, I saw a snapshot of our life and what it could have been, if not for Tower. What it might *still* be, if I pulled off the impossible and freed us both, after I freed Steven.

After I freed all *three* of us, because she wouldn't leave without her sister.

Kori fell asleep in my arms, in the dark, but rolled away from me in her sleep, so I curled around her, treasuring her warmth, wondering how so much woman could possibly fit into such a small, beautiful body.

Something woke me in the middle of the night, and I lay still, trying to figure out what I'd heard. Then I heard it again. Kori. I rolled over to find her mumbling in her sleep, half word, half moan of pain.

She was dreaming.

"No," she murmured, and when she started twisting, the covers tangled around her legs, which seemed to upset her even more. "No, *please...*" Her eyes were closed, but her head rolled back and forth, a vague outline in the dark room.

"Please," she begged in her sleep, and a tear rolled down her face, glittering in the moonlight shining between the cracks in the blinds. And that was all I could stand.

"Kori." I touched her arm, and she froze. Her eyes flew open and her hand slid beneath her pillow. "Are you—" Before I could finish the question, she'd shoved me down on my back and I felt the cold steel of a knife at my throat. My pulse roared in my ears, my heart thumping painfully.

She was awake, but unaware, still caught in the nightmare. Still trapped in the basement. Only this time she was armed with a knife from the room service tray.

"Kori, it's me," I whispered, afraid to move my throat much because there was actual pressure behind the blade. It was a miracle she hadn't yet broken skin. "It's Ian. Remember? We're in my hotel room."

She blinked, and some of the confusion cleared.

"See the window? Can you see the moonlight? Do you know where you are?"

Kori gasped and let go of my shoulder, then retreated across the bed with the knife still in hand. "I'm sorry. Fuck! I'm so sorry. I could have killed you."

"It's okay. We're both fine." I probably could have subdued her, but not without making her nightmare worse. "But maybe you could put the knife down?"

She lifted her hand and seemed surprised to see the knife still in it, the serrated edge shining in a thin beam of moonlight. "Shit." She dropped it onto the marble-topped nightstand, where it bounced and clattered, then went still. "I'm so sorry."

"It's okay. Do you mind if I put the knife away?"

"Get rid of it, please. I don't even remember bringing it in here."

"Do you sleep with one at home?" I stepped into my underwear, then rounded the bed toward the nightstand on her side.

"Yeah. Sorry. I guess I should have warned you."

I took the knife into the front room, and when I got back into bed, she was in the bathroom. A minute later, the toilet flushed, then water ran in the sink. When she came out, she left the door open and the light on, without even seeming to notice. And that's when I realized she was afraid of the dark. Or at least afraid of sleeping in it—surely a complicated problem for a shadow-walker.

She climbed back into bed next to me, wearing only plain black cotton underwear, and sat with her legs crossed beneath the covers, her hands over her face, visibly trying to collect herself. I reached out, aching to comfort her but hesitant to touch. Finally I laid my hand between her shoulder blades, and when she didn't flinch, I started to rub her back.

But my hand froze after a couple of inches, when my fingers skimmed over a smooth, thick line of skin. A scar.

An inch later, I found another.

I scooted toward the headboard for a better view of her back, and in the light from the bathroom, I saw more than I wanted to see. I saw it all.

Bruises, still healing two weeks after she was let out. Burn scars, small and round, like the tip of a cigarette. Long thin strips of scar tissue I couldn't identify. Teeth marks—an entire set of them—in three different places.

I don't know what I'd expected, but this wasn't it. She hadn't been punished. She'd been tortured.

Rage burned so hot in my gut I felt like I was roasting alive. I wanted to kill something. Someone. Everyone who'd had a hand in what happened to her. But I swallowed that rage. I held it inside, because my anger could trigger hers, and justice for Kori couldn't be had in that moment, in the middle of the night, with her still shaking from the latest bad dream.

But she *would* have justice. I would make sure of that.

"Do you have a lot of nightmares?"

She shrugged. "Sleep is overrated."

"You can tell me about it," I said, and her hands fell away from her face. She shook her head without looking at me. "It's not going to scare me or make me want you any less."

"I don't want to talk about it, Ian. That'll make *me* want me less."

"I don't understand."

"I know." She sounded so alone. So convinced that she had to be.

"I don't understand, but I *want* to. If you want to tell me, I want to hear."

For a long time, she didn't say anything. She didn't lie down. She didn't even move. She just wrapped her arms around her knees and stared at the end of the bed, breathing slowly. Deeply. Then she took one more deep breath, and her mouth opened.

"I don't know where to start."

"Can you tell me who did this?" I rubbed her back again, and I felt kind of guilty for my own ulterior motive in asking that question. I wanted to know who had done it so I could kill him. Even if killing the bastard who had hurt her didn't make her feel better, it would make *me* feel better.

"Doesn't matter who it was. Jake gave the orders. Jake told him he could do whatever he wanted with me, so long as I survived intact. Then he told me not to fight back."

"What?" My blood ran cold.

"That was my sentence. Before he left the day they locked me up, Jake looked right into my eyes and said, 'You like to fight, don't you, Kori? Then let's let the sentence fit the criminal. Don't fight back.'" She sucked in a choked breath and swallowed thickly. "Then he just left. I spent nearly every day at his side for the past six years, and he looked at me like I was worth less to him than the lint in his pocket. He just left me there, alone with—"

"With who?" She obviously didn't want to say the name. She probably didn't even want to think it. But she was seeing him in her head. I could tell that much. "Who did he tell you not to fight?" The very idea of which horrified me to no end.

"His brother. He told me not to fight Jonah. Six weeks, and I never lifted a fist, because the first time I tried, the resistance pain nearly killed me, and if I'd died, there'd be no one to protect Kenley. That, on top of the rest of it…it was just too much."

"Sadistic *bastard,*" I hissed. Just thinking about it made me feel sick and useless. The fierce ache in my chest rivaled the vicious twisting in my gut, and if hearing about it was that painful, I couldn't imagine how she'd held it together. How she'd come out of that cell traumatized, but mentally intact.

"I hate myself," she whispered, and I blinked, sure I'd heard her wrong. I wanted to hold her, to comfort her, but I didn't know how she'd react to being touched in the middle of remembered trauma.

"No, you don't. You don't hate yourself." How could she? None of it was her fault.

"Don't fucking tell me what I feel!" she snapped, her pale hair practically glowing in the light from the bathroom. "Do you want to hear this or not?"

"I want to hear whatever you want to say."

"I hate myself," she repeated, and if anything, she seemed to believe it more this time.

"You hate *him*," I insisted, because I couldn't help it. I hated hearing her say that.

"Yeah. I hate him more than anything else in the world. Except Jake. I hate Jake more. But that's normal."

"Normal?" How could any of this be normal?

Kori shook her head, confused, like she could feel what she was trying to say, but the words wouldn't come out right. "They're heartless. Cruel. Jake and Jonah are sadistic, and I knew that from the beginning. Sadistic people do sadistic things, so they were just being who and what they are."

My jaws ached from being clenched in anger. "That doesn't excuse anything they—"

"No, it doesn't," she agreed. "Nothing can excuse what they did to me, or to anyone else, and I'll hate them until the day I blow their heads into a million shards of bone and splashes of gray matter. And that day *will* come. But they aren't the ones who betrayed me. I betrayed myself."

"You didn't—"

"Yes, I did." She stared straight into my eyes, trying to make me understand. "Bad men do bad things. That's what they do and who they are. I fight. That's what *I* do, and who *I* am. But in the basement, I didn't fight. I couldn't."

"That's not your fault, Kori." She was killing me. She was carving out a piece of my soul with every word she spoke, and pain flowed in to fill the void.

"Don't…" She shook her head in frustration. "I can't explain what I mean. You can tell me it wasn't my fault until the earth cracks into a billion pieces of space dust, and in my head, I know that's true. But that doesn't change anything. I fight for Kenley. I fight for myself. I even fight for Jake, but that's really just another way of fighting for me and Kenley. But in the dark, I couldn't fight. I couldn't do what I do, and that means I failed. I wasn't strong."

"Kori, they took away your strength," I insisted, and she flinched, like my words actually hurt.

"Yeah. And if someone can take away your strength, you weren't strong enough in the first place. I wasn't strong enough to fight, and if I'm not a fighter, I don't know who I am. I don't know how to be me now. I don't know how to be *anything*. I lost myself in there, Ian." Her fists clenched around a handful of comforter, and her eyes watered. "The Kori who went into that cell isn't the Kori who came out. I can't find the old me, and I don't know how to be this new one." Her gaze held mine. I was captivated and devastated by the pain she was showing me. "I'm not the Kori Daniels you would have met if you'd come here two months ago."

"Good." I reached for her hand and she let me take it. "I'm so very sorry and angry about what happened to you, but I like this Kori. I might even love her." How could I not? She was a force of nature—a sudden fierce storm that had blown into my life, overturning everything I thought I knew about myself and exposing new truths. She was stronger than anyone I'd ever met, whether she could see that or not. "You may not know who you are, but I do. I know you, and I know you can be anything you want. What do you want to be? *Who* do you want to be?"

"I don't know!" She pulled her hand from mine and shoved blond tangles back from her face. "All I know is that I don't want to be her anymore. I don't want to be the woman I hear screaming and begging whenever there's nothing else loud enough to drown it out. I *hate* her. I hate what she said and what she let happen. I hate her so much that it actually makes me sick. She's there, in the pit of my stomach, rotting me from the inside out, and every time I think about it, I need to vomit. But no matter how many times I throw up, I can't purge her. She's in there, and she's scared and hurt, and I hate her."

"No." I shook my head and took her hands, and finally she looked at me again. "You may not be the woman who went into that cell, but you're not the woman who lived there for six weeks, either. That Kori died so you can live, and that's what you have to do. You have to live. And I want to be a part of that life. When the time comes for Jake and Jonah to die, I want to help you hunt them down, and slice them open, and watch their insides fall out."

"Again with the poetry." She managed a small smile. "That sounds so much prettier than blowing their brains out."

"I doubt Jonah would agree with you," I said returning her smile with a small one of my own. "But I think it's worth dreaming about. Why don't you try that? Try dreaming about what we're going to do to them, instead of what they did to you? I'll do it with you. We'll share the dream. Then we'll share the reality. I promise."

She blinked at me for several seconds, like she was trying to decide if I was serious. Then she nodded and kissed me, and we slid beneath the covers together. A few minutes later, she fell asleep in my arms again, and this time there were no nightmares. For her. I lay awake for three more hours, trying to figure out how to make my promise a reality. How to help her kill Jake and Jonah, without getting both of us killed in the process.

Her binding had to be broken. All roads led to that one conclusion. And there was only one person in the world who could make that happen.

Kenley Daniels. It all came back to her.

The next morning, I woke up to find Kori watching me, her fingers curled around mine on the comforter. There was something new in her eyes. Something fragile, but full of promise. After a moment, I realized what I was seeing.

Trust. She was trusting me. She *had* trusted me, and that couldn't have been easy, considering what she'd been through. And what I'd come to do. But she didn't know I'd come to kill her sister, and she *wouldn't* know, because I wasn't going to do it. If I'd had any doubts about that before, they were gone now. I could not betray this fragile new trust.

"Breakfast?" I asked.

She smiled, and my heart beat so hard it bruised the inside of my chest. How could she do that? How could one smile make me ache deep inside, in places I hadn't even known existed? How could she mean so much to me, in so little time?

"Yeah, but first—" Her sentence ended abruptly as her phone started beeping from somewhere on the floor. Kori popped upright like a jack-in-the-box, fear suddenly as clear in her features as satisfaction had been a moment before. "Shit!" She glanced at the bedside clock, which said it was seven-thirty in the morning, then scrambled off the bed and snatched her jeans from the floor, digging in one pocket in search of her phone. "I have to be in Tower's office in thirty minutes, or he'll lock me back up."

"What?" I rolled onto the floor and flipped up the lid on my suitcase, then snatched a pair of pants from the top of the pile.

"I'm in trouble for not reporting what happened at the park," she said, stepping into her jeans as I stepped into mine.

"Why didn't you tell me?"

"Because there was fighting, then there was sex, then I told you a whole bunch of other things, and this one just kind of slipped my mind. It's messy in there, you know."

"I'm coming with you." I pulled on my shirt, then sat on the end of the bed to shove my feet into a pair of socks.

"No, I have to go alone." She buttoned her pants, then took the bra I handed her and I fastened the hooks at her back while she dialed on her phone. "Kenley?" she said, when her sister answered. Kenley said something I couldn't make out, and Kori nodded. "I know. Twenty-five minutes." She shoved one arm into her sleeve, then transferred the phone to her other hand and slid the opposite arm in, too. "Is Van with you?" she said, and I buttoned her shirt, so she could hold the phone.

"I don't want to leave you alone," Kori said, in response to something else I couldn't hear, and I saw my opportunity.

"I'll stay with her," I said, and Kori looked up at me. And that trust faltered. I could see it. "She can come here, or I'll go there. Whichever's easier."

"I don't know..." Kori said, and I realized that her devotion to Kenley might be the only thing in the world strong enough to threaten the connection we'd just made.

Good thing I wasn't planning to kill her sister anymore.

"I swear on my life that I won't let anything happen to her," I said.

Kori closed her eyes and took a deep breath. "Okay." She wanted to threaten me. I could almost hear the words she was holding back, and I understood them. She was trusting me with the only thing she had left in the world, other than her heart, and I was hoping she'd trust me with that, too, if I kept Kenley safe from…whatever was threatening her at the moment.

"Kenni, I'm going to drop Ian off on my way to Jake's." Another pause, and Kori frowned. "He's not a babysitter. He's a friend, and I trust him. Just humor me, okay? We'll be there in a minute."

Thanks to the miracle of shadow-walking, she meant that literally.

Kori threw on the rest of her clothes, then we brushed our teeth and I helped wind the scarf around her neck again. Then we stepped from my bathroom into her sister's apartment.

Kori let go of my hand and a second later, light flared to life overhead, illuminating a cramped room stuffed with a twin bed, desk and dresser. A pile of free weights stood in one corner and a collection of handguns and knives were laid out on a towel stretched over her dresser, next to a squeeze bottle of gun oil sitting on an aluminum case that could only be a gun kit.

"Kenni!" Kori called, and an instant later Kenley Daniels appeared in the tiny hall. The three of us would hardly have fit in the bedroom together. "I have to go. I need you to stay here with Ian. He'll protect you."

"From what?" Kenley crossed her arms over her chest and glared openly at me. "There's a guard right outside the front door."

"We can't trust Jake's men. This is just in case."

"No way. We can't trust *him,* Kori! He's not bound. You hardly even know him."

"I know enough," Kori said, and I realized she was using my words. And that I loved hearing them in her voice. "Just stay with him until I get back." Then she turned to me, her hand already on the light switch, ready to step into the darkness once again. "If I'm not back in an hour, get her out of here. Same thing goes if anyone comes for her. Kill the bastard and get her as far away as you can."

I nodded, but she shook her head, like that wasn't enough. "Fucking promise me, Ian."

"What's going on?" Kenley demanded, but Kori didn't even glance at her.

"I swear, I won't let anything happen to her," I said, but Kenley's scowl didn't soften.

Kori watched me for a second, then went up on her toes and kissed me. "Thank you." Then she reached back and flipped the switch to kill the light, and as soon as she was gone, I realized that I could feel her absence, even though I couldn't see it.

Twenty-Five

Kori

I stepped out of my bedroom and into Jake's darkroom in an instant, my heartbeat measuring the seconds, burning through them faster than should have been possible. I had minutes to get out of the darkroom, down the stairs, and into Jake's office, and if I wasn't there when his timer went off, I might never see either the light of day or true darkness again.

I flipped the light switch up and pressed the button beneath the monitor mounted flush with the wall next to the door. Static buzzed on the screen for several seconds, while impatience buzzed beneath my skin. Then a familiar face appeared in its place, his broken nose and black eyes rendered in full color from the closed-circuit camera in the security room.

David. Shit. He'd been demoted to hall monitor because I'd taken him down twice in twenty-four hours.

"Kori Daniels, what an unpleasant surprise."

"Let me out. Jake's expecting me."

David leaned back in his chair, arms crossed over

his chest, and I realized that—at least from my vantage point—the security room was empty behind him. His supervisor was gone—cigarette? Bathroom?—and it was just the two of us, for the time being. "Apologize for re-breaking my nose with a fucking sucker punch, and I'll let you out."

"Sucker punch my ass." I crossed my arms over my shirt. "You fight like a twelve-year-old girl with menstrual cramps."

"Bitch!" he growled, leaning closer to the camera. "You know Jake won't let them set my nose? He wants me to see it every day as a reminder of my arrogance. Or some shit like that." His eyes narrowed in fury. "If I ever get another shot at you, I'm going to break every bone in your face. Then there'll be no jobs left for you, except as a freak in the haunted house on Halloween."

"Don't listen to the rest of them, David. Your threats are sounding more credible every day. Someday I might even tremble." I pulled my phone from my pocket and dialed Jake's number. "Hey, it's Kori," I said, when he answered. "I'm in the darkroom."

On the monitor, David scowled and pressed a button, and the darkroom door swung open into the hall.

"Be there in just a sec," I said, then hung up without waiting for a response from Jake. I had a minute and a half. I shoved the door open, and David's shout chased me halfway down the hall.

"You'll never see me coming, Daniels!"

Maybe not. But his angry bellow seemed to suggest that I'd hear him coming from a mile away.

I raced down the curved staircase, across the foyer, and into Jake's office with thirty seconds to spare, and his timer started beeping before I'd even caught my breath.

"Slow start this morning?" he said from behind his desk, one brow raised in amusement over my huffing and puffing.

"Nah. Traffic was a bitch, though."

"Well, *you* seem to have regained some of your former spunk." Julia crossed one leg over the other from her perch on the credenza to the left of Jake's desk. "It almost sounds like recruiting agrees with you, Kori." I spared one moment to visualize exactly how far through her face I'd like to shove my fist, then I dismissed her in favor of her brother, almost proud that I'd resisted rising to her bait.

"Tell me about the park," Jake said, and Julia scowled. She hated being ignored by anyone, and by her brother most of all.

I shrugged and dropped into a chair in front of his desk. "There's a swing set, and a slide, and on Thursdays, if you bring two dollars, you can get a cherry-pineapple snow cone from a clown with a red nose."

"Korinne..." Jake's angry voice was all the warning I'd get, but if I didn't at least try to push his buttons, he'd suspect something was up.

"Oh, fine. Cam and Olivia showed up with guns and tried to take Ian to the east side."

Jake's brows shot up again. "Cameron was there?"

"Yeah. Is it true you let Cavazos buy his contract?" I'd never heard of anyone else getting out of a contract with Tower early.

Jake folded his hands on his desk, and suddenly I felt like a kid called before the principal. "Korinne, it doesn't benefit you to remind me of the part you played in letting Cavazos into my home. In fact, it makes me want to lock you up again until I manage to forget just how badly behaved you've been."

My jaw clenched, and I fought to unlock it. "I'm more use to you here. On the outside."

Julia huffed and leaned forward, gripping the edge of the credenza on either side of her knees. "That remains to be seen."

"Well, it's not like I can compete with all that useful sitting around *you* do," I snapped, relishing the glower she aimed my way.

"I was well compensated for the loss of Mr. Caballero," Jake said, as if neither of us had spoken. "But please understand that no one will pay for you like Cavazos paid for him. Your Skill is common, your strength and range mediocre. You are worth more to me for your influence over your sister than as a Traveler, and you've never been worth less to me as a bodyguard." He leaned forward, eyeing me closely. "And to elaborate on the recent decline of your value, reports from the guards who protect your sister tell me she's had frequent company recently—a certain pretty former prostitute who seems quite taken with Kenley. You know what that means, don't you, Korinne?"

Yeah. I knew.

"That means that you're about to become obsolete," Julia supplied, and Jake nodded.

"So if you have any worth to claim, I suggest you start demonstrating it now. What happened with Caballero and Olivia Warren at the park?"

I sighed and swallowed the rest of the sarcasm burning in my throat. "They pulled guns on us, so Ian called up darkness, and I stepped us through it and into the wine cellar. We picked up a bottle of Cabernet for you, but I seem to have forgotten it in my rush to be threatened and insulted here today."

Okay, I swallowed *most* of the sarcasm. But neither Tower sibling seemed to notice.

"He made it dark in the middle of the day? Outside?" Julia said, and for once there was nothing in her voice but genuine surprise.

"Well, in the shade from some oak trees, but yeah."

"Amazing." Jake nodded, pleased. "Tell me about his fighting. He's good?"

"Yeah. He's fast, and strong, and accurate with a gun." I didn't want to increase Ian's value, but I wouldn't get away with lying. "We actually make a good team—he creates darkness and I use it. We could do good work for you." I flinched as soon as I heard the words falling from my own tongue. They reeked of desperation. But it's not like I was giving away my hand; we all knew what I stood to lose.

Jake leaned back in his chair, eyeing me in ruthless interest now. "Did you fuck him yet?"

I stared at the floor, silently refusing to answer. Hating how dirty the question made me feel. "He's going to sign. That's what you really want to know."

"Don't tell me what I want to know. This assignment is equal parts recruitment of Holt and punishment for you—an extension of your sentence in the basement."

I bristled, my temper flaring like heartburn. "I thought this was a chance for me to prove myself." To save my life and secure Kenley's future.

"It's all of that at once. Efficient, isn't it?" Jake smiled, and I wanted to break every tooth in his mouth. "Now, did you fuck him?"

I'd never hated Jake more.

"Yes," I said, fists clenched at my sides. I despised him for asking, and Julia for listening, and myself for answering. "But it wasn't like that."

"What was it like? Were there roses, and chocolates, and soft music?" Julia said, her words oozing saccharine venom. "Was it beautiful, Kori?"

"Fuck off."

Julia laughed. "You know, it's those clever, articulate retorts that tell me you're exactly where you belong in this organization, Korinne. On the bottom."

Jake rounded the corner of his desk to sit on the edge, less than a foot away from me now. So close he could kick me, if he wanted. Or I could kick him, if I went batshit insane in the next few minutes. "I don't give a damn what it was like, so long as it made him happy. Did you make him happy?"

"Yes." My stomach lurched over the truth of it. I *had* made him happy, and he'd made me happy, and Jake was soiling that. Defiling the memory. He was leaving his mark on a moment he'd had no part in, just by making me discuss it.

"Good. You may yet prove useful."

"I didn't do it for you," I spat, rage bubbling inside me, threatening to boil over. "I did it in *spite* of you."

He laughed out loud, not just a chuckle, but a great, full-bodied laugh. "Everything you do is for me. You're not privileged anymore, Kori, and those in the general population do what I tell them to do. And you'll fuck Holt again if I tell you to. Or *never* again, if I tell you not to."

"Oh, now, Jake, that would make the poor girl miserable!" Julia said, her voice dripping with fake sympathy. "She was telling the truth. I think she really likes him."

Jake's left brow rose. "Is that true? Do you like him?" When I didn't answer, he nudged my thigh with his foot. "Speak, Kori."

"Yes. I like him," I said through clenched teeth.

Julia closed her eyes and inhaled, like she was scenting the air. What she was really scenting was the truth of my statement. "It's more than that," she announced, glee dancing in every syllable. She loved seeing me suffer.

Jake frowned. "Is there more? Do you *love* him?"

"I don't know. Maybe." I swallowed the rest of what I'd almost said—the rest of how I felt—because it couldn't be captured in mere words. But that one word was enough for Jake.

"And he's going to sign?"

"Yes." *That* word, I wanted to take back. I wanted to chew it up and swallow it just so he couldn't have it. I didn't want Ian bound into the same hell I'd served in for the past six years.

Jake nodded, pleased. "Once he signs, you are done with him. You'll never touch him again, and you won't let him touch you. Understood?"

Tears formed in my eyes and rage burned in my chest. "Why?" I demanded, whispering to keep from shouting. "Just to make me miserable? To make him miserable? You're getting what you want. He's going to sign. What we do after that is none of your business."

Julia leaned forward in anticipation, and I could feel her watching me. Watching her brother. Waiting for him to snap. But that wasn't Jake's style.

"You're an investment, Kori. If you love him, you'll put him ahead of me in your heart, and that would be bad for business. So once he signs, you will stay away from him, and he from you. I'll send someone else to him.

Someone prettier. Someone nicer. Someone better in bed. He'll be with her and he'll forget about you, because none of this was ever real anyway. I created this little love connection, and I can take it apart just as easily."

"But you didn't," I said, when understanding surfaced with sudden brilliant clarity. "Ian and I clicked in spite of your involvement, not because of it, and you hate that. You're threatened by it, and that's why you're trying to tear us apart."

Jake stood and pulled me up by one arm, then leaned in to growl directly into my ear, and if I hadn't known he wasn't allowed to touch me, I might have missed the flare of pain behind his eyes. "If you don't watch your mouth, you might find yourself in another bed, performing a similar function for someone else who needs to be reminded that nothing and no one comes before the syndicate."

"Do it," Julia said, and the eager cruelty in her voice made me flinch. "Give her to someone else. She needs to be reminded who's the boss around here."

I held my breath, waiting for his decision, fighting the need to punch something.

Some*one*.

Julia.

Jake let me go and turned to her with a scowl, and I'd never seen him so close to losing his temper. "That *was* her reminder," he snapped. "She knows who the boss is, and she knows that's not *you*."

Julia flushed, but kept her mouth shut. A lesson I probably should have noted.

"Bring him in," Jake said. "I have a statement of intent already drafted and I want Holt here within the hour."

"An hour?" My heart thudded in my ears, racing in

panic. "I can't. I don't even know if he's out of bed yet. I need more time."

"Lies…" Julia hissed.

Jake glanced at me in surprise, and I cursed silently. Nothing in my contract actually forbade me from lying to him, but with Julia there, I wouldn't get away with it. I'd known better, but panic made me foolish and rash. I'd never been more afraid of anything than of signing Ian and losing him. Of seeing him every day, but not being allowed to touch him.

In that moment, facing monumental loss, I realized that I could love him. I might already. Either way I could no more lose him than I could lose Kenley.

I couldn't let this happen.

"One hour," Jake repeated, angry now. "He will sign, then you're done with him."

"You can throw women at him, but he won't touch them and he won't forget about me," I said, rage burning deep inside me, fueled by my terror at the thought of losing Ian. "And you can send me to whoever you want, but I won't fucking do it. I won't bring Ian in, either. If he wants to sign on his own, fine, but I won't be the one who hands him the damn pen. I want no part of it. I'll kill myself first."

Everyone had a limit, and Jake had just found mine.

"She means it," Julia said, her eyes flashing in anticipation.

"Well, she's wrong." Jake slid off his desk and onto his feet again, and he stepped so close I could smell the coffee on his breath. But I held my ground. "You won't kill yourself and you will bring Ian Holt in for the same reason you do everything else I tell you to. To keep your sister safe."

I glared back at him, my fists clenching and unclenching at my sides. Viewed through the red-tinted lenses of my own rage, everything suddenly seemed so clear. So simple.

"That threat won't work anymore. You already said I'm expendable." Kenley would be fine without me. Jake still needed her.

"You aren't afraid to die?" His gaze searched mine from a couple of inches away, and I stared back, letting him see the truth.

"There are days I fucking *wish* for death, Jake. Whether it comes from your hand or mine matters less every second, and your threat to kill me is starting to sound more like a promise."

His brows rose in interest, and he glanced at Julia, who nodded to confirm the truth in my statements, and her cruel smile was reflected on her brother's face. "Lia, go get Kenley Daniels and find a cell in the basement for her."

My pulse spiked painfully, but I refused to let my fear show. "That won't work." Why hadn't I seen it before? "If you're going to have her tortured anyway, what's her motivation to keep sealing bindings for you? Resistance pain doesn't seem so bad, when your whole world is pain."

Jake's smile gave me chills. "I'm not going to have her tortured. I'm going to have *you* tortured, and she's going to watch. How do you think your sweet little sister will react to seeing you beaten and humiliated, knowing there's nothing she can do to stop it? Do you think she'll still be psychologically stable after several days of hearing her only sister scream? Do you think she'll ever forgive herself for not being able to protect you like you protected her?"

I closed my eyes, horror rolling through me, deeper with every word he spoke. In six years, I'd never seen Jake Tower bluff. He would do it, just because I'd pissed him off. And he was right—even if I survived another stint in the basement, Kenley couldn't, even if no one laid a hand on her.

And he wouldn't let me die. There would be no out for me, and there would be no recovery for her. There was only one way to stop Tower from signing Ian, caging Kenley, and putting me back where I'd sworn I'd never go again.

We had to run. Even if we got caught. Even if we didn't get very far in the first place. Even if we spent the rest of our lives traipsing from one shadow to the next in search of peace.

"Stop," I said, when Jake waved Julia toward the door, on her way to send for Kenley. "I'll bring Ian in. Leave my sister out of this."

"She's lying," Julia warned, and Jake nodded perfunctorily, like that's what he'd expected from me all along. "Which is why she won't be going alone. Lia, ask Harris and Milligan to come in here please."

Julia stuck her head out of the office and gestured to someone I couldn't see. A minute later, she held the office door open and Milligan—one of my basement jailers—and Harris stepped into the office. Both were members of Jake's security team—men I'd worked with for years.

"You will escort Kori to pick up Ian Holt, then bring them back here. If she so much as hiccups without permission, haul her straight back to the basement, then bring me Holt and Kenley Daniels. Understood?"

Both men nodded. Neither looked at me.

Jake stepped close to me again, and every hair on my body stood on end. It was his calm that scared me. I knew people who'd killed in self-defense and many more who'd killed out of rage. But Jake was the only person I'd ever met who could order someone brutally tortured or slowly, viciously murdered without blinking an eye. Even someone he'd known for years and shared meals, and drinks, and conversations with. The suffering of others truly didn't touch him. That knowledge terrified me because it told me he wasn't human. Not in any way that counted.

And that meant there would be no mercy from him. No hope.

"This is your very last chance, Korinne," he said, so close to me his breath brushed my ear. "If you mess this up, I will bury you in the basement and forget I even have a key. Your binding will expire and your mark will die, but you'll stay buried, alone in the dark with the voices in your head, and no one will ask about you, because they'll all think you're dead. I will keep you there forever, Kori. Alive in body, but dead in every other sense of the word. If you want anything at all from the rest of your life—anything other than pain and dead shadows—think very carefully before you try to screw me over. Do you understand?"

"Yes." There was nothing more to say.

Jake nodded and stepped back, dismissing me without a word as he rounded his desk and sank into his chair. When I left the room, escorts in tow, Jake was already speaking into the phone, demanding that an Intent to Sign document be sent over for Ian Holt.

Milligan and Harris followed me silently across the foyer, up the stairs, and into the darkroom while I did my best to ignore the buzz of impatience and fury tingling beneath my skin. Jake meant what he said, but I'd meant what I said, too. I wasn't taking them to Ian, and they would never get their hands on my sister, either.

"Kori…?" Milligan said softly, as I pulled the door to the darkroom shut, closing us in with absolute darkness. "Whatever you're thinking about doing—"

"Shut the fuck up and give me your hand," I snapped, and a hand found each of mine in the dark, one thick and rough, the other smooth and strong. "When I tug, take two steps forward, then stop."

Without waiting for their acknowledgment, I pulled them forward as hard as I could and they stumbled alongside me, out of the darkroom and into Ian's bathroom, where I let them go and fumbled for the doorknob.

"Where are we?" Milligan asked, as I shoved the door open and stepped into the bedroom without them. Light flooded the bathroom, illuminating marble countertops, a hot tub and a dual-head shower.

"Holt's suite. Stay here. I'll go get him."

"Hell, no." Harris grabbed my arm and pulled me back into the bathroom. "I know what a Traveler can do."

I turned on him slowly, jaw clenched, eyes narrowed in fury. "You have no fucking idea what I can do. Let go of me."

"Not till we see Holt."

"Let her go, Harris," Milligan said, but I didn't need his help, and I knew better than to trust his words or even glance at him.

Focus. Power. Speed. Those were the tools of survival.

"She's not going anywhere without us," Harris insisted. "Start walking." He shoved me by the arm he still held, his fingers tight enough to bruise. I turned like I'd lead them into the living room, but instead I grabbed the hair dryer hanging from the wall by the door. Spinning, I jerked my arm from his grip, and swung the dryer at his head as hard as I could.

Harris reached for his gun instead of blocking my arm. The dryer slammed into his temple before he could draw his weapon, and he crumpled to the floor, unconscious, without even a whimper. Blood dribbled from the gash in his head, and pain ripped through mine—the beginnings of resistance pain for violating my oath of loyalty.

"*Damn* it, Kori," Milligan swore as his partner fell at our feet, one arm draped over my shoe. Milligan already had his gun aimed at my thigh. "Are you *trying* to make Tower kill you?"

"Yeah. But that won't do it." Trying to ignore the steady waves of pain deep inside my head, I bent and pulled the pistol from Harris's holster, and Milligan tensed, but didn't shoot. "Was he there? In the basement?" I asked, but Milligan only frowned in confusion. "Did he *fucking watch?*" I demanded, and Milligan nodded.

I flipped the safety switch off and shot Harris in the thigh with his own gun. I wanted to kill him. The only thing stopping me was the knowledge that the more I violated my oath, the worse I'd hurt.

"Motherfucker!" Milligan shouted, as the echo of violence thundered around us. He raised his aim to my chest. "Are you *insane?*"

"I might just be." I stepped over Harris's prone form and into the bedroom, and Milligan still didn't fire. Because unlike his partner, he wasn't an idiot. "I'm guessing we have about five minutes before building security gets here. I can tie you up or shoot you. Your call."

"Kori, stop!" he shouted as I bent over the nightstand and ripped the phone cord from the wall. "Don't make me shoot you!"

"Holt isn't here, and if you shoot me, you'll never find him." I glanced at him over my shoulder and shoved the nightstand back into place. "Tower's already gonna be pissed at me, but if you go back without Holt, you'll be on his shit list, too." I held up the cord in one hand, Harris's gun in the other, as Milligan considered, his aim steady. "But if you give me your gun, I'll take you someplace safe and you can start running. That's the only shot you have now."

"Where's Holt?"

I leaned against the glass-topped desk and glanced at the alarm clock next to the bed. "Tick tock, Milligan."

"What the hell is *wrong* with you?" he demanded, sweat beading on his forehead. He exhaled slowly and held my gaze. "Just give Tower what he wants, and we'll all walk away from this intact."

"Intact?" I grabbed the desk lamp and hurled it past his head and he flinched when it smashed against the wall at his back. "Do I sound intact to you? Did you miss the part where Jake tried to drive me insane with solitude and torture? Or maybe you missed the part where it fuckin' worked! Shoot me!" I shouted, advancing on him with my arms spread, gun held loosely in my right hand, my head throbbing so badly my vision was starting to blur.

Milligan lifted the gun again, aiming at my chest, but his finger wasn't even on the trigger. He knew what would happen if he killed me without finding out where Ian was.

"Shoot me, you fucking coward!"

"Take me to him," Milligan said, like we were bargaining. "Just take me to him, and you can go. I won't try to stop you."

I rolled my eyes and reached for his gun, and his finger finally found the trigger. "If you're going to shoot me do it. Otherwise, hand the damn thing over."

Milligan frowned, and I read determination in his eyes an instant before he lowered his gun, aiming for my leg. I threw a fist up and out, knocking his arm to the side. His shot went wild. The bullet tore a chunk of wood from the headboard to my left.

I slammed his gun arm into the edge of the desk as hard as I could. Bone crunched, and Milligan howled. He dropped his gun and I picked it up while he clutched his fractured arm to his chest.

"Kori…" he mumbled, as footsteps thundered toward us from the hall outside the front door.

"Did you watch?" I aimed both guns at his chest, but he only shook his head, not in answer, but in refusal to respond. "Did you fucking watch!" I demanded as the first fist pounded on the door to Ian's suite.

"Mr. Holt? Are you okay in there?" some hotel employee called from the hall. "We heard gunfire! The police are on their way!"

"Not for sport, Kori, I swear," Milligan said. "I was working. It made me sick, I swear on my life!"

"Good." I shot him in the left shoulder with Harris's

gun and in the right with his own. "That's why you're still alive."

Milligan stumbled back into the desk, sucking in deep breaths, face already pale from shock. I staggered on my feet as the pain in my head echoed deep in my stomach, and my hands started to shake. Then I pulled in a deep breath and stepped past him and into the bathroom, as something slammed into the front door. Security was trying to break it down.

Harris's feet were blocking the bathroom door, so I had to shove him over to make it close. Armed and surrounded by true darkness, I sucked in one deep, calming breath, trying to get a handle on the agony my body had become. Then, as wood splintered and the front door gave way, I stepped over Harris's body and out through the darkness.

Twenty-Six

Ian

When Kori was gone, her sister glared into the dark bedroom at me, though I was pretty sure she couldn't actually see me. And for just a moment, the opportunity I was passing up made my head hurt and my fingers itch for action. I was alone with Kenley Daniels. I could kill her in seconds, and my brother's body would stop shutting itself down and finally start to heal.

As a bonus, I'd be permanently crippling Tower's empire. He'd never find another Binder as strong as Kenley, and with her blood no longer flowing, actively reinforcing the bindings she'd sealed for him, most of them would break. Flesh marks would die. People would go free.

That was the very least he deserved, for what he'd done to Kori.

But if I killed Kenley, I wouldn't just be crippling one monster—Tower—I'd be creating another one. Myself. And Kori would never forgive me.

Before I could master my thoughts enough to speak,

Kenley stomped out of sight and I followed her through the tiny square of hallway, across a small living area and into the kitchen, where she waved one hand at a bar stool across the counter. I sat, and she watched me, assessing me, like I was an obstacle to be overcome. Though she probably had no idea how close to right she was.

"Coffee?" she said at last, and I nodded. Kenley opened a drawer and pulled out both a bag of coffee grounds and the cutest little .22 pistol, then set them side by side on the counter. "I don't trust you."

It took most of my self-control to keep from laughing. Her gun was a peashooter, and if she'd been any good with it, she never would have set it within my reach. But I respected her intent.

"Good. You shouldn't trust anyone."

"I trust Kori," she said, running water in the coffee carafe.

"And Kori trusts me," I pointed out, voicing the part of the equation that was obviously troubling her.

She turned off the water and set the full carafe on the counter, eyeing me skeptically. Then she pulled a push-pin from the corkboard hanging on one side of the fridge, and before I realized what she was doing, she'd grabbed my left palm and shoved the pin into it.

"Whoa!" I tried to snatch my hand back, but she wouldn't let go, and I couldn't get loose without hurting her. Which was sorely tempting, considering she'd just breached my skin and spilled my blood—the greatest affront possible against anyone who understood the power inherent in blood. "What the *hell* are you doing?"

"Shh." Kenley held her left index finger to her lips, smiling behind it with a glance at the front door, beyond which—I gathered—one of Tower's men stood guard.

Then she swiped that same finger across the drop of blood welling from the hole in my palm.

"Whatever you're about to do, don't," I growled as she let go of my wrist and tossed me a paper tower for my bleeding hand. Instead of answering, she grabbed a notepad from the front of the fridge and a pen from the countertop and jotted three words on the paper.

"Speak only truth," she mumbled as she scribbled, and my blood chilled in my veins.

"No!" I whispered fiercely, but before I could grab the paper, she pressed her bloody index finger onto it, leaving a smear of my blood beneath the words. Binding me to them.

"Son of a bitch!" I hissed. My heart beat against the inside of my chest like a captive beast demanding freedom. I'd never been bound to anyone or anything, and the sudden caged feeling pissed me off and made me want to strike out just to prove I still could. I lunged across the counter, grabbing for the impromptu binding, but she snatched the paper out of reach before my fingers had more than brushed the edge.

Kenley folded the paper and stuffed it into her back pocket, and I realized two things at once. First, I'd have to hurt her to take the binding and destroy it, and I'd sworn to Kori I wouldn't let anyone hurt her sister. Second, Kenley Daniels was not the sweet, naive young woman her sister had described. Not entirely, anyway. She was fast, and she was smart. And she had guts.

Just like her sister.

"It won't hold," I said, though I was virtually certain I was wrong about that. An involuntary binding—especially one sealed without the Binder's blood—wouldn't hold for most Binders, but Kenley wasn't most Binders.

If she had been, neither of us would have been in Tower's territory in the first place.

Kenley flipped open the top of the coffeepot and poured the water in without spilling a drop, though she watched me the whole time. "Based on your reaction, Mr. Holt, one might think you have something to hide."

"Everyone has something to hide," I growled, angry, but not sure what to do about it, a dilemma I'd only previously experienced with Kori, who was enough to drive a man mad and make him love the journey.

She set a coffee filter into its cup. "True. But some secrets can get you killed. Are you sleeping with my sister?"

"I don't have to answer that," I said when I realized she'd left me a loophole. Had she done that on purpose? If I spoke, I could only tell the truth. But I could choose not to speak at all.

"No, you don't. But a refusal to answer is as revealing as the answer itself. So, have you had sex with my sister?"

"Yes." She was right. Silence was as good as an admission. "But for the record, you're invading her privacy as well as mine with questions like that."

Kenley's brows shot up in surprise, then she nodded again. "Fair enough. One more question, and we'll leave that issue alone. Did she want it? Did she have the chance to say no?"

"That's two questions. And yes to both." I leaned closer to catch her gaze. I wanted her to understand that I was answering not because I had to, but because I wanted her to know. "I'm not one of your heartless syndicate thugs, Kenley. I would never hurt her. Never. In fact, that's the only reason I haven't already taken your juvenile little oath and burned it."

Her gaze held mine, and I felt like we were facing off at high noon, in some long-abandoned Western town. "We all use the weapons at our disposal, Mr. Holt. This is the only way I have to look out for her, and I'm damn well going to do it."

"Fine." I could respect that. "Ask what you want to know."

"Are you going to sign with Jake?" Kenley said, and I blinked in frustration. I'd expected more questions about me and Kori. Stuff I could answer without getting anyone hurt.

"No." She'd know the truth whether I answered or not, and I didn't like being forced into things any better than Kori did.

"Does Kori know that?"

"No. I had to tell her I would sign, to protect...her." I'd almost said "you both." *To protect you both.* But I couldn't be sure Kenley knew she was in real danger, especially considering she didn't know why Kori had brought me over in the first place. "I lied to keep her from having to tell Tower something he wouldn't want to hear."

"If you're not going to sign, why did you come here?"

I exhaled, suddenly eager for some of the coffee she hadn't yet started brewing. "I won't answer that, and for the record, you're putting all three of us at risk with this line of questioning." She now knew I was in Tower's territory under false pretenses, and if and when he asked her, she'd have to tell him what she knew.

"Something's wrong," Kenley said. "More wrong than usual. How am I supposed to know how much danger any of us are in if I don't ask questions?" She pressed the brew button and coffee began to drip into the pot. Kenley stared at it, her forehead furrowed, her lips pressed together as she thought, obviously trying to decide which verbal land mines to avoid and which to hit head-on. "Does you being here have something to do with my sister?"

"She's not the reason I came to the city. But she's the reason for nearly everything I've done since I met her."

"Why does Kori think I need to be protected, today in particular?" she asked, and I picked at the edge of the Formica where it was starting to lift from the countertop, trying to decide whether or not to answer that. "Please. If it involves me, I have a right to know."

"Because Tower threatens you to keep Kori in line."

Kenley rolled her eyes. "I've known that from the beginning. What's different about today? What does any of it have to do with you?"

I exhaled slowly, hoping Kori wouldn't hate me for what I was about to say. Because Kenley was right—she did have a right to know. "If I don't sign on, Tower's going to kill Kori and put you in the basement in her place."

Her face paled so fast I thought for a minute that she'd pass out. "I don't... I can't..." She didn't seem to know how to finish either sentence.

I carried my stool into the kitchen and set it on the floor behind her, then started opening cabinets in search of coffee mugs.

"Kill Kori?" she said, sinking onto the stool, and I could only nod. "And put me...?"

"In the basement. But we're not going to let that happen." I pulled two mugs from the third cabinet I'd tried and pressed the pause button on the coffeepot, then filled them both.

"You can't stop it," she whispered, accepting the mug I pushed toward her. "You can't stop Jake."

"No. Not on my own, anyway. At first I thought I could just kill Tower, but—"

"No, you can't!"

"Because of his successor. I know."

"You know who it is?" She reached absently for a container of powdered creamer, and her hand shook as she lifted it.

"No. Do you?"

Kenley nodded. "I can't tell you who it is, but I can tell you that things will be worse for us both—maybe for all three of us—if Jake dies."

Jonah. It had to be. Who else would both Kori and her sister be so terrified of?

"We don't have to kill Jake." Though, personally, I was on board with killing both him *and* Jonah. "I can stop him from hurting Kori—with your help." And if she could break the seal binding Kori, she could break the seal binding Steven, too.

She poured the creamer but forgot to stir it. "How?"

But she wasn't ready to hear that just yet. I'd have to work up to it. "Kori loves you more than anything, you know," I said, and Kenley nodded, still dazed with shock, sipping from her mug, and when she lowered it, a clump of powdered creamer stuck to her upper lip. "She's given up her whole life to protect you, and because of that, she's been through things I can't imagine."

"There was nothing I could do." Her voice shook. "Jake wouldn't tell me where she was. I couldn't help her."

"She's melting down, Kenley. They fucked her up in that cell. She's out now, but it's not over for her. One minute, she's spitting nails and throwing punches, and the next, she's cowering in the corner, fighting flashbacks and panic attacks."

Kenley nodded miserably. "I know. She screams in the middle of the night, and the first time I tried to wake her up, she punched me before she even had her eyes open. I've done everything I can think of to help her, but she won't talk about what happened, and therapy isn't covered under Tower's medical plan. Not that she'd go if it was. Not that he'd let her. He wants her to suffer."

"We can help her. You and I." I held her gaze, trying to emphasize the importance of what I was saying. "She's given up everything for you. It's time to give something back."

"How?" Her mug shook in her hands.

"Let her go, Kenley. Break the binding keeping her here."

Her head swiveled back and forth, her eyes wide with terror. "I can't."

"Yes, you can. You're the *only* one who can. It's time to set her free."

She shook her head, and I could see her thoughts flicker over her face before they fell from her tongue. "I can't. I can't be here alone. I'm not strong like she is."

"Bullshit." My hand slammed into the counter. "You pulled a gun on me, then stole my blood. You are as strong as you need to be, and you *can* survive this place. I couldn't say it if I didn't believe it was true, right?" I said, holding up my palm to remind her of the binding she'd sealed without my consent. "You can even survive the basement. But if you free Kori, she and I will do everything within our power to make sure you never wind up there. You know she'd never abandon you, and she'll be even better able to help you when she isn't bound to obey Tower. Do this for her. Do this for all three of us."

Kenley studied whatever she saw in my eyes for one long moment, then she closed her own in thought. Or maybe in prayer. "Yes," she said finally, and when her gaze met mine again, I recognized the determination shining in her eyes. I'd seen that same look on Kori at least a dozen times since we'd met. "What do I have to do?"

"I've heard that a Binder can break her own seal if she remembers enough specifics about the particular contract." Which was what worried me about Steven's binding—if my hunch was correct, she'd never even seen the binding her blood had sealed.

But Kenley shook her head. "I've tried. I tried for years to break the seal binding Kori to three of her friends, and I can't do it. And I remember every word of that oath. I wrote it."

"Try it," I insisted. "Just think about Kori's contract, as specifically as you can, and remove your will from the seal."

"Okay." She set her coffee down and took a deep breath, then closed her eyes and laid her hands flat on the counter. Her forehead furrowed and her lips pressed together. And she sat like that for nearly a minute, her eyes rolling behind closed lids as she thought.

Then, finally, she looked at me again, and I could read the outcome in her slumped shoulders and the disheartened way she rubbed her forehead, fighting resistance pain, because what we were attempting was no doubt a violation of her oath of loyalty to Tower. "Try it again," I said, before she could tell me she'd failed. "You have to do it. You have to set her free, or she's going to die."

"I tried!" Kenley's eyes watered, and though she and Kori were only two years apart, she suddenly looked much younger than her twenty-six years. "I don't know how to remove my will. I don't even know what that means."

"It means you have to want to break the seal." And as soon as the words left my mouth, I realized what was wrong. "You don't want to, do you? Deep down, you don't want to break the seal because you're scared of being alone here."

She blinked and those tears rolled down her cheeks. "What they did to her in the basement—they broke her. And if they can break Kori—the strongest person I've ever known—they can break me. I want her to be free. But I'm terrified of being here without her."

"Okay." *Patience, Ian.* I'd been a soldier when I was younger than Kenley, and Kori had obviously been fighting all her life. But we were the exceptions, right? Kenley's fears were rational; who wouldn't be scared of what Kori had been through? She just needed the proper motivation—a dose of the raw truth.

"If you don't set her free, you're going to be alone anyway, because they'll kill her. They'll fucking kill her, Kenley, and then you *will* be sent to the basement. And there's nothing she can do for you from beyond the grave."

More tears fell, and her chin started to quiver.

"Try it again," I insisted, and she closed her eyes as the first tear rolled down her cheek and fell onto the countertop. "This is what she needs," I whispered, as she breathed slowly in and out. "This is what *you* need. You *have* to want this."

"I'm trying…"

"Try harder," I demanded. "If you don't free her, they will lock Kori in a basement cell and they'll put you in the one next to her. They'll shoot her, or stab her, but somewhere not immediately fatal, because they want her to suffer awhile. They want you to hear her scream."

"Stop," Kenley whispered, clutching the edge of the counter.

"That's good. Get used to saying that, because it'll be the last thing Kori hears. You, screaming for it to stop. Because whoever Tower sends into that cell with you will beat you to within an inch of your life. He'll strip you and humiliate you. He will fuck you while you scream, and Kori will hear it all while she bleeds out on the floor in the room next door, and she'll know exactly what's happening to you, because that's what happened to her."

"Stop it!" Kenley cried, tears pouring down her face, the guard outside forgotten.

"You stop it!" I hated myself for what I was saying almost as much as I hated her in that moment. I hated us both for our inability to help Kori, not to mention Steven and Meghan. For our weakness, where they had nothing but strength and sheer determination to live. But their own strength wasn't enough to save them. They needed help. *"You* make it stop, Kenley. Only you can do it. Free her so she can fight, and we can help her. Break the binding, for both of your sakes. Save your sister. You owe it to her."

Kenley gasped, and her eyes flew open. She turned to me, eyes wide, jaw slack, tears still running down her face. "I think I did it. Something...snapped. Inside. I think I broke the seal."

A rustling noise drew my gaze up, and I found Kori staring at us from across the room, a gun clutched in each fist, the back of one hand pressed to the chain marks tattooed on her upper arm. "What the *fuck* did you just do?"

Twenty-Seven

Kori

Flames licked my upper left arm, a brief burst of pain that died almost as soon as it had flared to life. I tried to touch it, to feel the heat, but I still held Harris's gun, and that was just as well, because the burning had already stopped. But I could still feel the shape of it, like an echo on my skin, in the form of two chain links.

My headache was gone, in spite of the guns I still held. My stomach felt fine, though I'd disobeyed Jake on purpose this time.

My marks were dead.

"Kenley? What happened?" I demanded, trying to process her tears, and Ian's look of shocked relief, and the newly dead marks on my arm, all while the clock ticked in my head, counting down the minutes until either Jake or the police came looking for me.

"Where'd you get those?" Ian rounded the end of the counter and crossed the room toward me, eyeing my new double handfuls of death. "Whose are they?"

"Jake sent a couple of men back with me. I ditched them at your hotel. What just happened to my arm?"

"Kenley broke the seal on your oath."

I blinked, stunned, though I could feel the truth of his statement.

"You're serious?" I hadn't expected to see my marks die. Ever. I'd been sure *I* would die first.

"Of course I'm serious. Are Tower's men alive?" Ian took Milligan's gun from my left hand, checked the safety, then tucked it into the waistband of his pants.

"They were when I left. Hope you didn't need anything from the suite. Pretty sure it's all being logged into police evidence as we speak." Ian's eyes widened. "Don't worry." I stepped past him on my way to the kitchen, where my sister was bent over the counter clutching her head in both hands, eyes squeezed shut in pain. "They know you had nothing to do with it. I left a conscious witness."

"Kori, what the hell happened?" Ian demanded, staring after me.

I set Harris's gun on the counter, then pulled a clean rag from the drawer to the left of the sink and ran cold water on it. "Jake told me to bring you in. Immediately." I helped Kenley onto the bar stool and pressed the cold rag to her forehead, offering what little comfort I could for what was obviously severe resistance pain from breaking her oath of loyalty to Jake.

I could hardly even process what she'd done, but I knew exactly how badly she must be hurting. "You okay? I need you to breathe through it, Kenni. We're leaving in five minutes and you have to pack."

"I'm trying." Kenley took the rag from me, and her hand shook. "Are we running? There's nowhere to go."

She moaned and clutched her stomach, and her rag fell to the floor. Then her hand slid into her back pocket and pulled out a folded scrap of paper, which she set on the counter, then pushed toward Ian. "Burn it."

Ian grabbed a match from the box on the counter, then lit it and set the paper on fire. When the flames reached his finger and thumb, he dropped the charred scrap into the sink and exhaled slowly.

"What was that?" I asked, bending to pick up the rag.

"Nothing. How long will this last?" Ian asked, watching Kenley.

"I don't know. I've never seen her disobey before, and she picked a hell of a way to start. Fortunately, it's a terminal breach of her oath, so if she can ride this out, she'll be fine." Unlike an ongoing breach—such as refusing to obey an order—for which she'd suffer until she either gave in or died.

I contorted my shoulder for a good look at my left arm, where the two interlocking chain link tattoos had faded from iron-gray into a dull, muted gray. "How'd she do it? Did she burn my contract?" How the hell had she even gotten hold of it?

Kenley shook her head, one fist pressed against her gut, as if she could physically stop the pain. "I unsealed the binding." Her voice was strained and her legs were shaking on the stool. "You're free, Kori."

I blinked at her. Then I glanced at Ian, brows raised in question. He nodded. I burst into tears. "How? Why?" Sniffling, I wiped my cheeks, but the girly fuckin' tears just kept coming.

Kenley was crying now, too, but obviously trying to hold it back. "He said if I didn't break your binding, Tower would kill you and put me..." Her words faded into unspoken thought and her mouth twisted into a grimace beneath another wave of agony. "So I just... I stopped wanting you to be bound to him."

"What?" When had she ever wanted me bound to Jake?

"She removed her will from the seal," Ian said as I rewet her rag and blotted her face. "The only way I could explain that to her was to tell her she had to stop wanting you to be bound to Tower." He shrugged, hands shoved into the pockets of his jeans, claiming no credit for an event he'd obviously set into motion. "So, now you're free."

I smiled—I couldn't help it—and for one short moment, I enjoyed the most wonderful words I'd ever heard.

Then I realized that in securing my freedom, Ian and Kenley had just screwed things up for his brother.

"Jake will never help you now." I rubbed the dead marks on my arm, horrified by what my freedom had cost him.

Ian glanced at the ground, and guilt left deep lines in his forehead when he met my gaze again. "I don't need him," he said, his voice soft and low, like he was making a confession. "I never did. I need her." He glanced at Kenley again, and I frowned as her grip on the countertop began to ease, the resistance pain finally ebbing.

Kenley's mouth opened, and I could almost see the question hanging on her lips, but before she could ask what we both wanted to know, her front door opened and the guard-of-the-day stepped into the living room, gun drawn, but aimed at the floor.

"I'm supposed to take you all to Tower. Now."

Shit. I was hoping to be gone before Jake got his ducks in a row.

"And if we won't go?" I stepped in front of Harris's gun on the counter, so he wouldn't see it. If I used it, others would hear and come running. Ian had Milligan's gun—also absent silencer—tucked into the back of his pants, out of view unless he turned.

"I shoot you and take them," Kenley's guard said. "You're acceptable collateral damage."

"Always good to hear." I turned toward the hall. "Just let me grab my phone."

"Stop." He raised his gun, aiming for my chest, and I tried not to look like my breath had frozen in my throat. "One more step and I'll shoot you."

"I need my fucking phone. I want to talk to Jake on the way."

"Let her get it." He nodded at Kenley, his aim never wavering from my chest. "Jake said not to let you two out of my sight," he added, glancing from me to Ian, who looked alert, but seemingly unarmed with his hands at his sides.

"Fine." I turned to Kenley, so that the guard couldn't see my face. She sat up straight, carefully hiding the last of her resistance pain. "The phone's on my dresser. It's on silent." I didn't dare emphasize that last word—even a stupid guard might pick up on what I was really asking for—so I lifted both brows instead, hoping she understood.

Kenley nodded solemnly, eyes wide with fear, hands still shaking as she stepped into my bedroom. The light went on, and I turned back to the guard, ready to capture and hold his attention.

"I can't believe they let you carry a gun. I mean, how can you see where you're aiming, with your head stuck so far up Jake's ass?"

The guard glared at me and started to speak, then something over my shoulder caught his attention. He raised his gun, but before he could squeeze the trigger, a *thwup* echoed behind me and he stumbled backward into the door, one hand over the new hole in his gun arm, blood pouring between his fingers.

He started to raise his gun again, in spite of the pain. I turned and took the silenced nine millimeter from my sister and squeezed the trigger twice more. Two new holes appeared in the guard's chest, and he slid down the door to sit on the tiled entry, his eyes sightless, his mouth hanging open. His fingers relaxed, and the gun fell to the tile between his thighs.

Something thumped behind me, and I turned to see my sister on the floor, leaning against the living room wall. "Kenley?" I crouched next to her as I flicked the safety on my gun, and Ian was there with us in an instant.

"I shot him," she mumbled.

"Your aim's definitely improving."

"Kori, I *shot* the man who was here to protect me." Her hands were shaking harder now, and I couldn't tell how much of that was from resisting standing orders from Jake and how much was shock.

"You didn't kill him," Ian pointed out. "You just kept him from shooting Kori."

"Anyway, he wasn't here to protect you. He was here to do whatever Jake told him to do, and Jake told him to bring you in. That's the opposite of protecting you." I reached down for her arm and hauled her up. "Hold it together, Kenley. We have to get out of here."

She tried to pull her arm free, but I held on to it, looking right into her eyes to emphasize the importance of what I was going to say. "Call Van, if you want to bring her with us. It's her choice, but if you can break my binding, you can break hers, too, right? And your own? We'll all run, and when we're safe, we'll see what we can do for Ian's brother."

My range wouldn't be great with three other people in tow, but I could take them, even if we had to make several layovers to get where we were going.

"What's wrong with his brother?" Kenley asked, already digging her phone from her pocket. But before I could answer, Ian shook his head.

"She can free...Van?"

He glanced at my sister, and she nodded. "Assuming she sealed Van's contract and remembers enough specifics about it. But I'm guessing Kenley didn't seal her own binding." He turned to her again for confirmation, and Kenley nodded again.

"Barker did it." He'd been Jake's top Binder until Kenley was recruited as a naive, twenty-year-old prodigy.

"Then only Barker can break the seal." Ian frowned at her. "How do you not know any of this?"

"Jake wouldn't teach her anything she could use against him," I said as the ramifications of what Ian had just explained sluggishly came together in my head. "So wait. I'm free, and Van can be free. But Kenley can't?"

"Not right this minute, no." Ian sighed and met my gaze with a somber one of his own, and the clock in my head kept ticking, driving me as surely as my own pulse did. "There are three ways to free Kenley. We can find her contract and burn it. We can kill the Binder who sealed the contract. Or—and this is a long shot—we can convince him to break the seal himself, just like Kenley did for you."

"Okay, we don't know where the contract is, and I don't want to kill anyone," Kenley said.

"Do you know where Barker is?" Ian asked, and we both nodded.

"Tower keeps him protected, but he's not as hard to get at as Kenley is." Especially for me.

"Do you think you can convince him to break the seal?"

I held up my silenced nine millimeter. "I can be pretty damn convincing." But I was running out of places to stick guns. I needed a holster. A double.

Ian shook his head. "You can't scare him into it. He can't remove his will as long as he wants her to be bound to Jake, and scaring him won't change that."

"So we explain that he only lives if she goes free. He'll want to break her binding to save his own life, right?"

Ian shrugged. "I guess it's worth a try."

I turned back to Kenley. "Throw some clothes and essentials into a bag and call Van while you pack. Don't tell her what's going on, though, or she'll have to rat us out. Just tell her you want to see her. You can break her binding once we're on our way." I was afraid if she tried to break it without telling Vanessa what she was doing, Vanessa would feel the burn on her arm and accidentally give us away before she understood what was going on.

Kenley nodded sluggishly, and I laid one hand on her arm. "You okay? Resistance pain?" I asked. The pain from unsealing my oath had passed, but as long as we were actively working against Jake, she would be hurting, and if we couldn't break her bindings soon, that hurt would quickly become unbearable.

"Just a headache so far." Kenley dialed as she crossed

the living room, then stopped cold less than a foot from the hall, phone pressed to her ear.

"Kenley? What's wrong?" I asked, and she turned slowly, eyes wide in terror, index finger pressed to her lips in the universal sign for "shh." She pressed a button on her phone, and Jake Tower's voice greeted the entire room, on speakerphone.

"I heard her, Kenley. I know your sister's there. Is Holt there with you?"

Kenley glanced at me, the phone shaking in her hand, and I shook my head.

"No," she said, phone held near her mouth.

"I know you're lying, but I'm not angry," Jake said, and Kenley swallowed nervously. "I understand why you'd want to protect them both. I also understand that you're not responsible for the massive clusterfuck your sister has just laid on my doorstep. Did she tell you what she did in Holt's hotel suite?"

Kenley nodded, then when she realized he couldn't see that, she whispered, "Yes."

"Avoiding police interference cost me quite a bit of money. More than your sister's service is worth to me. More than her life is worth. Do you understand?"

"Yes," Kenley said, her voice no stronger now.

"Good. Then you'll understand how very generous I'm being with the offer I'm about to extend to her. Korinne, can you hear me?"

"Fuck off, Jake," I snapped, picking up the gun on the counter, just for the comforting feel and weight of it.

"Kori, I'm willing to let you live if you bring your sister and Ian Holt to me right now. Walk them right into my darkroom, and you will all three live. You have my word."

"No way in hell," I said, more than loud enough to be heard.

Jake chuckled, but there was no true amusement in the sound. "That must hurt. Why don't you be a good girl and do as you're told, and that nasty headache will go away."

I glanced from Kenley to Ian in surprise, and we all seemed to come to the same conclusion—Tower didn't know my marks were dead. And I saw no need to tell him.

"I'd rather die from resistance pain than bring either of them to you," I said, careful that every word I said was true, in case Julia was listening.

"Okay, we tried this the civilized way," Tower said, evidently speaking to all three of us. "Now I'm going to give you one guess where I'm standing, and who's with me. I'll even give you a hint."

There was a moment of quiet over the line, then a scream cut through the silence like a scalpel through flesh. I knew that voice.

"Vanessa!" Kenley screeched, and Tower laughed again.

"Good guess. Vanessa and I are in the basement, and she's just had her first taste of my displeasure. Tell them what happened, Vanessa," Tower said, and Van's ragged, uneven breathing grew louder as the phone was moved closer to her.

"Cut," she gasped, and the word was bitten off, like she'd swallowed back sobs. "Fucker cut me."

"And I'll let him do it again," Tower said as Vanessa's shocked pants faded. "Once every fifteen minutes until you show up. If the three of you aren't here in ninety minutes, the last cut will be across her throat."

"Kenley, don't—" Vanessa shouted, but her words were swallowed by another scream of pain, and tears rolled down Kenley's face.

"Ninety minutes," Tower repeated. Then the phone went dead.

"Oh, shit. Shitshitshit." Kenley sank onto the couch in shock, her phone still cradled in her hands. She was pale from ongoing resistance pain, and her hands were starting to shake again. "What are we going to do?"

"Surely he won't kill her," Ian said. "If she's dead, what's our motivation to turn ourselves in?"

If Jake said he'd kill her, he'd kill her. Then he'd find new motivation. But I couldn't say that with my sister listening.

"But he'll cut her!" Kenley shrieked.

"There's nothing we can do about that," I said, brushing past her and into my bedroom. "But we're going to get her back, and then we're out of here. All four of us. You can break her binding, and we'll figure out how to break yours, even if it means killing Barker."

"The minute someone sees your dead marks and reports them, Tower will know Kenley broke your binding," Ian said, following me into my room. "And he'll know you're going after Barker to free Kenley. Beyond that, if we get caught and Vanessa's binding is already broken, he'll have no reason to keep her alive."

I settled my double holster onto my shoulders and adjusted the straps, watching him in the mirror. "So Kenley won't break Van's binding yet, and he won't know she broke mine." I turned to my sister as I slid the silenced nine millimeter into the custom left hip holster. "Kenni, get a black permanent marker."

While she rooted through kitchen drawers, I handed

Ian a spare double holster and he chose one of my extras to go along with Milligan's gun, which he obviously meant to keep.

When Kenley came back with the marker, I exchanged it for a slim folding knife. I would have given her a gun, except that she was still bound to Jake, and the gun would be easier for him to make her use against us.

Then I turned to Ian with my left sleeve pulled up over my shoulder and handed him the marker. "Try to stay inside the lines."

Twenty-Eight

Ian

"How does it look?" Kori asked as I put the cap back on the marker.

"Not bad. Unless he carries a magnifying glass, he'll never know the difference. How did you know that would work?"

She stood and examined her arm in the bathroom mirror. "I used a wig and a black permanent marker to sneak around the east side a couple of times when I first came to the city, before anyone really knew who I was."

"So, what's the plan?" Kenley asked from the doorway, twisting her fingers together. She hadn't stopped fidgeting since Tower hung up on her, and she kept ducking into the living room to check the clock hanging over the door.

I'd been checking the time, too. Eight minutes until her girlfriend would get cut again. No wonder she was melting down.

"Well, even if Jake doesn't know my marks are dead,

I'll never make it to the basement like this," Kori said, patting her guns in their holsters.

"What if we go in from the basement?" I said, from my seat on the edge of the tub. "If I could get down there on my own and call up true darkness, you could come through it, right? We could grab Vanessa and go."

"Can you do that?" Surprise shone through the shock still lingering in Kenley's eyes. "Can you make darkness deep enough to blind the infrared lights?"

Kori's brows rose. "Kenni, he can block out the fuckin' *sun.*"

"Not the *whole* sun," I amended. "Just a little of its light."

"Daylight?" Kenley gaped at me. "You can kill daylight?" she said, and I nodded. "No wonder Jake wants you."

"Well, he's not going to get me. He's not going to get any of us."

Kori nodded, obviously thinking. "Okay, we'll drop Kenley somewhere safe, then you'll turn yourself in to Jake. Once you're in the house, find some excuse to go to the basement. Say you won't sign until you know Van's okay, and if that doesn't work, do whatever it takes to get down there, and I'll come get you both. But take this gun and leave that one here." She pulled the pistol from my right holster and replaced it with one from her dresser.

"Why this one?"

"Because they'll confiscate your weapons, but if you don't try to bring some in, you'll look weak. And I don't mind losing that one."

I gave her a grim nod, trying not to show how much this plan was growing on me. If Van was in the basement, Jonah would be, too. I would get a shot at him, and that would make the whole thing worth it. But...

"But my brother comes first."

Both Daniels sisters looked at me like I'd lost my mind. "Ian, Van's being tortured," Kori said.

"So is Steven. He's been on the verge of death for two weeks. His organs are failing. He can't talk. He can't sleep. He's so pale you can almost see through his skin. He's dying, and I've made him suffer two days longer than he had to because I didn't want to hurt either of you. But now that I know Kenley can break his binding, we have to go help him. Now."

"Wait, he's in *breach?*" Kori's eyes were so big the rest of her features looked smaller in comparison. "You said he was bound, but you never said he was in breach of his binding. How could he survive that for two weeks?"

"Meghan's a Healer."

"Who's Meghan?" Kenley asked, and Kori answered with only a brief glance at her.

"Steven's girlfriend." She turned back to me. "Meghan's been healing him for two weeks?"

I nodded. "Almost two and a half, now. They're both hanging on by a thread, and I came here to break the binding. And for that I need Kenley."

"What the hell are you talking about?" Kenley said, crossing her arms over her chest so I couldn't see them shake—a clear sign of the resistance pain she was fighting.

Kori's hard gaze flicked from me to the clock over the microwave—we were all counting the minutes. "But you said she can only break bindings she actually sealed..."

"Yeah. She's the one who bound Steven. We don't know what or who she bound him to, but we know it was her. The Tracker recognized her psychic signature—he evidently sees it a lot in this area." Because Kenley had bound nearly three quarters of Tower's current employees, according to Aaron's sources.

"Whoa." Kori stepped away from me, eyes narrowed on me in suspicion. "You never said Kenley was the one who bound your brother."

"I couldn't. I couldn't tell you any of this while you were still bound to Tower." And now Kenley was suffering the resistance pain I'd tried so hard to spare Kori.

"He works for Jake?" Kenley frowned in both confusion and pain. She hadn't caught on yet to the truth already surfacing through her sister's ambient anger. "Because I haven't bound anyone to anything except service to Jake in six and a half years."

"This would have been sometime before that," I said, watching Kori even as I answered her sister.

"Why are you here, Ian?" Kori demanded, her voice as soft and dangerous as I'd ever heard it. "Why are you *really* here?" Her hand hovered at her hip, ready to draw on me like a Wild West outlaw. A tiny, scary, blonde outlaw.

"Kori, wait..."

"At least have the balls to admit it. You didn't come for her help. You came here to kill her," Kori said, and Kenley stared at us both, pain and confusion warring for control of her expression. "That description you gave Jake—that wasn't me, it was Kenley. You requested her so you could get close enough to kill her."

"That doesn't make any sense," Kenley said, hunched over now from the pain in her stomach. "I didn't bind your brother. I've never even heard of him."

Kori drew her gun. "Kenni, go to your room." Tears

filled her eyes, but her aim didn't waver. And I didn't draw against her. I couldn't.

"I'm not going to hurt her." I held my hands up, palms out, demonstrating how harmless I was. "I gave you my word."

"What good is your word, if you've been lying the whole time?" Kori demanded, rage flashing behind her eyes, fueled by something even stronger. Something she didn't want to admit to.

"I had no choice!" Anger rose through me slowly, winding its way up my spine. "You'd do anything to protect Kenley. So how can you blame me for being willing to do the same for my brother? I didn't know her." I spared a glance at Kenley, who still watched us in shock. "I didn't know you. All I knew was that killing her would save Steven, and he's my *brother*. We shared the same fucking *womb!* But then I met you, and you were horrible, in the most wonderful way."

"Don't…" Her aim held steady, but her eyes were watering again.

"You were tactless, and scary, and funny, and easy to provoke, but I knew from the start that you were *so strong*. You're a fighter, and I loved that about you from the beginning, and I knew I couldn't hurt you, even to save my brother. So I found another way, and I had to do it without telling you. To protect you. I did what had to be done, and if you'll just put the damn gun down and think about this for a second, you'll realize that you would have done the same thing."

"No, I wouldn't." She lowered the gun. "I would have gone through with it. I wouldn't have hesitated to kill your brother to save my sister."

For a moment, we stared at one another, a silent brutal

understanding passing between us. Then she blinked, and one more tear rolled down her face. "And I would do the same for you."

My chest ached like someone had tried to pry my ribs open and pull my heart out through the gap.

"I don't know what's going on here." Kenley sank onto the couch, drawing both her sister's attention and mine. "I don't remember binding anyone named Steven Holt, but if this doesn't stop, I'm going to ask you to reconsider shooting me." Her face was twisted with pain, her arms clutching her stomach in obvious agony.

"Come with me." I dropped into a squat in front of Kenley, to catch her gaze. "If you can break Steven's binding while Meghan has anything left in her, she can help you, at least long enough for us to work on your binding." I glanced up at Kori, appealing to her mercenary logic. "We can't stay here anyway. Tower's probably already sent men after us."

"What about Van?" Kenley demanded, and I recognized the angry flush in her cheeks—she looked just like her sister in that moment.

"I'm not going to let the princess die in the dungeon. Kori and I will go after her as soon as Steven's unbound."

"But…" Her foot began to jiggle—a very bad sign. And every minute she didn't turn herself in to Jake, it would get a little worse.

"No more arguments. We're going. Ian, get the lights." Kori wrapped one arm around her sister and carefully pulled her up from the couch while I crossed the room to flip switches in the kitchen and by the front door, where I had to step over the dead guard's body. When the room was dark enough to travel through, I took Kori's free hand and gave her the address. She spared a moment to visualize the general location and search for a pocket of darkness. Then she stepped forward and Kenley and I went with her.

Two steps later, I banged my shin on the toilet in the house Meghan grew up in. They'd kept the house when they moved out a few years earlier, but it was currently unrented, which made it a decent hideout. Though Tower's Trackers would find us, if we stayed too long.

Kori's foot hit something and she cursed, while I felt around on the wall for the light switch.

Something clicked behind us just as I found the light, and I was still half-blind when I turned to find Aaron aiming a gun at me from the hall. He exhaled in relief when he recognized me, and his aim shifted to Kori.

"We haven't met." Kori half held her sister up with one arm, leaving her left hand free to go for her gun. "I'm Kori Daniels. If you don't get that gun out of my face, I'm gonna take it, then I'm gonna break your jaw so I can unhinge it and shove your own pistol down your throat. That way the bullet goes through the long way."

I groaned and gestured for Aaron to holster his gun, but he looked distinctly disinclined. "She believes in making a strong first impression. But she's here to help. They both are."

Aaron held his position for another second, then reluctantly lowered his gun and stepped aside, so we could enter. I took Kenley from her sister and carried the Binder in both arms down the hall and into Steven's room, where he lay on the bed, a skeleton wrapped in skin so thin it looked like it might tear at the slightest pressure.

"Oh, hell," Kori whispered. "He should be dead."

"Don't ever say that again," Meghan said from her recliner next to the bed. The circles beneath her eyes had darkened and swollen. Her arms were thin and pale, and the veins stood out like dark tree branches, stretching beneath her skin.

Kenley gasped when I set her in a chair on the opposite side of the bed and she got her first look at my brother. "Twins?" she asked, and I nodded, surprised she could see the resemblance in what little was left of him.

"He's nine minutes my junior." I knelt next to the bed, searching for something familiar in the living skeleton that used to be my brother. I wanted to take his hand so he'd know I was there, but I was afraid to touch him.

Steven's eyes rolled beneath his lids, and he groaned in his sleep. Only he wasn't really sleeping—he was barely clinging to consciousness.

"I don't know him." Kenley's eyes filled with tears and she sounded half-choked by them. "I thought when I saw him I'd remember, but I've never seen him before. I didn't bind him."

I pulled up a folding chair and sat next to her, while Aaron and Kori hovered near the doorway. "You may not have personally bound him, but your blood and your will sealed the binding."

Kenley blinked in confusion, but then comprehension surfaced so hard and fast her body actually jerked, like someone had slapped her. She turned to her sister, anger and guilt warring behind her eyes, pain evident in every movement she made. "Nadia? You told him about Nadia?"

Kori shrugged. "I was explaining how we got involved with Jake in the first place."

"Who's Nadia?" Aaron asked.

"Her college roommate," Kori said. "Years ago Kenley

gave a sample of her blood to some bitch she had a crush on, who abused the fuckin' privilege."

"But Jake fixed all that. None of those bindings are still intact."

"I don't care who made the mess and who cleaned it up," Aaron said from the edge of the room. "His bindings are obviously still intact, and your blood is keeping it that way. So break the fucking seal now, or I'll end this once and for all." He drew his gun and pointed it at Kenley's head, and she gasped.

Kori burst into motion so fast I hardly saw her move. She shoved his gun arm up, startling Aaron, who accidently fired into the ceiling, and the rest of us ducked. Kori threw her knee up and into his groin, and when Aaron fell to his knees, too shocked to make a sound, she took his gun hand in both of hers and twisted viciously. I heard his bone crack from across the room, and I flinched when Aaron howled in pain.

Kori plucked the pistol from his grip, then kicked him in the stomach for good measure.

"You ever point a gun at my sister again, and I'll strangle you with your own intestines. Got it?"

Aaron moaned from the floor, and Kori must have accepted that as a reply, because she checked the safety on his gun, then kept it, and suddenly I understood where most of her weapons collection had come from.

"Carry on," she said, waving her empty hand at both Kenley and Steven, but when Meghan stood to help her brother, Kori shook her head and raised the gun again. "Sit. Save your healing juice for my sister. He'll be fine," she added, with a contemptuous glance at Aaron, who was still curled up on the floor.

Meghan sank back into her chair reluctantly, and I turned back to Kenley.

"I don't even know how to start," she said. "Breaking Kori's seal was hard, but at least I knew what I was doing. I don't know what Steven was bound to, so I don't know what to remove my will from."

"Okay…" Kori came close, obviously thinking, and I didn't miss the glance she threw at the alarm clock next to the bed. Vanessa's time was slipping away, along with Steven's. "Whatever this binding is, he only breached it a couple of weeks ago, right?" she said, and I deferred to Meghan. I wasn't even in the country when the whole thing started. I'd been gone for nearly seven years.

"Um, yeah." Meghan sniffled. "I'll never forget because it was the night he proposed. We had a wonderful dinner, then there was the question, and the ring…" She held her hand out and studied the diamond on her left ring finger. "Half an hour later, he got a migraine, and we had to leave in the middle of dessert."

"Oh, hell," Kori said, turning to see if I'd come to the same conclusion. And I had. Only I knew more than she did. More than any of them could possibly know. "Love Knot," she said, and I nodded. But the name was a misnomer—you can't control someone's emotions, no matter what you bind them to. But that didn't stop the occasional love-sick adolescent—or desperate college student—from preventing the object of her affection from marrying—or proposing marriage—to anyone else.

Kenley watched us, obviously trying to think through her own pain to follow the conversation. "You're saying the Love Knot my college roommate used my blood for six years ago was targeting your boyfriend's twin brother? What are the chances?"

Kori shrugged and shook her head slowly. "I stopped asking that years ago. How did Jake break the seal?"

"He didn't. He said he *couldn't*," Kenley said, and my temper flared.

"He only said that because he didn't want you to know you could break your own bindings."

"So, what, he just lied and said the binding was broken, when it wasn't?" Kori asked.

Kenley shook her head. "He helped me transfer it."

I frowned. "You can't transfer a binding."

Kenley shrugged. "Evidently you can, under certain circumstances. In this case, he said the target had a dead brother, close in age. And Nadia didn't have a sample of Steven's blood, so she used a name binding. Jake's man showed me how to transfer the binding to the dead brother, where it couldn't hurt anyone." She gave another little shrug, brow furrowed from the headache. "Dead people don't fall in love, you know." Then she turned to me, frowning. "Except that you're not dead."

"He's not bound, either," Meghan pointed out. "If you transferred the binding, why is Steven still bound?"

I exhaled heavily and rubbed my own forehead, leaning back in my chair. "Because she transferred the binding *to* Steven, not *from* him."

"I don't understand," Kori said.

"Oh, shit. Your names," Aaron said, and I looked up to see him still sitting on the floor, his fractured arm clutched to his chest. He wouldn't take care of his own injuries until he knew his sister was safe.

"What about your names?" Kori asked. "The quick version," she added, with another glance at the clock.

"My mom raised us to be paranoid," I said. "She told us from the time our Skills manifested that people would want to use them. She said we'd have to hide our Skills, and possibly hide ourselves. Turns out she was right. When we left home for college—we picked schools on opposite sides of the country—we switched names, to help protect our true identities. That way, if someone tried to track me by my name, they'd actually be tracking him, and he was so far away even the best Tracker in the world couldn't pick up his signal."

Fortunately, Steven's skill as a Reader was more common and less powerful than mine, which was why he'd felt safe enough just hiding his name, whereas I'd had to hide my entire existence.

"So, you're not really Ian?" Kori said.

"No, I'm Ian. But in college, I called myself Steven, and I registered with his records and ID. So when Nadia bound Steven, she was actually binding me—Ian— because he was using my name. He got his degree as Ian—my brother really *is* a systems analyst—got his first job as Ian, and applied for his mortgage as Ian Holt. He still uses my name to this day," I said, glancing at Meghan for confirmation, and she nodded. "And I joined the Marines as Steven Holt."

"*You're* the dead serviceman?" Kori's eyes were narrow, her voice unsure. She was trying to untie a knot of identification my brother and I had worked for years to tangle. To keep each other safe. But that had obviously backfired. "You faked your own death?"

I shrugged. "I just took advantage of the opportunity when the Corps thought I died, along with most of the rest of my unit. Steven chose to hide in plain sight. I chose to hide in Australia. In Steven's name, which now belonged to a dead U.S. serviceman."

Kori sat on the end of the bed, eyes closed, thinking

out loud. "So, Nadia bound Steven, but she used your name—Ian—so she was actually binding you. Then, when Kenley transferred the binding to you—in Steven's name—she was actually transferring it back to the intended target. Is that right?"

"Yeah. I think so." I turned back to Kenley. "Does that give you enough information to break the seal?"

"I sure hope so."

"Please, do it," Meghan begged as Kenley closed her eyes. Her hands shook in her lap as she concentrated, and I wondered how much harder this would be, with so much resistance pain already crippling her. Her eyes moved behind her eyelids, and her hands clenched around the arms of her chair

The rest of us waited, hardly breathing. I watched my brother—my twin—trying to find some change in him to indicate her success. Or her failure. His breaths were shallow, his chest hardly moving. He'd grown way too thin, especially in the past week, when food became too hard to keep down, even when Meghan managed to get it in him. He'd stopped letting me help. In fact, he'd kicked me out of his room eight days earlier—that was the last time he'd had the strength to shout—and it took me a while to understand that seeing me was hard for him, because I looked like he remembered himself, even as he wasted away a little more every day.

Finally Kenley gasped and her eyes flew open. "I think I did it."

Meghan burst into tears and pushed herself out of her recliner to sit on the edge of Steven's bed. I couldn't see a change, but she looked happy. Relieved. She laid one hand on his cheek, then touched his arm. Then she turned the sheets back to touch his bare, gaunt stomach. And when she finally looked up, silent tears poured down her cheeks.

"They're working. They're all working again." She turned to Kenley, wiping her face with both hands. "Thank you."

"I'm so sorry," Kenley said, clutching her own stomach. "I didn't mean to hurt anyone."

"He's going to be fine soon," Meg said, and I stood, already turning to Kori.

"Ready?" We had twenty-five minutes to get to Vanessa.

Kori turned to Meghan, who was fussing over Steven, trying to make him more comfortable, obviously eager for him to wake up. "Swear you'll take care of her." The gun in her right hand made it kind of hard to hear her request as anything less than an order, complete with implicit threat.

"What's wrong with her?" Meghan turned to look critically at Kenley for the first time.

"She's in breach of her oath to Jake Tower just by being here."

"If she dies, three-quarters of Jake Tower's private army will go free. His empire will collapse," Aaron said from the floor near the door, injured arm still cradled at his chest, and I started to reconsider my original assessment of his IQ.

Kori turned to him slowly, pistol aimed at his head. "If she dies, you die, even if I have to chase you across the fuckin' planet. And you should know that one of the best Trackers in the country owes me a favor." She lowered her gun, and Aaron looked up at me, anger smoldering in his eyes.

"You're with her on this? You're gonna pick some

bitch you just met over a friend you've known all your life?"

"I'm hoping I won't have to. Don't be stupid, Aaron. Kenley just saved your sister's life."

"She's the one who put it in danger!"

"No, I put my own life in danger," Meghan said, rounding the bed for a closer look at Kenley. "I chose to heal Steven. And now I choose to heal the woman who saved him." She turned to Kori, as she knelt next to Kenley. "She'll be fine as long as I am. But I don't know how long that'll be. I've been doing this too long as it is."

"It won't be long," Kori said, and I could see the solution in her eyes. In the set line of her jaw. She was going after Barker. In killing one of Tower's Binders, she'd be freeing the other. The king's castle would come crumbling down on top of him. "Let's go."

Twenty-Nine

Kori

I walked us out of Meghan's bathroom and back into Kenley's living room, and neither of us bothered with the light. "I need to be gone before Jake's men get here, and it'll look better if you go in voluntarily."

"Where will you be?" Ian asked.

"Recruiting backup."

"You know, if you hadn't broken Aaron's arm, we could have used him as backup."

I huffed. "If he was that easy to disarm, he wouldn't have done us any good."

"So who are you calling?" Ian asked as I dug my phone from my pocket.

"My brother. And Olivia. I trust them both at my back."

"Olivia Warren?" I could hardly see his frown in the deep shadows. "*Cavazos's* Olivia?"

"She was *my* Olivia before she was his, and I know how to avoid his claim to her." I glanced at the microwave clock. It had been seventy-five minutes since Jake called Kenley's phone. In the basement, Vanessa was being cut again. I couldn't hear her scream, but I could almost feel it.

I dialed Liv's number from memory, then pressed the speaker button and my phone rang out into the room. After four electronic bleats, Olivia answered, her voice thick with suspicion. "Hello?"

"Will you help me?" I said, in lieu of a greeting.

"Kori?" Liv was pissed. I could hear it in her voice, in the way she bit my name off at the edges. But she was also worried; she knew I wouldn't call unless I was in trouble. "What's wrong?"

"I need sanctuary. Are you at your office?"

"Yeah."

"Turn off the light. I'm coming over."

Olivia sighed. "Fine."

I hung up and turned to Ian. "I'll see you in the basement."

"Be careful." He pulled me close for a kiss, and I didn't want to let him go. Ever. But this wouldn't be over until Van and Kenley were free. Hell, it might never be over. And Van was running out of time.

I took a deep breath, then made myself let him go and step into the shadows.

The moment I stepped into the darkened bathroom in Olivia's tiny two-room office, I could see her. And hear her. She sat on the couch opposite her desk, fully visible in the well-lit main room.

"Kori's here," she said into her phone as I rounded the desk toward her. "Yeah, I'll let you know when—"

"You still bound to Cavazos?" I asked, and she nodded, scowling at the interruption.

I snatched the phone before she could finish the

aborted sentence and threw it at the ground as hard as I could, where it broke into several large plastic pieces.

"Damn it, Kori! Do you have any idea how many phones I go through in a good year?"

"Sorry," I lied, shoving her stapler over so I could sit on her desk. "I can't chance Cavazos calling you while I'm here." He'd use her against me.

"That was Cam, not Ruben."

"He'll understand. Text him from my phone." I tossed my cell to her and she started typing with both thumbs, pausing frequently to glare at me.

"What's this about?" she said as she handed my phone back.

"As of about an hour ago, I am a free woman, and the best part is that Jake doesn't know yet."

Olivia reached over and pushed up my left sleeve. "Your marks aren't dead."

"Black permanent marker." I sat next to her on the couch. "Take a closer look."

She leaned down, squinting at my arm from two inches away. "Wow. How'd it happen?"

"Ian taught Kenley how to break her seal. It's no piece of cake, but she pulled it off."

"Is she still bound?"

"Yes, and she's in a lot of pain, but a friend of Ian's is a Healer, so she's in good hands, at least until I can kill the Binder that sealed her to Jake."

"If you're killing Tower's men, I'm in."

I grinned without bothering to hide my relief. "I was hoping you'd say that. But first I have to bust Kenley's girlfriend out of Jake's basement."

"Her girlfriend?"

"Yeah." I stood and shoved my phone into my pocket. "She was a friend of Cam's. You two might have met."

"Van?" Olivia sounded horrified, and I nodded from the bathroom doorway. "Why would Tower torture her?" Cam had obviously told her what goes on down in Jake's basement.

"To get to Kenley. And by extension, me and Ian."

"How are you going to get her out?"

"I sent Ian in to bust a hole in Jake's infrared grid. Once he has, I'm gonna walk in alone, and walk out with Vanessa. Then we're going after Barker, Tower's secondary Binder."

"Want some help in the basement?"

"Thanks, but I'll have Ian and Van on the way out." And if she got too close to Ian, she'd be obligated to try to take him from me. "I do need another favor, though. Are you under any standing orders to give Kenley to Cavazos?"

"Nope." She smiled, and I welcomed the sight. "Obviously he knows Tower has a Binder, but he doesn't know who that is, to my knowledge. Or that I have any connection to her."

"Good. If you can do it, I need you to call Kris, so he can get both Van and Kenley somewhere safe, as soon as we're done with Barker." Because Jake was probably already tracking Kenley, and the farther away she was, the harder that would be for him. And she couldn't stay with Liv, because if Cavazos got his hands on my sister, the mess we were already in would be infinitely worse. And bloodier.

"No problem," Olivia said.

I thanked her, then closed my eyes and mentally reached out toward Jake's house, ignoring all the other pockets of darkness between. As usual, his house was an inferno of infrared light burning beyond the visible spectrum, except for the cool, dark sanctuary of the dark-room. But I reached deeper, lower, hoping against all hope that Ian had already found his way to the basement, and that I wasn't too late to take advantage of it. Because once he'd created darkness, they'd realize what he was doing and they'd try to stop him.

So when I actually found that spot of true dark in the basement, I nearly choked on my own surprise. We'd caught another break.

"Hopefully this won't take long," I said, backing into the bathroom. Then I took another step backward, and this time my shoe landed not on cheap, faded linoleum, but on gritty concrete.

The basement.

"Ian?" I whispered, because I'd need him to let go of the dark long enough for us to find Vanessa and take care of whoever was with her. I was close. My bindings were dead and I'd broken into the impenetrable Tower fortress. I was minutes from true freedom.

I might just survive the day after all.

A footstep whispered on the concrete behind me and I started to turn, my heart thumping. Then something slammed into the side of my head and the world spun around me, unseen in the dark. The floor crashed into my back and the lights came on overhead. Stunned and out of breath, I could only blink as a foot pressed into my neck and someone pulled my guns from their holsters.

I blinked again, and a face came into focus against the glare of the lights overhead. Jonah.

"Welcome home, Kori. We've missed you."

Thirty

Ian

After Kori left Kenley's apartment, I double-checked the clips in both of the guns she'd lent me—not that I'd have a chance to use them—then took the jacket off the dead guard still slumped against the front door. The jacket was a size too large and had an uneven spot of blood near the hem on the right side and a blood-soaked bullet hole in the right sleeve, but neither would be easily visible in the dark material, which would hide the fully loaded double holster.

Satisfied with the functionality of the jacket, I hauled the guard into the kitchen, then went downstairs to catch a cab, intending to report to Tower's fortress for Trojan horse duty. But as I stepped onto the sidewalk, a sleek black car pulled to a stop at the curb in front of me. The window rolled down to reveal Julia Tower. Alone, except for her faceless driver.

"Mr. Holt, may I offer you a ride?" Her head was tilted slightly to the left, but her cool smile was on straight.

I crossed my arms over my chest. "You say that like I have some choice in the matter."

"In fact, you have three choices. You may ride in here with me, up front with the driver, or in the trunk."

"And if I decline all three options?"

"My brother Jonah is in a basement cell right now, hoping that's exactly what you'll do. The young woman with him is no doubt praying you'll show better sense."

"Vanessa?" I asked, and Julia nodded. "What makes you think I care what happens to a woman I've never even met?"

"I know you care, because I know the *real* Ian Holt— the man who doesn't own a personal computer and doesn't even know what kind of systems he supposedly analyzes." She paused a moment to let me truly experience the shock of her words. "I know Ian Holt, the soldier who defied a direct order to pull an injured friend out of the line of fire. The brother who rose from the grave— feigned though that grave was—and stepped back into his own identity to save his twin from certain agonizing death. That Ian Holt can't help himself—he's at the mercy of a ruthless hero complex."

"How…?" I started to ask how she knew. Then I realized that didn't matter. What mattered was, "How long have you known?"

"Mr. Holt, we would never have asked you to become one of us if we didn't already know how many fillings are in your teeth and how you broke your arm in the third grade."

I *had* broken my arm in the third grade… "Lila Sobresky—"

"Pushed you off the slide. I know." She folded her hands in her lap, and I couldn't take my gaze from her face. From eyes that saw more than they should and ears that seemed to hear my very thoughts. "I also know that your mother is first-generation Irish-American, which is where you get those striking green eyes, and your father is fifth-generation African-American, the source of your lovely dark skin. You and your brother are fraternal twins, but you looked virtually identical until he began wasting away in excruciating pain two weeks ago. Steven was named for your paternal grandfather, who spelled his name with a *ph* instead of a *v.* Your mother named *you* after her older brother. Sweet, but stupid. Almost as stupid as it was for you and your brother to keep the names. But switching them...?" Julia laughed, and the sound bounced around inside my head like nuts and bolts clanging in the dryer. "That was clever. We might never have figured that part out, if you and your brother hadn't already pinged our radar years ago, thanks to the younger Miss Daniels."

Her gaze trailed over my face and down the front of my shirt, like she could see the flesh beneath, and my teeth ground together so hard my jaw ached. "You are quite a prize, Mr. Holt. A soldier with a philosophy degree under a stolen identity. A thinker and a fighter, with a strong, thick—" her gaze traveled lower "—protective streak. No wonder Korinne fell for you."

My anger built with every word she spoke, like my secrets were worth less than the lipstick staining the mouth that spilled them. I'd rarely wanted to punch a woman, but I wanted to drive Julia Tower's straight, white teeth through the back of her skull, just so I wouldn't have to hear another word come out of her mouth.

"Get in the car, or Vanessa loses a finger."

I hesitated, gripping the car door where the window

had receded into it, letting my anger swell a little more. Grow a little more useful. Then I opened the door, not because Julia had told me to, but because she represented the most direct path through Tower's heavily guarded headquarters to the basement, where Vanessa and Kori needed me to be. But before I could sit, Julia held up a hand to stop me. "Place your weapons in the front seat." Where they would be beyond my reach, thanks to the panel separating driver from passengers.

But that was not unexpected.

I opened the front door and dropped both guns on the seat, then slid onto the backseat next to Julia Tower. Before I'd even closed the door, I wondered if I'd made a tactical error. If bending to her will, even for my own purpose, was the first of many steps in the devouring of my soul by the beast that was her brother's organization.

"Kori didn't know any of that, did she?" I asked, twisting to face Julia on the bench seat. Why would they keep their recruiter in the dark about her own recruit?

"Korinne knew only what she needed to know," Julia said as the car pulled away from the curb. "But Jake and I knew why you really accepted our invitation from the beginning. And we knew you would never go through with your cold-blooded mission because at your core, pulsing where your heart should be, is a stubborn kernel of chivalry, rotting you alive like a cancer. You didn't kill Kenley Daniels when you had the chance because you couldn't. And you fell for Kori like a schoolboy in love the moment you got that first glimpse of her poor, abused, damaged heart. Just like Jake knew you would."

My fist clenched around the door handle. "If Tower knew I had no intention of joining, why send Kori to recruit me?"

Julia laughed, like she'd never heard anything truly amusing until that very moment. "Korinne wasn't re-cruiting you. She was living out her sentence. Jake got bored with her in the basement." Julia frowned in thought. "That's what he says, anyway, but he's lying."

And suddenly, studying her expression—the first raw, unfiltered look I could remember seeing from Julia Tower—I understood what Kori hadn't been free to tell me. Julia was a Reader. She'd heard—and no doubt reported—every lie she'd heard me tell. But now that I knew what she was, she'd lost her advantage. The key to fooling a Reader is to tell two lies at once, and make one of them obvious. That way the Reader doesn't know there's a bigger untruth buried beneath the surface lie. I'd learned that, if nothing else, from growing up with Steven.

"The truth is that he started to hate her, because Jonah couldn't break her and Jake couldn't do it himself. That's in his vows, you know." Julia's eyes sparkled with bitter amusement. "The only thing he promised his wife—that he would never touch another woman. Not ever. So when you came along, he saw a possibility involving you both. For Kori, the impossible task. Recruit the man who cannot be recruited. The immovable object."

My blood burned in my veins like liquid fire. "He set her up to fail."

Julia nodded. "And to hate every single debasing, hu-miliating moment of it."

"And me?"

Her smile grew smaller, tighter. "For you, the irresist-ible force. Korinne, our own shattered doll, pretty, yet fierce. Delicate, yet dangerous. The damaged woman who cannot be fixed—Kryptonite to any man with a hero complex."

"He played us." The truth of it echoed inside me, ringing over and over, resonating in every bone in my body.

She nodded again. "He did. And he watched you both struggle and flail for two days, butting heads and bruising egos for his entertainment, knowing that in the end, you would sign with him for the same reason you came out of hiding—to protect those you care about. My brother is cruel and smart, and he is without mercy. Which is why I can tell you without a doubt in my mind that if you don't sign whatever contract he offers you, he will cut poor Vanessa in places that should never feel pain. And if that fails to motivate you, he will move on to your brother, and your brother's fiancée, and—"

Before she could finish threatening everyone I'd ever met, Julia's phone started ringing and she frowned, then reached into a slim purse and pulled out her cell. Her frown deepened when she glanced at the display, then she pressed a button and held the phone to her ear. "Hello?"

She listened in silence for several seconds while a voice I didn't recognize said words I couldn't understand. Then Julia's brows rose in sudden interest. "Yes, I'll show him. We're on the way."

She ended the call, then started pressing more buttons on her phone. "You're a very lucky man, Mr. Holt. As it turns out, Jake won't have to target what remains of your family after all," she said, and a cold ball of dread formed in my stomach, growing with every second of silence from Julia Tower. But I wasn't going to beg for information.

Finally she looked up and her usual smug smile was

absent. She looked almost somber. Instead of offering me an explanation, Julia simply handed me her phone.

I took it, dread churning in my stomach. But when I glanced at the screen, my rage swallowed all other emotions like the ocean swallows a single raindrop. Kori stared out at me from the display on Julia Tower's phone. She was shouting, but I couldn't hear her, because there was no sound. But I could see her gesturing in fury, her mouth open wide with each enraged shout. Behind her were a toilet, a curtainless shower stall, and a rollout mattress on a raised concrete block.

"That's a live feed. From Jake's basement," Julia said. And as badly as I wanted to believe this was old footage, even on the tiny black-and-white screen I could see that Kori was wearing what she'd put on that morning, including the double holster, though the guns—and no doubt the knives—were gone.

"Let her out." I could hear the rage roiling in my voice.

"That's beyond my authority. The only way for you to help Kori is to sign the contract."

I pulled the phone out of reach when she tried to take it. "Can you honestly tell me that if I sign, he'll let Kori out?"

Julia watched me closely for a second, like she was sizing me up. Trying to decide whether or not to gift me with the truth. Or maybe to curse me with it. "No," she said at last. "We both know Korinne will never set foot outside that cell again. There's nothing I can do about that."

"Get her out, or I won't sign."

"Sign, or she'll suffer before she dies," Julia countered. "And if you do it quickly, I might be able to arrange a visit with her."

"That's not good enough." I dropped the phone on the leather between us and grabbed her by the throat, pinning her to the opposite door, letting my fury echo in my growl. "Get. Her. Out."

Something hard pressed into my stomach and I looked down to find her holding a gun, the barrel digging into my navel.

"You're not going to shoot me. Your brother needs me."

"And you're not going kill me, because you need *me,*" she insisted hoarsely, using the fingers of her empty hand to pry at mine, trying to free her neck.

"You just said there's nothing you can do for Kori."

"There isn't—as long as Jake's in charge."

I blinked in surprise. Then I frowned. Then I frowned harder and loosened my grip on her neck. It almost sounded like... "Are you asking me to kill your brother?"

"I'm not asking anything of the sort." Because she couldn't. She was no doubt contractually prohibited, just like the rest of Jake's employees.

"But you can speak in hypotheticals, right?"

"As can you," she said, and I let her go.

"If Jake were out of power, you could help Kori?"

"I could." She rubbed her neck with her free hand, but her gun remained pointed at me.

"Why should I believe you care one way or another about what happens to her?"

"I don't." Julia shrugged, like that should have been obvious. "I care about what happens to me." Her brows rose in question, silently asking if I was understanding the things she wasn't allowed to say.

"You're not happy under your brother's reign?"

"You mean under his thumb? I'm chained to him just

like Korinne is, only I've been serving since I was sixteen. Since before service came with a time limit." She lifted her left sleeve to show me her binding marks, which seemed to ring her entire arm. "As long as these marks are live, I'll never have a family or a home of my own. I can't leave the city without authorization, which never comes. I can't even leave the *room* without permission. All because of one stupid oath I took as a kid, in exchange for my older brother's protection."

"Protection from what?"

Her lips pressed together for a second before she answered. "There's a skeleton in every closet, Mr. Holt."

"Fair enough. What about his heir? Do you honestly think it'll be better with Jonah pulling your strings?"

Her brows rose again, and her smile was back, small and reticent this time, like she was about to tell me a secret. "I can handle Jonah, Mr. Holt. His bark and his bite are both fierce, but I know how to leash him."

I thought about that for a moment, weighing my options and her sincerity. "If I were to give you that opportunity, you'd make sure Kori goes free? Immediately?"

"You have my word that if Jake is removed from power, Kori Daniels will go free immediately." I wasn't sure I believed her, but since I planned to kill both Jake *and* Jonah anyway, Kori would go free whether or not Julia kept her word. What I really needed to know was...

"Can you get me a second alone with Jake?"

She nodded without hesitation. "My contract predates time-in-service limits, but it also predates the stricter obedience clauses. I have more leeway than most employees. But I'm going to need some reassurance from you, Mr. Holt. A handshake won't do."

"What do you want?"

"Protection. When people find out that I helped rid the world of Jake Tower, those loyal to him—or to his wife—will be out for my head. I want your word—signed and sealed—that you'll protect me until that threat is gone."

"No bindings," I insisted. Kori's bindings had gotten her tortured. Kenley's had gotten her caged. Steven's had nearly gotten him killed.

"Then no deal," Julia countered. "It's a simple promise, Mr. Holt. Not a service agreement. Jake's secondary Binder is bitter about being replaced by Kenley Daniels and he's loyal to me."

Secondary Binder? A glimmer of an idea surfaced on the horizon of this new complication. "Is his name Barker?"

Julia frowned. "Yes. And I assure you, he's heavily guarded. Especially with Kenley currently on the run. Though that won't last long."

"I have no plans to harm your Binder." Big lie—if Kori couldn't take him out, I damn well would. "In fact, I'm looking forward to working with you both." Smaller, obvious lie, to cover the larger fib.

Julia rolled her eyes, and I knew I had her. "I know you don't want to be bound, Mr. Holt. But I assure you this is the least painful solution for all involved. I've already drafted the binding, and we can strike through and initial minor points of compromise before we sign. Then when we get to Jake's house, you will play your part. After that, you and Kori can walk off into the sunset, if that's the kind of cheesy, happy ending you sentimental types like."

"Just like that?" I studied her face, searching for the catch. "It sounds too good to be true."

"I assure you it's not. Jake knows how to defend himself, and even if you're successful, you'll have to fight your way out. I'll do my best to rein Jonah in immediately, but in moments of passion and fury, men are often uncontrollable."

A fact I was personally familiar with. But if Jonah was so uncontrollable, what made her think she could control him? Especially once he'd inherited her binding from Jake?

There was something she wasn't saying, and I wouldn't trust Julia Tower even if my *own* marks had been tattooed on her arm.

"This Binder? How far away is he?" I asked as that idea on the horizon came into even clearer focus.

"Less than a mile." She pressed a button on the glass separating us from the driver, then gave him an address. "I'm pleased we could come to an agreement."

Barker turned out to be a grizzly looking man in his mid-sixties who subsisted on nothing but pizza and beer, if the garbage covering his kitchen counters was any evidence.

I was sorely tempted to kill him where he stood, to free Kenley, which would cut Kori's last tie to Tower. But if I killed Barker, Vanessa was as good as dead, and Kenley would never forgive me. Which meant Kori might never forgive me. So I watched in silence as the Binder read aloud from the document Julia had produced from a briefcase taken from the trunk of her car.

The document was short and to the point. It said that I would protect Julia Tower from any threat rising from the demise of her brother until such threat was over. I insisted that Barker add an expiration date—Julia wanted five years, but I whittled her down to two, max—as well as a statement that both Vanessa and Kori would be released from the basement the moment Jake Tower died.

I tried to end their terms of service, too, along with Kenley's—why not shoot for the moon?—but Julia insisted she didn't have the authority to do that. And we both knew she wouldn't have freed them even if she could have.

The phrasing was all very careful, because Julia could not actually ask me to kill her brother or offer to reward me directly for that service.

Julia signed. I signed. Barker stamped the agreement with a bloody thumbprint, symbolizing his own will to seal the deal. And after several tense moments, we agreed to leave the document with him, because neither of us was willing to trust the other with it. Then we got back in the car and rolled steadily toward Jake Tower's fortress of a home, while I tried to think about exactly how I wanted to end his life instead of how dirty I felt, like I'd just signed over a piece of my own soul.

Thirty-One

Kori

"Let me the hell out of here or I'm going to rip your head off and finger paint with your fucking gray matter!" I shouted, roughly the twentieth variation of the same threat. Plausibility and creativity had expired about six versions earlier.

"That's gonna be kinda hard to pull off, with you in there and me out here," Jonah called back over the intercom, and I pounded on the glass again.

"Then come face me like a man!" My demands were useless—the glass pounding even more so—but I was alive with rage that had no outlet. My fists *itched* for Jonah's face. I was finally free to fight, but couldn't reach the target.

"Honey, if I go in there, only one of us is coming back out," Jonah said.

"That's the general idea!"

Silence answered me, and my rage burned on, unspent. I whirled around and scanned the cell for something to throw. Something to break. But there was nothing. I couldn't even tell if this was the same room I'd occupied before, or just a neighboring look-alike.

Either way, there was nothing that wasn't bolted to the floor, except for the worthless two-inch-thick mattress and... My gaze hovered over the toilet, one of the few differences between Jake's homemade prison and a real one. This toilet was commercial, not detentional. The tank had a lid. A heavy, porcelain lid.

Someone was going to get his ass reamed for overlooking that security risk.

I picked up the tank lid and hefted it, getting used to the weight. If it would kill a Hollywood zombie, it would kill an actual asshole.

"You're scared, aren't you?" I demanded, stalking closer to the glass, my porcelain weapon hanging at my right side. "You're scared to face me, now that I'm armed and free—" I bit off my own words in a sudden belated spasm of common sense. They didn't know I was unbound, and telling Jonah would mean giving up my only advantage.

"Now that I'm free to fight back," I finished instead. Because Jake hadn't ordered me not to, this time. "Does your brother know what a sniveling coward you are?" I pounded the glass with one fist. "Is there anyone else out there? Can you guys actually *see* Jonah's balls shrivel up and retreat indoors, or are they so small to begin with that you can't tell any difference?"

"Keep talking, Kori," Jonah said over the intercom, fury riding his voice like light rides a bolt of lightning. "Every word you say buys you a little more pain." But beneath his worthless threats, I heard what I really wanted to hear. Laughter. He wasn't alone, and the other men were laughing at him. Helping me taunt him into disobeying orders, at least long enough to open the door to my cell.

I glared at the one-way glass, pissed off that my reflection was all I could see. "A *little* pain, huh? If memory serves, a little's about all you have to offer."

I couldn't hear the laughter that followed from the peanut gallery, but I could practically feel it.

"You know you're in there because of your own stupidity, right?" Jonah said over the staticky intercom, obviously trying to claim the verbal upper hand. "You walked right into a trap."

Unfortunately I couldn't argue with that. But...

"It wasn't your trap, though, was it? Leaving me in the dark last time wasn't your idea, either, right? Was it Jake? No, it was Julia, wasn't it? The ideas come from Julia. The orders come from Jake. But what good are *you,* Jonah? What do you contribute to the Tower team effort?" I paused to give him time to answer, but I wasn't the least bit surprised when he didn't.

"Nothing. That's what you contribute," I shouted. "They could give your job to a fucking monkey and the result would be the same. How does it feel to know you contribute *nothing?*"

The intercom buzzed with static for a moment before he spoke. "It's not going to work. I'm not coming in there."

"Because you're a fucking coward!" My vision started to darken with fury and I swung the tank lid without thinking, smashing it against the glass. The glass cracked but held. The porcelain shattered into several large chunks and a zillion tiny slivers of white glass.

Shit! My fearsome bludgeoning weapon had been reduced to half a dozen mediocre stabbing weapons. Still, any one of them was sharp enough to open a vein if wielded with enough enthusiasm. But to even have a shot at Jonah, I'd have to get him in the room.

"Are you gonna cower and quake out there with your guns and knives because you're scared of one unarmed woman? Did Jake actually *say* you couldn't come in, or are you using your binding as an excuse to cower out there in the hall? We all know you bend the rules when you want to. You thread the loopholes like a seamstress threads a fucking needle. Don't tell me you don't!"

In another fit of fury, I reared back and kicked the glass, but it didn't budge. The crack didn't even widen. So I kicked it again. And again. And finally the crack started to spread, and a jolt of triumph burned the length of my spine.

Then the door opened.

Jonah stood in the doorway, one hand on the butt of his gun, like the idiot deputy from any old spaghetti Western. His jaw was clenched in fury and his eyes were narrowed in rage. "Are you trying to make me kill you? Because you know death is the only way out of here."

I squatted without taking my focus from him and felt around on the ground for a large chunk of broken toilet tank lid, desperately wishing I had something to wrap it with, to keep it from cutting my hand. The last thing I wanted was to leave a sample of my blood behind— Jonah had taken my pocket-size bleach bottle along with my weapons.

"You're bigger and better armed," I said, hoping the men in the hall could hear. "But I'd lay money on me to win, any day of the week."

"Arrogant little *bitch!*" But he didn't move. And that's

when I realized he actually *did* have orders not to touch me. Or at least not to shoot me.

Jake still needed me, no matter what he'd said about me being obsolete. He needed me to draw Ian and Kenley back into the fold.

I couldn't let that happen.

I clutched the three-inch splinter of porcelain and curled my other hand into a fist. I could kill Jonah caveman style, but I'd need his gun—and a lot of luck—to take out whoever was watching from the hall.

But before I could rush him, Jonah pulled the handheld radio from his belt clip and pressed a button. "Go ahead," he said, and I froze when Jake's voice invaded the cell, staticky, but perfectly audible.

"Why do you do this to yourself, Korinne?" he asked. But he didn't wait for my answer, and Jonah didn't let go of the button, which would have let him hear me. "You know the drill. Don't fight back. And don't touch the damn glass."

For a moment, the old terror washed over me, and it actually took me a moment to remember that I didn't have to obey Jake. His orders were worth less than the breath it took to say them, forgotten before the last syllable even faded from my ears.

Jake held no power over me. But my initial thoughtless fear probably saved my life. If I hadn't looked scared, Jonah would have realized something was wrong, and my advantage would have faded into nothing, like Jake's worthless order.

"Thanks," Jonah said into the radio, teeth clenched in resentment. He hated needing his brother's help.

"Move her to another cell and this time don't leave the fucking toilet tank lid. Mess this up again, and you'll be in the cell next to her, where you'll have plenty of time to think about the fact that you can't control one small woman without needing her muzzled first."

Jonah seethed and clipped the radio to his belt again without answering. I waited. Watching him. Trying to remember how I'd looked and acted when I was actually scared of him. The memories were there, but they were disjointed and clouded by fear.

"Let's go." Jonah stalked toward me, even angrier than usual because of what I'd just overheard.

"Don't touch me." I backed up until my spine hit the wall, then slid the hand clutching the shard of porcelain behind my thigh, even as I scooted to the left, avoiding his reach like I had no better options.

Jonah grabbed my arm and a slimy smile appeared at the corner of his mouth—an instant mood-lift in response to my fake fear. He hauled me across the cell and I let him, biding my time.

When he got close to the door, I began to drag my feet, resisting, but not truly fighting back. Jonah jerked me forward and pulled the door open with his free hand.

I sucked in a deep breath and swung my right arm as a primal screech of rage erupted from my throat. His eyes widened, but I buried the three-inch chunk of white porcelain in his jugular before he could make a single sound. "There's a reason I was his bodyguard and you were his lapdog," I said as his mouth opened and closed, gasping uselessly.

Blood dribbled between my fingers, most of it his. He gurgled and grasped at my fingers, but he was already weak from massive blood loss.

"Don't fight back," I whispered, throwing Jake's words at him as I pulled the glass free and stabbed him again, and when he slid to the floor, propping the door open with his weight, I knelt with him. "Beg me to stop." I didn't realize I was crying until the first tears dripped onto his shirt. "Does it hurt? Tell me how much it hurts."

He blinked up at me, his eyelids sluggish, and then he stopped breathing. He just *stopped,* and my tears fell faster.

Finally, it was over.

Distantly, I heard men shouting my name, rounds being chambered, safety switches clicking off.

I hunched over Jonah's body, my back to the other men, crying tears of joy and relief they no doubt mistook for some weaker, more primal emotion. And while they watched me sob, waiting for me to stand and face the inevitable consequences of my actions, I pulled Jonah's gun from his holster and checked the chamber, then flicked off the safety. Then I stood, the pistol hidden by my own body. I turned slowly, sliding the weapon behind my thigh, and counted the men aiming guns at me while I sniffled, displaying my trauma.

There were only three.

"Kori, we need you to turn around and put your hands behind your head," the guy in the middle said. Roscher. I'd known him since he signed on two years ago, but now he was talking to me like I was a child. Or insane. They thought I'd lost it.

I could work with that.

"He was right," I said, letting my voice go light and shaky as I stepped forward. "Death was the only way out."

"Stay there," Roscher said, as they all three aimed at my chest. "Turn around and show us your hands."

"My hands?" I stepped into the hall and took a moment to be grateful they were all on my right. As was the exit. No one could sneak up behind me. "You want to see my hands?" I held up my left hand, red and slick with Jonah's blood. "See?"

When they all glanced at my bloodstained hand, I dropped into a squat and swung Jonah's gun up, firing twice in rapid succession. Roscher and the man to his left stumbled back, hit, their bullets whizzing over my head.

"Drop it!" The third man called, aiming at my head, no doubt picturing how grateful Jake would be when he'd caged me where his coworkers failed.

His mistake.

I fired again, and a hole appeared in his shirt, right over his heart. He was dead before he hit the ground, and his bullet shattered the glass I'd already cracked.

I felt bad about killing them. But not too bad. They would have locked me back up. They would have helped Jake use me to get to Ian and Kenley. They would have let more bad things happen to Vanessa. And if our positions had been reversed, they would have killed me in a heartbeat.

Pulse racing, I snatched the key ring from Jonah's belt and checked the other basement cells one by one until I found Vanessa, huddled in the corner on her bed in her underwear, holding one arm out from her body, because of the series of bright red cuts marching up her forearm in neat, bloody rows. She had a black eye and bruises on both legs. But she looked intact.

Van burst into tears the moment she saw me.

"Are you okay?" I asked as she crawled to the edge of the bloodstained mattress.

She nodded, in spite of obvious pain. "Are you alone?"

"Not anymore. Cover your ears." She put both hands

over her ears and I shot into the ceiling, using bullets four through six from Jonah's full clip to shatter at least three of the infrared bulbs. Then I helped her off the bed and leaned outside the door to flip the switch controlling the regular lights. Her cell fell into shallow darkness, and I felt my way into the only patch of true dark, beneath the hole in the infrared grid. There was only room for a single step.

I closed my eyes, took a deep breath, and squeezed her hand. Vanessa stepped into the deeper darkness with me and out into the bathroom in Olivia's office.

Someone yelped, startled, and I opened my eyes to find myself staring at my brother, Kris, who'd been about to step into the bathroom. I hadn't seen him in nearly two years, but nothing had changed except for his hair, which he now wore in short, dark blond waves. "Kris!" I dropped Vanessa's hand and threw my arms around my brother.

He hugged me back, so tight I could hardly breathe. Then he let go and held me at arm's length. "Why are you covered in blood every time I see you?"

"Be fuckin' grateful it's someone else's," I said, smiling in spite of the grim circumstances of our reunion.

"Still got that dirty mouth," a gruff, shaky voice said, and I looked over Kris's shoulder to find my grandmother frowning at me in gray slacks and a cardigan over a white blouse.

"I learned every four-letter word I know from you, Gran," I said, and couldn't resist a smile, even as I leaned closer to whisper into Kris's ear. "Why the hell did you bring her here?"

"She thinks it's 2004. Where was I supposed to leave

her?" he asked, and I shrugged, conceding the point, then tugged him away from our grandmother.

"Have you talked to Kenley?" I asked, sinking onto Olivia's office couch as Van followed my grandmother into the office.

"Yeah." Kris sat next to me while Olivia handed Van a spare set of clothes. "She's in a lot of pain, and that Meghan woman's about out of juice."

"Okay, Ian wasn't in the basement when I was there, so I'm going back for him—"

"Who's Ian?" Kris asked before I could finish my sentence.

"He's...complicated. But he saved Kenley's life and he helped her break my binding to Jake, so I'm not going to leave him there."

"Okay. What can I do?"

"Um...get me George Barker, Tower's other Binder. He's the one who sealed Kenley's oath. We'll give him a chance to unseal it voluntarily and save his own life. If he won't...there's always plan B."

"The B stands for bullet?" Kris said, grinning.

"What else. I'm going to take Gran and Vanessa to Kenley, then I'm heading back to Jake's, through the hole I punched in his infrared grid in the basement."

"How much security does Barker have?" Liv asked, perching on the edge of her own desk while across the room my grandmother was interrogating Vanessa under the misguided assumption that she was Kris's new girl-friend.

"Probably more than usual, now that Kenley's MIA. Kris could use another gun if you're interested." But I wouldn't ask her. I wouldn't force her to help me, when I could very well be leading us both to our deaths.

Olivia shrugged and grabbed a loaded extra clip from her top desk drawer. "I have nothing better to do at the moment, and since I have yet to replace my phone, I don't anticipate any orders getting in the way."

"Thanks, Liv."

Kris glanced back and forth between us. "Aren't you two on opposite sides of the turf war?"

Olivia shrugged. "With friends like Kori, who needs enemies?"

"Ain't that the fuckin' truth!" Gran called from across the room, and Vanessa burst into teary laughter.

"Okay, I have my phone. Let me know how it goes with Barker," I said to Liv and my brother as I ushered Gran and Vanessa into the darkened bathroom.

Kris nodded and closed the door behind us as I took one of their hands in each of mine. Two steps later, we emerged in Meghan's bathroom. "Nobody shoot, we come in peace!" I shouted, and Aaron stepped into sight in the hall, still clutching the broken arm he obviously hadn't yet sought treatment for.

"Well, you can just step right back into that shadow and take your sister with you. If Tower tracks her here, we're all as good as dead."

"I'll be back for her as soon as I can. For now, I need you to watch a couple of valuables for me while I go storm the castle."

"No. No more women with prices on their heads…" Aaron started, shaking his head firmly, but his sister shouted over him from the bedroom.

"Bring them in here!"

I led Vanessa and Gran toward Meghan's voice. Kenley struggled up from her chair in spite of obvious pain the moment she saw Van.

"This isn't Europe," Gran said as Kenni and Vanessa embraced. "You don't have to kiss everyone you meet on the mouth, Kenley."

I would have laughed, if I weren't so close to tears.

"This is *not* a home for wayward women!" Aaron insisted.

"They'll be out of your hair soon," I said as Meghan gently began to examine Vanessa's butchered arm. She obviously didn't have the strength to heal three people at once—which explained Aaron's persistent fracture—but most Healers knew more than a little about first aid, to supplement their natural Skills.

I took a deep breath, double-checked the gun I'd taken from Jonah, then marched back into Meghan's bathroom, then into Jake's basement through the hole I'd blown in the infrared grid. Vanessa's cell was still dark, so I peeked into the hall cautiously. The bodies were all still there. Nothing had changed. I'd been gone less than ten minutes.

I spared a moment to grab extra guns from the downed men. Two went into my holsters and a third stayed in my hand, while I shoved their extra clips into my pockets. I'd never actually made an action-movie-style assault on a heavily guarded modern fortress, but I was pretty sure Hollywood was dead-on with at least two of the typical clichés: bullets would fly and blood would flow.

Properly armed, I walked right by the elevator—installed for easy transport of prisoners—and took the stairs instead. I didn't want to be surprised by a room full of men aiming guns at me as soon as the doors slid open.

At the top of the stairs, I opened the door just wide

enough to peek out. The foyer was empty, except for the usual guards, one at the foot of either staircase. No one in the basement had lived long enough to sound the alarm, but they'd be found as soon as Jake discovered he couldn't raise Jonah on his radio. If not sooner.

I pushed the door open and stepped into an alcove off the foyer, my heart thumping painfully with each step. I glanced toward Jake's office just as Julia pushed the door open and stepped out. A second later, movement from across the foyer caught my eye. Two armed men were getting on the elevator.

Shit. The elevator only went to the basement, and they would sound the alarm the minute they saw the bodies.

I turned back to Julia as she rounded the corner into the back hall, without noticing me—a blessing that would die with the first screech of the security siren. Then I stepped into the foyer.

"Hey!" the guard at the closest staircase shouted, drawing his gun, and I shot a hole through his left shoulder. He stumbled back onto the stairs as I shot his counterpart from across the room. But my silencer turned out to be pointless, because no sooner had the second guard fallen than the brain-skewering screech of the security alarm started wailing from everywhere.

Time was up.

Thirty-Two

Ian

"Won't this look suspicious?" I whispered as Julia led me up the steps and into Jake Tower's house, and I couldn't help remembering the first time I'd walked that very path, only two days earlier. How could everything have fallen apart in such a short time?

"No, it'll look like I've done my job," Julia said, her steps bold and confident. "Jake sent me to pick you up, and that's what I've done."

"I don't suppose you can sneak me in with a gun?"

She glanced at me in disdain, and I bristled even before she spoke. "You're going to have to contribute *something* to this effort on your own."

"You mean, other than pulling the trigger?"

"I mean finding a trigger to pull." She opened the front door and marched inside like she owned the place. Like we hadn't just been plotting the assassination of her brother, leash holder and the man who signed her paychecks. "I'll take you into the office," she whispered as we crossed the foyer, accompanied by the click of her heels on the marble. "But then I'll have to go. If I'm there when you make your move, I'll be obligated to stop you."

I nodded, my hands steady, my spine steeled. With one shot, the man who'd sentenced Kori to six weeks of a living hell would be dead. Then I'd make my way to the basement and kill the man who'd delivered that hell, and both Kori and her sister would be free for good.

No doubt easier said than done, but never had a challenge promised a better reward.

"Wait here for a minute," Julia said, and while she crossed the foyer for a private word with the guards at the stairs, I pulled my phone from my pocket and texted like a madman. I hit Send as she turned back to me and motioned for me to follow her.

Julia threw open the door to Jake's office and marched inside, then held the door for me. "Out," she said to the two extra men in the room, one standing guard at Jake's back, the other seated in a chair in front of his desk. "Mr. Holt has come to negotiate his contract."

Tower didn't even stand. "My men are sworn to secrecy on private matters," he said. "Anything you say will stay in this room."

"But they won't," I insisted. "Or this negotiation is over."

Jake's left brow rose. "You'd walk out over a little compromised privacy?"

"I'd walk out over too little ice in my whiskey." I turned to Julia. "Four cubes."

She scowled, but made no complaint. I'd given her the excuse she needed to leave the room.

Tower looked more amused than truly threatened, but he waved the men out of the room. "Go check on Kori Daniels. She was giving Jonah fits a few minutes ago."

I tried not to laugh, hoping whatever fits she'd given Jonah hadn't resulted in any more bruises for her.

"Can I get you anything?" Julia asked her brother, one hand on the door as the men crossed the foyer toward the elevator behind her.

"Call Barker and find out where that Intent to Sign document is. I want Mr. Holt bound by Kenley Daniels, but Barker will do for the preliminary document."

Julia nodded and stepped out of the room.

"Oh, and, Lia, pay a visit to Kori and explain exactly what will happen to her if she doesn't give up her sister. Quickly."

Julia nodded again and disappeared into the foyer.

"Nothing will happen to her," I said, sinking into one of two chairs in front of Tower's desk.

"What?"

"Nothing will happen to Kori," I repeated. "I want that written into the contract. You will release her and swear that she will have no further contact with you or anyone in your organization. Ever. When I have that written and sealed, I will sign."

"No deal." Jake stood and rounded his desk to sit on one corner of it, and his jacket parted to reveal the gun at his hip. If I could get it, this would all be over.

"You don't need her," I said, waiting for opportunity to knock. Negotiation was pointless, since I wasn't going to sign. "You've already got me here, and your Trackers can find her sister without Kori's help. Assuming Kenley can stand the resistance pain long enough to get out of the city. Kori's useless to you."

"Korinne is a living object lesson, Mr. Holt. My people know what she did, and if I don't make sure she lives and breathes pain until the instant she dies, someone else will think they can get away with what she did. And I can't let that happen."

I shrugged. "So tell them she's dead."

Tower folded his arms over his chest. "They need to see her die."

"I think *you* need to see her die. But I swear on my own life that if you kill her, you will never have my service."

Tower watched me carefully. Thinking. Hopefully weighing his options. While I bided my time. My moment hadn't yet come.

"Why Kori?" he asked at last, studying my face like he couldn't quite make sense of it. "I'm afraid I don't see the attraction."

"That's because you are threatened by her strength, while I am bolstered by it. But you don't have to understand that," I said, pleased to hear that my voice sounded much calmer than the rest of me felt. "You just have to let one of us go. Which do you want more, my service or her death?"

Tower's eyes narrowed, and his jaw clenched in anger—a first from him, at least that I'd seen. But before he could answer, a screeching siren echoed from all over, visibly startling us both.

Tower stood, eyes wide. "Security breach!" he shouted into the radio he'd grabbed from his desktop. And suddenly I realized what had happened. Kori was free. Everyone would be gunning for her.

My time had come.

"Lock the door," Tower said, reaching for the phone on his desk—no doubt an internal, secure line.

I lunged for his gun instead. Tower fought me and the gun went off in its holster.

He screamed and blood ran down his leg. Tower slapped one hand over the wound and I took the gun.

I backed up, aiming at him, and Tower leaned over his desk, fumbling for the top drawer. I fired before he could get it open, and blood poured from the new hole in his chest.

"No!" Kori shouted behind me, and I spun to see her standing in the doorway, gun drawn. Kori raced around me and pressed her free hand to the wound in Tower's chest. Blood ran between her fingers, but she was already covered in blood anyway, though I couldn't find any wounds, at a glance. "No, don't die!"

She turned to me, still trying to stop the bleeding, and the siren stopped screeching as suddenly as it had begun. But it rang on in my head. "I told you not to kill him!" Kori shouted, like she could still hear the ringing, too, as footsteps pounded toward us from the foyer. "He has an heir clause!"

"Yes, he does," a new voice said, and I turned to find Julia in the doorway, two large men at her back. "Or rather, he *did*." She glanced pointedly at her brother and I followed her gaze to find Jake's eyes open and staring blankly at some point near the top of the wall. "Call the police and report a break-in," she ordered, and the men stepped past her. "Speak to our man in Homicide. He'll take care of the details."

The first guard brushed Kori aside, and she sank onto her knees next to the wall, defeat dulling her eyes as one man picked up Tower's desk phone and began dialing.

"Don't fret, Korinne," Julia said. "The evil king is dead, thanks to your loyal lover." She spread her arms and gave me a broad smile. "Long live the queen." She stepped closer and ran one hand up my arm, practically purring. "Jonah was never Jake's heir." She trailed her fingers over my shoulder and across my chest, and the movement became bold as she watched my face for shock, or anger, or whatever she'd expected me to feel in the face of her betrayal.

"I know," I said, and her hand fell away. Her eyes narrowed, then her jaw clenched as she read the truth in my statement. "Jonah's a sadistic monster, but not overburdened by brains. Jake wasn't stupid enough to leave his kingdom in reckless hands, and *you're* not stupid enough to think you could control Jonah—unless he was bound to you."

"None of that matters now," Kori said, standing, still stunned by Jake's death, and still holding her gun. "Jonah died voiceless, in a pool of his own blood. In the basement. I'd call that irony, except it seems so fucking fitting."

Julia's eyes narrowed further, and her fists clenched at her sides.

"What do you want us to do with her?" The remaining guard asked, aiming at Kori even as Kori took careful aim at Julia. And behind her, I caught a blur of motion and a brief glimpse of a welcome, familiar face in the foyer.

"Nothing. You are free," Julia said to Kori. "I suggest you go out the way you came in, now, before the police arrive and start to draw the inaccurate conclusions I have every intention of fostering."

"Sure." She chambered a round in her gun and shifted her aim up to Julia's head. "Right after I send you after your brothers."

The sudden bolt of pain in my head was almost enough to paralyze me, but I'd been expecting it. "I can't let you shoot her." I stepped between Kori and Julia, whom I'd sworn to defend.

"Ian?" Kori stared at me, confused. Heartbroken.

"Ian is my new bodyguard." Julia ran one hand lightly over my shoulder from behind, and I hated her touch almost as much as I hated the pain and betrayal shining in Kori's eyes. "My own personal bringer of the night. You'll have to kill him to get to me. And I don't think you want to do that, do you, Korinne? In fact, I don't think you want anyone else to do that, either, do you?"

Kori lowered her gun, but didn't holster it. "What did you *do?*" she whispered, her eyes alive with pain.

"I did what I had to do. I can't let you hurt her. But you're more than welcome to hurt *him*."

"What?" Julia demanded as I turned, and she spun to follow my gaze. Olivia Warren and a tall blond man stepped into sight in the foyer, with Barker between them, still wearing the grease-stained shirt he'd worn an hour earlier.

"Ian?" Kris said, and I nodded. "Kenley gave me your message. Here's what you asked for." He pushed Barker forward a single step, without letting go of the Binder.

Julia's men raised their guns, but Kris and Olivia were faster, even with each holding one of Barker's arms. Their silencers *thwupped,* and Julia's men fell, their guns unfired.

Julia gasped, then she opened her mouth to shout for more help.

"Don't." Olivia aimed at her head. I pulled Julia out of reach of both Kori and Olivia—I had no other choice.

"Break Kenley's and Ian's bindings, and I'll let you live," Kori said, aiming her gun at Barker now.

"If you even think about it, I'll have your tongue cut

out and shoved down your throat so that you drown in your own blood," Julia spat.

Barker stared at her, terrified and confused.

Kori shrugged. "At least my way's quicker and less painful. I'm sorry." She aimed, and her gun *thwupped* once. A neat hole appeared in Barker's head, and he fell over backward in the middle of the foyer.

Kris and Olivia both stepped away from him as Kori took aim at Julia. And this time, I let her. Because I could.

"I'm unarmed," Julia said, her tone reasonable, her fear almost hidden by steady hands and a firm jaw.

"You'll never be unarmed as long as there's a tongue in your mouth and a brain in your head," Kori spat. "It was your idea to turn the lights off wasn't it? In the basement. It was your idea to let me rot in the dark."

"Jake wanted to kill you," she said, arms held out, displaying her defenselessness. "I saved your life."

"Because you wanted me to suffer."

Julia couldn't argue with that.

"Don't worry," Kori said as the first police sirens wailed in the distance. "I want you to suffer, too. Everyone's gonna know you betrayed the king of the castle. And Kenley's going to take away your loyal subjects, one at a time."

Across the foyer, a door opened, and armed men came running toward us. Kris and Olivia ducked into Jake's office, but Kori didn't seem to notice. She moved closer to Julia with every word, threatening the new queen with her very presence. "And when you fall from the throne, and the castle comes crumbling down on you, I want you to remember who pulled down the first stone."

Kori holstered her gun as I began to gather shadows

from the corners of Jake's office. Julia backed slowly away. Kori smiled. Then she kicked Julia square in the chest.

Julia flew backward into the foyer with an *oof* of stolen breath. She landed hard on her ass, her mouth open, her legs sprawled in front of her.

Kori slammed the office door shut as the first bullets whizzed toward us, over Julia's head. Glass shattered, and we all ducked. Kori grabbed my hand while Kris took Olivia's. I pulled the shadows up and around us, and Kori exhaled, her hand warm in mine. I could feel her smile, even if I couldn't see it.

Then she pulled me forward, and we stepped out of Tower's hell and into the rest of our lives. Which looked suspiciously like Meghan's bathroom.

Kris and Liv tripped over one another in their haste to check on the others, but I pulled Kori back before she could go. Then I kicked the door closed and pulled her closer, wrapping the shadows around us again. "You're free," I whispered, running my hands over her back, while hers slid beneath my shirt. "So what do you want to do now?"

She kissed me, then her lips trailed over my chin toward my ear. "Now?" she whispered, and chills shot up my spine. "Nothing. Everything. Isn't that the whole point? From now on, we can do whatever the hell we want."

* * * * *

Acknowledgments

Thanks, as always, to my critique partner, Rinda Elliott, the first to read everything I write. Thanks most of all for your willingness to tell me when I suck. The truth is greatly appreciated.

Thanks to #1, my husband, for endless patience. This book and the subsequent revisions took up a crazy three and a half months of our lives and I may not have been the most pleasant person during that time.

A huge thank-you to the MIRA Art department for the *SHADOW BOUND* cover art. The models are perfect. The colors are beautiful. The tone is dead-on. I love it.

And, of course, thanks to all the readers willing to give this dark and twisted world a chance. I promise, there is a light at the end of the tunnel....

They say blood is thicker than water. They have no idea.

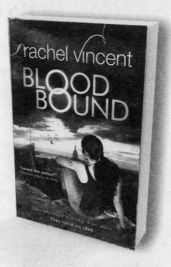

As a blood tracker, Liv is extremely powerful.
And Liv only survives by her own rules.

Rule number one? Trust no one.

But when a friend's daughter goes missing, Liv is
bound by a potent magical oath. She has to find her.
And that means trusting her dangerous ex, Cam.

A prophecy tells that she and Cam will be the death
of each other, yet Liv's tired of being a slave to destiny.
She's ready to play the forces controlling her world
at their own game…

www.mirabooks.co.uk

CONFRONTING THE PAST, CONTROLLING THE FUTURE

With an execution order on her head, Yelena must escape to Sitia, the land of her birth. She has only a year to master her magic – or face death.

But nothing in Sitia is familiar. As she struggles to understand where she belongs and how to control her rare powers, a rogue magician emerges – and Yelena catches his eye.

Suddenly she is embroiled in a battle between good and evil. And once again it will be her magical abilities that will either save her life…or be her downfall.

www.mirabooks.co.uk

MIRA

THE APPRENTICESHIP IS OVER – NOW THE REAL TEST HAS BEGUN

When word spreads that Yelena is a Soulfinder – able to capture and release souls – people grow uneasy. Then she receives news of a plot rising against her homeland, led by a murderous sorcerer she has defeated before.

Honour sets Yelena on a path that will test the limits of her skills, and the hope of reuniting with her beloved spurs her onward. Yelena will have but one chance to prove herself – and save the land she holds dear.

www.mirabooks.co.uk

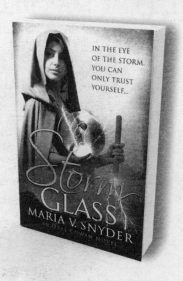

HER POWER REMAINED HIDDEN – UNTIL CHALLENGED BY ENEMY FORCES

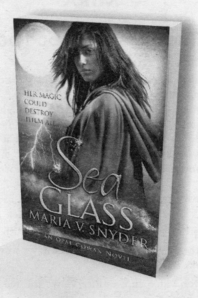

Student glass magician Opal Cowan's newfound ability to steal a magician's powers makes her too powerful.

Ordered to house arrest, Opal dares defy her imprisonment. In hostile territory, without proof or allies, Opal isn't sure whom to trust.

And now everyone is after Opal's special powers for their own deadly gain…

www.mirabooks.co.uk

MIRA